P9-BZE-647

PENGUIN CLASSICS

SEVEN VIKING ROMANCES

HERMANN PÁLSSON studied Icelandic at the University of Iceland and Celtic at University College, Dublin. He is now Professor of Icelandic at the University of Edinburgh, where he has been teaching since 1950. He is the General Editor of the New Saga Library and the author of several books on the history and literature of medieval Iceland; his more recent publications include *Legendary Fiction in Medieval Iceland* (with Paul Edwards) and *Art and Ethics in Hrafnkel's Saga*. Hermann Pálsson has also translated *Hrafnkel's Saga*, and collaborated with Magnus Magnusson in translating *Laxdæla Saga*, *The Vinland Sagas*, *King Harald's Saga* and *Njal's Saga* for the Penguin Classics.

PAUL EDWARDS read English at Durham University, Celtic and Icelandic at Cambridge, and then worked in West Africa for nine years. He is now Reader in English Literature at Edinburgh University. He has written several books on Icelandic studies with Hermann Pálsson, and has published books and articles on African history and literature, and on English literature, mainly on nineteenth-century poetry.

Hermann Pálsson and Paul Edwards have also translated *Egil's Saga* and the *Orkneyinga Saga* for the Penguin Classics.

SEVEN
VIKING ROMANCES

Translated with an introduction by
Hermann Pálsson and Paul Edwards

Penguin Books

Penguin Books Ltd, Harmondsworth, Middlesex, England
Viking Penguin Inc., 40 West 23rd Street, New York, New York 10010, USA
Penguin Books Australia Ltd, Ringwood, Victoria, Australia
Penguin Books Canada Ltd, 2801 John Street, Markham, Ontario, Canada L3R 1B4
Penguin Books (N.Z.) Ltd, 182–190 Wairau Road, Auckland 10, New Zealand

First published 1985

Copyright © Hermann Pálsson and Paul Edwards, 1985
All rights reserved

Made and printed in Great Britain by
Cox & Wyman Ltd, Reading
Filmset in 10/12½ Linotron Aldus by
Rowland Phototypesetting Ltd, Bury St Edmunds, Suffolk

Except in the United States of America,
this book is sold subject to the condition
that it shall not, by way of trade or otherwise,
be lent, re-sold, hired out, or otherwise circulated
without the publisher's prior consent in any form of
binding or cover other than that in which it is
published and without a similar condition
including this condition being imposed
on the subsequent purchaser

Contents

Seven Viking Romances

Introduction

The imaginative literature of medieval Iceland which we call 'the sagas' displays a remarkable diversity of modes and materials, ranging from naturalistic stories about farmers and farmhands in the authors' native Iceland to tales of pure fantasy, the adventures of imaginary kings and princes in strange and distant lands. The stories in this volume lie somewhere between the extremes of, on the one hand, the social realism of *Hrafnkel's Saga* and, on the other, the naïve romance of *Gibbon's Saga*. They tend, however, towards the romance end of the spectrum, and we wish to begin by making clear some of the differences between such romances and naturalistic narrative such as *Hrafnkel's Saga*.

One variety of saga may well display features of others, but in *Hrafnkel's Saga*, even though we have no external evidence that the events which it describes actually happened, we recognize a distinct historical aspect. It is set in a tenth-century world which, though it existed some three hundred years before that of the author, was not essentially different from it; and the title-hero bears the name of one of the original settlers of Iceland recorded in the historical *Book of Settlements* (*Landnámabók*). It ought not to be regarded too literally, simply as a straightforward record of the killing in days gone by of an innocent shepherd and of its consequences; the narrative also has an ethical aspect, very much the concern of the age in which it was written. But it clearly differs a great deal from the more apparently naïve romances, with their idealized heroes and conventional villains. *Hrafnkel's Saga* offers no clear instance of either hero or villain, and is concerned with the moral dilemmas of its naturalistic characters, not with the adventures of supermen. Like other sagas in what is thought of as the 'great tradition',[1] it

1. Generally, the more famous sagas: *Njal's Saga, Grettir's Saga, Eyrbyggja Saga, Laxdæla Saga, Egil's Saga* and others, several of them published by Penguin.

reflects a world of experience, in realistic-seeming human images: a shepherd on horseback searches the uplands for his straying flock; girls milk the ewes the following morning; a servant washes her linen by the lakeside; a group of travellers drive their pack-horses over the heath. The author of *Gibbon's Saga*, on the other hand, did not attempt to describe things that he had experienced himself, and was concerned neither with the history of his society nor with current moral issues. His purpose appears to have been to create an entertaining tale from the materials of romance.

Nevertheless, even among the most 'realistic' of the sagas, we find fanciful elements, particularly when the hero journeys over-seas. Though the audience of the naturalistic saga may have lived two or three hundred years after the events described, it lived in an Iceland sufficiently similar to the world of the tale to compel the narrator to present a plausible and recognizable environment. But once the hero sets out from his native shore, he often enters an alien world, of kings and courts, and of martial exploits on a scale quite different from the local conflicts of the Icelandic settlements; and so we may find – in, for instance, *Egil's Saga* – a shift into something akin to romance fiction. In Iceland, Egil is the troublemaking son of a rich farmer, and there is always a homely quality about his experiences. But on his travels overseas, we find him rescuing a helpless maiden from the clutches of an ill-intentioned berserk, saving a sick girl from a magic spell cut in runes, demonstrating near-superhuman fighting skills while defending England from the invading Scots, and composing a praise-poem overnight despite the interruptions of a twittering bird which turns out to be the shape-changing Queen Gunnhild, his old enemy. Characteristically such exploits do not figure in the episodes set in Iceland, where the killings, however fearsome, remain believably domestic. The same might be said of the supernatural elements in the two varieties. The hauntings in *Grettir's Saga* or *Eyrbyggja Saga* are described natu-ralistically in terms of a commonly held belief, despite their weirdness: in romance saga, the author deliberately displays a world of wonder and spectacle.

The adventures abroad in *Egil's Saga*, then, could be seen to have an affinity with the 'viking' element in our seven tales, but in other ways these romances are very different from the 'great tradition'. The Scandinavian past is more dimly remembered in the romances; the realism of an Icelandic setting gives way to the fantastic, exotic and geographically remote. The conventions of European romance narrative, of castles and courtesy, the battlefield and the boudoir, influence the Icelandic narrator. Though most of the action continues to take place in northern Europe, strange places appear on the map, and many episodes are set in more distant lands, real or imagined. Broadly speaking, these stories offer the same picture of the vikings and their activities as that still imprinted on the European imagination: ruthless, uninhibited northerners, plundering in every direction – north to Lappland and Permia, east to Russia, south to Germany, France and the Near East, west to the British Isles. Beyond rational geography, the longships and dragon-headed galleys of the adventurers make raids on the Otherworld of pagan Scandinavia, on Geirrodstown, Gjallandi Bridge and Noatown of the *Poetic Edda*, and on the ambiguous Glasisvellir, Glasir or Shining Plains, a barren region thought to lie somewhere between the geographical *Ultima Thule* of Permia and the super-natural Geirrodstown. In one of the romances not included here, *Samson's Saga*, there is a brave attempt to rationalize the position of the mythic lands of the Arctic:

Glasir Plains are situated to the east of Giantland, which lies to the east and north of the Baltic and extends in a north-easterly direction. Then there is the land known as Jotunheim, inhabited by giants and monsters, and from Jotunheim to Greenland extends a land called Svalbard [i.e. Spitzbergen].

While most of the fantastic elements seem to emanate from a native tradition going back to pagan preliterate times, others derive from foreign learning. Of particular note is the description of the giant in *Egil and Asmund* (Chapters 9–10), which ultimately derives from the Polyphemus story in Homer's *Odyssey*, though it would have reached Iceland in a Latin version. But in the world of *Egil and Asmund*, there is nothing incongruous about this Greek legend. The authors of the Icelandic romances were eclectic; they gathered their materials freely from myth and romance, folklore, fragments of history, old heroic tales – wherever they could be found.

Icelandic antiquarians in medieval times took great pride in their pagan past, and consequently a large body of pagan poetry has survived. Particularly relevant to the viking romances are those poems dealing with mythological and legendary themes, now usually gathered under the general heading of the *Poetic Edda*. Later, Snorri Sturluson (d. 1241), Iceland's greatest medieval writer, retold some of these in his *Prose Edda*, and further evidence of his interest in the remote past is in the *Ynglinga Saga*, based largely on ninth-century poems, which forms the first section of his *Heimskringla*, or *History of the Kings of Norway*. *Ynglinga Saga* describes the legendary history of the royal house of Sweden and, in the final chapters, of Norway too, down to the ninth century. The opening chapters of two of our tales, *Bosi and Herraud* and *Halfdan Eysteinsson*, show that their authors must have known *Ynglinga Saga*, in which Odin is given the status of a mortal king. Here, as elsewhere in legendary literature, it is not clear whether men have been turned into gods, or gods into men. One of our tales, *King Gautrek*, has affinities with the late-twelfth-century *Skjöldunga Saga*, another source of legendary materials which deals with the early history of Denmark, but only exists now in a Latin summary and an Icelandic fragment. Finally, yet another medieval work, Saxo Grammaticus' massive *History of the Danes* (*Gesta Danorum*), is relevant to three of our sagas – *King Gautrek*, *Thorstein Mansion-Might*, and *Helgi Thorisson*. Saxo, who died in 1216, paid tribute – as did a Norwegian contemporary – to the Icelanders historical learning, and acknowledged his use of their 'saga treasures' (*thesauri historiarum*). The first nine books of Saxo's *History* deal with the legendary and mythological past of Denmark, and it is in Books V, VI and VIII in particular that we find parallels to our Icelandic tales.

Just as the geography of the viking romances is kept indistinct, so too is their historical content. Two of the tales, *Thorstein Mansion-Might* and *Helgi Thorisson*, are associated with the historical King Olaf Tryggvason of Norway (995–1000), but also with the legendary King Godmund of Glasir Plains, who appears too in *Bosi and Herraud*, and about whom we shall say more. One of the characters in *Halfdan Eysteinsson* is said to have been a settler in Iceland (c. 900), and the medieval audiences of these tales might have recognized in such names as Ketil Trout, Harald War-Tooth, Starkad and Gautrek shadowy eighth-century figures from the genealogical records, such as those of the *Book of Settlements*. But such characters are on the historical fringes, and these tales have little to do with history. The women of the naturalistic saga tradition, for instance, such as Njal's wife Bergthora, or the dominating figure of Gudrun in *Laxdæla Saga*, have their roots in history and are presented powerfully and credibly in human terms, for all the fictional art that goes into their creation. There is nothing quite like them in the viking romances, where we can distinguish three principal representations of womanhood. First there is the valkyrie type, exemplifying the heroic mode (though often with more than a touch of grotesque comedy), such as Brynhild in *Bosi and Herraud*. Her name echoes that of the archetypal Brynhild Buðli's-daughter of the *Nibelungen* legend, whose maidenhood was guarded by a sacred flame. Ingigerd in *Halfdan Eysteinsson*, who disguises herself as a man and takes up arms to avenge her father, evidently belongs to this category too, despite her more obvious romantic features. So does one of the heroines of a tale not included here, *Hrolf Gautreksson*, a princess named Thornbjorg who dresses in armour and insists on being called 'Sir'. The second recurrent type is the courteous lady of romance, and the third is the ingenious, often promiscuous, servant or peasant girl. This is not to say that these figures are presented artlessly: within the romance convention, they emerge with wit and vigour, but they are closer to folk-narrative than to the art of the naturalistic saga. Here are Ingibjorg, daughter of Godmund of Glasir Plains, from *Helgi Thorisson*, and her equivalent from British folklore, the Fairy Queen of 'Thomas the Rymer':

Then Helgi saw twelve women come riding through the wood, all of them on red-coloured horses and wearing red costumes. They dismounted, and all their riding-gear shone with gold. One woman was far lovelier than all the others, and they were in attendance upon this great lady.

They put out their horses to graze, then the women set up a splendid with stripes of alternating colours and embroidered everywhere The points of the tent were ornamented with gold, and which stood up through the tent there was a grea women had made these preparations, they set up a table and laid it with all kinds of choice food. Then they took water to wash their hands, using a jug and basins of silver, inlaid everywhere with gold.

Helgi was standing near the tent watching them, and the great lady said to him, 'Come over here, Helgi, have something to eat and drink with us.'

So that's what he did, and he could see that the food and wine were delicious and the cups quite splendid. When the table had been cleared, and the beds were made – these beds were much more ornate than those of other people – the great lady asked Helgi whether he would prefer to sleep alone or share a bed with her. He asked her name.

'I'm called Ingibjorg. I'm the daughter of Godmund of Glasir Plains,' she said.

'I'd like to sleep with you,' he said.

So they slept together for three successive nights. (*Helgi Thorisson*, Chapter 1.)

> True Thomas lay on Huntlie bank,
>   A ferlie he spied wi' his ee,
> And there he saw a lady bright,
>   Come riding down by the Eildon Tree.
>
> Her skirt was o' the grass-green silk,
>   Her mantle o' the velvet fyne,
> At ilka tett of her horse's mane
>   Hang fifty siller bells and nine.
>
> . . . .
>
> 'Harp and carp, Thomas,' she said,
>   'Harp and carp along wi' me,
> And if ye dare to kiss my lips,
>   Sure of your bodie I will be.'
>
> 'eside me weal, betide me woe,
>   weird shall never daunton me;'
>   e has kissed her rosy lips,
>   derneath the Eildon Tree.

homas the Rymer' in Scott's
y of the Scottish Border.)

the Rymer' overlaid by European
adition of saga narrative, that we
rms that we should read them.
th regard to the figures of

Starkad in *Gautrek's Saga* and the title-hero of *Grettir's Saga*. Both are essentially warriors, but they are also poets and men of exceptional sensibility; both live out tragic destinies under a curse. It is said of Grettir, and might equally well be said of Starkad, that his life showed the difference between great talents and good luck. But Grettir's doom reveals his incompatibility with the society in which he lives, whereas Starkad's is stated in terms of mythology. Starkad is taken by his foster-father to a certain island. There, suddenly, the foster-father casts off his disguise to reveal himself as Odin, and introduces Starkad to a circle of seated gods, who make a formal declaration of his destiny. So the gods are seen to create the contrary impulses which are to agonize and destroy the hero, out of their own conflicts and jealousies, and a rather different perspective is given to the choice which Starkad has to make – to kill his lord and friend Vikar, and break the codes of human society; or to keep faith with Vikar and defy the will of the god Odin. In both cases the narrative mood is dictated by the heroism of the man whose choices continue to be made in the face of what appears to be inexorable and fatal, but the perspectives in which destiny is seen are very different.

One of the principal manifestations of the Starkad legend is Saxo's *History of the Danes*, in which another figure important to these romances, King Godmund of Glasir Plains, also appears. Godmund enters into three romances, but performs very diverse roles, and is in different tales benefactor, devil and fool. In *Helgi Thorisson*, Godmund emerges as the enemy of the virtuous Christian King Olaf, and it is his daughter Ingibjorg – like her father, an amiable enough figure in the early stages of the relationship – who in the end gouges out the hero's eyes. Nevertheless, the story is inconclusive and ambiguous. In *Bosi and Herraud*, Godmund is something of a figure of fun, an incompetent villain, and his sister Hleid becomes Herraud's beloved and loving wife. But in *Thorstein Mansion-Might*, Godmund is a large, friendly figure, and enemy of the forces of evil represented by Geirrod. He befriends Thorstein, and when they part he sends valuable gifts to King Ol[...] he has every respect for what he calls King Olaf's 'l[...] promises that if Thorstein were to become his follow[...] interfere with Thorstein's Christian faith.

Godmund, then, is clearly a mythical figure, and his visit to Geirrod echoes Thor's journey to the same imaginary place, Geirrodstown, as told by the tenth-century poet Eilif, and later by Snorri in the *Prose Edda.* The formidable river Vimur corresponds to the Hemra in *Thorstein Mansion-Might.* According to both Eilif and Snorri, Geirrod was a giant hostile to the gods, and the ambiguous presentation of Godmund in romance narrative appears to reflect a stubborn clutching of the old gods and spirits by way of popular beliefs much older than the settlement of Iceland around 900, and the establishment of Christianity around 1000.

Yet another significant element of the literary tradition derives, as we have said, from European romance, in particular the French romances, several of which were translated into Norse in the thirteenth century; the first was the Tristram story in 1226.

In our viking romances, then, the reader must not expect to find a literature in quite the same tradition as that of the great family sagas of the Icelandic settlements. They were intended as entertainments of a less serious nature: yet they have their own virtues, and draw upon a vigorous tradition of storytelling, which allowed for wide-ranging digression contained within a carefully planned overall design, best illustrated in this volume perhaps by *Arrow-Odd*, some of the sources for which are discussed in the Appendix. The tale's ultimate shape is dictated by its second chapter, in which a prophecy is made about the hero's life which, despite all appearances, is to be fulfilled. The prediction is in three parts: first, that Odd is to live for three hund— years; second, that he will never put down roots in any soci— —hird, that the skull of his horse will be the death of him— —en he hears the prophecy is to kill the horse and —und under a mound of rocks, and in that way, —pletely. But what he has in fact done is to —the prophecy can be fulfilled.

—y the horse's skull, his life is stretched —him, suspended, and it is no longer —gh the normal process of youth, —Are you that Odd who went to —who went to Permia a long time ago?' At the same time, he becomes a figure of decay and regeneration: he discovers death through the loss of his friends; tries, in a sense, to die by shedding his heroic role and dressing himself in tree-bark, telling the king, 'I'm older than anything you can think of.' But we are in a world of folklore again: this 'Barkman', as the saga calls him, is well known as the Wild Man of the Wood, discussed in Frazer's *Golden Bough*, who dressed in leaves or tree-bark (compare Lear's fantastic dress of wild flowers) and had to undergo a test of endurance and survival. 'The killing of the tree-spirit', says Frazer, 'is associated always (we must suppose) implicitly, and sometimes explicitly also, with a revival or resurrection of him in a more youthful and vigorous form'.[2] So, by the end of the episode, the bark has been stripped away and Odd is young again: 'Under the bark he was wearing a red tunic of costly material, lace-trimmed; his hair fell down over his shoulders, there was a gold band round his forehead, and he looked very handsome indeed.'

The second element of the prophecy – that Odd cannot put down roots but is fated to wander – is of course a prescription for romance geography, which shifts between actual places and purely imagined ones. The normal can appear strange because of the perspective in which it is seen. Thus Odd and his men find themselves in Aquitaine, a favourite land of romance, where they see 'a house built in quite a different way from any other they had ever seen. Up they went to the house. It was built of stone and the door was open.' They see people flocking into it, and from it comes 'a noise like nothing they'd ever heard before', so they start asking questions of those who come out:

'What's this house for, where you've been all this time?'
'We call it a minster or a church,' he said.
'What was all that noise you were making?'
'We call that the Mass,' he said.

Odd moves on from Aquitaine to the River Jordan, where he bathes; then later he is picked up by an enormous vulture and rescued by a giant who happens to be rowing past in a stone boat – 'one', we told, 'of the giants of Giantland'. The second element of t ecy, then, ensures that both Odd and the narrative ke

2. Sir J. G. Frazer, *The Golden Bough* (London, 1947, abrid

The third element predicts that Odd will be killed by the skull of his horse, Faxi. Odd's efforts to cheat destiny, the killing and burying of the horse, and his wanderings which keep him away from its burial place (and his birthplace) Berurjod seem wholly adequate, but are in fact quite futile. The prophecy is central to the state of anticipation created by the narrative, preparing the way for the final chapter and the working out of Odd's destiny. Only near the end is Odd drawn back to his almost forgotten birthplace, his decision never to return overruled by some impulse stronger than his desire to cheat the fatal prophecy. His careful disposal of Faxi's remains in a pit full of heavy rocks has been mocked by time itself, the same three hundred years that the first element of the prophecy gave him to live. In those three hundred years the surface of the earth has been eroded, and the skull lies on the surface waiting for him, to fulfil the prophecy and, we hope, the reader's expectations.

The fourteenth-century scribes and tellers of these tales have given a number of indications as to what such expectations might be. The story is seen primarily as an entertainment, and if the storyteller glances at the high ethical purposes of the great saga tradition, he appears to do so with his tongue in his cheek:

Since this tale nor anything else can be made to please everyone, nobody need believe any more of it than he wants to believe. All the same the best and most profitable thing is to listen while a story is being told, to enjoy it and not be gloomy: for the fact is that as long as people are enjoying the entertainment they won't be thinking any evil thoughts. Nor is it a good thing when listeners find fault with a story just because it happens to be uninformative or clumsily told. Nothing so unimportant is ever done perfectly.

Such imers as this one, by the storyteller of *Göngu-H* both a frame to, and an internal commentary le, and it would be a heavy-handed critic parisons with *Njal's Saga* or *Laxdæla u-Hrolf* concludes:

tened and enjoyed the story, and since satisfied, let them enjoy their own

slated by Hermann Pálsson and Paul

FINNMARK

NORWAY

SWEDEN

TAFESTALAND

KARELIA

Orkney

SCOTLAND

ESTONIA

Novgorod

Rostof

Suzdal

Murom

PERMIA

Dvina R.

North
Sea

Skaane

Baltic Sea

LIVONIA

IRELAND

ENGLAND

Polotsk

Vitebsk

KURLAND

RUSSIA

SAXONY

NORMANDY

FLANDERS

POLAND

Kiev

ALSACE

FRANCE

AQUITAINE

Black Sea

M e d i t e r r a n e a n   S e a

GREECE

Antioch

Jordan R.

Europe of the Viking Romances

0   500 miles

Europe of the Viking Romances

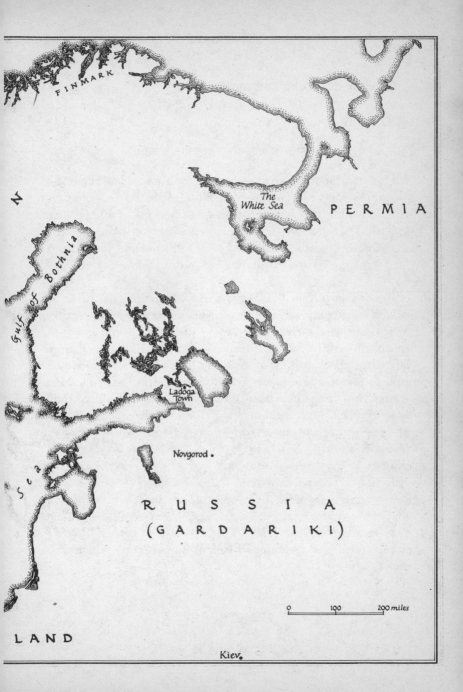

FINMARK

N

PERMIA

The
White Sea

Gulf of Bothnia

Ladoga
Town

Sea

Novgorod.

R U S S I A
(G A R D A R I K I)

0   100   200 miles

LAND

Kiev.

Note on the Texts and Translations

All the translations in the present volume are based on the text of Guðni Jónsson's editions. (See the Bibliography below.) The present translation of *Halfdan Eysteinsson* is the first to appear in English. The other tales in the volume are revisions of our previous translations, *Gautrek's Saga and other medieval tales* (London and New York, 1968) and *Arrow-Odd: A medieval novel* (New York, 1970).

Arrow-Odd (*Örvar-Odds saga*) exists in two versions, the earlier of which was composed about the middle of the thirteenth century. *King Gautrek* (*Gautreks saga*) was written towards the end of the thirteenth century, but it survives only in manuscripts of much later date. *Halfdan Eysteinsson* (*Hálfdanar saga Eysteinssonar*) belongs to the beginning of the fourteenth century and survives in manuscripts from the fifteenth century. *Egil and Asmund* (*Egils saga einhenda og Asmundar saga berserkjabana*) was written around 1300 and is preserved in three vellum manuscripts of the fifteenth century. *Bosi and Herraud* (*Bósa saga og Herrauðs*) belongs to the same period, surviving in manuscripts from the following century. *Thorstein Mansion-Might* (*Þorsteins þáttr bæjarmagns*) was probably composed in the first half of the fourteenth century, although the earliest surviving manuscripts date from the fifteenth. *Helgi Thorisson* (*Helga þáttr Þórissonar*) is preserved in a magnificent vellum codex written about 1390 (*Flateyjarbók*).

Bibliography

For fuller details, see H. Hermannsson, *Islandica*, vols. 5 (1912) and 26 (1937), and H. Bekker-Nielsen, *Bibliography of Old Norse-Icelandic Studies* (1963– ; in progress).

I Editions

C. C. Rafn, *Fornaldar sögur Norðrlanda*, I–III (Copenhagen, 1829–30).
Guðni Jónsson, *Fornaldarsögur Norðurlanda*, I–IV (Reykjavík, 1950).

II General

Inger M. Boberg, *Motif-Index of Early Icelandic Literature* (Copenhagen, 1966).
Peter Buchholz, 'Fornaldarsaga und mündliches Erzählen zur Wikingerzeit', *Les vikings et leur civilisation* (Paris, 1976), 133–78; *Vorzeitkunde . . .* (Neumünster, 1980).
Paul Herrmann, *Die Heldensagen des Saxo Grammaticus* (Leipzig, 1922).
Anne Holtsmark, 'Heroic Poetry and Legendary Sagas', *Bibliography of Old Norse-Icelandic Studies* (Copenhagen, 1966), 9–21.
Finnur Jónsson, *Den oldnorske og old islandske litteratur*, vols. II and III (Copenhagen, 1923–4).
Knut Liestøl, *Norske trollvisor og norrøne sogor* (Oslo, 1915).
Axel Olrik, *The Heroic Legends of Denmark*, trans. Lee M. Hol-

lander (New York, 1919); *Kilderne til Sakses oldhistorie* (Copenhagen, 1893–4).

Hermann Pálsson and Paul Edwards, *Legendary Fiction in Medieval Iceland* (Reykjavík, 1970).

H. Reuschel, *Untersuchungen über Stoff und Stil der Fornaldarsagas* (Bühl-Baden, 1933).

Margaret Schlauch, *Romance in Iceland* (London, 1934).

H. Schneider, *Germanische Heldensage* I–II (Berlin and Leipzig, 1928–34).

Einar Ol. Sveinsson, *Verzeichnis isländischer Märchenvarianten* (Helsinki, 1929); 'Celtic Elements in Icelandic Tradition', *Béaloideas* XV (Dublin, 1959), 3–24; *Dating the Icelandic Sagas* (London, 1958).

M. C. van den Toorn, 'Über die Ethik in den Fornaldarsaga', *Acta Philologica Scandinavica* XXVI (1963–4), 19–26.

E. O. G. Turville-Petre, *Myth and Religion of the North* (London, 1964); *The Heroic Age of Scandinavia* (London, 1951).

III Individual Tales

1 Arrow-Odd

R. C. Boer (ed.), *Örvar-Odds saga* (Leiden, 1888); (ed.), *Örvar-Odds saga* (Halle, 1892); 'Über die Örvar-Odds saga', *Arkiv för nordisk filologi* VIII (1892), 97–139, and 'Weiteres zur Örvar-Odds saga', op.cit. 246–55.

N. K. Chadwick, *The Beginnings of Russian History* (Cambridge, 1946).

Lars Lönnroth, 'The double scene in Arrow-Odd's drinking contest', *Medieval Narrative* (Odense, 1979).

A. S. Ross, *The Terfinnas and the Beormas of Ohtere* (Leeds, 1941).

Archer Taylor, 'The death of Örvar-Oddr', *Modern Philology* VIII (1921), 93–106.

2 King Gautrek

Wilhelm Ranisch (ed.), *Die Gautreks saga in Zwei Fassungen* (Berlin, 1900).

Lee M. Hollander, 'The Gautland cycle of sagas', *Journal of English and Germanic Philology* 9 (1912), 61–81; 'The relative age of the Gautrekssaga and the Hrólfs saga Gautrekssonar', *Arkiv för nordisk filologi* 29 (1913), 120–34.

James Milroy, 'Starkaðr: An Essay in Interpretation', *Saga-Book of the Viking Society* 19 (1975–6), 118–38; 'The Story of Ætternis-stapi in Gautreks saga', *Saga-Book of the Viking Society* 17 (1967–8), 206–23.

3 Halfdan Eysteinsson

Franz Rolf Schröder (ed.), *Hálfdanar saga Eysteinssonar* (Halle a/S, 1917).

4 Bosi and Herraud

O. L. Jiriczek (ed.), *Die Bósa saga* (Strassburg, 1893).

Alex. H. Krappe, 'La source de la Saga af Herrauði ok Bósa', *Neuphilog, Mitteil* 29 (1928), 250–56.

Claibourne W. Thompson, 'The Runes in *Bósa saga ok Herrauðs*', *Scandinavian Studies* 50 (1978), 50–56.

5 Egil and Asmund

Åke Lagerholm (ed.), *Drei Lygisögur* (Halle, 1927).

Donald K. Fry, 'Polyphemus in Iceland', *The Fourteenth Century. Acta* 4 (1977), 65–86.

6 Thorstein Mansion-Might

Jacqueline Simpson, 'Otherworld Adventures in an Icelandic Saga', *Folklore* 77 (1966), 1–20.

Marlene Ciklamini, 'Journeys to the Giant-Kingdom', *Scandinavian Studies* 60 (1968), 95–110.

7 Helgi Thorisson

C. R. Unger (ed.), *Flateyjarbók* I (Copenhagen, 1860), 359–62.

Arrow-Odd

1. Odd's Childhood

There was a man called Grim, nicknamed Hairy-Cheek because he was born with a certain peculiarity, and this is how it happened: when Grim's father, Ketil Trout, went to bed with Hrafnhild Bruni's-daughter (as in the tale told earlier), her father Bruni spread a hide over them because he'd invited a number of Lapps in. During the night Hrafnhild happened to look out from under the hide and caught a glimpse of one of the Lapps who was hairy all over. That was how Grim got this mark: for people think he was conceived at that very moment.

Grim lived at Hrafnista. He was a rich man and wielded a great deal of power throughout Halogaland and many other parts too. He was married to a woman called Lofthæna, the daughter of the chieftain Harald of Oslofjord in the east.

One summer, after the death of his father-in-law Harald, Grim got ready for a journey east to Oslofjord where he owned valuable property. When Lofthæna learned about this, she asked to go with him, but Grim told her it was out of the question as she was expecting a child at the time.

'I won't be satisfied unless I go,' she said.

Grim loved her very dearly, and he let her have her way. She was very good-looking, and in all she did the cleverest woman in Norway.

They fitted themselves out in great style, and Grim sailed with two ships from Hrafnista east to Oslofjord. When they were sailing past the district called Berurjod, Lofthæna asked the men to reef the sails as she could feel her labour pains coming on, so they made for land. A man called Ingjald was living there with his wife and a son called Asmund, a good-looking youngster.

When the ships had landed, messengers were sent up to the farm to tell Ingjald that Grim and his wife had arrived. Ingjald had a team of draught-horses hitched to a cart and went himself to meet Grim and his wife, offering them all the hospitality they needed and whatever they would take, after which they went home to Ingjald's farm. While Lofthæna was shown to the women's quarters, Grim was ushered into the hall and invited to sit on the high-seat. Nothing that Ingjald could do to show respect to Grim's party was too much trouble. Lofthæna's labour pains increased till at last she gave birth to a boy and the women who took care of him thought they'd never seen such a fine baby.

Lofthæna looked at her son and said, 'Take him to his father, he must give the boy a name.' And that's what was done. The boy was sprinkled with water and given the name Odd.

When they had stayed there for three days, Lofthæna told her husband that she was ready to carry on with the journey, so Grim told Ingjald he wanted to leave.

'I've been thinking,' said Ingjald, 'I'd very much like to have some mark of your respect.'

'You deserve one,' said Grim. 'Choose your own reward, I'm not short of money.'

'I've plenty of that myself,' said Ingjald.

'Then you'd better have something else,' said Grim.

'I'd like to be your boy's foster-father,' said Ingjald.

'I don't know how Lofthæna will take that,' said Grim.

But she replied, 'If you take my advice, we ought to accept such a handsome offer.'

So Grim and Lofthæna were seen on their way down to their ships while Odd stayed behind at Berurjod. They carried on with their journey till they arrived east in Oslofjord, and stayed there as long as necessary. After that they made ready to sail back, and had a fair wind all the way to Berurjod. Then Grim told his men to reef the sails.

'Why shouldn't we go on with our voyage?' asked Lofthæna.

'I thought you'd like to see your son,' said Grim.

'I took a look at him before we parted,' she said, 'and it seemed to me that he had little love in his eyes for us people of Hrafnista. So we'll go on our way,' she said.

Grim and his wife arrived back home at Hrafnista, and Odd grew up with Asmund at Berurjod. Odd was trained in all the sporting skills of the time, and Asmund followed him in everything that he did. Odd was better looking and smarter than most other men.

Odd and Asmund had become blood brothers. Every day they used to swim or practise at the butts, and there was no one who could match Odd at any sport. But Odd would never play like other children and Asmund used to go along with him wherever he went. In everything, Ingjald was fonder of Odd than of Asmund.

Odd got every good craftsman he met to make him arrows, but he didn't take much care of them so they used to lie around in people's way, on seats and benches. A number of people were hurt by them when they came inside after dark and sat down. That was the one thing that made Odd unpopular, and people complained to Ingjald that he ought to have a word with Odd about it.

Ingjald mentioned this to Odd one day: 'There's one thing, foster-son, that gets you a bad name.'

'What's that?' asked Odd.

'You don't take proper care of your arrows like other people,' said Ingjald.

'I'd have thought you could only blame me if you'd given me something to keep them in,' said Odd.

'Whatever you want, I'll give you,' said Ingjald.

'I don't think you will,' said Odd.

'That's not so,' said Ingjald.

'You've a black three-year-old goat,' said Odd. 'I want it killed and the skin flayed off in one piece, with the horns and the hooves.'

So it was done just as Odd wanted, and he was given the skin-bag when it was ready. Then he gathered his arrows into it, and stopped only when the bag was full. He had more and bigger arrows than other men, and a bow to match. Odd always wore a red scarlet tunic, and a gold-embroidered headband round his forehead. He carried his arrow-bag with him wherever he went. Odd cared little for sacrifices to the gods, but trusted his own strength, and Asmund followed his example even though Ingjald was a great man for sacrifices. The two of them often used to row together out to sea, Odd and Asmund.

2. The Prophecy

There was a witch woman called Heid who had second sight, so with her uncanny knowledge she knew all about things before they happened. She would go to feasts, telling people their destinies and forecasting the weather for the coming winter. She used to have a following of fifteen girls and fifteen boys, and as it happened she came to visit someone not very far from Ingjald's farm.

One morning Ingjald got up early and went to see Odd and Asmund who were still in bed. 'I want to send you off on an errand today,' he said.

'Where are we to go?' asked Odd.

'You're to invite the sorceress over here, now there's a feast ready for her,' said Ingjald.

'That's an errand I'm not going on,' said Odd, 'and I won't thank you for it if she comes here.'

'Then you can go, Asmund,' said Ingjald, 'I can give you orders.'

'I'm going to do something,' said Odd, 'as little to your liking as this is to mine.'

Asmund went off and invited the sorceress to the feast, and she accepted and came with all her following. Ingjald went to meet her with his men and invited her into the hall. Then they got things ready for the performance of the witchcraft on the following night. After the meal was over, people went to sleep, but the prophetess and her company went to carry out their night-rituals. In the morning Ingjald came to see her and asked how the witchcraft had turned out.

'I think I've found out all you want to know,' she said.

'Then everyone had better go to his seat and take turns to hear you,' said Ingjald, and he was the first man to come before her.

'It's good to see you here, Ingjald,' she said. 'I can tell you this much, that you'll live in honour and respect till your old age, which should please all your friends.'

Then Ingjald stepped down, and Asmund took his turn. 'It's good to see you here, Asmund,' she said, 'for your reputation will spread throughout the world. You won't have to wrestle with old age, but you'll be judged a brave man and a great warrior wherever you go.'

Then Asmund went back to his seat, and the rest of the household went in turn to the prophetess. She told each of them what the future held for him, and they were all pleased with their prospects. Then she predicted the weather for the following winter and a lot more that was not previously known. Ingjald thanked her for her prophecies.

'Has everyone in your household been to see me now?' she asked.

'I think most of them have,' said Ingjald.

'What's that lying on the bench over there?' said the prophetess.

'It's a cloak,' said Ingjald.

'It seems to stir a bit whenever I look in that direction,' she said.

At that moment the one lying under the cloak sat up and said, 'It's just as you think, there is someone here, and what that someone would like would be for you to shut your mouth at once and stop babbling about my future, for I don't believe a word of it.'

Odd was holding a stick in his hand, and he went on, 'I'll give you one on the nose with this wand if you start making any prophecies about me.'

She said, 'I'm going to speak up, all the same, and you'd better listen.' Then she spoke these verses:

> You'd better not try
> to bully me, Odd,
> with your bit of bough,
> even though I babble:
> the words of the witch
> were wise, you'll see,
> foretelling the future
> and fate of all.
>
> It won't matter whether
> you wander on your way
> by the broad sea-firths,

pacing the beaches,
or surf-borne
by the driven spray,
here your body will burn
at Berurjod.

The snake will spit,
venom-full, will stab
sharp from the age-worn
skull of Faxi:
the serpent will strike
at the sole of your foot,
when, lord, you have lived
your allotted time.

'I can tell you this, which should please you, Odd,' she carried on.
'There are more years in store for you than for any other man.
You'll live for three hundred years, wandering from land to land,
and wherever you go you'll always be the greatest of men. You'll
have a reputation all over the world, but no matter how far you
travel, you're going to die here at Berurjod. There's a grey black-
maned horse, Faxi, standing near the stable. His skull will be the
death of you.'

'Damn you for making this prophecy about me,' said Odd. And as
soon as she'd finished speaking, he sprang up and struck her so
hard on the nose with the stick that her blood gushed onto the
floor.

'Get my clothes,' said the prophetess, 'let me out of here; I've
never been to any place before where I've had to suffer a beating.'

'Don't go,' said Ingjald, 'there's compensation for every injury.
Stay here for three nights and I'll give you some fine presents.'

She took the gifts, but didn't stay for the celebrations.

3. Odd Visits His Father

After that, Odd asked Asmund to come with him. They put a bridle
on the horse Faxi, and led him after them till they came to a certain
hollow. There they dug a pit so deep that Odd could hardly climb out

of it, then killed Faxi and pushed him in. Odd and Asmund got the biggest boulders they could find, and piled them on top of the horse, then poured sand between each of the boulders until they'd built a mound over Faxi.

When they'd finished their task, Odd said, 'I think it's fair to say that it'll be trolls' work if Faxi ever gets out of this. It seems to me I've cheated my destiny, because that horse is never going to kill me.'

Then they went back home to see Ingjald. 'I want some ships,' said Odd.

'Where are you going?' asked Ingjald.

'I'm leaving,' said Odd, 'and as long as I live, I'm not coming back to Berurjod.'

'This can't be what you want,' said Ingjald. 'You couldn't do anything worse to me. Anyway, what men are you taking?'

'Asmund and I, just the two of us,' said Odd.

'Send Asmund back to me soon,' said Ingjald.

'He'll not come back any sooner than me,' said Odd.

'You're being very hard,' said Ingjald.

'I'll do all I can to pay you back for inviting the prophetess here when you knew how much I was against it,' said Odd.

So Odd and Asmund got ready for the voyage. They said their farewells to Ingjald and he wished them luck. Then they went down to their ship, launched it and rowed out to sea.

'Where shall we go?' said Asmund.

'Wouldn't it be a good idea to visit the family at Hrafnista?' said Odd.

They rowed past the islands, then Odd said, 'Our voyage is going to be a bit of a bore if we have to row all the way north to Hrafnista. Well, I'm going to see whether or not I've my family's luck. I'm told Ketil Trout used to hoist sail in calm weather, so I'll try hoisting sail myself.'

As soon as they had unfurled the sail, they got a fair wind all the way, and came early one morning to Hrafnista. They hauled their ship ashore and went up to the farmstead. Odd carried his arrow-bag on his back and the bow in his hand, and these were the only weapons he had. When they arrived at the farm, there was a man standing outside the house who gave them a friendly welcome and asked who they were.

'That's none of your business,' said Odd.

Odd asked if Grim was at home, and the man said he was. 'Then tell him to come outside,' said Odd.

The man went in, and told Grim that there were two men outside. 'They said you were to come out,' he said.

'Why don't they come in?' asked Grim. 'Tell them to come inside.'

The man went out and repeated what he had been told. 'You'd better go in again,' said Odd, 'and tell Grim to come outside and see us.'

The man went back and told Grim. 'How do these men look?' asked Grim.

'They're fine-looking men,' he said, 'very tall, and one of them carries a great bag on his back.'

'From what you tell me about them, they must be the foster-brothers Odd and Asmund.'

Then Grim went outside with all the people of the house to welcome Odd and Asmund. Grim asked them into the hall, and they accepted his invitation. After they had settled down, Odd asked about his kinsmen, Gudmund and Sigurd. This Gudmund was the son of Grim and Lofthæna and Odd's brother, but Sigurd was Grim's nephew. They were both handsome men.

'They're sheltering on the north side of the island on their way to Permia,' said Grim.

'I want to see them,' said Odd.

'But I want you to spend the winter here,' said Grim.

'I'm going to see them first,' said Odd.

Grim came along with him, and when they reached the north side of the island, there they saw two ships. Odd called on his kinsmen to come ashore. They gave him a good welcome and asked him the news.

'Where are you thinking of going?' inquired Odd.

'To Permia,' said Gudmund.

'We'd like to go with you,' said Odd.

Gudmund spoke for the others, and said, 'It can't be done,

kinsman Odd, your coming along with us this summer. We've already made all the arrangements. Next summer you can come with us wherever you like.'

'That's very kind of you,' said Odd, 'but maybe by next summer I'll have my own ships, and won't need to be your passenger.'

'Well, you're not joining us on this expedition,' said Gudmund, and with that they parted.

4. *To Permia*

Odd went back to his father and accepted his invitation to stay. Grim set Odd beside him on the high-seat, with Asmund on Odd's other side, and offered them every hospitality.

For a fortnight Sigurd and Gudmund lay at anchor to leeward of the island waiting for a fair wind. One night Gudmund was very restless in his sleep, and the men argued whether or not they ought to wake him, but Sigurd said they should let him dream out his dream. Just then Gudmund woke up.

'What were you dreaming about?' asked Sigurd.

'In my dream,' said Gudmund, 'I seemed to be on board my ship here to leeward of this island, and when I looked up I could see a polar bear lying in a circle around the island. Its head and tail met just above the ships. It was the grimmest-looking bear I've ever seen. Every hair on its body was standing on end. It seemed to me as if the bear was just about to hurl itself at the ships and sink them both, but then I woke up. Now try interpreting the dream,' he said.

'It seems to me,' said Sigurd, 'that there's not much need for interpretation, for when you believed you saw this savage bear lying there with all its hairs turned forward and looking as if it was about to sink the ships, then it's clear to me that it was Odd's fetch, and he's angry with us. That's why the bear seemed to feel so wolfish about us, and I can tell you this, we'll never get a fair wind to sail out of here unless he joins us.'

'He won't join us now even if we ask him,' said Gudmund.

'What can we do, then?' said Sigurd.

'It's my advice that we go ashore and ask him to come with us,' said Gudmund.

'What shall we do about the voyage if he won't?' asked Sigurd.

'Rather than leave him behind,' said Gudmund, 'we'll have to give him one of the ships.'

They went ashore to look for Odd and asked him to come along with them. He said he was definitely not going. 'If you join us,' said Gudmund, 'we're ready to give you one of our ships.'

'Then I'll go,' said Odd. 'I'm all set.'

Grim went with them down to the ship to see them on their way. 'There's some treasures here I'd like you to have, kinsman Odd,' said Grim, 'three arrows called Gusir's Gifts,' and he gave him the arrows. Odd looked at them. 'Precious gifts, these,' he said. They were feathered with gold and flew of their own accord from the bowstring and back again, so there was never any need to search for them.

'Ketil Trout took these arrows off Gusir, king of the Lapps,' said Grim. 'Because dwarfs made them, they bite anything they're told to.'

'I've never in my life received a gift to compare with these,' said Odd. He thanked his father for them and they parted the best of friends. Odd stepped aboard and said they should start their travels away from the island, so they unfurled sails first on Odd's ship and then on the other.

They sailed north with a favourable wind, but when they were north of Lappland the wind dropped, so they made for a harbour there where they spent the night. There were plenty of Lappish huts farther up. In the morning the crew on Gudmund's ship went ashore, raided every hut, and robbed the Lapp women. The women took this in very bad part and started screaming noisily. The crew on Odd's ship wanted to go ashore too, but he wouldn't hear of it. In the evening Gudmund and his men came back to the ship.

Odd said, 'You went ashore then?'

'I did that,' said Gudmund, 'and I've had the time of my life, making the Lapp women squeal. Would you like to come along with me tomorrow?'

'Not in the least,' said Odd.

They lay there for three days, then got a fair wind, and there's nothing more to tell till they reached Permia. They brought their ships up the river Dvina. This river has a great many islands, but the place they cast anchor was off a headland jutting out from the mainland. Then they noticed crowds of people leaving the forest and assembling.

Odd said, 'What do you think those people are doing up there, Gudmund?'

'I don't know,' he said. 'What's your opinion, Odd?'

'I'd think this must be either a big sacrificial rite or a funeral feast,' said Odd. 'This time, Gudmund, it's your turn to guard the ships while Asmund and I go ashore.'

When they reached the forest, they saw a large building. Darkness was coming on. They went up to the door and took a good look round to see what was happening. Inside, people had been settled on benches along both sides of the hall, and by the door there was a vat. The house was so well lit there wasn't a shadow to be seen except behind the vat. It sounded as if the people in the house were enjoying themselves.

'Do you know anything about the language of these people?' asked Odd.

'No more than the twittering of birds,' said Asmund. 'Can you make anything of it?'

'About as much as you,' said Odd, 'but you see that man there serving the drinks to both benches. I've an idea he knows how to speak Norse, so I'm going into the house to look for some likely place to take up position, and in the mean time you're to wait for me here.'

Odd went inside, took up his position near the door and waited there until the serving man happened to pass by. The first thing the serving man knew, Odd had grabbed him and lifted him above his head. He started yelling and shouting to the Permians that he'd been caught by a troll. Up they jumped, and made for Odd on one side but he warded them off with the serving man. In the end, Odd and Asmund managed to get him outside, and the Permians didn't feel confident enough to chase after them.

They brought the serving man down to the ships. Odd settled the man on the seat beside him and started questioning him, but he didn't say a word.

'There's no point in keeping your mouth shut,' said Odd, 'I know you can speak Norse.'

'What do you want to know?' asked the man.

Odd said, 'How long have you been here?'

'Some years,' he said.

'What do you think of it?' asked Odd.

'I've never been anywhere I've liked less,' said the serving man.

'What would you say was the worst trick we could play on the Permians?' said Odd.

'That's a good question,' he said. 'There's a mound further up on the banks of the river Dvina, made up of two parts, silver and earth. A handful of silver has to be left there for every man who leaves this world, and the same amount of earth for every one who comes into it. You couldn't play the Permians a nastier trick than go to the mound and carry off all the silver.'

Odd called to Gudmund and Sigurd and said, 'You and your crew follow the serving man's directions and go to the mound.'

They got ready to go ashore, but Odd stayed behind to guard the ships and kept the serving man there with him.

5. Encounters with Permians and Lapps

Off they went to the mound and there they began gathering loads for themselves, for there was plenty of silver. When they were ready, they went back to the ships. Odd asked them how things had gone. They were very pleased with themselves and said there was no shortage of plunder.

'Now,' said Odd 'take the serving man and watch him carefully. He keeps looking ashore as if he doesn't dislike the Permians as much as he'd have us believe.'

Odd went up to the mound while Gudmund and Sigurd guarded the ships. They kept the serving man between them and at the same time they tried to sift the silver from the earth, but before they knew what was happening he was off and ashore, and that was the last they saw of him.

Meanwhile, Odd and his men had reached the mound. 'Now,' said Odd, 'we'll gather loads, each according to his own strength, so that our journey won't be wasted.'

Dawn was breaking when they left the mound, and they travelled on till the sun was up. Suddenly Odd came to a halt.

'What are you stopping for?' asked Asmund.

'There's a crowd swarming down from the forest,' said Odd.

'What can we do now?' asked Asmund.

Then they all saw the crowd. 'This doesn't look too promising,' said Odd. 'My arrow-bag's back at the ship. I'd better turn off into the wood and cut myself a club with this axe I have, but you carry on to that headland jutting out into the river.' And that was what they did. When he got back to them he had a great club in his hand.

'What's the cause of this crowd, do you think?' asked Asmund.

'It's my guess the serving man must have got away from Gudmund and Sigurd and then carried tales about us to the Permians,' said Odd. 'I've a feeling that he wasn't as unhappy here as he pretended to be. Now we'd better spread out in a line across the headland.'

Then the mob swarmed towards them, and Odd recognized the serving man well to the fore. Odd called out to him and asked, 'What's your hurry?'

'I wanted to find out what would please you best,' he answered.

'Where did you go?' asked Odd.

'Further inland to tell the Permians what you were up to,' he said.

'How do they like this affair?' asked Odd.

'I've put your case so well for you,' said the serving man, 'that they want to do business with you.'

'We'd like that,' said Odd, 'as soon as we get back to our ships.'

'The Permians think the least they could ask for is to finish the business here and now.'

'What's our business to be then?' asked Odd.

'They want to exchange weapons with you, silver for steel.'

'We're not interested in that sort of bargain,' said Odd.

'Then we'll just have to fight it out,' said the serving man.

'That's for you to decide,' said Odd.

Then Odd told his men to throw all their dead enemies into the river. 'Otherwise, if they can get back any of their dead, in no time they'll start using their magic against our people.'

So the fight began. Odd hacked his way through the enemy wherever he could get at them, and cut down the Permians as if they were saplings. It was a long hard fight, but the outcome of the battle was that the Permians fled, with Odd at their heels. Then he turned back to find out what had happened to his own men and saw that only a few of them had been killed, though the natives had fallen in large numbers.

'Now we can do business,' said Odd. 'We'll collect silver weapons in loads.'

That was what they did, and then went down to their ships. But when they arrived, the ships had vanished. Odd seemed rather put out by this.

'What can we do now?' asked Asmund.

'There are two ways of looking at it,' said Odd. 'Either they must have brought the ships round to the lee of the island, or else they've let us down worse than we could ever have expected.'

'That couldn't be,' said Asmund.

'I'll try to find out,' said Odd.

He went up to the edge of the wood and set fire to a large tree. It was soon ablaze, and flames reached high in the air. Next thing, they saw the ships coming back to land. The kinsmen were delighted to meet again. After that they set off with their loot and there's nothing to tell of their journey till they reached Lappland, putting in at the same harbour as before.

After nightfall they were woken by a great din in the sky, louder than anything they had ever heard. Then Odd asked Gudmund and Sigurd if they knew of any stories about this sort of thing, but while they were discussing it there was another crash, as loud as the first, and then a third, the loudest of all.

'What do you think is behind this, Odd?' asked Gudmund.

Odd said, 'I've been told that two contrary winds sometimes start to blow at the same time and then clash, and their collision produces loud bangs. We'd better get ready, there's some rough and ugly weather coming our way.'

They built a bulwark across their ships and took other precautions according to Odd's instructions, and no sooner had they made themselves ready than a gale burst upon them, so savage that they were driven out to sea. Their ships ran out of control and they had to keep on bailing. The weather was so rough they expected their ships to founder beneath them at any moment.

Then Gudmund shouted to Odd from his ship. 'What can we do now?' he called.

'There's only one thing,' said Odd.

'What's that?' asked Gudmund.

'Take all the Lappish stuff and throw it overboard,' said Odd.

'What good will that be to them?' asked Gudmund.

'Leave that for the Lapps to decide,' said Odd.

This was what they did. All the Lappish loot was thrown overboard, and they could see at once how some of it drifted forward along the one side of the ship, and some backwards on the other side, till it formed a cluster; then it thrust hard against the wind and was soon out of sight. A little later they sighted land, but the gale carried on blowing and they were driven up to the coast. By this time almost everyone aboard was exhausted, apart from Odd and his kinsmen, and Asmund.

They made land, but it's not said how long they were at sea. They carried their belongings ashore, then Odd asked them to beach their ships and make them secure. Once that was done they built a shelter for themselves and set out to explore the land. Odd guessed that this must be an island. They saw that there was no shortage of animals there, and they shot all they needed to keep themselves going.

One day Odd saw a huge bear in the forest, and took a shot. There was no missing it. When he'd killed the bear, he flayed off the whole skin and put a spike into the mouth right through its body. He stood the bear in the middle of the road facing the mainland. Odd took things easy on the island.

They were out one evening when they noticed a number of people on the mainland crowding together on a headland, people of all sizes, great and small.

'What do you think, Odd?' asked Gudmund. 'What are these people up to?'

'I don't know,' said Odd, 'but I'm going ashore to find out what they're arguing about.'

Odd asked Asmund to come with him. They went down to the beach, boarded a boat and rowed up to the headland. There they put up their oars to listen to the debate.

The chieftain of the giants was speaking. 'As you know,' he said, 'some children have turned up on our island yonder, and they've done us a great deal of harm. I've come here to propose the extermination of these squatters on our property. I've a bracelet on my arm that I'll give to anyone who's willing to kill them.'

A woman stepped forward and spoke to the assembly.

'Give me the bracelet,' she said, 'We're keen on trinkets, us women.'

'Good,' said the giant. 'You'll make a proper job of anything you do.'

Odd and Asmund started back home and told their men what they had discovered. Sooner than they expected they saw a woman wading across the sound from the mainland and over to the island, wearing a leather tunic. She was so big and evil looking, they thought they'd never seen a creature like her. She went up to the ships, took hold of their prows, and shook them so fiercely they thought the ships would break into pieces. Then she strode ashore. Odd had stationed himself behind the bear. Beforehand, he had put glowing embers into the creature's mouth. Now he took an arrow and shot it right through the bear. She saw the arrow coming and stopped it with the palm of her hand, but the arrow bit no more than if it had hit a piece of rock. Then Odd took one of Gusir's Gifts and shot it like the first one. The giantess put up her hand, but the arrow went straight through it into her eye and out through the back of her head. Still she kept coming on, and Odd shot the third arrow. She spat in her other palm and held it up, but the arrow went the same way as the earlier one, into her eye and out at the back of the head. Then she turned around, splashed her way back to the mainland, and told them about the rough treatment she'd been given.

Odd and his men stayed on the island for some time.

6. The Giants

One evening when they were standing outside their house, they saw that a crowd had gathered on the headland, just as before. Odd and Asmund rowed over to the mainland, and rested on their oars. Up on the headland, the chief giant was speaking. 'It's very peculiar,' he said, 'that we can't kill these children. I sent a lady of real quality against them, but they've got a creature that blows out arrows and fire through its mouth and nostrils. I'd better go home, I feel so sleepy suddenly.'

Odd and Asmund did the same. Two evenings later they saw the same thing taking place on the mainland, so they rowed across to listen. The same man as before was talking up on the headland.

'As you know,' he said, 'we've already passed sentence on these children; and nothing much has come of it. But now I have a vision.'

'What do you see, then?' asked his companions.

'What I see,' he said, 'is two small children who've come here in a boat and are listening in on our conversation, so I'll send them a little something.'

'Now's the time to be on our way as fast as we can,' said Odd, and at that very moment a rock came hurtling down from the headland and landed just where the boat had been. They started rowing back towards the mainland.

'This is very queer,' said the giant's leader. 'Their boat's still undamaged and so are they. I'll try throwing another stone and a third, and if that doesn't work I'll let them alone.'

The third stone was so enormous they were nearly swamped, but Odd and Asmund managed to row away from the land. Then the giant said, 'They're still safe, and so is their boat. I'm so sleepy now, I just can't stay awake.'

Then the giants went back home.

'Now we'd better go and haul our boat ashore,' said Odd.

'What do you want to do?' asked Asmund.

'Find out where this tribe lives,' said Odd.

They went ashore and walked until they came to a cave with a fire burning inside. They took up position there and saw giants seated on the benches along both sides, and on the high-seat a fiendish looking character, huge and ugly. He had a thick head of hair, black as a whale's gill-combs, a running nose and nasty-looking eyes. His wife sat next to him, and to describe one is to describe them both.

The chieftain spoke: 'Now I have a vision, I can see across to the island. Now I know who they are, the men who have come, they're the brothers Odd and Gudmund, sons of Grim Hairy-Cheek. I can see it's the Lapps who've sent them here for us to kill, but I know we can never manage that because Odd's fate is to live much longer than other men. So now I'm going to give them as fair a wind to sail away with as the Lapps gave them to come here.'

'Gifts be damned,' muttered Odd. 'Man or monster, you're the meanest.'

'I can see something else,' said the giant. 'Odd has the arrows with him called Gusir's Gifts, so I'm going to give him a nickname and call him Arrow-Odd.'

Then Odd took one of Gusir's Gifts and drew the bowstring with the idea of paying back the giant for his fair wind. When the giant heard the whizz of the arrow coming towards him, he jerked violently to one side and gave himself a crack on the rock face, but the arrow caught his wife under one armpit and came out through the other. She flew at her husband, clawing him. The giants on both benches jumped to their feet, some to help the woman, others her husband. Odd shot the second of Gusir's Gifts into the giant's eye, and after that he went back to the ships. Gudmund and the others were glad to see Odd and Asmund. 'How far did you go, Odd?' asked Gudmund.

Then Odd spoke this verse:

> I sought my goal
> with Gusir's Gifts
> between the cliff
> and kindling flame.
> I hit an ogre
> in the eye
> and his rock-woman
> in the ribs.

'Something out of the ordinary is the least we'd expect of you,'

said Gudmund, 'considering how long you were gone. Did anything
else happen to you on your trip?'

'I was given a nickname,' said Odd and recited this verse:

> I won my nickname,
> just what I needed!
> giants called it
> from the cliff,
> rewarded me fairly
> with fine weather,
> for Arrow-Odd
> to cross the ocean.

'A good wind is what we've been promised to get away from here,
and I've heard the breeze won't be any worse than the one the Lapps
gave us when we came.'

They got themselves ready to sail away with as fine a show as on
the previous occasion, and off they went. When they were some
way from land, the same gale as before overtook them and swept
them out into open sea. They had to spend all the time bailing, and
the weather only let up when they came to the same harbour they'd
drifted from before. All the Lappish huts there were in ruins. As
soon as the breeze was favourable they made their way home to
Hrafnista, where they arrived late in winter. Grim was delighted to
see them and invited them with all their men to stay with him, an
offer they accepted. They handed all their loot over to Grim, and
spent the rest of the winter with him.

7. The Viking Halfdan

Odd gained such a reputation for this voyage, people think none
like it has ever been undertaken from Norway. They had a good
time at Hrafnista that winter, and a lot of drinking went on.
In the spring Odd asked his kinsmen what they wanted to do
next.

'You can decide for us,' they said.

'I'm going on a viking expedition,' said Odd.

He told Grim that he wanted four ships equipped to sail abroad.

When Grim heard this he took complete charge and told Odd when the ships were ready.

'Now,' said Odd, 'I'd like you to put us in the way of some viking you think worthy of us.'

'There's a viking called Halfdan,' said Grim. 'He's got thirty ships and uses the Elfar Skerries as his base.'

When they were ready, they sailed south, rounded the south coast of Norway and reached the Elfar Skerries. They found anchorage for their ships not far away from Halfdan. Once Odd and the rest had pitched their tents, he set off with a few men and went over to the place where the vikings lay. Odd saw that there was a great dragon ship in the fleet. He called out to the ships and asked who was in charge.

The vikings lifted the awnings. 'The leader of this fleet is called Halfdan,' they said, 'but who's asking?'

'Odd's the name.'

'Are you the Odd who went to Permia?'

'I've been there,' said Odd.

'What do you want from me?' said Halfdan.

'I want to find out which of us is the greater man,' said Odd.

'How many ships have you got?' asked Halfdan.

'We've three ships, all big ones and a crew of a hundred and twenty on each. I'll come here in the morning and see you again.'

'I won't be losing any sleep on that account,' said Halfdan.

Odd rowed off back to his men and told them what had happened. 'Now we've plenty of work on our hands,' he said. 'I've decided what we're going to do. We'll unload all our cargo and put it ashore to make the ships as light as possible. Then we'll fell some trees, the biggest and leafiest we can get, and put two on each ship.' And that was what they did.

When all was set, Odd said, 'I want you two, Gudmund and Sigurd, to board the dragon ship from one side.'

They agreed and started rowing quietly towards the ships which were lying at anchor farther down the creek. Odd rowed up to the other side of the dragon ship, so that they flanked it, and the vikings were taken completely by surprise, for the attackers swung the trees against the dragon ship, with a man on every branch. They struck at the vikings through the awnings, and Odd and Asmund fought with such ferocity they cleared the deck all the way to the poop before Halfdan could get to his feet. They killed him there in the poop, and after that Odd gave the survivors a choice, either keep fighting, or surrender. They made the easy choice and surrendered to Odd. From them he picked out all the toughest-looking men; the dragon ship and one other ship he kept for himself, the rest he gave to the vikings, but he took all the valuables there. He gave the dragon ship a name and called it Halfdan's Gift.

After this great victory they sailed back home to Hrafnista and stayed the winter there. In the spring Odd got ready to sail abroad, and when everything was prepared he asked his father, 'Where can a man find a viking who's really out of the ordinary?'

Grim said, 'There's a viking called Soti, and I'll tell you where you can find him, south off Skien, with thirty ships, all big ones.'

8. The Viking Soti

Odd and his kinsmen sailed from Hrafnista in five ships, south off Skien. Late in the summer Soti heard about Odd's movements, and set out to search for him night and day until they came face to face. Then Soti ran into difficult weather.

'Now we'll lay our ships in a line,' he said, 'one alongside the other, with my own ship right in the middle. I've heard that Odd's a very ambitious man and I think he'll make straight for our ships. As soon as they come up with us and reef their sails, we'll surround their ships and not one of them will get away.'

Meanwhile, this is what Odd was planning. 'I know what Soti and his men are planning to do,' he said. 'They're assuming that we'll sail right up to their fleet.'

'Wouldn't that be unwise?' asked Gudmund.

'We mustn't disappoint Soti,' said Odd, 'but we'd better take some countermeasures too. I think I'll lead the attack in my dragon ship and make first for Soti. But we'll have to clear the deck before the mast.'

That's what they did, and off went Halfdan's Gift at high speed. It was protected with iron right round the prow, so that the ship's keel was just touching bottom.

'My idea is to make straight for Soti with my dragon ship,' said Odd, 'and you can sail in my wake. I think it's likely the ropes between their ships will snap.'

Odd got up all the speed he could in his dragon ship, and before Soti realized what was happening it had penetrated his fleet, cutting the links between his ships, and Odd and Asmund were running towards the prow fully armed. They took Soti and his men completely by surprise, leapt aboard his dragon ship and cleared it, and before Gudmund arrived on the scene with his men Soti was dead. Then Odd gave the vikings a choice, either to accept a truce, or carry on fighting, and they opted for a truce. He took the dragon ship but gave them the rest of the fleet.

After that Odd and his men sailed back to Hrafnista with a great deal of loot. Grim was glad to see them, and they stayed there over winter enjoying great respect, but when spring came round again Odd and his men began getting their ships ready for a voyage. Odd was very particular in his choice of men. He gave the dragon ship Soti's Gift to Gudmund and Sigurd, then had the whole of Halfdan's Gift painted and the dragon heads fore and aft gilded, along with the weather vane.

When they were ready to set out, Odd went to see his father Grim and said, 'Now tell me where to find the greatest viking you know.'

'You're not satisfied with being great men,' said Grim, 'you really believe nobody could possibly stand up against you. So I'm going to tell you where you can meet up with the two greatest vikings I know, the greatest in everything they do. One of them's called Hjalmar the Brave, and the other Thord Prow-Gleam.'

'Where are they?' asked Odd, 'and how many ships do they have?'

'Fifteen ships,' said Grim, 'with a hundred and twenty men aboard each of them.'

'What's their home territory?' asked Odd.

'There's a king in Sweden called Hlodver. Over winter they stay with him, but they spend summer aboard their fighting ships.'

As soon as they were ready, away they went with Grim to see them off. Father and son parted great friends.

9. *Hjalmar and Odd*

Now, as to Odd, as soon as the wind was favourable he and his men put out to sea from Hrafnista, and there's nothing to say of their voyage till they reached a certain headland jutting out to sea from the mainland of Sweden. There they put up the awnings, and Odd went ashore to look around. On the other side of the headland he saw fifteen ships, and a camp on shore, with games being played near the tents. The leaders of this outfit were Hjalmar and Thord.

Odd went back to his ships and told what he had seen. Gudmund asked him what they should do.

'We'll divide our men into two groups,' said Odd. 'You bring your ships round the headland and call to the men ashore. I'll take my half by land up into the forest, and then at the same time we'll shout a war cry at them. I daresay this will shake them. Now I come to think of it, they might even run off into the forest and save us any more trouble.'

But as it happened, when Hjalmar and his men heard Gudmund's war cry they didn't pay the least attention, and when they heard the second war cry from the land they just stopped playing as long as it lasted, then carried on with their games.

So both attackers went back to the headland. When they met, Odd spoke to Gudmund. 'I'm not so sure these men we've found are so easily scared,' he said.

'What do you want to do next?' asked Gudmund.

'I'm making a snap decision,' said Odd. 'We're not going to attack these men by stealth. We'd better rest here tonight to lee of the headland and wait till morning.'

Next morning they went ashore to meet Hjalmar, and as soon as Hjalmar's men saw these vikings they put on their armour and went towards them. When they met, Hjalmar asked who the leader was.

'There's more than one leader here,' said Odd.

'What's your name?' said Hjalmar.

'My name's Odd, the son of Grim Hairy-Cheek of Hrafnista.'

'Are you the Odd who went to Permia? What do you want here?'

'I want to find out which of us is the greater man,' said Odd.

'How many ships have you got?' said Hjalmar.

'I've five ships,' said Odd, 'how many have you?'

'We've fifteen,' said Hjalmar.

'That's heavy odds,' he said.

'Ten of my crews can sit back,' said Hjalmar, 'we'll fight it out man to man.'

Each side prepared for battle, then the armies lined up and fought as long as daylight lasted. In the evening a truce was agreed and Hjalmar asked Odd what he thought of the day. Odd said he was pleased with it.

'Do you want to go on with this game?' said Hjalmar.

'I wouldn't consider anything else,' said Odd, 'I've never met better and tougher fighting men. We'll start the fight again as soon as it's daylight.'

Everyone agreed with Odd's suggestion, and in the evening they dressed their wounds and went back to their camps. Next morning both sides lined up for battle and fought all day. Late in the afternoon they made a truce, and Odd asked what Hjalmar thought of the battle that day. Hjalmar said he was pleased with it.

'Do you want us to play this game a third day?' he asked.

'That would really settle matters between us,' said Odd.

Then Thord broke in: 'Is there plenty of money and treasure aboard your ships?'

'Far from it,' said Odd, 'we haven't won any loot all summer.'

'What I think,' said Thord, 'is that there can't ever have been a meeting of such stupid people before. We're fighting over nothing but our own pride and ambition.'

'What do you suggest we do about it?' said Odd.

'Don't you think it would be a better idea,' said Thord, 'to pool our resources?'

'It would suit me very well,' said Odd, 'but I don't know what Hjalmar would think.'

'All I insist on are those viking laws I've always kept,' said Hjalmar.

'When I've heard your laws,' said Odd, 'I'll know what I think of them.'

Then Hjalmar said, 'The first point I want to make is that I and my men refuse to eat raw meat. Plenty of people are in the habit of squeezing a bit of flesh in a piece of cloth and then calling it cooked meat, but in my opinion it's a habit more fit for wolves than men. I never rob merchants or peasants beyond the occasional raid to cover my immediate needs. I never rob women, even when we meet them on the road with plenty of money, and no woman is ever to be brought to my ship against her own free will. And if she can show that she's been taken to the ship against her will, the one who took her, whether he's rich or poor, shall be put to death.'

'I think your laws are very good,' said Odd, 'and they're not going to stand in the way of our alliance.'

So they joined forces. People say that their combined armies were just about the size of Hjalmar's before they met.

10. In Sweden

After that Odd asked where they could expect to get any plunder. 'I know of five berserks based on Zealand,' said Hjalmer, 'the toughest men I ever heard tell of. Here are their names: one's called Brand, the next Agnar, the third Asmund, the fourth Ingjald, and the fifth Alf. They're brothers, and they have six large ships. What do you say we do now, Odd?'

'I say we make straight for the berserks,' said Odd.

They arrived at Zealand with their fifteen ships, and learned that the berserks had gone ashore to see their concubines. Then Odd went ashore by himself to meet the berserks, and as soon as they met, fighting broke out. The outcome was that he killed all the berserks without suffering a single wound.

When Odd had gone ashore Asmund missed him. 'Yes,' he said to Hjalmar, 'there's no doubt about it, Odd must have gone ashore and we're not going to be idle while he's away.'

Hjalmar sailed with six ships to where the other vikings were, and a fight started at once. Just as Odd came down to the shore, Hjalmar had taken the viking ship. They told each other their news, for each had earned himself a great deal of fame and plunder.

After that Hjalmar gave Odd and his men an invitation, which they accepted, to come with him to Sweden. But Gudmund and Sigurd, the men from Halogaland, went north to Hrafnista with their men. They agreed to meet later east at Gota River. When Hjalmar and the others arrived in Sweden, King Hlodver welcomed them with open arms. They stayed there over winter, and Odd was shown great honour for the king thought there was no one to compare with him. Shortly after Odd arrived there, the king gave him five estates.

The king had a daughter called Ingibjorg. She was exceptionally beautiful and clever in everything proper to women.

Odd kept asking Hjalmar why he didn't ask permission to marry Ingibjorg. 'I can see how much you love one another,' said Odd.

'I have proposed to her,' said Hjalmar, 'but her father won't marry her to anyone who doesn't have the title of king.'

'Then we must get our army together next summer,' said Odd, 'and give the king a choice, either to fight or else give you his daughter.'

'I'm not so sure about that,' said Hjalmar, 'I've enjoyed sanctuary here for a long time.'

They stayed there quietly over the winter, and in the spring as soon as they were ready, they set out on a viking expedition.

11. Death in Ireland

There's nothing to tell of their journey until they all met at Gota River and discussed where they should be going that summer. Odd said he wanted most of all to sail west across the North Sea. They now had twenty ships altogether, and Odd commanded Halfdan's Gift. They reached Scotland and made forays into the country, raiding and burning everywhere they went, and there was no stopping them until they had levied a tax on the entire land. From there they sailed to the Orkneys, took over and stayed there throughout the winter. In the spring they crossed to Ireland, harrying there along the coast and also further inland. Odd never went anywhere without taking Asmund along with him. Men, women, and children took to their heels before them into the woods and forests, trying to conceal their possessions and themselves.

One day it happened that Odd and Asmund were alone together some distance inland. Odd was carrying his arrow-bag on his back, and had his bow in his hand. They were looking to see if they could find anyone. Before Odd suspected anything, a bowstring suddenly twanged, and an arrow came flying out of the trees. It was a direct hit on Asmund. He fell down and died almost at once. To Odd this was the most terrible loss he had ever suffered in all his days on earth.

Odd left Asmund lying there and went deeper inland. So fierce was his rage, his only thought was to hurt the Irish in any way he could, no matter what entered his head. He came upon a clearing in the wood where he saw a large crowd of people gathered, men and women. He caught sight of a man there wearing a costly tunic, a bow in his hand, and beside him arrows stuck in the ground. Odd was sure that this was where he should direct his vengeance, against this man. So he pulled out one of Gusir's Gifts, drew the bowstring and took aim at him. The arrow caught the man in the waist, and he dropped dead. Now Odd shot arrow after arrow, killing three more men, and then all the people ran off into the forest. Odd was in such a rage against the Irish, there was no limit to the damage he meant to do. He followed the main track through the wood, tearing up by the roots all the bushes that happened to be in his way. One of the bushes was less firmly rooted than the rest, and he saw a door underneath. He pulled it open and went underground. Inside this underground chamber he saw four women, one of them much more beautiful than the rest. He grabbed her by the arm and tried to force her outside.

Then she spoke. 'Let go of me, Odd,' she said.

'What sort of a troll are you, that you know my name's Odd and not something else?' he said.

'The moment you came here,' she said, 'I knew who you were, and there's another thing I know – Hjalmar is with you, and I'll know what to say to him if I'm taken down to the ships by force.'

'You'll come all the same,' he said.

Then the other women took hold of her and tried to keep her back, but she told them not to do so. 'I want to make a bargain with you, Odd,' she said. 'Let me go in peace, I'm not short of money.'

'Your money's the last thing I want,' said Odd, 'I'm not without silver myself or gold either.'

'Then I'll make you a shirt,' she said.

'The answer's still the same,' said Odd. 'I've more than enough of shirts and shirt-making.'

'You're in no position to get a shirt like the one I'll make for you,' she said. 'It will be made with silk and embroidered with gold. And I'll endow the shirt with certain qualities you've never been offered before.'

'Tell me more,' said Odd.

'You'll never be cold in it, either by sea or land. You'll never be tired when swimming, never hurt by fire, never troubled by hunger, and no iron will bite you. It will protect you against everything, with one exception.'

'What's that?' said Odd.

'Iron will bite you if you run away,' she said, 'even though you wear the shirt.'

'I've better things to do than run away from battles,' said Odd. 'When can the shirt be ready?'

'Next summer,' she said, 'at noon as now, in precisely one year, to the day. Then we shall meet in this same clearing.'

'Have you any idea,' said Odd, 'what I'll do to the Irish if you don't keep your promise, with so much to pay back for the killing of Asmund?'

'Since you've killed my father and three brothers,' she said, 'don't you think you've had your revenge already?'

'As I see it, their deaths don't bring me any closer to vengeance,' said Odd.

They settled the agreement, then went their separate ways. Odd went back to Asmund, lifted him up and carried him on his back down to the sea. Hjalmar had just come ashore with all his men intending to make a search for Odd. They met not far from the ships. Hjalmar asked Odd what had happened, and Odd told him.

'Did you avenge him?' asked Hjalmar.

Then Odd made this verse:

> I raced on my way
> upon the wide road,
> then set my face
> to the fierce arrows.
> To have Asmund alive
> along with me now,
> all of my gold
> I'd gladly give.

'What shall we do now?' said Hjalmar. 'You must be keen to plunder and do all the damage you can here.'

'Far from it,' said Odd, 'I want to get away from here as fast as possible.'

The vikings could make little sense of this, but Hjalmar said they must do as Odd wanted. They raised a burial mound for Asmund. The vikings were so angry over all this, they started criticizing Odd behind his back as soon as he was out of earshot, but he pretended not to notice anything.

They sailed back east as far as Læso Island. A certain earl, who is unnamed, was lying there with a fleet of thirty ships. They decided to attack there and then, and at once made a fierce assault, in which Odd cleared his name of the cowardice the vikings had accused him of in Ireland. Odd and Hjalmar won the victory in this battle.

From there they sailed to Denmark, where they learnt that a force had been gathered to avenge the five berserks they had killed before sailing to Ireland. Two earls were the leaders of this force, and by the end of the encounter they had killed both earls and taken tribute from the land.

12. A New Shirt

After that they broke up their forces. Gudmund and Sigurd sailed north to Hrafnista and settled down to a quiet life, for they wanted to give up their fighting career. Odd stayed behind in Denmark over winter, while Hjalmar went with his men across to Sweden, and they agreed to meet east in Skaane the following spring. Now they both spent a quiet winter. In the spring Hjalmar came from the east with Thord Prow-Gleam at the time agreed, and when they met, Hjalmar asked Odd where he wanted to go that summer. Odd said he wanted to go to Ireland.

'You didn't want to plunder there last summer,' said Hjalmar.

'Whatever happened then,' he said, 'that's where we're going now.'

They put out to sea and had favourable winds until they reached Ireland. Then Odd said, 'We're going to camp here now, and I'm going alone into the country.'

'I'll come with you,' said Hjalmar.

'I'm going by myself,' said Odd, 'I've a rendezvous with some women in the forest.'

Odd went on his way until he came to the clearing where Olvor had agreed to meet him, but as yet she hadn't arrived. This made him so angry at the Irish that he decided to start raiding the country right away, but before he had gone far he heard some carts coming towards him.

It was Olvor, and when they met she was first with her greetings.

'Now I hope you're not going to be angry with me,' she said, 'even though I am later than I promised.'

'Is the shirt ready?' said Odd.

'No doubt about that,' she said. 'You'd better sit down beside me, because I want to see how well it fits you.'

He did as he was asked, took the shirt, unfolded it and put it on. It was a perfect fit.

'Do all the qualities you spoke of go with the shirt?' he asked.

'Certainly,' she said.

'How's that?' said Odd. 'Did you make this fine garment all by yourself?'

Then she spoke a verse:

> This shirt is sewn
> from six lands' silk,
> one arm in Ireland,
> north the other, by Lapps:
> Saxon maids started it,

Hebrideans spun it,
Welsh wives the weavers,
on Othjodan's-mother's warp.

Then Odd spoke a verse:

Not like the byrnie,
the blue ringed mail-coat
feeling like frost
upon my flesh,
when about my sides,
gold-stitched,
the silken shirt
slipped close.

'How do you like the shirt anyway?' she asked. Odd said he liked it very much.

'And now,' he said, 'I'd like you to choose a reward for your shirt-making.'

'Things have been so troubled here since my father was killed,' she said, 'I'm afraid the kingdom will slip out of my hands. So the reward I choose is for you to stay here three years.'

'Then we'll have to make another bargain,' said Odd. 'You can go along with me and be my wife.'

'You must think I'm very keen to get a husband,' she said, 'but I'll accept your offer.'

Then Odd looked around and saw near by a group of fighting men. He asked if these had been sent to kill him. 'Far from it,' she said. 'These men are to attend you down to the ship. You'll be travelling away from here with much more ceremony than you did last summer.'

He went back to his ship attended by these fighting men, and met Hjalmar at the camp. Odd asked him to stay with him over these three years, and he agreed. So now Odd married Olvor. In summer Odd and his men used to stay aboard their ships and kill the vikings who were attacking the country. By the time they completed their three-year stint they had rid Ireland of vikings, far and near. Some were killed and others made off. By then, Odd had grown so tired of being there that it was useless trying to hold him back.

Olvor and Odd had a daughter called Ragnhild. An argument

arose between them, as Odd wanted to take the girl with him, but Olvor refused this. In the end the matter was referred to Hjalmar, and he said the girl should grow up with her mother.

As soon as Odd and Hjalmar were ready, off they sailed and made their way to England. They heard that a viking called Skolli was lying there with forty ships. After they had anchored their ships, Odd took off in a small boat, as he wanted a word with Skolli. When they met, Skolli asked Odd what business he had in that part of the world.

'I want to fight you,' said Odd.

'What have I ever done to you?' said Skolli.

'Nothing at all,' said Odd, 'but I want to have your property and your life because you've been plundering the kingdom of the ruler here.' This king was called Edmund.

'Are you the Odd who went to Permia a long time ago?' said Skolli.

'The same,' said Odd.

'I'm not so conceited as to start thinking myself your equal,' said Skolli. 'But you must want to know why I keep plundering Edmund's kingdom.'

'Maybe I do,' said Odd.

'This king killed my father and many of my kinsmen in the land, and then he stole my father's throne. But I've sometimes managed to conquer half of the land, and sometimes a third. I think it would do your reputation some good if you were to join forces with me; then we could kill King Edmund and take the kingdom for ourselves. I'd like to seal our agreement with witnesses.'

'In that case,' said Odd, 'summon eight farmers from the land to swear oaths on your behalf.'

'So be it,' said Skolli.

Odd went down to the ships to see Hjalmar and tell him that if everything turned out as Skolli had said, they must give him their support. They slept through the night, and in the morning they went ashore with all their men. Skolli had been busy during the night, and now he had come down from the country with the farmers, who swore oaths to support him. After that they joined forces and marched up into the country, looting everywhere, burning and destroying wherever they came. The inhabitants fled before them and sought help from King Edmund. The two armies met in the south of the country, and at once fighting broke out. The battle lasted for three days, but the outcome was that King Edmund was killed. Odd and Skolli took over the country and stayed there through the winter.

In the spring Skolli offered to give them the kingdom. However, Odd refused it – 'though my advice is that you offer it to Hjalmar.' But he wouldn't accept it either.

'In that case I suggest we give the kingdom to Skolli,' said Odd. This he accepted, and told them they were welcome to stay there any time, whenever they pleased, in winter or summer. Then they equipped twenty ships to sail abroad, and there's nothing to tell of that voyage until they arrived south of Skien.

13. *Ogmund Eythjof's-Killer*

There were two kings called Hlodver and Haki at anchor there with thirty ships. As Odd and his men were lying in-shore with their fleet, ten ships came rowing at them. When they met they didn't bandy words, and fighting began at once. Odd had twenty ships. Never had Odd found himself in a tougher spot, the clash was so fierce, but the outcome was that all ten ships were taken.

Then Odd said, 'These people have been made out to be worse than they are.'

'Is that what you think?' said Hjalmar. 'These were only the scouts the enemy were sending out.'

After they'd been resting for a while, twenty ships rowed towards them from the coast and at once fierce fighting broke out. Never before, on sea or land, had Odd and his men met fighters like these, yet the battle ended with both kings dead and all their armies, though it is said too that by then, Odd and Hjalmar had so few men left that they sailed away in a small boat. They reached some isles called Elfar Skerries; inlets called Tronu Creeks cut into these skerries, and it was there they saw two ships draped with black awnings. This was at the beginning of summer.

'I don't want us to let them know that we're here,' said Hjalmar. 'These vikings seem to be lying quietly under the awnings.'

'I'm not standing for that,' said Odd. 'I want a word with people when I run into them!'

So Odd called out and asked who was in charge of the ships. Someone lifted the hem of the awning and said, 'He's called Ogmund.'

'Which Ogmund's that?' said Odd.

'Where have you been that you've never heard of Ogmund Eythjof's-Killer?' said the man on the ship.

'I've never heard your name before,' said Odd, 'and I've never seen an uglier-looking man.'

This, so we're told, is how the man looked. He had black hair, a thick tuft of it hanging down over his face where the forelock should have been, and nothing could be seen of his face except the teeth and the eyes. There were eight men with him, all looking just the same. No weapon could bite them, and for size and ugliness they were more like monsters than men.

Then Ogmund said, 'Who's this man finding fault with me?'

'Odd's the name,' he said.

'Are you that same Odd,' said Ogmund, 'who went to Permia a long time ago?'

'Some such fellow,' said Odd, 'has arrived.'

'That's very good,' said Ogmund, 'I've spent most of my life looking for you.'

'What do you have in mind for me?' said Odd.

'Where do you want to fight, by sea or land?' said Ogmund.

'I'll fight at sea,' said Odd.

Then Ogmund and his men pulled down the awnings. Elsewhere, Hjalmar and his crew made their preparations, loading their ship with stones. When both sides were ready, they clashed fiercely, their ships grappling alongside one another. It was a long, hard battle. After some time, Ogmund hoisted a flag of truce and asked Odd what he thought of it all. Odd said he thought very poorly of it.

'Why's that?' asked Ogmund.

'I'll tell you why,' said Odd. 'Up till now I've always believed I've been fighting men, but this time I seem to be fighting demons. I struck at your neck just now with the sword I'm holding, and it seemed an easy chance, but it didn't bite at all.'

'Each of us can say the same about the other,' said Ogmund, 'that he seems more like a troll than a man. I struck at your neck when I had an easy chance and the sword I was using has never faltered in a blow before, but it didn't bite at all. Shall we carry on fighting or part now, because I can tell you how our battle is bound to end. Your sworn-brothers Hjalmar and Thord will both fall here, and so will every one of your followers. All my warriors will be killed, too, only the two of us will be left standing, and then, if we fight it out, you will be the death of me.'

'On with the game then, till all our men and yours are dead,' said Odd.

So they thrust shield against shield once more and fought until only three on one side were left standing, Thord, Hjalmar and Odd, though there were still eight with Ogmund.

'Do you want us to part now, Odd?' he asked. 'I think we've killed equal numbers on both sides. It will turn out just as I told you, but you're fated to live much longer than other men, and you've a shirt to protect you from harm.'

'I'd rather part from you sooner than later,' said Odd, 'as long as you don't lay the name of coward on my back.'

'Then let's break off,' said Ogmund, 'now our killing scores are equal.'

Odd said he wanted to get away from the creeks, so they moved over to a certain islet. Odd said there were three things to be done: one was to go into the wood and shoot animals, the second to look after the ship.

'And I'll light a fire and take care of the cooking,' said Hjalmar.

Odd went into the forest, and Thord guarded the ship. When the others came back, Thord had disappeared, so they went to look for him. Since they found the boat tied securely, they kept searching for Thord and found him in a cleft in the hillside, sitting there dead.

'This is an evil business,' said Odd, 'we haven't suffered such a loss since Asmund died.'

They looked for what had killed him and saw that a spear was stuck into one armpit with its point coming out through the other.

'That blackguard Ogmund seems to have thought our scores weren't equal after all,' said Odd. 'We must go straight back to the creeks to look for them.'

And that's what they did, but Ogmund had vanished without a trace. They scoured all the skerries for him and the forests and islands and headlands for a whole week, but they neither found him nor heard anything of him. So they went back to Thord and brought him home to Sweden and raised a burial mound over him. After that they went to Uppsala, where the king received them with open arms. They told him what had happened. They stayed there for a time, and when summer came round again the king asked them to stay on. 'I'll give you a ship and crew so you can sail along the coast and enjoy yourselves,' he said.

14. The Death of Hjalmar

To continue with the story of Odd and Hjalmar, they fitted out two ships, with a crew of forty aboard each, and went sailing along the coast. It so happened that they ran into rough weather and looked for shelter at an island called Samso. There are creeks there known as Munar Creeks, where they found anchorage for their ships and put up the awnings. During the day it happened that the gable head on Odd's ship had broken, and in the morning Hjalmar and Odd went ashore to cut down a tree to replace it. It was Hjalmar's custom to have on all the armour he wore in battle. Odd had left his arrow-bag down at the ships, but he used to wear the shirt day and night. All their men were asleep.

Suddenly some vikings under the leadership of a man called Angantyr made a surprise attack; twelve of them there were, all brothers, and never more than twelve in all. By this time they had travelled all over the world and never met with any real resistance. They came upon the ships of Odd and Hjalmar and attacked the men on board, and, to make a long story short, they killed every man on the ships.

Then the brothers started chatting and said, 'The way it looks, our father Arngrim never told us a bigger lie than when he said these men were savage vikings and no shield could stop them. In all the places we've been, nobody has ever borne themselves worse or shown less fight. Let's go back home and kill that old shit of a father to pay him back for his lie.'

'There's another way of looking at it,' said some of the others. 'Either Odd and Hjalmar have been very much over-praised, or else they must have gone ashore because of the fine weather. Rather than give up and go home, we ought to be looking for them.'

So that's what the twelve brothers did, screaming and running about in a berserk fit. This time even Angantyr was seized with one, which had never happened before. Just then, Odd and Hjalmar came down from the forest. Odd stopped and hesitated a bit, and Hjalmar asked what was the matter.

'Something queer keeps happening to me,' Odd said. 'Sometimes I seem to hear a bull bellowing or a dog howling, and sometimes it's like people screaming. Do you know anybody who behaves like that?'

'Yes,' said Hjalmar, 'twelve brothers I know of.'

'Do you know their names?' said Odd.

Then Hjalmar spoke this poem:

> Hervard, Hjorvard,
> Hrani, Angantyr,
> Bild and Bui,
> Barri and Toki,
> Tind and Tyrfing,
> the two Haddings:
> These are the issue
> of Arngrim and Eyfura,
> born they were
> on Bolm in the east.
>
> These men I have learned
> the most malevolent,
> the last of all
> to act with honour.
> They are berserks,
> bringers of chaos,
> from our ships they swept
> our loyal fellow-sailors.

Then Odd saw the berserks coming, and spoke this verse:

> I see war-hungry
> ones walking
> from Munar Creeks,
> men in grey corselets.
> Foul the battle
> these fellows have fought
> and on the beach,
> battered, our boats.

Then Odd spoke again. 'It's a pity,' he said, 'that my arrow-bag and bow were left behind on the ships, and I've nothing but this little wood-axe.'

Then Odd made a verse:

> One time I shivered,
> when, shouting and screaming,
> from our ships
> they strode upon the island,
> the most treacherous,
> so I've been told
> of men, eager
> for any mischief.

Odd went back into the forest and cut himself a club, while Hjalmar waited for him. When he came back, up ran the berserks. Then Hjalmar said:

> No matter what fearsome
> fighters they seem,
> never shall we fall
> back before them:
> Tonight we'll be guests
> of the god Odin,
> but the berserks will live,
> the band of twelve.

Then Odd said:

> There was a time once
> I proved your words wrong.
> They'll drink Odin's brew,
> this bunch of berserks,
> you and I, Hjalmar,
> have years to live.

Then Angantyr made this verse:

> Things go sadly
> for you two seamen,
> all your comrades
> killed before you,
> now you must follow
> to feast with Odin.

Then Odd said:

> Here they come, twelve
> tramping together,
> men without honour,
> evil and mad,
> but face to face
> is the fashion of the hero,
> fighting alone
> unless his heart fails.

'Who are these fellows we're meeting here?' asked Odd.

'There's one called Angantyr,' the others said, 'and he's the leader. We're twelve brothers, the sons of Earl Arngrim and Eyfura from eastern Flanders.'

'Who's asking?' said Angantyr.

'One of us is called Odd, the son of Grim Hairy-Cheek, and the other is Hjalmar the Brave.'

'Well met,' said Angantyr, 'we've been looking for you everywhere.'

'Did you visit our ships?' said Odd.

'We did indeed,' said Angantyr, 'and we've taken everything there for ourselves.'

'What do you think about this meeting of ours?' said Hjalmar.

'I think we ought to do what you were suggesting just now,' said Angantyr, 'fight it out in single combat. I want to take on you, Odd, because you've a shirt that prevents any weapon from wounding you, and I've a sword called Tyrfing, made by dwarfs, who swore it could bite anything, even iron and rock. We divide our band into two groups, seven in one, and four plus myself in the other. By myself I'm supposed to be the equal of the two Haddings, and then there's one more to balance up with Tyrfing.'

'I want to fight against Angantyr,' said Hjalmar. 'I've a mail-coat made of fourfold rings that's always kept me free of wounds.'

'That wouldn't be very clever,' said Odd, 'we'll do well as long as I'm the one that fights Angantyr, but otherwise it'll be hopeless.'

'I don't care, I'm getting my own way,' said Hjalmar.

'If anyone survives,' Angantyr said, 'I'd like him to promise not to rob the dead of weapons. If I'm killed I want to take my Tyrfing into the mound with me. And in the same way, Odd must keep his shirt and arrows, and Hjalmar his mail-coat.'

And they agreed that the survivors should raise burial mounds over the dead.

The two Haddings were the first to come forward. Odd struck each of them a blow with his club, and that was all they needed. One after another rose to fight Odd, and the outcome was that he killed all who came against him. Then he took a rest and Hjalmar stood up. Someone came to fight him, and it wasn't long before the challenger was dead. The second came forward, and the third and the fourth. Finally Angantyr rose to his feet, and they fought a long hard duel, but in the end Angantyr was killed by Hjalmar. Then Hjalmar went over to a hummock and sat on it and sank down against it. Odd went up to him and spoke this verse:

> What is it, Hjalmar?
> How wan your face:
> your wounds, I see,
> wear down your strength.
> Your helmet's shattered,
> your mail-coat split,
> your strength, I think,
> is slipping away.

'It's been proved right,' said Odd, 'what I told you; it would never do for us if you were to fight Angantyr.'

'That's neither here nor there,' said Hjalmar. 'Everyone has to die.' Then he said:

> I've sixteen sword-cuts,
> my mail-coat's split,
> all is black
> before my eyes:

> no path is clear:
> tempered in poison,
> Angantyr's point
> has pierced my heart.

'This is a loss that will never be repaired, no matter how long I live,' said Odd. 'See where your obstinacy has brought you; we'd have won a great victory if only I'd had my way.'

'Settle down,' said Hjalmar, 'I want to compose a poem and send it with you back home to Sweden.'

Then he made this poem:

> The ladies back home
> shall never learn
> that ever I cringed
> at the clash of swords:
> the smart young woman
> at Sigtun won't ever
> giggle at me
> for giving ground.
>
> I travelled, leaving
> the lovely songs
> of the women; with Soti
> I wandered joyless.
> When I joined
> the journeying band,
> and left my loyal friends,
> I shortened my life.
>
> My dear one, the king's
> fair daughter led me
> out by the hand
> to Agnafit;
> her prophetic words
> work to their end –
> Hjalmar will never
> return to his home.
>
> I deserted her,
> my dear Ingibjorg –
> a moment of decision,

the day of my destiny.
She will mourn for me
with bitterness of mind
but nevermore
shall we meet again.

Carry my helm
and my coat of mail
to the court, show it
in the King's hall.
Tears will his daughter
drop at the sight,
the byrnie, broken
upon my breast.

Five lordships
lay under my rule,
yet I was not happy
there at home.
Now I lie prostrate
and powerless here
on Samso Island,
slashed by swords.

Take the ring from my arm,
the red bracelet,
the gift given
to the girl Ingibjorg:
deep in her mind
the maid will mourn
that nevermore
we two shall meet.

Well I remember
the women, seated,
persuading me – don't
set out from Sigtun:
ale and good company
in the king's hall
will never again
gladden Hjalmar's heart.

'Now I want you to give my greetings to all our comrades, and I'm
going to name their names:

We talked and drank
deep many a day:
Alf and Atli,
Eyvind, Trani,
Gizur, Glama,
Gudvard, Starri,
Steinkell, Stikill,
Storolf, Vifill.

Hrafn and Helgi,
Hlodver, Igul,
Stein and Kari,
Styr and Ali,
Osur, Agnar,
Ormr and Trandil,
Gylfri and Gauti,
Gjafar and Ragnar.

Fjolmund, Fjalar,
Frosti and Beinir,
Tind and Tyrfing,
the two Haddings.
Valbjorn, Vikar,
Vemund, Flosi,
Geirbrand, Goti,
Guttorm, Sneril.

Styr and Ari,
Stein and Kari,
Vott and Veseti,
Vemund, Hnefi.
We shared the ale-bench,
idled at ease;
I'm not ready now
to run for my life.

Svarfandi, Sigvaldi,
Sæbjorn, Kol,
Thrain, Thjostolf,

Thorolf and Sval,
Hrappi and Hadding,
Hunfast, Knui,
Ottar, Egil
Yngvar and all.

'Now I want to ask you a favour,' said Hjalmar to Odd. 'Don't have me buried in a mound next to nasty devils like these berserks. I think I'm a much better man than they were.'

'You'll have your wish,' said Odd, 'just as you ask. I can see you're slipping away.'

'Pull the bracelet off my arm,' said Hjalmar. 'Give it to Ingibjorg. Tell her I sent it her as I lay dying.' Then Hjalmar spoke this poem:

The earls are all
eager at the ale-drinking,
easy in the king's
companionship at Uppsala;
many a warrior
weakens at the ale:
on the isle I weary,
alone with my wounds.

A raven flies, beating
from a tall southern branch,
and after the raven
a ravenous eagle.
Eagle, I offer you
every hospitality,
a last bowl
of my life-blood.

After that Hjalmar died. Odd heaved all the berserks into a single heap and piled timber around them. It was close by the sea. Then he laid their weapons beside them and their clothes, and he stole nothing. After that he covered the heap with turf, and finally topped the whole mound with sand. Then he took Hjalmar, lifted him on his back, carried him to the shore and there he laid him down. He went aboard the ships, carried all the dead ashore and built a burial mound over all his men there on the beach. People who have been there say that the signs of Odd's work can still be seen.

15. The Lovers' Burial

After that Odd carried Hjalmar aboard and put out to sea. He resorted to his magic, hoisted sail in calm weather and journeyed back home to Sweden with Hjalmar's body. Odd landed at a spot he had picked out, beached his ship, lifted Hjalmar on to his back and walked over to Uppsala. He laid the body beside the door of the hall and walked inside, carrying Hjalmar's mail-coat and helmet, threw them down on the floor in front of the king and told him what had happened. Then he went up to the chair where Ingibjorg was sitting sewing a shirt for Hjalmar.

'Here's a bracelet,' said Odd, 'which Hjalmar sent you with his greetings on the day he died.'

She took the bracelet and looked at it in silence. Then she leaned back against the chair posts and died.

Odd burst out laughing. 'Not many pleasant things have happened lately,' he said, 'and when they do we'd best welcome them. Since they weren't allowed to while they lived, these two can enjoy each other in death.'

Odd lifted her up and laid her in Hjalmar's arms before the door of the hall. Then he sent someone into the hall for the king so that he could see how everything had been laid out. After that the king made Odd welcome and invited him to sit on the high-seat beside him. When Odd had rested, the king said he wanted to hold a funeral feast for Hjalmar and Ingibjorg and then raise a burial mound for them. The king arranged to have everything done just as Odd had suggested. When the helmet and armour which Hjalmar had owned were displayed, everyone was deeply impressed by all that he had achieved and the spirit in which he had defended his life. Hjalmar and Ingibjorg were laid in one mound, and all the people came to view this marvel, for Odd had seen to it that everything was done with great honour.

Odd took it easy over the winter at King Hlodver's court and in the spring the king let him have some men and ten ships. In the summer Odd went off once more in search of Ogmund Eythjof's-Killer, but could find him nowhere.

16. The Viking Sæmund

In the autumn it happened that Odd came to Gotaland and there he heard about a viking called Sæmund. People said this viking was the hardest of men to deal with, and he had fifty-five ships. With his ten ships Odd came upon the vikings, and as soon as they met a battle flared up, long and fierce, with no shortage of action. The outcome was that in the evening all Odd's ships had been swept clean of men, and he was left alone. When it was almost dark Odd jumped overboard, but one of the vikings saw this and hurled a missile after him, catching him in the calf so that it stuck right into the bone. It occurred to him that, the way things were, he could be said to be on the run, so he swam back to the ships, and when the vikings saw him they hauled him aboard. Sæmund told them to shackle Odd's feet, and tie his hands with a bowstring, and they did as he ordered.

Odd sat there in chains, with twelve men guarding him, but Sæmund had himself ferried over to the mainland and camped there.

Then Odd said to the men who were guarding him, 'What's your choice, shall I entertain you or will you entertain me? It's very dull as things are.'

'It seems to us you're in no state to entertain anybody,' said their leader, 'with your feet in chains and waiting to be executed in the morning.'

'That doesn't bother me,' said Odd. 'Everybody has to die.'

'In that case we'd like you to do the entertaining,' they said.

He started singing to them and kept it up till they were all asleep, then crawled over to an axe that lay on the deck and managed to shift it a bit so that the edge was turned upwards. Then he twisted his shoulders and rubbed his hands against the edge till they were free. He untied the shackles and got them off his feet. Once he was free he felt he had room to move. He went up to the sleeping men, prodded them with the axe handle and told them to wake up. 'While you've been sleeping like idiots, the prisoner's broken loose.'

Then he killed them all, took his arrow-bag, got into a boat and rowed across to the mainland. He first went into the wood, pulled out the spearhead and dressed his wound.

Meanwhile, Sæmund woke up in his tent and sent some people out to the ships to the watchmen, but they were all dead and Odd was gone. They were not too pleased at what they found and told Sæmund what had happened. He scoured the whole of Gotaland looking for Odd, but by that time Odd was elsewhere, and looking for Sæmund.

Early one morning Odd came out of the wood. He saw Sæmund's camp and his ships floating in the harbour. Odd turned back into the wood and cut himself a club, then went up to Sæmund's tent, pulled it down over him and his men, and killed Sæmund and fourteen others. Afterwards he gave the men on board the ships the chance to submit and accept him as their leader, and that is what they chose. Now Odd sailed back home to Sweden, and stayed there over winter with only a small band of followers.

17. Baptism

Odd sent a message north to Hrafnista asking his kinsmen Sigurd and Gudmund to come and help him in the spring. They were glad to do this, so off they went to meet Odd, and there was a happy reunion. After that they put out to sea and sailed southwards, getting into shallow waters, for Odd had never sailed there before. They went plundering in the south through Normandy, France and Alsace, creating havoc everywhere.

There is nothing to tell of their expedition till they wrecked their fleet on a certain coastline. They marched their men ashore, and there they saw a house built in quite a different way from any other they had ever seen. Up they went to the house. It was built of stone, and the door was open.

Odd said, 'What sort of a house have we got here? What do you make of it, Sigurd?'

'I've no idea,' he said. 'What do you think, Odd?'

'I don't know,' he said, 'but I suppose there must be some people living in it and they'll be coming back to it soon, so we'd better not go in just yet.'

They settled down somewhere near the house. After a while they saw people flocking towards it, and not only that, heard a noise like nothing they'd ever heard before.

'It seems to me the men of this country are a very queer lot,' said Odd. 'Let's wait here till these people leave the house.'

Just as Odd had guessed, after a while they began to stream away from the house. One of the local people went up to Odd and his men. 'Who are you?' he said.

Odd told him. 'But what's the name of this country where we are now?' he asked. The man told him it was Aquitaine.

'What's this house for, where you've been all this time?'

'We call it a minster or a church,' he said.

'What was all that noise you were making?'

'We call that the Mass,' he said. 'But what about you, are you really a complete heathen?'

'We don't know anything about any religion,' said Odd, 'except that we believe in our own power and strength, and we don't believe in Odin. What's your faith?'

'We believe in Him who created heaven and earth, the sea, the sun and the moon,' said the man.

'He must be very great, if he's made all that,' said Odd. 'That much I can understand.'

Odd and his men were shown to a hostel. They spent several weeks there and had meetings with the local people, who asked Odd and the others whether they were willing to embrace the faith, and eventually Gudmund and Sigurd did so. Then they tried to find out if Odd was willing to do the same.

He said he would offer them terms. 'I'll take your faith, but keep my old habits. I won't offer sacrifices to Thor or Odin or any other idols, but I'm not so keen to stay here. I want to roam about from land to land, sometimes among the Christians and sometimes among the heathen.'

All the same, in the end Odd was baptized, and there they stayed for a time.

One day Odd asked Gudmund and Sigurd if they were keen to get away. They said, 'We like it better here than anywhere we've ever been.'

'We couldn't disagree more then,' said Odd. 'I've never been so bored in my life.'

So without asking leave of his kinsmen, he stole away alone, and left them behind with all their followers.

On his way out of the town he saw a large group of men coming towards him. One of them was riding and the rest were on foot. They were all elegantly attired, and none of them carried arms. Odd stood beside the road as they passed by, and neither spoke to the other. Then Odd saw four men come running, all carrying long knives in their hands. They rushed up to the rider, cut off his head, and then ran back the way they had come, right past Odd, one of them carrying the victim's head. It seemed to Odd that these men had committed a particularly nasty crime, so he ran after them into the forest, down into some underground chamber. Odd leapt into the chamber behind them. They tried to defend themselves, but Odd attacked them without pause until he had killed them all. He cut off their heads, tied them together by the hair, and left the cave carrying all the heads with him, including the one they had brought there. Back in town, Odd found that the people had gone to the church with the body of the man who had been killed.

Odd flung the heads into the minster. 'There's the head of your man who was killed,' he said, 'but I've avenged him.'

They were very impressed by what Odd had done. He asked them what sort of a man the one whom he had avenged had been and they told him he was their bishop.

'In that case, what I did was better than nothing,' said Odd.

They kept close watch on Odd because they wanted him to stay, and, bored as he had been staying there, things were even worse now he realized they were keeping an eye on him: so he waited for a chance to get away.

One night the chance came, and off he stole. From land to land he wandered until at last he reached the river Jordan. There he took off all his clothes, shirt and all, waded into the river and bathed just as he liked. When he came out of the river and put on his shirt again, it kept all its magic just as before. Carrying his arrow-bag on his back, he went from land to land till at last he found himself in a wild wood, in such a state that he had nothing to live on but the animals and birds he managed to shoot for food; and this was how matters stood for a while.

18. In Giantland

One day, it is said, Odd came to a cliff-top overhanging a steep, rocky gorge, through which cascaded a great river, roaring in full spate. He tried to think how to get over to the other side, but saw no way, so he sat down. He'd not been sitting there long when something caught hold of him violently and lifted him into the air. A vulture had come flying at Odd and snatched him up so fast in its talons that there was nothing he could do to stop it. This creature flew with him across many a land and sea till it came at last to a precipice, and settled there on a grassy ledge in the cliff face where its young waited. When the vulture loosed its hold on Odd, he was still unharmed, for his shirt had protected him from the vulture's talons, as from everything else that has been spoken of.

Odd was left with the vulture's young in the eyrie, a high cliff above and a deadly sheer drop below down to the sea. There seemed no way for Odd except to take his life in his hands and plunge into the sea, but there appeared to be little chance of getting ashore anywhere, as he couldn't see beyond the cliffs on either side. The young were still unfledged and the vulture was seldom in the eyrie, as it spent most of the time searching for food, so Odd bound up the beaks of the young, and hid himself in a cleft behind the nest. The vulture started bringing even more food – fish, fowl, human flesh, game and meat of all kinds. Eventually it brought some cooked meat, and as soon as the vulture had gone, Odd started eating, though he kept himself in hiding between meals.

One day Odd saw a great giant rowing up toward the nest in a stone boat.

'That's a wicked bird nesting here,' he said in his very loud voice. 'It's begun to make a habit of stealing my fresh cooked meat every day and now's the time to get my own back. When I took the king's oxen, it wasn't any part of my plan that this bird should get them.'

Then Odd stood up, killed the young vultures, and called out to the giant: 'Here's everything you're looking for. I've been taking care of it.'

The giant climbed up into the lair, picked up his meat and carried it into the stone boat.

'Where's that little infant I saw here just now?' he asked. 'There's no need to be frightened, step forward and come with me.'

Odd showed himself, and the giant picked him up and put him in the boat.

'What's the best way to kill this monster?' asked the giant.

'Get some fire and set it to the nest,' said Odd. 'When the vulture comes back it'll most likely fly close, then its feathers will catch fire and that's when we can kill it.'

It happened just as Odd had calculated, and they finished off the vulture. Odd cut off its talons and beak, and took them with him. Then he boarded the boat and the giant started rowing away.

Odd asked him his name. The giant said he was called Hildir, and that he was one of the giants of Giantland. He had a wife called Hildirid and a daughter by her called Hildigunn. 'I've a son, too, called Godmund, born yesterday. I'm one of three brothers. Ulf's the name of one and Ylfing's the other. We've arranged to hold a meeting next summer to decide who's going to be king of Giantland. It's to be the one who performs the most heroic action and has the most savage dog in the dog-fight at the assembly.'

'Who do you think most likely to win the kingdom?' asked Odd.

'One of the others is bound to win,' said Hildir. 'All my life I've been the least of us brothers, and that's how it's sure to be.'

'What would you choose yourself? What would suit you best?' asked Odd.

'I'd choose to be king,' answered Hildir, 'but that's not very likely, because Ulf has a wolf more savage than anything. There isn't a dog can stand up against him. Ulf himself has killed a creature they call the tiger, and has the head to prove it. But my brother Ylfing is even harder to deal with. He owns a polar bear that nothing can beat. Ylfing's killed a creature called the unicorn, and I can't produce any deeds to match theirs, nor any dog either.'

'That's a very interesting story,' said Odd, 'but I think it might be possible to find a solution if someone really applied himself to it in a friendly spirit.'

'I've never met a child as small as you who was so arrogant and crafty as well,' said Hildir. 'I think it would be fair to say that there's little else to you but sheer intelligence. I think you're a real treasure even though you may be a smart alec. I'm going to let my daughter Hildigunn have you to play with, and she can rear you and nurse you with my son Godmund.'

Then Hildir settled down to the oars and rowed home to Giant-land. Odd was quite surprised how fast the stone boat went. When the giant got back home, he showed people the infant he had found and asked his daughter to look after him with his own baby son. Hildigunn took Odd, and as he stood there beside her he barely reached her mid-thigh, yet Hildir was a lot bigger than she was, as you would expect of a man. When Hildigunn had picked Odd up and sat him on her knee, she turned him around to look at his face and said:

> Though this tiny little pip
> May have down upon his lip,
> Godmund's bigger, far away,
> Born only yesterday.

Then she laid him in the cradle beside the giant's baby and sang lullabies to them. She started caressing him, and when she thought he was becoming too restive in the cradle, she put him in her bed beside her and embraced him. Eventually Odd played all the games he felt like, and after that they got on very well together. Then Odd told her that although he was so much smaller than the local people, he was no child. The people of Giantland may be a lot bigger and stronger than any other race, and more handsome than most other people too, but they aren't any more intelligent.

Odd stayed there over the winter, and in the spring he asked Hildir what he would do for the man who could lead him to a dog capable of beating his brothers' animals.

'I'd be very generous to him indeed,' said Hildir. 'Maybe you can put me in the way of one?'

'I can show you, but you'll have to catch the dog yourself,' said Odd.

'I'll get the dog,' said Hildir, 'if you'll take me within sight of him.'

'There's a creature in the Wolf Isles called a hibernating bear, with this peculiarity,' said Odd. 'It lies asleep all winter, but in the summer it wakes up and then it's so greedy and wild that there's nothing safe from it, people, cattle, anything it comes across. There's a good chance this creature might beat your brothers' dogs.'

'Show me where this dog is,' said Hildir, 'and if things turn out the way you say, I'll pay you back handsomely when I come to power.'

So they got ready for the journey. Hildigunn spoke to Odd. 'You'll be coming back from this trip?' she asked.

He said he didn't know for certain.

'It would mean a lot to me,' she said. 'I love you very dearly, small as you are, and I can't fool myself any longer that I'm not pregnant, though it must seem unbelievable that a useless little thing like you could do so much. But there's no one else involved who could be the father of the child I'm carrying. Still, though I love you so much and find it hard to let you go, I won't stop you, wherever it is you want to travel. I can see it goes against the grain for you to stay here with us much longer, but don't you doubt it, you'd never get away from here unless I agreed to it. Yet I'd rather bear my sorrow and pain, mourning and withering with emptiness, than for you not to be where you wish. What is it you want me to do about our child?'

'If it's a boy, send him to me when he's ten years old,' said Odd. 'I'll have great hopes for him. But if it's a girl, bring her up here and look after her yourself, for I shan't want anything to do with her.'

'You'll have your own way in this as in everything else between us,' she said. 'Goodbye and good luck.' And as Odd went aboard, she wept bitterly.

Hildir started rowing, but Odd thought him too slow with the oars, for there was a long way to go. So he fell back on that magic the men of Hrafnista had, hoisted sail, got a fair wind in no time and off they sailed along the coast. Before long Hildir scrambled to his feet in the boat, went for Odd, took hold of him, laid him flat on his back and said, 'If you don't stop this magic of yours, I swear I'll kill you. The shore and the mountains race along as if they're off their heads and the boat's going down beneath us.'

'Better clear your mind,' said Odd. 'You're dizzy because you're not used to sailing. Just let me stand up, and you'll soon see I'm telling the truth.'

The giant did as Odd asked, and as soon as Odd had reefed the sail, the shore and the mountains stood still. Odd told him not to be surprised if this should happen to him again on the voyage and said he could stop the ship whenever he wanted to. This calmed Hildir down and he accepted what Odd said, as he realized they had been going much faster than by rowing. Odd hoisted sail again and off they went. Now Hildir kept quiet.

There is nothing to tell of their journey until they arrived at Wolf Isles and went ashore. There was a massive scree there, and Odd told Hildir to stretch his hand down among the rocks and see if he felt anything.

He did as he was told, and squeezed his arm right up to the shoulder into the rocky scree. 'There's something strange here inside,' he said, 'I'll get my oar glove.' He did so, and pulled out a bear by its ears.

'Now,' said Odd, 'you'd better take my advice about how to treat this dog. Take it home with you and make sure you don't let it loose until the meeting when the dogs are to fight. Don't feed it before summer, keep it in a separate house but don't tell anyone where. On the first day of summer, set it against your brothers' dogs. If that doesn't work, come here next summer. I'll give you another piece of advice if this is no use to you.'

Hildir had been badly bitten all over his hands. 'There's just one thing I'd like you to do for me, Odd,' he said. 'Come to this place next spring but one, at about the same time.'

Hildir went back home with the animal, and did everything precisely according to Odd's instructions. Odd went in the other direction, and there's nothing to tell of his deeds and daring till the next spring but one, when he came back to the spot where they had agreed to meet. Odd was the first to arrive. He hid among some trees near by to avoid the risk of Hildir seeing him. Odd was afraid the giant would be looking for revenge if things had not gone precisely according to plan.

Shortly afterwards Odd heard the loud splashing of oars and saw Hildir coming ashore, carrying in one hand a cauldron filled with silver, and two heavy boxes in the other. Hildir came to the appointed place and waited for some time. When Odd failed to show up, the giant said, 'It's a great pity, Odd my foster-son, that you're not coming. I haven't the time to hang about here since there's nobody in charge of my kingdom while I'm away. So I'm going to leave these boxes, both filled with gold, and this cauldron full of silver, and if you should come later it's all yours. I'll lay this slab of stone upon it so it won't be blown away by the wind, and in case you happen not to notice it, I'm placing on top these precious things: a sword, a helmet and a shield. But if you're close enough to hear what I'm saying I want to tell you I won the kingship over my brothers. My dog was by far the most savage, for it bit my brothers' dogs to death and a good many of their men too, who tried to come to the rescue. I produced the beak and the talons of the vulture, and people thought that a much greater deed than those of my brothers, and now I'm the sole ruler of the land that used to belong to the three of us. I'm going back home now to my kingdom. If you should ever come and see me, you'll have the best of everything. Another thing, my daughter Hildigunn's had a son called Vignir, and she tells me that you're the father. I'll bring him up like a lord. I'll teach him sporting skills and do everything for him just as if he were my own son, and foster him till he's ten years old. Then he'll be sent to you, in accordance with your instructions to his mother.'

After that the giant rowed away in his stone boat. When he had gone, Odd went over to the treasure under the slab, but it was such a great lump of rock that a team of men would have been unable to lift it. So Odd could only get the goods on top of the slab, though even these were worth a fortune. The treasure having been taken, just as the story says, Odd went on his way into the dark forest.

19. Red-Beard

One day Odd came out of the forest very tired, and sat down under an oak tree. Then he saw a man walking by, about middle height, wearing a blue-striped cloak and high boots, and carrying a reed in his hand. He wore gold-emblazoned gloves and had a courteous look about him, though a hood concealed his face. He had large moustaches and a long beard, both red in colour. He turned towards where Odd was sitting, and greeted him by name. Odd returned his greeting in a friendly way and asked who he was.

He said his name was Beard and that he was known as Red-Beard. 'I know all about you, Arrow-Odd,' he said, 'and it's good to hear. You're a remarkable man and a great champion, but you're rather short of followers now and travelling like a pauper. It's a pity to see a great man like you reduced to such a sad state.'

'It's a long time now since I've been in charge of men,' said Odd.

'Would you like to swear blood-brotherhood with me?' asked Red-Beard.

'It's hard to refuse a generous offer,' said Odd, 'so I'll accept it.'

'Your luck hasn't quite run out yet,' said Red-Beard. 'I'm telling you, now, there are two warriors east of here with twelve ships. They're my foster-brothers; one of them's a Dane and he's called Gardar, the other comes from Gotaland and he's called Sirnir. I know of no fighting men like them this side of the sea, they're best at almost everything. I'll see to it that you enter into blood-brotherhood with them, and you'll have the greatest say of us all, though the best thing would be to follow my advice. Where would you like to go if it could be arranged as I've just been saying?'

'I can never get it out of my head that the man I want to meet is Ogmund Eythjof's-Killer, otherwise known as The Tussock.'

'Stop, stop,' said Red-Beard, 'don't say it. You won't be fighting a human being if you fight him, and if you meet Ogmund again you'll come off even worse than the last time. Get this idea of meeting him again right out of your head.'

'I'm going to avenge my blood-brother Thord,' replied Odd, 'and if that's to be my fate, I'll never give up until I face Ogmund.'

'Do you want me to tell you how Ogmund came to be born?' said

Red-Beard. 'Once you know his background, I think you'll realize he's beyond human power.'

'First I should explain that there was a king called Harek who ruled over Permia about the time you went there on your viking expedition. You'll remember all the damage you did the Permians? Well, after you left, the Permians thought they'd had the worst of it and wanted, if they could, to get revenge, and this is how they went about it. They took an ogress living under this great waterfall, loaded her with magic and sorcery and put her in bed beside King Harek, so he had a son by her. The boy was sprinkled with water and called Ogmund. Even as a young child he wasn't like ordinary mortals, as you'd expect from the kind of mother he had, and anyway his father was a great sorcerer too. When Ogmund was three he was sent over to Lappland where he learned all sorts of magic and sorcery, and as soon as he'd mastered the arts, he went back home to Permia. By that time he was seven and already as big as a full grown man, immensely strong and very hard to cope with. His looks hadn't improved during his stay with the Lapps. He was dappled black and blue, with long black hair, and had a rough tussock hanging down over the eyes where his forelock ought to be. That's why he was called Ogmund Tussock. The Permians meant to send him to kill you, though they realized that the ground had to be carefully prepared before they could put you under it. The next step they took was to have him strengthened with witchcraft, so that ordinary weapons couldn't bite him, then they carried out their rituals over him and turned him into a proper troll, like nothing on earth.

'There was a viking called Eythjof, a fine berserk and a fighting man with no equal. Eythjof never had fewer than eighteen ships on his viking expeditions, and never set up a base on land, but stayed at sea, winter or warm summer. Everyone was terrified of him, wherever he went. He conquered Permia and forced it to pay tribute. At that time Ogmund had eight companions. They all used to wear thick woollen cloaks, and iron couldn't touch them. Here are their names: Hak and Haki, Tind and Toki, Finn and Fjosni, Tjosni and Torfi. Then Ogmund joined forces with Eythjof and they went on campaigns together. Ogmund was ten at the time, and he was with Eythjof for five years. Eythjof grew so fond of him, he could refuse him nothing, and because of Ogmund, Eythjof exempted Harek from paying any tributes from Permia. The best Ogmund could do to repay Eythjof was to kill him asleep in his bed and then conceal the murder. It was an easy thing to do. Eythjof had shared his own bed with him, had never done anything against him, and was even thinking of making him his adopted son. Afterwards Ogmund separated from Eythjof's men. They went wherever they wanted, while Ogmund took two ships, fully manned. From then on he was called Ogmund Eythjof's-Killer. That was the same summer you fought him at Tronu Creeks, when he was fifteen years old. It didn't please him at all that he'd not been able to get his own back on you. That's why he murdered your blood-brother Thord Prow-Gleam. Afterwards Ogmund went to see his mother the ogress, called Grimhild when she's with humans, but by then she'd turned into a monster. Her head looks human enough, but further down she's an animal with enormous talons and a tremendous tail, and she's a killer, men or cattle, beasts or dragons. Ogmund tried to get her to finish you off and now she's living out in the woods with the wild creatures. She's come from the north over to England and she's looking for you. That's just about all the light I can throw for you on Ogmund.'

'If he's as bad as you say,' said Odd, 'I can see why most men find him hard to fight, but I still want to meet him.'

'He's even worse,' said Red-Beard, 'he's more of a phantom than a human being and I don't think he'll ever be killed by man. But first, let's go down to our ships.' And that was what they did.

When they came down to the sea Odd saw a number of ships floating off-shore. They went aboard, and Odd noticed two men there who stood out from all the others. They rose to their feet and greeted Red-Beard as their blood-brother. He settled himself down between them and told Odd to sit too.

Red-Beard said, 'Here's a man you fellows must often have heard mentioned. Odd's his name, Arrow-Odd. I want him to be our blood-brother, and to have the most say, since he's the one who's done the most fighting.'

Sirnir answered, 'Is this the Odd who went to Permia?'

'Yes, it's him,' said Red-Beard.

'In that case, if we have him as our blood-brother it's very much our gain,' said Sirnir.

'It suits me fine, too,' said Gardar. So they made a binding agreement.

Then Red-Beard asked Odd where he wanted to go. 'First,' said Odd, 'let's sail west to England.'

And that was what they did. When they reached land, they put up the awnings over their ships and rested there for some time.

20. Death of a Monster

One fine day it happened that Gardar and Sirnir went ashore with a number of their men to amuse themselves, but Odd stayed behind aboard the ships. Red-Beard was nowhere to be seen. The weather was extremely hot, so the blood-brothers stripped and went swimming in a certain lake near a forest. All the men were playing some sport or other. Late in the afternoon they saw an enormous creature coming out of the trees. It had a human head and huge fangs, a long, thick tail, and talons of fantastic size with a great gleaming sword in each claw. When this monster got close to the men, she started to make a loud howling noise, then killed five of them stone dead in one swoop. Two of them she killed with the swords, a third she bit with her fangs, and two more she struck dead with her tail. In no time at all she'd killed sixty men. By then Gardar had dressed and turned out to meet the monster, giving her a blow that knocked one of the swords out of her claws and into the lake. But with the other she made a stroke at Gardar knocking him flat, then threw herself on top of him. At that moment Sirnir came up with Snidil, the best of all swords, which never faltered in battle, and gave the creature such a blow that her other sword flew into the lake too. Then the monster got on top of him and knocked him senseless.

The survivors ran down to the ship to tell Odd that his blood-brothers had been killed along with many others. They said no one could stand up against this monster. 'Let's put out to sea right away, Odd,' they said, 'and save our lives if we can.'

'That would be a shameful thing to do,' said Odd, 'to leave without avenging the blood-brothers, brave men that they were. I'm not having that.'

Then he took his arrow-bag and went ashore. He had not gone far when he heard a fearful noise, and soon saw where the monster was raging. He strung one of Gusir's Gifts on the bow and shot the monster in the eye, right through the back of the head. Then the monster came at him so hard that he had no time to use the bow again, and went for his chest so fiercely with her claws that he was nearly flattened, but as usual the shirt protected him and the claws could do him no harm. Then he drew the sword at his waist, and gave the monster a good stout blow, cutting off her tail as she tried to strike him with it, while he prevented her with his other hand from biting him. When she lost her tail she ran screaming into the trees. Then Odd shot the second of Gusir's Gifts. It caught her in the back, went right into the heart and out through the breast, and she fell to the ground dead. Now all the men who had not dared to come anywhere near before rushed up to the monster, hacking and hewing, but by that time she was finished. Odd had the monster burnt, and brought the blood-brothers down to the ship to be healed.

After that they went away from there, and stayed the following winter in Denmark, then spent a good many summers plundering. They raided in Sweden, Saxony, France, and Flanders until Sirnir and Gardar got tired of fighting and settled down in their kingdoms. Red-Beard went along with them, having come down to the shore when they were about to sail off after Odd had killed the monster. Red-Beard was seldom around when there was any danger, but he was a great man for giving advice whenever it was needed, and rarely dissuaded them from performing great deeds.

21. Family Reunion

Now Odd went off on a viking expedition, with three ships at his disposal, all well manned, and set out once again in search of Ogmund Eythjof's-Killer. Ten years had gone by since Odd left

Giantland. One evening Odd was anchored off a headland with a tent ashore, when he saw someone rowing a small skiff. The man looked amazingly big and rowed powerfully. He rowed up to Odd's ships so hard that he smashed everything in his way.

When he reached the shore, he went up to the tent and asked who was in charge of the ships. Odd gave his name. 'Who are you?' he asked.

The stranger said he was called Vignir. 'Are you the Odd who went to Permia?'

'Yes, that's true,' said Odd.

'I'm at a loss for words,' said Vignir.

'Why's that?' asked Odd.

'I can't believe such a puny-looking little wretch as you could be my father,' said Vignir.

'Who's your mother?' asked Odd. 'How old are you?'

'My mother's called Hildigunn,' said Vignir. 'I was born in Giantland, that's where I've been brought up, and now I'm ten. My mother told me that Arrow-Odd was my father, and I had the idea he was a proper man, but you look like a nobody to me, and so I daresay you'll turn out.'

'Do you really think you'll ever do bigger and better things than me?' said Odd. 'But I'll acknowledge our kinship, and you're welcome to stay with me.'

'I'll accept your offer,' said Vignir, 'though I think it's very degrading to mix with you and your men – they seem to me more like mice than men – and in my opinion it's very likely, if I live, that I'll do greater things than you ever did.'

Odd told him not to insult his men.

In the morning they got ready to sail. Then Vignir asked Odd where he wanted to go. He said he wanted to look for Ogmund Eythjof's-Killer.

'It won't do you any good to meet him,' said Vignir, 'he's the worst troll and monster ever born in the northern hemisphere.'

'I can hardly believe it!' said Odd. 'You've ridiculed my strength and that of my men, and now you're too scared to go and look for Ogmund Tussock.'

'There's no need to start questioning my courage,' said Vignir, 'but I tell you this, one of these days I'll pay you back for these words, and you'll be just as sorry as I am now. But I can tell you where Ogmund is. He's with his nine tussocked mates in the fjord called Skuggi that lies in Slabland Waste. He's there because he doesn't want to meet you, but if you like you can pay him a visit and see how things go.'

Odd said he would do just that.

They sailed all the way to the Greenland Sea, and skirted the country south and west. Then Vignir said, 'Today I'll sail ahead, and you can follow me.'

Odd told him to have it his way. By that time, Vignir was captain of one of the ships. During the day they saw two rocks rearing up out of the sea, and Odd thought this very strange. They sailed between the rocks. Later in the day they saw a large island, and Odd told them to sail up to it. Vignir asked why they should. Odd told five men to go ashore and look for water. Vignir said there was no need for that and forbade anyone from his ship to go. Odd's men landed on the island, and they'd only been there a short while when the island sank and they were all drowned. Covered with heather the island had been, but they never saw it again, and when they looked, the two rocks had vanished as well.

Odd was flabbergasted and asked Vignir what he made of it.

'It seems to me you're about as clever as you are tall,' said Vignir. 'I'll tell you about it: these were two sea-monsters, one called Sea-Reek, and the other Heather-Back. The Sea-Reek is the biggest monster in the whole ocean. It swallows men and ships, and whales too, and anything else around. It stays underwater for days, then it puts up its mouth and nostrils, and when it does, it never stays on the surface for less than one tide. Now that sound we sailed through was the space between its jaws, and its nostrils and lower jaw were the two rocks we saw in the sea. The island that sank was the Heather-Back. Ogmund Tussock sent these creatures against you with the aid of his witchcraft, to kill you and your men. He expected more men would go the same way as those who drowned, and he meant the Sea-Reek to swallow all of us, too. But I sailed through its mouth because I knew it had just come to the surface. So far we've been able to see through Ogmund's trickery, but I've a feeling you're going to suffer more from him than from any other man.'

'That's a risk I'll have to take,' said Odd.

22. Death of Vignir

They sailed the whole way to Slabland, and up the fjord called Skuggi. After they had tied up their ships, Odd and his son went ashore, then over to a stronghold they had sighted, a well-fortified place it seemed to them. Ogmund came out onto one of the flanking-walls, along with his men. He greeted Odd and his son in a friendly way and asked what they wanted.

'There's no need for you to ask that,' said Odd, 'it's your life I want.'

'It would be a better idea,' said Ogmund, 'for us to be properly reconciled.'

'No, I'm not having that,' said Odd. 'That's not what I'd in mind the day you had my blood-brother Thord Prow-Gleam so shamefully murdered.'

'I only killed him because I thought I hadn't killed as many as you,' said Ogmund. 'But even though you've caught up with me, you'll never beat me while I'm inside the stronghold. So I'll make you an offer: either you two fight me and all my companions, or we'll stay in the stronghold.'

'So shall it be,' declared Odd. 'I'll fight you, Ogmund, and Vignir will fight your companions.'

'So shall it not be,' said Vignir. 'Now I'm going to pay you back for the charge of cowardice you laid at my door the first time we met, that I wouldn't have the courage to fight Ogmund.'

'That's something we'll long have cause to regret,' said Odd, 'but you'll get your own way this time.'

After that they started fighting, and a close thing it was. The struggle between Ogmund and Vignir, both powerful fighting men and skilled at arms, was fierce. Vignir pressed Ogmund so hard that he began running north along the sea-cliffs with Vignir after him. Then Ogmund leapt down over the cliff, landing on a small grassy ledge, with Vignir still close behind. The place where they grappled was forty fathoms above the sea. Hard and bitter their struggle was and they tore up earth and rocks like fresh fallen snow.

Now back to Odd. He had a great club in his hand, since none of the Tussock lads could be wounded with iron weapons, and laid about him so hard with the club that soon he had killed every one of the men he was fighting, though he himself was unhurt and only feeling a little tired: his shirt saw to that.

Then Odd thought he should see what had happened to Vignir, so he went along the edge of the cliff until he reached just above where Vignir and Ogmund had been fighting. At that moment Ogmund threw Vignir on his back and in a flash bent his face right down over Vignir, and tore out his throat. That was how Vignir died. Odd said it was the most horrible thing he had ever seen, and the most shattering.

'Now,' Ogmund said, 'don't you think it would have been better, Odd, if you'd taken my offer and been reconciled? For you've suffered a loss at my hand from which you'll never recover. Your son Vignir is dead, the man I think would have turned out to be the bravest and toughest in all Scandinavia. He was only ten and still he'd have beaten me had I been an ordinary human, but I'm as much a phantom as a man. He squeezed me so hard that nearly every bone in my body is broken, they're rattling inside my skin, and I'd be dead, had that been in my nature. I'm not afraid of any man in the world but you, Odd, and it's through you that sooner or later I'll meet my own ill fortune. You've reason enough now for taking revenge on me.'

By this time Odd was wild with anger and jumped down over the cliff, landing on his feet on the grassy ledge. Ogmund moved quickly and plunged down into the sea head first so that the white sea spray came splashing up the cliff-face. He never surfaced again as far as Odd could see, and so, on this occasion, Odd and Ogmund parted.

23. Encounter with Ogmund

Odd took it all very badly. He went back to his ships and sailed off without stopping till he got to Denmark, where Gardar his blood-brother gave him a very fond welcome.

Odd stayed in Denmark over winter, and in spring went with Gardar on a raiding excursion, sending word to Sirnir in Gotaland. He came to meet them, and with him Red-Beard, who asked Odd where he wanted to go. Odd said he wanted to set eyes on Ogmund Eythjof's-Killer, and keep up the search for him.

'You're just like that old nag,' said Red-Beard, 'that always sought the place where it was badly treated. You keep looking for Ogmund, yet whenever you meet him you suffer shame and misery. Don't think Ogmund has improved since you parted. But I can tell you where he is now, if you really want to know. He's journeyed east to the giant Geirrod of Geirrodstown and now he's married the giant's daughter Geirrid. They're the most grisly trolls, the pair of them, and I wouldn't recommend you to go there.'

Odd said it was where he meant to go all the same.

Then all the blood-brothers got ready to sail to the Baltic. When they came east to Geirrodstown they saw someone sitting in a small boat, fishing. It proved to be Ogmund Eythjof's-Killer with a shaggy cloak thrown over himself. After Ogmund and Odd parted, Ogmund had gone east and become Geirrod the giant's son-in-law. From all the kings east of the Baltic he took tribute – every twelve months they all had to send him their beards and moustaches. With these he had a cloak made for himself and that was the one he was wearing. Odd and his men made for the boat, but Ogmund kept retreating, rowing very strongly. The blood-brothers all jumped into a skiff and rowed after him furiously, but Ogmund was such a powerful oarsman it was all they could do to maintain the distance between them. When they came to land, Ogmund ran ashore and left his boat at high-water mark. Odd was the quickest of all the men to get ashore and next to him, Sirnir; both of them ran after Ogmund, and when Ogmund realized they were going to catch up with him, he spoke this verse:

I call on Geirrod,
greatest of warriors,
to assist me
supported by the gods
and along with him
let my wife come
quickly: I need all
the aid they can offer.

The old proverb is true that when someone speaks of the devil he's never very far away. Geirrod came up with his household, fifty of them all told. Then Gardar and Odd's men arrived, and a savage battle began. Geirrod kept swinging hard so that in a short time he'd killed fifteen of Odd's men. Then Odd looked for Gusir's Gifts; first he picked out the arrow called Hremsa, put it on the bowstring and took a shot at Geirrod, hitting him in the chest so that it pierced right through him. Still Geirrod came on even after taking the arrow, and killed three men before he fell dead. His daughter Geirrid was a menace too, killing eighteen men in no time at all. So Gardar turned to meet her and exchanged blows but he ended up beaten to the ground, dead. When Odd saw this, he went wild with rage, put one of Gusir's Gifts on the bowstring and shot it into Geirrid's right armpit straight through to the left one. As far as anyone could see this had not the slightest effect on her. She carried on wading through the troops and killed five more men. Then Odd shot the second of Gusir's Gifts. It hit her in the smallguts, and came out through the loins. Not long after that she was dead.

Ogmund was wasting no time in the battle and soon killed thirty men. Sirnir turned towards him. They attacked each other ferociously, and very soon Sirnir was wounded. Not long afterwards, seeing that Sirnir was backing away before Ogmund, Odd turned that way, but Ogmund saw him coming and started running off at high speed. Odd and Sirnir went chasing after him, both of them moving very fast. Ogmund was wearing his fine cloak, and when the pursuers were almost on top of him, Ogmund threw down the cloak and spoke this verse:

I must cast off
my cloak, made

with the beards of kings,
lace-fringed at the border.
Now that I'm wary
I'll throw it away.
Odd and Sirnir
occupied themselves, both
busy chasing me
from the battlefield.

Now that he was less impeded, Ogmund began to draw ahead. Odd did his best and started to pull ahead of Sirnir. When Ogmund saw that, he turned to meet Odd and they came to grips, wrestling and battling long and hard. Odd was not as strong as Ogmund, but still Ogmund could not bring him down. Then Sirnir came up with his sword Snidil, meaning to strike at Ogmund, but seeing that, Ogmund held Odd between himself and the blow, and Sirnir had to hold back. So it went on, with Ogmund using Odd as a shield, so that Sirnir's attacks came to nothing. But even when Odd was hit he could not be wounded because of his good shirt.

Once it happened that Odd braced both feet against a boulder sunk in the ground, and pushed so hard against Ogmund that he brought him to his knees. At that moment Sirnir struck, and this time Ogmund wasn't able to parry the blow with Odd: the sword landed on Ogmund's backside, cutting off a slice of his buttocks so big it would have made a full horse-load. This shook Ogmund so much that he plunged straight down into the earth right where he was. Just as he did this, Odd got hold of his beard with both hands and jerked it so hard that he ripped off the whole beard with the skin underneath right down the bone, including the entire face and both cheeks, up the forehead and back to the middle of the crown. So they went their separate ways as the ground opened up, and Odd kept what he was holding. The ground closed over Ogmund's head, and that was how they parted!

Odd and Sirnir went back to their ships with a heavy death-toll. Odd grieved bitterly for the loss of his blood-brother Gardar. Red-Beard had vanished, and Odd and Sirnir never discovered what had become of him after they had found Ogmund in the boat. It was as true as ever, that he never risked his own life, though he was the toughest of men when it came to giving advice. As far as is known they never saw Red-Beard again, and people believe that he was very likely none other than Odin himself.

The blood-brothers went away, and everyone thought Odd had again got the worst of it in his dealings with Ogmund, having lost his blood-brother, the high-spirited Gardar. But with the help of his friends Odd had once more achieved something remarkable by killing those monstrous companions of Ogmund. Geirrid had a son by Ogmund Eythjof's-Killer, called Svart. He was three years old at the time, a very big child who promised to turn out an evil man.

24. King Herraud

Odd went back home to Gotaland with his blood-brother Sirnir who invited him to stay the winter there. As winter wore on, Odd became very dejected, for his thoughts kept turning to the miseries Ogmund Tussock had brought upon him. He was determined never again to risk the life of his blood-brother in the fight with Ogmund, for the losses he had suffered already were sore enough, so he made up his mind and stole away one night by himself. He managed to get transport wherever he needed, travelling on through woods and wildernesses and stumbling over long mountain tracks, his arrow-bag on his back, through one country after another, and the time came when he was forced to shoot birds in order to survive. He fastened birch-bark round his body and feet, and then he made himself a big hat with the bark. He stood out from all other men, for besides being much bigger than anyone else he was all covered with bark.

There's nothing to tell of him till he emerged from the forest, and found settlements coming into view. He saw a big farmstead there, and another smaller one not very far away. It came into his mind to try the smaller farm, though he had never done anything like that before, so up he went to the door. Outside a man was chopping firewood, a small man with white hair.

The old man greeted the stranger warmly and asked his name.

'I'm called the Barkman,' said Odd. 'What about you?'

He said he was called Jolf. 'You'd like to stay here overnight, I suppose,' he said.

'Yes, I would,' said Odd the Barkman.

The old man showed him into the living-room, where there was an old woman sitting on a chair. 'We've got a visitor,' said the old man, 'you entertain him, I'm too busy myself.'

The old woman began to complain and said this wasn't the first time he'd promised hospitality to people '– and nothing for us to offer,' she said.

The old man went away, and Odd stayed behind with the old woman. In the evening Jolf came back home and a table was laid before them with one plate. The Barkman put down on his side a fine knife, with two rings on it, one of gold and the other of silver.

When Jolf saw the knife he stretched out his hand for it and examined it. 'You've got a splendid knife there, friend,' said the old man. 'How did you come by anything so valuable?'

'When I was young,' said the Barkman, 'a number of us used to make salt. One day a ship was driven on to the rocks just where we were, and smashed to pieces. The crew were washed ashore very weak, so it didn't take us long to finish them off, and I got this knife as my share of the loot. If you should happen to have any use for this knife, old fellow, I'll give it you.'

'The best of luck to you!' said the old man and showed it to his wife. 'Here's something worth looking at,' he said, 'it's just as good as my old one.'

Then they settled down to eat, and after that the Barkman was shown to bed. They slept through the night, and when the Barkman woke up, Jolf had disappeared and his bed was already cold.

'Wouldn't it be best for me to get up and look for breakfast somewhere else?' he asked. But the old woman said that the old man wanted him to wait.

About noon when the old man came home, the Barkman was already up. Then the table was laid, with one plate on it. On his side the old man put down three stone arrows beside the plate. These arrows were so big and fine the Barkman thought he'd never seen their like.

He picked one up to examine it. 'That's a well-made arrow,' he said.

'It's good if you like them,' said the old man, 'because then I'll give them to you as a present.'

The Barkman smiled, and said, 'I don't think there's any need for me to haul these stone arrows around.'

'You can never tell when you might need them,' said the old man, 'I know that you're called Arrow-Odd and that you're the son of Grim Hairy-Cheek of Hrafnista in the north. I know too that you've three arrows called Gusir's Gifts, and you'll be surprised to learn that one day you may find yourself in a situation where they'll be useless and the stone arrows will save you.'

'Since you know without being told that my name's Odd,' he said, 'and that I've arrows called Gusir's Gifts, what you predict may well turn out to be true. So I'll accept the gift of the arrows,' and he put them into his arrow-bag.

'What can you tell me about this country?' asked Odd. 'Does it have a king?'

'Yes,' said the old man, 'his name's Herraud.'

'Who are his most important men?' said Odd.

'There are two of them,' said the old man. 'One's called Sigurd and the other Sjolf. They're the king's leading men, and great fighters.'

'Has the king any children?' said Odd.

'One beautiful daughter called Silkisif,' said the old man.

'Is she really beautiful?' asked Odd.

'Yes,' said the old man, 'there isn't a woman as beautiful in the whole of Russia and beyond.'

'Tell me something, old fellow,' said Odd. 'What kind of reception will I get if I go there? You're not to let them know who I am.'

'I can hold my tongue,' said the old man.

Then they went over to the king's palace, but the old man put his foot down and refused to go any further.

'What are you stopping for?' asked Odd.

'The reason's this,' said the old man. 'I'll be put in chains if I go inside, and I'll be a lot happier when I get away from here.'

'No,' said the Barkman. 'We're going to enter side by side, and I won't hear a thing about your not coming with me.' At this he seized hold of the old man.

They went into the palace, and when the retainers saw the old man they started bunching up on him, but the Barkman gave him such firm support that they just bounced off. The two made their way across the floor until they got to the king. The old man greeted the king courteously and the king returned the greeting in a friendly way. Then the king asked who was walking behind him.

'That I can't say,' said the old man, 'he'll have to tell you himself who he is.'

'I'm called the Barkman,' said Odd.

'Who are you, fellow?' said the king.

'One thing I do know,' said Odd. 'I'm older than anything you can think of, but I've neither wit nor memory in my head, for I've been living out in the woods nearly all my life. Beggars always want to be choosers, king, and I'm asking you to take me in for the winter.'

'Are you good at anything?' said the king.

'Not a thing,' he replied, 'I'm the clumsiest man on earth.'

'Are you willing to do any work?' said the king.

'I don't know how to work, and I'm too lazy to do it,' he said.

'This doesn't look very promising,' said the king, 'for I've made a vow only to take in skilled men.'

'Nothing I ever do will be the least use to anyone,' said the Barkman.

'You ought to know how to collect the game for the hunters,' said the king. 'Maybe I'll be going hunting some time.'

'Where do you want me to sit?' said the Barkman.

'Take a seat on the lower bench near the door, between the freed men and the slaves,' said the king.

The Barkman saw the old man off and then he went to the seat he had been offered. Two brothers, called Ottar and Ingjald, were sitting there.

'Come over here, fellow,' they said, 'sit between us,' and so he did.

They sat close at his knee, one on either side, and asked him about different countries, whatever came to mind, but no one else understood what they were talking about. The Barkman hung his arrowbag on a peg, and put his club beneath his feet. They kept asking him to take the bag away, as they thought it a nuisance, but he said he'd never let it be taken away from him, and that wherever he went he carried the bag with him.

They offered him bribes if he would take off the bark. 'We'll give you fine clothes,' they said.

'I couldn't do it,' he said, 'I've never worn any other clothes, and as long as I live I never shall.'

25. Hunting

So there the Barkman sat. He would drink very little in the evening and go early to bed, and that was how things stood till the hunting season began in the autumn.

One evening Ingjald said they'd have to get up early next morning.

'What's happening?' asked the Barkman.

Ingjald said they were going hunting, and they lay down to sleep. In the morning the brothers got up and shouted at the Barkman, but he slept so soundly they couldn't wake him. When finally he did wake up, everyone who wanted to go hunting had already left.

'What's going on?' asked the Barkman. 'Are the men ready?'

'Ready?' said Ingjald, 'They've all gone. We've been trying to wake you all morning. We'll never shoot a single animal today.'

Then the Barkman asked, 'Are Sjolf and Sigurd such great sportsmen?'

'We'd find out,' said Ingjald, 'if they had someone to compete with.'

When they came to the mountain a herd of deer ran past them and Ottar and Ingjald drew their bows and tried to hit the deer, but missed every time.

Then the Barkman said, 'I've never seen anyone make such a mess of it. Why are you so clumsy?'

'We've told you before,' they said, 'we're the clumsiest men on earth. We were late getting ready this morning, and the only deer we come across are those the other hunters have already startled.'

'I don't believe I could be any worse at it than you. Give me the bow and let me have a try,' said the Barkman.

They did so and he drew the bow. They told him not to break it, but he drew the arrow up right to the very tip and the bow snapped in two.

'Now you've done it,' they said. 'This really is a nuisance. There's no chance now that we'll shoot any deer today.'

'Things haven't gone too smoothly,' he said. 'But don't you think my stick would do for a bow? And don't you want to know what's in my bag?'

'Yes,' they said, 'we're very curious.'

'Then spread your cloaks, and I'll empty everything out,' said Odd.

Ottar and Ingjald did as he asked, and he emptied the bag on to the cloaks. Then he drew his bow, put an arrow on the string and shot it right over the heads of all the hunters. He kept this up throughout the day, always trying for the deer Sigurd and Sjolf were after. He shot all his arrows but six, the stone arrows the old man had given him and Gusir's Gifts. He didn't miss a deer all day, and Ottar and Ingjald ran along beside him admiring his marksmanship.

In the evening when the hunters came back home, all their arrows were brought before the king. Everyone had marked his own so that the king could see how many deer each man had shot during the day.

'Go over there and claim your arrows, Barkman,' said the brothers, 'from on the table before the king.'

'You go,' he said, 'say they're yours.'

'We'd never get away with it,' they said, 'the king knows what sort of sportsmen we are, the worst shots on earth.'

'Then we'll go together,' he said, and so they went before the king. 'Here are the arrows that we three are claiming,' said the Barkman.

The king looked at him and said, 'You're a fine archer.'

'That I am, sir,' he said. 'I'm accustomed to shooting birds and beasts for my own table.' Then they went back to their seats.

So now time passed.

26. Contests

One evening after the king had retired to bed, Sigurd and Sjolf rose to their feet, went over to the brothers Ottar and Ingjald with a horn each and offered them a drink. When they had drunk up, they brought two more. The brothers took them and drank.

Then Sjolf said, 'Does that mate of yours spend all his time lying down?'

'Yes,' they replied, 'he thinks it's better than drinking himself silly, like we do.'

'Is he a very good archer?' asked Sjolf.

'Yes, he is,' they said, 'as good as he is at everything.'

'Do you think he can shoot as far as we can?' asked Sjolf.

'The way we see it, he could shoot a lot further and straighter,' they said.

'Let's have a bet on it,' Sjolf said. 'We'll stake a bracelet weighing half a mark if you'll stake two of the same weight.'

It was agreed that the king and his daughter should be there to watch the shooting contest; and they were to take the bracelets beforehand and give them to the winner. After the wager had been agreed on, they slept through the night, but when the brothers woke up next morning, they felt they'd made fools of themselves over the wager, and told the Barkman everything.

'It doesn't look like a very promising bet to me,' he said. 'I may be able to shoot animals, but that's nothing compared with taking on archers like these. Still, I'll have a go and do my best since you've risked your money.'

So everyone had a drink, and after that they went outside as the king wanted to see the shooting contest. First Sigurd stepped forward and shot as far as he could. A pole was stuck into the ground there, and Sjolf went up to it. A spear shaft was set up with a gold chess-piece on top, and Sjolf shot the gold piece off the shaft. Everyone thought this was fantastic marksmanship and said it was hardly worth the Barkman making the effort.

'Good luck often alters bad prospects,' said Odd. 'I'm going to have a try.'

The Barkman went to the place where Sigurd had stood and aimed his arrow. He shot it up in the air so that it was long out of sight, but eventually it came down again straight through the middle of the gold piece and into the spear shaft without disturbing a thing.

'The first shot may have been a fine one,' said the king, 'but this is much better. I tell you, I've never seen a shot like it!'

Then the Barkman took another arrow. He shot it so far that no one could see where it landed and everyone agreed that he had won the contest. After that people went back home, and the brothers were given the bracelet. They offered it to the Barkman, but he said he didn't want to take what was theirs.

Some days went by, then one evening after the king had left the hall, Sigurd and Sjolf went over to the brothers with one horn each and offered them a drink. The brothers drank up. Then they brought the brothers two more horns.

'The Barkman's still lying there, and not drinking,' said Sjolf.

'He's still better mannered than you,' said Ingjald.

'But I think there's more to it,' said Sjolf. 'He won't have mixed much with the better kind of people, living so long like a pauper out there in the wilds. Is he a good swimmer?'

'We think he's just about as good at any sport you'd care to name,' they said. 'And in our opinion he's a pretty good swimmer.'

'Would he be a better swimmer than the two of us together?'

'That's what we think, he's a better swimmer,' said Ottar.

'Let's have a bet on it,' said Sjolf. 'We're ready to stake a bracelet weighing a mark if you'll wager two bracelets, each a mark in weight.'

It was agreed that the king and his daughter should watch their swimming contest, and all the arrangements were just as before. They slept through the night, but in the morning when they woke, news of the wager spread through the benches.

'What's everybody talking about?' said the Barkman. 'Did you accept another wager last night?'

'Yes, we did,' they said and told him all about it.

'This doesn't look too promising,' said the Barkman, 'I can't swim a stroke, and when I tried I couldn't even keep myself afloat. It's a long time since I came in contact with cold water. Have you staked much money?'

'We have,' they said, 'but there's no need for you to try, unless you want to. It would serve us right if we had to pay for our stupidity.'

'I'm not having that,' said the Barkman. 'You've shown me too much honour for me not to try. As the king and Silkisif will see I'm certainly going to swim.'

When the king and his daughter had been told, everyone went down to the large lake a short distance away. At the lake, the king and his retinue sat themselves down, and the contestants started swimming in their clothes. The Barkman was dressed as usual. As soon as they were some way from the shore, Sigurd and Sjolf swam up to him and tried to force him under, and held him down for a long time. At last they let him surface again, and took a rest themselves. Then they went for him a second time. He reached out towards them, took them one in each hand, forced them down and kept them under for so long that no one expected them to come up again. He gave them only a short breather, then got hold of them a second time and forced them down, then a third time for so long no one expected them to get back to the surface alive. All the same, they reappeared. Both the royal gentlemen had blood trickling from their noses, and needed to be helped back to land, so the Barkman took hold of them and hurled them ashore. Then he started swimming again, and put on a show of well-known swimming tricks. In the evening he returned to land and came before the king.

'Aren't you a better sportsman at archery and swimming than anyone else?' asked the king.

'Now you've seen these, you've seen all the skills I have,' said the Barkman. 'My name's Odd, if you want to know, but I can't tell you anything about my family.'

Then Silkisif gave him the bracelets, and everyone went back home. The brothers said Odd should have all the bracelets, but he wouldn't take them. 'Keep them for yourselves,' he said.

So time passed, but not long. The king was very troubled about what had happened and who this man staying with him could be.

27. A Drinking Contest

Staying with the king, and much honoured by him, was a man called Harek, an old man. He had fostered the king's daughter, and the king would talk over this business with him. Harek told him that he had no answer but thought it likely that the man came from a noble family.

One evening after the king had retired, Sjolf and Sigurd went down to the brothers with two drinking horns, and they finished them off.

Then Sjolf asked, 'Is Odd the Great asleep?'

'Yes,' they answered, 'and it makes more sense than drinking yourself out of your wits like us.'

'It could be he's had more practice at lying out in the lake and forest country than drinking with respectable people. A great drinker, is he?'

'Yes,' they said.

'Would he be a greater drinker than the two of us together?' asked Sjolf.

'We think he could drink a lot more,' said Ottar.

'We'll have a bet on it,' said Sjolf. 'This twelve-ounce bracelet against your heads.'

They made a binding agreement about this just as before. In the morning Odd asked the brothers what they had been discussing and they told him.

'Now you've made a really stupid bet,' said Odd. 'Risking your own heads is adding a lot to the previous stakes. I'm not sure I can hold all that much more than other men, though I'm a lot bigger than they are. Still, I'll go to the drinking match and take them on.'

The king was told that Odd was willing to compete, and that the king's daughter and her foster-father Harek were to sit with him and watch. Sigurd and Sjolf went up to Odd.

'Here's a horn,' said Sigurd, and then he sang this verse:

> Odd, you've never burst
> mail-coats in battle
> when helmed warriors
> took to their heels.

> The war raged,
> fire raced through the town
> when our king won
> victory over the Wends.

Sjolf gave him another horn and asked him to drink up. He recited this verse:

> Odd, you weren't there
> at the weapon-clash when
> we gave the king's troops
> a taste of death.
> Fourteen wounds
> I fared home with,
> while you were begging
> your bread from the farmers.

Then they went back to their seats. Odd rose to his feet and went before Sigurd with a horn and gave another one to Sjolf. He sang one verse to each of them before he went away:

> Listen to my song
> you seat-warmers,
> Sigurd and Sjolf,
> it's time to serve you
> for your nasty piece
> of knotty poetry –
> you're a pretty
> pair of milksops!

> Sjolf, you were flat
> on the kitchen floor
> no sign of daring,
> not a single deed –
> you had faced nothing
> when I felled four
> in Aquitaine
> and ended their lives.

They drained their horns, and Odd went back to his seat. Then Sigurd and Sjolf went over to him again, and Sjolf gave him a horn with this verse:

> Odd, you've busied yourself
> with a band of beggars,
> taking titbits
> from the table.
> But I bore
> back alone,
> home from Ulfsfell,
> my hacked shield.

Sigurd brought him another horn, and said:

> Odd, you weren't
> with the Greeks, when
> we reddened our swords
> on the Saracens;
> we made the martial
> music of steel,
> the fighters we felled
> in the folk-flame.

Odd drained the horns, and they went back to their seats. Then he stood up and went with a horn to each of them, and sang this:

> Sjolf, you were gossiping
> with the girls, while we
> sent the fires raging
> through the fortress.
> The fierce Hadding,
> we defeated;
> we lopped the length
> of Olvir's life.

> You, Sigurd, were lying
> enchambered with the ladies,
> while twice we clashed
> in combat with the Permians.
> Hawk-minded, we won
> our war like heroes,
> while you lay dozing
> under the linen.

Then Odd went back to his seat and drained the horns. Everybody thought this great entertainment and was giving it a good hearing.

Next, Sigurd and Sjolf went up to Odd and gave him two horns.
Then Sjolf said:

> Odd, you weren't
> on Atalsfell
> when we gathered
> the bright gold.
> We bound up
> the berserks; many
> the king's men
> that we killed.

Then Odd drained the horns and they sat down. Odd brought
them a horn and said:

> Sjolf, you weren't
> there when we saw
> the mail-coats washing
> in blood like water.
> Spear-points dug
> deep in the chaincoats;
> more to your taste
> tripping round the king's hall.

> You couldn't have been there,
> Sigurd, when we cleared
> the six high-pooped
> ships off Hauksness;
> you weren't with us
> west, in England
> when Skolli and I
> shortened the king's stay.

Then Odd sat down, and they brought him the horn, but with no
poetry this time. He drank up, and they sat down. Odd brought
them a horn and said:

> You weren't around,
> Sjolf, when we reddened
> our steel on the earl
> off Læso Island.
> Mad for sex, you
> sat at home wondering

whether to cuddle
the calf or the kitchenmaid.

Where were you, Sigurd,
when on Zealand I slew
the battle-hard brothers
Brand and Agnar,
Asmund and Ingjald,
and the fifth one, Alf?
You were lounging
at home with the lordings,
the tall-story teller,
the comic turn.

Then he went back to his seat. Sigurd and Sjolf stood up and
carried over to him the drinking horns. Odd finished them both off,
then he brought them a horn, and said:

Where were you, Sjolf,
when south at Skien
the kings fought,
crushing the helms?
Ankle-deep
we dabbled in blood,
I was killing men:
but you were missing.

Where were you, Sigurd?
Not at Svia Skerries
when we paid back Halfdan
for his hostility:
our swords carved
the war-seasoned shields,
Halfdan himself dropped
dead to the earth.

Odd sat down, Sigurd and Sjolf brought him the two horns, and
he drank up, and they went back to their seats. Then Odd brought
them a horn, and said:

We sailed our ship
through Elfar Sound,
contented, carefree,

> to Tronu Creeks,
> where Ogmund lay,
> Eythjof's-Killer
> slow to flee,
> in two fighting ships.
>
> We pelted shields
> with hard stones,
> with sharp swords
> we struck them.
> On our side, three,
> and nine on theirs
> survived. Why so silent,
> captive scum?

Then Odd went back to his seat and Sigurd and Sjolf brought him two horns. He drained these down, then offered them two more, and said:

> Sigurd, you weren't
> on Samso Isle
> when I hewed blow
> for blow with Hjorvard;
> two of us only,
> twelve of them.
> I conquered,
> you sat quiet.
>
> I went across Gotaland
> grim at heart
> for seven days
> till I met Sæmund.
> Before I left
> I took eighteen lives,
> while you, poor wretch,
> were reeling your way
> through the black night
> to the bondmaid's bed.

There was loud cheering in the hall when Odd had spoken this, then Sigurd and Sjolf drained their horns and Odd sat down. The king's men couldn't get enough of this entertainment. Sigurd and

Sjolf gave Odd two more horns, and he finished them off in no time. Then he rose to his feet, went up to them and saw that the drink had completely defeated them, and that poetry was beyond them. He gave them the horns and said:

> Where will you ever
> be estimated worthy
> company, Sigurd
> and Sjolf, for a king?
> But I bear in mind
> Hjalmar the Brave,
> who brandished his sword
> more briskly than any man.

> Thord forced his way forward
> each time we fought,
> no protection,
> never a targe:
> the heroic king
> Halfdan and his companions,
> Thord laid the lot of them
> low on the earth.

> In our boyhood
> together, blood-brothers
> Asmund and I,
> we were always there.
> Many's the time
> I managed a spear
> when the kings
> clashed in war.

> I've fought enemies,
> the Irish, the English,
> the Swedes and the Saxons,
> and once, the Scots:
> I've fought against Frisians
> and Flemings and French.
> To all these people
> I've been like a plague.

I'll let you have
a list of them now,
those fierce fighters
who used to follow me:
never again,
no, never, for sure,
shall we see such brave men
go into battle.

I have listed all
the exploits now
which we performed
in the far past:
rich in victories
we reached our homes,
to sit on the high-seats.
Now, Sjolf, have your say.

After that Odd went back to his seat. Sjolf and Sigurd collapsed and fell asleep, and had nothing more to do with the drinking, though Odd kept going for a long time. Then everyone went to bed and slept through the night.

In the morning, by the time the king had come to the high-seat, Odd and his companions were already outside. Odd went down to one of the lakes to wash himself, and the brothers noticed that the bark cuff on one sleeve was torn. Underneath there was a red sleeve and a thick gold bracelet on the arm. Then they tore all the bark off him, and he made no attempt to stop them. Under the bark he was wearing a red tunic of costly material, lace-trimmed; his hair fell down over his shoulders, there was a gold band round his forehead, and he looked very handsome indeed.

They took him by the hand and led him into the hall up to the king's high-seat, and said, 'It seems that we haven't fully appreciated who we've been entertaining here this winter.'

'That could be so,' said the king. 'But who is this man who's been hiding his identity from us?'

'I still call myself Odd, as I told you a while ago, and I'm the son of Grim Hairy-Cheek of Hrafnista in north Norway.'

'Are you that Odd who went to Permia a long time ago?'

'I'm the man who went there.'

'It's no wonder then that my leading men didn't do so well against you at games,' said the king. Then he stood up and welcomed Odd and invited him to sit on the high-seat beside him.

'I'll not accept the offer unless my comrades and I all go together,' said Odd.

It is said that they changed their seats and Odd sat next to the king, while Harek moved over to a chair in front of the king. The king heaped honours upon Odd, showing greater respect for him than for any other man.

28. A Mission

Odd and Harek often talked things over with one another, and Odd asked him if anyone had made an offer of marriage to the king's daughter.

'No doubt about it,' said Harek, 'the two leading men have both proposed to her.'

'What did the king say to that?' asked Odd.

'He told them there's a chance.'

'What sort of chance?' asked Odd.

'The king wants to collect tribute from a land called Bjalka, ruled by a king called Alf, nicknamed Bjalki. Alf's married to a woman called the Priestess, and like him, she's a great worshipper of the gods. They've a son called Vidgrip. They're such great sorcerers, they could hitch a stallion to a star. King Herraud has a tribute to collect from there that hasn't been paid for ages, and he's offered to give his daughter to the man who collects it. But it hasn't come to anything, because they asked to go with such an army, the king thought he wouldn't be able to defend the land against attack.'

'It looks to me,' said Odd, 'that either the tax won't ever be collected, or it will have to be gathered with a much smaller force. Do you think that the king would give me the same chance as the others if I managed to collect the taxes?'

'The king's a shrewd man,' said Harek, 'and my guess is he'll recognize the difference between you and the other suitors.'

This matter was mentioned to the king, and the long and short of it was for Odd to go on this mission and collect the tribute, and, if he completed the mission and recovered the tribute, to get the king's daughter. There were a good many witnesses present when she was promised him.

Odd made ready for the journey, and mustered all the forces he wanted. When he was ready the king went to see him off. Odd and his men were to travel overland.

'There's something valuable I want to give you,' the king said.

'What's that?' said Odd.

'It's an amazon who's been with me for a long time,' the king said, 'and she's been my shield in every battle.'

Odd smiled and said, 'I've never been where I've needed women to shield me. Still, I'll take your gift since you mean well.'

The king and Odd parted, and Odd went on his way till he came to a big swamp, which he cleared with a long running jump. The amazon was just behind him and when she came to the swamp, she hesitated.

'Why didn't you jump after me?' Odd asked her.

'I wasn't ready,' she said.

'Oh, yes?' he said. 'Well, make yourself ready.'

She tucked up her skirt and ran up to the swamp a second time, and it went just the same as before, as did her third effort. Odd jumped back over again, grabbed her by the hand and threw her into the swamp. 'Clear off, the trolls can have you,' he said. Then he cleared the swamp for the third time and waited for his men. The bog was so broad and hard to cross, they had to go round the far end of it.

Odd pressed on with his men. He sent spies ahead, who reported that Vidgrip had gathered a massive army and was marching against him. The two confronted each other on a certain plain, and by then it was evening.

Both armies camped there, and during the evening Odd kept watch to see where Vidgrip would pitch his tent. When everyone was asleep, and all was quiet and still, Odd got up and went outside, a sword in his hand, but with no other weapon. He kept going till he came to the tent where Vidgrip was sleeping and stood outside for a

long time waiting to see if anyone would come out, and finally
someone did. It was very dark.

'What are you hanging about here for?' asked the man. 'Come
into the tent or clear off.'

'All right,' said Odd, 'but I've got myself into a mess. I can't find
the place where I lay down to sleep last night.'

'Do you remember whereabouts it was in the tent?'

'I'm positive I was supposed to sleep in Vidgrip's tent, with one
man between me and him. But as things are, I can't find my way
back, and I'll be everyone's laughing-stock unless you help me out.'

'All right,' said the other, 'what I can do is lead you up to the bed
where Vidgrip's sleeping.' And that's what he did.

'Good,' said Odd, 'don't make any noise now, all's well, I can see
my bed quite clearly.'

The man walked away and Odd stood there until he thought the
other was asleep. Then Odd drove a peg of wood through the tent
just above Vidgrip's bed. After that he went outside and round to
the back where the peg jutted out. There he lifted the edge of the
tent, pulled Vidgrip outside and cut his head off on a log. Then he let
the body fall back inside, and closed the tent. He went back to his
own tent, lay down and acted as if nothing had happened.

29. Marriage

In the morning when the vikings woke up they found Vidgrip dead
and his head missing. This struck them as such a marvel they were
totally baffled and decided after some deliberation to make another
man their leader, call him Vidgrip, and have him carry their banner
during the day.

Odd and his men woke up and put on their armour. The way Odd
arranged things was this: he had a standard made, and on top of it he
put Vidgrip's head. Then both armies drew up. Odd went before his
men – he had a much smaller force – and made a speech. He called
out to the local army and asked whether they recognized the head
that was being carried before him. All the people thought it looked
like Vidgrip's head and they were dumbfounded as to how this could

be. Odd gave them a choice, either to fight him, or submit. They thought the way things had gone, their prospects looked rather bleak even if they wanted to try, so in the end they all submitted to Odd. He took charge of the whole army and marched on until he faced Alf Bjalki. Each of them had a big army, but Odd's was smaller than Alf's. Fighting broke out right away, so fierce that Odd thought he'd never seen such slaughter, and it wasn't long before he realized his force had been badly reduced in numbers. 'And another thing,' said Odd, 'while I can scythe my way right up to Alf's banner, still I can't seem to see the man himself.'

Then one of the local men who had been with Vidgrip said to Odd, 'I don't know what's up with you that you can't see him, because he's marching just behind his banner and never moves away from it. If you want any proof, he's the one shooting an arrow from each of his fingers who kills a man with every one of them.'

'I still can't see him,' said Odd.

Then the man raised his hand above Odd's head and said, 'Now have a look, under my hand.'

At once Odd could see Alf and all the other things he had been told about him. Odd said, 'Keep your hand like that for a while.' The man did as he was asked.

Odd felt around for Gusir's Gifts, took one of them, set it on the bowstring and shot it at Alf Bjalki, but Alf just put the palm of his hand in the way and the arrow didn't bite at all.

'Off you go, the lot of you,' said Odd, 'even though none of you is any use.'

He shot all the Gifts, and every one of them dropped into the grass. 'I don't know,' said Odd, 'it may have come true what old Jolf told me, that Gusir's Gifts are gone for good. So I'd better try the old fellow's stone arrows.' He took one of them, set it on the bowstring and shot it at Alf Bjalki. When Alf heard the whizz of the approaching arrow he put out the palm of his hand against it, but the arrow flew straight through and came out at the back of his head. Odd took another arrow, set it on the bowstring and shot. Alf put up his other hand meaning to protect his remaining eye, but the arrow went straight for the good eye and out through the back of his head. Still Alf didn't fall, so Odd shot the third arrow, and this one

hit Alf in the waist, and then he fell. The stone arrows the old man
had given him vanished, for as he had told Odd, they could only be
shot once and after that they would never be seen again.

The battle was soon over, for the army was routed and had started
fleeing to the city. The Priestess stood between the city gates
shooting arrows from all her fingers.

The fighting died down as the enemy began surrendering to Odd
everywhere. The temples and shrines which stood close to the town
Odd had set on fire, and everything near by he burnt.

Then the Priestess said:

> Who commands this fire,
> this clash of arms, who
> in the other troop wields
> weapons yonder?
> The shrines are ablaze,
> the temples burn:
> who has reddened the edge
> on Yngva's men?

Then Odd replied, and said this:

> Odd burnt the temples
> and broke the shrines
> and waded into
> your wooden idols.
> Little aid they could offer
> to their own selves,
> without skill to save
> themselves from a scorching.

Then she said:

> That's laughable, Odd,
> to learn how you
> have earned the fury,
> the anger of Frey.
> Now, all you great
> gods and goddesses!
> You Powers, support
> me, your Priestess.

Then Odd said:

> I don't care,
> curse me
> with Frey's fury,
> you filthy old female.
> I saw your fairies
> aflame in the burning:
> may the trolls get you!
> My trust is in God.

Then she said:

> Who fostered you
> to be such a fool,
> as not to offer
> sacrifice to Odin?

Then Odd spoke up and said:

> In my boyhood, Ingjald
> brought me up
> the lord of Eikund
> who lived in Jæderen.

Then she said:

> I'd feel a wealthy
> woman if I ever
> could see Alf again,
> the apple of my eye:
> I'd make sacrifice – four
> farms I'd offer,
> and into the flames
> he'd fling the lot of you.

Then Odd said this:

> When Odd bent
> his bow, the arrow,
> Jolf's handiwork,
> hammered your husband.
> I don't think Alf
> will accept your offer:
> the ravens are feasting
> on his flesh.

Then she said:

> Who aided you
> on your way eastward?
> a terrible journey,
> and treacherous.
> Keenly you must
> have sought conflict
> when you dealt Alf
> the death-arrow.

Then Odd said:

> My arrows aided me,
> and my all-powerful bow –
> mighty the missiles
> made by Jolf –
> and lastly the fact
> that I never befriended
> these gods of yours,
> I give you my word.
>
> First there was Frey,
> then Odin followed:
> I had them blinded
> and sent to the burning.
> Off ran the idols
> out of sight
> whenever we flushed out
> a flock of them.

And he said again:

> These gutless gods
> ran like scared goats
> before a wolf
> wherever I worried them.
> Odin's bad
> as a bosom friend:
> so we'll do away
> with devil-worship.

Then Odd went after the Priestess with a great oak club, and she ran off into the town with all her men. Odd chased after the fleeing people killing all those he was able to, but the Priestess escaped into the main temple which stood in the town, and as she ran inside she said:

> Now, all you great
> gods and goddesses!
> You Powers, support
> me, your Priestess.

Odd came to the temple but, not wanting to go inside after her, he climbed on to the roof and looked through the skylight to see where she was, then picked up a large boulder and hurled it through the skylight. The stone caught the ogress in the back, crushing her against the stalls, and there she died. Odd fought a battle right through the city. He came to where Alf lay, and since he was still alive, Odd beat him to death with his club. Then he collected tribute all over the country and appointed chieftains and governors. In his poem, Odd says it was in Antioch that he killed Alf and his son.

When everything was ready, he departed with such a quantity of gold and riches that no one could estimate its value. There is nothing said of his journey till he came back to Greece.

While he was away things had changed in the land, for King Herraud was dead, and had been laid to rest, with a mound over him. Odd had a funeral feast prepared as soon as he landed, and when everything was ready Harek betrothed his foster-daughter Silkisif to Odd, so that the same feast served both for the wedding and the funeral. At this feast Odd was given the title of king, and now began ruling his kingdom.

30. Last Meeting with Ogmund

It had so happened seven years before that the king who ruled over Novgorod had died suddenly, and a stranger called Quillanus had taken the land by force and ruled over it. He was a sinister-looking man, for he wore a mask covering his face so that it was never exposed. People thought this very strange. No one knew anything about his family or ancestral land or where he had come from. There was a great deal of talk about this, and the news spread far and wide until it reached the ears of Odd in Greece. It struck him as very remarkable that on all his travels he had never heard anything about this man before, so Odd stood up in public and swore to find out who the ruler of Novgorod really was. Some time passed, then he gathered forces and got ready for a journey, sending word to his blood-brother Sirnir to come and join him. Sirnir met him east of Wendland with forty ships, and Odd had another fifty, all well-equipped with weapons and men. So they sailed east to Novgorod.

Russia is a vast country, with a number of different kingdoms. There was a king called Marro who ruled over Muram, which is a part of Russia. A king called Rodstaff ruled over a land called Rostof, and another king, Eddval, ruled a kingdom called Suzdal. The king who had ruled over Novgorod before Quillanus was called Holmgeir. There was a king called Paltes who ruled over Polotsk; and one called Kænmar ruled over Kiev where the first settler had been Magog, the son of Japhet, Noah's son. All these kings who have just been mentioned paid tribute to King Quillanus.

The three years before Odd arrived in Novgorod, Quillanus had spent mustering forces. It seemed obvious to everyone that he must have known about Odd's coming. All the kings mentioned above supported Quillanus. Another one there was Svart Geirrid's-son, a name given him after the disappearance of Ogmund Eythjof's-Killer. There were also huge armies from Karelia, Tafestland, Refaland, Virland, Estonia, Livonia, Vitland, Kurland, Lanland, Ermland, and Poland. This army was so enormous that it could not be counted in hundreds. Nobody could imagine where such a multitude could have been gathered from.

When Odd came ashore he sent messengers to King Quillanus challenging him to a tournament. King Quillanus wasted no time and hurried to meet him with all his army. As usual, he was wearing the mask over his face. As soon as they came together they made preparations for the tournament. They had great long lances, and tourneyed for three days, breaking four lances, but achieved nothing more.

Then Quillanus said, 'I think we've tried each other out, and my guess is there's nothing to choose between us.'

'I'd say that's about right,' said Odd.

'Then I think it best if we broke it up,' said Quillanus, 'let's stop fighting, I want to ask you to a feast.'

'There's only one drawback,' said Odd.

'What's that?' said Quillanus.

'I don't know who you are,' said Odd, 'and I've sworn to find out who is king over Novgorod.'

Then Quillanus took the mask from his face, and said, 'Can you guess who this ugly head belongs to?'

Then Odd realized that this gentleman was Ogmund Eythjof's-Killer all right, for he could still see the marks he'd given Ogmund when he tore off his beard and face back to the middle of the crown. The flesh had healed over the bones but not a single hair grew there.

Odd said, 'No, Ogmund, I'll never come to terms with you, you've done me too much harm. I challenge you to battle in the morning.'

Ogmund agreed, and the next day fighting started again. It was a hard and brutal battle, with great slaughter on both sides. Sirnir as always fought a good hard fight and killed a lot of men, for his sword Snidil bit everything that came his way. Svart Geirrid's-son turned to meet him and there was a fierce clash between them, but then Snidil failed to bite even though Svart had no armour. But Svart had no lack of strength, or malice either, and by the time the duel was over, Sirnir had gained great honour, but Svart had killed him.

By this time Odd had slaughtered all the tributary kings who served under Quillanus, shooting some and hewing down others. When he saw Sirnir was dead he flew into a great fury, for it seemed to him history was repeating itself, another comrade lost at the hands of Ogmund and his men. Then he set an arrow to the string and aimed it at Svart, but Svart just put up his hand against it and the arrow failed to bite his palm. The second and third arrows went the same way. It passed through Odd's mind how much he felt the lack of Gusir's Gifts. He turned away from the battlefield into the forest, cut himself a great club and went back to the fight against Svart. Odd struck him blow after blow with the club, not stopping till he had broken every bone in Svart's body and left him lying there dead.

Meanwhile, Quillanus had not been idle. For each of the arrows that flew from every one of his fingers, so it is said, a man died; and with the help of his men he had killed every single one of Odd's. Quillanus himself had lost so many men that no one could count the dead. Odd was still on his feet and fighting, because of his shirt neither tired nor wounded. Then night came between them, for it was too dark to fight. Quillanus went back to the town with those of his men who were still alive, only about sixty of them, every one wounded and worn out. After this he was nicknamed Quillanus Blaze, and he ruled over Novgorod for a long time.

Odd went off, straying through wilds and woodlands until he came to Gaul. There were two kings reigning there at the time, one called Hjorolf and the other Hroar, although formerly there had been twelve kingdoms. They were the sons of two brothers. Hroar had killed Hjorolf's father to get the throne and, apart from one province which Hjorolf had, he ruled the whole kingdom. It was to Hjorolf's coast that Odd had come.

He was a young king, and used to amuse himself trying his hand at archery, but he wasn't much good at it, and Odd said the people there were poor shots.

'Can you shoot any better?' said the king.

'There's nothing to it,' said Odd. He started shooting and never missed. The king was very much impressed with Odd and formed a high opinion of him.

The king told Odd how he had been treated by King Hroar. Odd said he ought to ask for an equal division of the kingdoms, so they sent twelve messengers to Hroar with letters. After he had looked the letters over, he said he hardly thought the request they were making a modest one, and the thing to do was to send the messengers back in such a state that no one would ever want to make the same request again. After that both kings gathered their armies, Odd and Hjorolf having less than a twelfth of Hroar's force. Odd asked people to point out King Hroar, then took an arrow and shot it at him. It caught Hroar in the waist, and he fell there without a fight. Hjorolf offered the throne to Odd, but he wasn't happy there for long and crept away one night. After that he stayed out in the woods, until he got back to his kingdom and settled down there in peace.

Some time later Quillanus sent expensive presents to Odd, gold and silver and many other treasures; and along with all this, words of friendship and offers of reconciliation. Odd accepted the gifts, for he was smart enough to realize that Ogmund Eythjof's-Killer, or Quillanus as he was called now, could never be beaten, being, as you might say, as much a phantom as a man. It's not known that they had any further dealings, so that is the end of their quarrel.

31. Back to Childhood

Odd stayed in his kingdom for a long time. He had two sons by his wife, one called Asmund after his blood-brother, and the other Herraud after the boy's grandfather. They were both likely-looking fellows.

One evening when Odd and his queen came to bed, Odd said, 'There's one journey abroad I want to make.'

'You want to go where?' asked Silkisif.

'Up north to Hrafnista,' he said. 'I want to find out who's looking after the island, since it belongs to me and my family.'

'It seems to me you've enough property here,' she said, 'now that you've won the whole of Russia and can take land and goods from anybody you want. I don't see any sense in hanging on to a scrap of an island that's quite useless anyway.'

'It may be true that the island's not worth much,' he said, 'but I want to have my say about who's going to be in charge of it. There's no point in trying to put me off, for I've made up my mind to go. I'll only be away a short time.'

Then he got two ships ready for a voyage abroad, with a crew of forty aboard each. There's nothing to tell of his journey till he got to Hrafnista in the north of Norway. The people there gave him a good welcome and laid out a feast for him, and he was fêted for two weeks. They offered him the island and all that was on it, but he gave them everything back and wouldn't stay there any longer. He made preparations to leave, and the people saw him on his way with fine presents.

Odd sailed away south from Hrafnista until he was off Berurjod, which people say lies in Jæderen. Then Odd told his men to reef the sails. Along with his men Odd went ashore there and up to the place where Ingjald's farmstead had once stood, but now there were only ruins with grass sprouting everywhere.

He looked the place over, and said, 'It's a fearful thing to see, the farm in ruins and instead of all that used to be here, only a wilderness.'

He went over to the place where he and Asmund used to practice shooting, and explained how different the two of them had been. Then Odd took his men over to where they used to go swimming and pointed out every landmark.

'Now we must be on our way,' he said, after they'd looked at this. 'It won't do us any good to stand gazing here at the land, no matter what we may feel about it.'

They went down to the sea, and everywhere they went the soil had been eroded away, though there used to be lush grass there when Odd was young.

And as they were walking down, Odd said, 'I think hopes must be fading about it ever coming true, the prophecy that wretched old witch made about me so long ago. But what's that over there? What's that lying there? Isn't it a horse's skull?'

'Why, yes,' his men said, 'terribly old and bleached, a real giant, all grey on the outside.'

'What do you think?' asked Odd. 'Could this be the skull of Faxi?'

Odd prodded the skull with the shaft of his spear, the skull shifted a little to one side, and then from under it a snake wriggled out, right up to Odd, and struck at him above the ankle. The venom started to work on him at once and the whole leg swelled up to the thigh. It took Odd so suddenly that they had to help him down to the shore.

When they got there, Odd sat down. 'You'd better split up into two halves,' he said. 'Forty beside me while I compose a poem about my life; and the other forty can build me a stone coffin and collect firewood. When I'm dead, set fire to it and burn everything.'

32. *Odd's Death*

Then he started composing the poem, and the one group set about
making the stone coffin and collecting firewood, while those who
had been chosen memorized the poem. So Odd recited:

Warriors, attend well
to the words
I give form to, frame
now of my friends:
too late
for self-delusion,
no foolery
when fate rules.

My boyhood was spent
at Berurjod;
fostered just as
my father wished,
soon I learned to like it,
nothing was lacking
that led to my happiness,
if Ingjald could help.

Asmund and I
passed our infancy
both spent our boyhoods
at Berurjod:
shaping arrows,
sharpening darts,
building boats,
a life of bliss.

The prophetess
spoke plainly,
with true words,
but I lacked wisdom.
I told young Ingjald,
son of Asmund,
that I would fare
to my father's house.

Asmund said
he'd ever be eager
to follow my lead
as long as he lived:
so I spoke my fill
to his old father,
told him I'd never
return again.

We cruised our craft
across the ocean,
no hand needed
to navigate:
girded with cliffs
was the isle we came to,
where Grim was owner
of great estates.

I remember how
his men greeted me
with affection, favoured
me at the farmstead:
there I had fellows,
friends to have fun with,
sharing our gold,
our songs and stories.

In the spring
I learned that Sigurd
and Gudmund were going
against the Permians:
so I told them,
these two trusted
warriors, that I wished
to wander with them.

These, my kinsmen,
had command
over a fleet
of fighting ships,
and their crews
were keen to conquer

and take the treasure
of the Tervi-Lapps.

We approached the Permian
people's settlements,
sailing our trading
ships in safety:
we flayed the Permians
with flame and fire,
we took captive
the Tervi-Lapps' servant.

The servant said
that he could show us
where to look
for a load of loot:
told us further
to follow the road
if we wanted
to win more wealth.

Soon the Permian
people appeared
to defend their mound –
formed up their men –
but well before we
went on our way,
lots of them lost
their lives, with our help.

We sprang with speed
down to our ships,
flying on foot
across the fen:
we reached the shore
but saw no sails,
no sign of spoils,
not a single man.

Quickly then
I kindled wood,
fire flared

in the dense forest:
we tended the fire
until it touched
the sky above us,
a bark-burning flame.

Soon we saw
splendid ships,
with richly clad
crews racing shoreward:
my kinsmen
showed very clearly
how glad they were
to greet us again.

We were forced to leave
our lives to fortune,
brave bold men
in the bitter storm:
we seemed to carry
a cargo of sand,
for all our labours
no land we sighted.

Late in summer
we came to a shore
and reefed our sails
off the rocky isle:
we hurried then
to haul up
our boats briskly
on to the beach.

We made camp
while those of our comrades
who bent their bows well
went hunting bears:
we fashioned a fine
fire on the isle,
and before the bonfire
set the body of a bear.

If we wouldn't go willingly,
into the waves
they threatened to cast us,
the cliff-people:
we didn't reckon
the rock-dwellers' promise
all that pleasant
to contemplate.

But once we were all
established on the isle,
we didn't feel
afraid of a thing:
some of us built
a strong bastion
up on the cliff –
I was one of that company!

I sought my goal
with Gusir's Gifts
between the cliff
and kindling fire:
I hit one ogre
in the eye
and his rock-woman
in the ribs.

I won my nickname –
just what I needed!
– giants called it
from the cliff,
rewarded me fairly
with fine weather
for Arrow-Odd
to cross the ocean.

So we were ready
to set out to sea
away from the island
with our good wind:
unharmed, we heroes
sailed back home,

kindly our trusted
kinsmen greeted us.

Warriors together,
we passed the winter
enjoying a good time,
glad of our gold:
in spring the ice
started to split,
our decorated ships
we dragged down to the shore.

We sailed away
south by the shoreline,
twenty-and-one
and all on watch
expectantly,
to pillage and plunder,
to sack all
of the Elfar Skerries

Just off the coast
we came at last
on those two heroes,
Hjalmar and Thord.
They asked us whether
we'd prefer
to set up agreements
or start to grapple.

We talked of treaties,
coming to terms,
the chance of profit
seemed pretty poor,
so we judged it best
to join our bands
together, we found this
the fitter choice.

We sailed our ships
to any shore
that offered the best

hope of booty;
we feared
no fellow on earth,
we were fit, we fought
in the battle-fleet.

Raging, we
ran right into
the bold heroes
off Holmsness:
from six ships
we seized
all the gear
of those gallants.

We all stood
in the west with Skolli,
where he ruled, the lord,
over his lands.
His foes were sliced
apart with swords, soaked
in blood it was we
who won the battle.

The earl's warriors
laid waste the headland,
hard men ran, harried,
hounded like foxes.
Hjalmar and I set
their ships ablaze,
burned their boats
and won the battle.

Gudmund inquired
if I'd care to go
and keep him company
in the north country.
But I told Gudmund
that never again
could I come
home to my kinsmen.

We all agreed
to gather next summer
east at Gota River
and go raiding:
the warrior Hjalmar
wanted with him
my soldiers
to stride southward.

They split
in two sections,
the fierce fighters,
when the wind was fair:
we sailed our ships
first to Sweden,
to visit Ingvi
the King at Uppsala.

Hjalmar the fierce
hero gave five
estates of land
to me totally.
I took pleasure
and pride in my property,
when others proffered
peace and gold rings.

A wonderful day
it was when we –
Sigurd of the north
and the Swedish warriors –
all robbed the islanders
of their riches,
forced them by flame
to feel suffering.

From there we sailed
our speeding ships
across the waves
westward to Ireland:
once we had arrived,
women and men

all hastened
away from their homesteads.

On my way I raced,
upon the wide road,
then set my face
to the fierce arrows:
all of my gold
I'd gladly give,
to have Asmund alive
along with me now.

At last I saw
where the stout Irish
and their girls
were gathered together:
I gave aid to four
of Olvor's family –
I helped them to lose
their precious lives.

From the chariot the fairy-woman
cried her farewells,
making me a promise
of precious things.
She said that I should
return next summer
to win the reward
awaiting me.

Not like the byrnie,
the blue-chain breast-coat
feeling like frost
upon my flesh,
when about my sides,
gold-stitched,
the silken shirt
slipped close.

We sailed back eastward
searching for loot.
My men were calling

me a coward:
then we set upon
the sinister brothers
at Skien, there
it was that we slew them.

Soti and Halfdan
were the slaughterers
of many a soul
at Svia Skerries:
before we separated
we cleared sixty
of their fighting ships
from stem to stern.

After we left
our travels led
to some crafty fellows
at Tronu Creeks.
Not yet doomed
to die was Ogmund,
nine of his men lived,
three were left of ours.

By and by, when we
came back to our boats,
I could lay claim
to the killing of men,
hot with anger
were Hjalmar and I
when we found Thord
thrust through.

So we, the heroes,
journeyed home,
raised a burial mound
over Thord's body:
no one was eager
to act against us,
we had our will
in every way.

Hjalmar and I
saw happy times,
we steered our fleet
and stayed fit:
but when we set on
the warriors at Samso,
well they knew
how to wield weapons.

We forced them under
the feet of eagles,
the bestial band
of twelve berserks:
I suffered the death
on that doom-day,
the cruel loss
of my close comrade.

I have never known
a nobler man,
more lion-hearted,
in all my life,
I who bore him
home on my back,
the helm-battering
hero, to Sigtun.

I did not allow
long to pass
before seeking
Sæmund out:
but his men cleared
the decks of my craft,
and to save myself
meant swimming for it.

Six days I roamed,
raging through Gotaland,
before I could find
the fierce Sæmund:
I confronted him
and his fourteen men,

forced him to stand
and face my sword.

Far to the south
I fared by sea
until I came
to the shallow creeks:
others roamed
the road to Hel,
I travelled
my own track.

Several cities
I saw in Aquitaine,
ruled by men
of a mighty race:
there I killed
four men of courage –
take good note
of where I am now.

Once upon a time
word was sent
to my own folk
in the far north:
I was just as glad
to greet those men
as a greedy hawk
to ease its hunger.

Many the mark
of high estimation
offered there
to all of us three:
both my brothers
kept back and stayed there,
I carried on
in spite of kindness.

I travelled quickly
away from the crowd,
journeyed to the spacious

city of Jerusalem,
down I raced,
right into the river:
my conduct made clear
how Christ should be served.

I remember well
how the Waters of Jordan
gushed o'er me, far
from the land of Greece:
as I had expected,
my special shirt
kept secure
all its qualities.

Near the ravine
I met with a vulture
that flew with me
over field and forest,
until it came
to the lofty crag
where it laid me down
to lie in its nest.

Hildir the giant
helped me then,
a brawny brute
in a rowing-boat:
this sturdy warrior
said I could stay
at his home
for the whole year.

I was helpful
to the huge
and handsome girl,
daughter of Hildir:
she gave birth
to a fine brave
son, the best
boy of his breed:
the lad was unique,
none like him.

Slain in the stony
wastes of Slabland
was my son, by Ogmund
Eythjof's-Killer:
I crushed
his nine comrades;
never a viler
viking than Ogmund.

He also slaughtered
Sirnir and Gardar,
my own blood-brothers –
I ripped off his beard,
so he looked unlike
any living soul:
Quillanus Blaze
they called him then.

Mcn held me to be
great-hearted,
a brave battler
at Brow Plains:
when Hroar called
for the wedge-shaped column,
Odd the wanderer
was the warrior-leader.

A little later,
ruling the land,
I encountered
resolute kings:
I chose to help
the young chieftain,
to win his birthright
back again.

At last I came
to that king's country
where Sigurd and Sjolf
felt so sure of themselves:
the other retainers
urged me to test

my skills against theirs,
at sports and at shooting.

My arrows flew further
than those fine fellows',
the spear in my hand
was a subtler shaft;
next I skirmished
with them at swimming,
bloody noses
I bestowed on them both.

I was ordered to stay
by the amazon's side
as we went on our way,
marching to war:
far off, I know,
men were falling in Antioch
while we won
vast wealth for ourselves.

I struck down many
a soul with my sword,
I whacked away
at their wooden gods:
at the burgh-gate
I beat down Bjalki,
with an oak club
I crushed him.

Then Harek offered
his hand in friendship,
chose me to marry
his foster-child:
I wedded Silkisif
the wise princess,
together we ruled
our realm righteously.

But my luck wasn't destined
to endure as long
as a warrior would

have wished it to:
about my travels,
I could have taught you
many a lesson –
but this is my last.

Go briskly now
down to the boats,
we must say farewell
as our ways divide:
to Silkisif
and my sons I send
my last message –
We'll meet no more.

When it was finished, Odd was getting very weak, and they led him over to where the stone coffin was ready for him.

Then Odd said, 'Now it's all coming true, what the sorceress said would happen. I'm going to lie down in the stone coffin and die there. Then you're to set fire to it, and burn everything.'

He lay down in the coffin and said, 'Carry my greetings home to Silkisif and my sons and my friends.' And with that he died.

They set fire to the wood and burnt everything, and stayed till it was all reduced to ashes. Most people will tell you that Odd was twelve ells in height, because that was the measure of the stone coffin on the inside.

Then Odd's companions got ready for the voyage and sailed back east. They had fair winds all the way home. They told Silkisif everything that had happened during their travels and brought her Odd's farewell, sad news for her and her people. After that she took charge of the kingdom, along with her foster-father Harek. They governed the land until Odd's sons were able to take over, from whom Odd's progeny in Russia are descended.

The daughter Ragnhild whom Odd had left in Ireland went east from there after her mother's death, and then north to Hrafnista. She married there, and many people trace their ancestry from her. Ragnhild's descendants have lived there ever since.

And that's the end of the saga of *Arrow-Odd*, just as you've heard it now.

King Gautrek

1. In the Backwoods

Here we begin an entertaining story about a king called Gauti. He was a shrewd sort of man, very quiet, but generous and plain-spoken. King Gauti ruled over West Gotaland, which lies east of the Kjolen Mountains between Norway and Sweden and is separated from the Uplands by the Gota River. There are immense forests in that part of the world, very difficult to get about in except when the ground is frozen.

This king we're speaking of, Gauti, used to go into these forests with his hawks and hounds, for he was a keen huntsman and took a great deal of pleasure in the sport.

At this time the deep forests were thickly populated, as many settlers had cleared the land to establish farms far away from the world. A number had abandoned society because of some underhand dealings; others had left to avoid the consequences of youthful escapades and adventures. They thought the best way to escape scorn and mockery was to hide themselves from men's ridicule, and so they lived the remainder of their lives without seeing a soul other than their own companions. As these men had gone to live right off the beaten track, hardly anyone ever came to visit them, unless from time to time someone lost in the forest might stumble on their homes, wishing he'd never set foot there.

This King Gauti we spoke of started out with his retainers and his best hounds to hunt deer in the forest, and sighted a fine stag. Setting his heart on getting it, he unleashed his hounds and spent the whole day chasing hard after it. By evening he had lost touch with his fellow huntsmen and was deep in the forest. He realized that he wouldn't be able to get back to them, as it was already dark and he'd covered so much ground during the day. Not only that, he'd hit the stag with his spear, and it had stuck fast in the wound. On no account did he want to lose the spear if he could possibly help it, since it seemed to him a great disgrace to abandon one's weapon. Gauti had been hunting so hard he had thrown off all his clothes except for his underwear. He'd lost his socks and shoes, and his legs and feet were badly cut by stones and branches, but still he had not caught up with the stag. By now it was night and very dark, and he had no idea where he was going, so he stopped to listen for any sound, and after a little while he heard the bark of a dog. Since it seemed most likely that where a dog barked there would be people about too, he walked on in that direction.

Soon he saw a small farmstead, and standing outside it a man with a woodcutter's axe. When he saw the king approaching, the man attacked the dog and killed it.

'That's the last time you show a stranger the way to our house,' he said. 'Anyone can see from the man's size that he'll eat the farmer out of house and home once he gets inside. Well, that's not going to happen if I can help it.'

The king heard what the man said and smiled to himself. He realized that he wasn't at all suitably dressed for sleeping out; on the other hand, he wasn't sure what sort of hospitality he would be offered if he waited for an invitation, so he walked up boldly to the door. The other man ran into the doorway with the idea of keeping him out, but the king forced his way past him into the house. In the living-room he saw four men and four women, but there was no word of welcome for King Gauti. So he sat himself down.

One of them, evidently the master of the house, spoke up. 'Why did you let this man in?' he asked the slave at the door.

'I was no match for him,' said the slave, 'he's too strong.'

'What did you do when that dog started barking?' said the farmer.

'I killed it,' said the slave, 'I didn't want it to lead any more roughnecks like this to the house.'

'You're a faithful servant,' said the farmer, 'and I won't put the blame on you for this tricky situation. It's difficult to find a fitting reward for the trouble you've taken, but tomorrow I'll repay you by taking you with me.'

It was a well-furnished house and the people were good-looking but not particularly big. It struck the king that they were frightened of him. The farmer gave orders for the table to be laid, and food was served. When the king saw that he wasn't going to be invited to share the meal, he took a seat at the table next to the farmer, picked up some food and settled down to eat. When the farmer saw this, he stopped eating and pulled his hat down over his eyes. Nobody said a word. After the king had finished eating, the farmer pushed up his hat and ordered the platters to be cleared from the table – 'since now there's no food left,' he said.

The king lay down to sleep, and a little later on one of the women came up to him and said, 'Wouldn't you like me to give you a bit of hospitality?'

'Things are looking up,' said the king, 'now you're willing to talk to me. Your household isn't a very talkative one.'

'Don't be surprised at that,' said the girl. 'In all our lifetime, we've never had a visitor before. I don't think the master is too pleased to have you as a guest.'

'I can easily compensate him for his trouble,' said the king, 'as soon as I get back home.'

'I'm afraid this odd affair is going to bring us something from you other than compensation,' said the woman.

'Tell me what you people are called,' said the king.

'My father's called Skinflint,' she said, 'the reason being he's so mean he can't bear to watch his food stocks dwindle, or anything else of his. My mother is known as Totra because she'll never wear any clothes that aren't in tatters. She thinks herself very thrifty.'

'What are your brothers called?' asked the king.

'One's called Fjolmod, the second Imsigull, and the third Gilling,' she said.

'What about you and your sisters?' asked the king.

'I'm called Snotra, because I'm the brightest. My sisters are called Hjotra and Fjotra,' she said. 'There's a precipice called Gillings Bluff near the farm, and we call its peak Family Cliff. The fall is so steep, no creature on earth could ever survive it. It's called Family Cliff because we use it to cut down the size of our family whenever something extraordinary happens. In this way our elders are allowed to die without delay, and suffer no illnesses, and go straight to Odin, while their children are spared all the trouble and expense of having to take care of them. Every member of our family is free to use this facility offered by the cliff, so there's no need for any of us to live in famine or poverty, or put up with any other misfortunes that might befall us. I hope you realize how extraordinary my father thinks it, your arrival at our house. It would have been remarkable enough for any stranger to take a meal with us, but this really is a marvel, a king, cold and naked, coming to our house. There's no precedent for it. So my father and mother have decided to share out the inheritance tomorrow between me and my brothers and sisters. After that they're going to take the slave with them and pass on over Family Cliff to Valhalla. My father feels the least reward he could give the slave for trying to bar your way into the house is to let the fellow share this bliss with him. Besides, he's quite sure Odin won't ever receive the slave unless he goes with him.'

'I can see that you're the most eloquent member of your family,' said the king, 'and you can rely on me. I take it you're still a virgin, so you'd better sleep with me tonight.'

She said it was entirely up to him.

When the king woke next morning, he said, 'I'd like to remind you, Skinflint, that I was barefoot when I came to your house, so I wouldn't say no to a pair of shoes.'

Skinflint made no reply but gave him a pair of shoes, though he pulled out the laces first. The king said:

> A pair of shoes was Skinflint's gift,
> But he kept back the laces, just for thrift.
> Whatever these penny-pinchers proffer,
> There's always a drawback to the offer.

After that the king got ready to go, and Snotra came to see him off.

'I'd like to ask you to come with me,' said King Gauti, 'I think our meeting may have certain consequences. If you have a boy, call him Gautrek, to remind you of me and all the trouble I've caused your family.'

'I think you're close to the mark,' she said. 'But I shan't be able to go along with you now. Today my parents mean to divide their property between me and my brothers and sisters. When that's done my father and mother intend to move on over Family Cliff.'

The king said goodbye to her and told her to come and see him whenever she felt like it. Then he went on his way until he came up with his men, and now he took it easy.

2. Over the Cliff

But to get on with the story, when Snotra came back to the house, there was her father squatting over his possessions.

'What an extraordinary thing to happen,' he said, 'a king has paid us a visit, eaten us out of house and home and then taken away what we could least afford. It's clear we won't be able to stay together any longer as a family now we're reduced to poverty, so I've gathered together all my things, and now I'm going to divide them up between my sons. I'm going to take my wife and slave along to Valhalla with me, since the least I can do to repay him for his faithful service is to let him go there with me. Gilling is to have my fine ox, to share with his sister Snotra. Fjolmod and his sister Hjotra are to have my bars of gold, Imsigull and his sister Fjotra all my cornfields. And now I want to implore you, my children, not to add to the family, for only thus will you be able to preserve what you've inherited.'

After Skinflint had said all he wanted, the family climbed up to Gillings Bluff. The young people helped their parents to pass on over Family Cliff, and off they went, merry and bright, on the way to Odin.

Now that the young people had taken over the property, they decided they'd better set things right. They cut some wooden pegs and used them to pin pieces of cloth round their bodies so that they couldn't touch one another. They felt this was the safest method of controlling their numbers.

When Snotra realized she was going to have a baby, she loosened the wooden pins that held her dress together, so that her body could be touched. She was pretending to be asleep when Gilling woke or stirred in his sleep. He stretched out his hand and happened to touch her cheek.

Once he was properly awake, he said 'Something terrible has happened, I'm afraid that I've got you into trouble. You seem to be much stouter now than you used to be.'

'Keep it to yourself as long as you can,' she said.

'I'll do no such thing,' he said, 'once there's an addition to our family there'll be no hope of hiding it.'

Not long after, Snotra gave birth to a beautiful boy. She chose a name for him and called him Gautrek.

'What an odd thing to happen,' said Gilling, 'there's no hiding this any longer. I'm going to tell my brothers.'

'Our whole way of life is being threatened by this remarkable event,' they declared. 'This is indeed a serious violation of our rule.'

Gilling said:

> How could my brain have been so weak,
> To let me touch that woman's cheek.
> But if that's the way such deeds are done,
> It's not very hard to beget a son.

They said it wasn't his fault, particularly since he had repented and wished it had never happened. He said he'd willingly pass on over Family Cliff, adding that this little affair might be only the start. His brothers told him to wait and see whether anything else would happen.

Fjolmod used to herd his sheep all day, carrying the gold bars with him wherever he went. One day he fell asleep and woke up to find two black snails crawling over the gold. He got the idea that the gold had been dented where it was really only blackened, and he thought it much diminished.

'What a terrible thing,' he said, 'to suffer such a loss. If this should happen once more I'll be penniless when I go to see Odin. So I'd better pass on over Family Cliff just to make sure it never happens again. Things have never looked so black, not since my father handed over all this money.'

He told his brothers about his ominous experience, and asked them to share out his part of the property. Then he added:

> Whate'er I do is of no avail,
> My gold's consumed by a scrawny snail!
> Stripped of my wealth I'm sorely troubled,
> Now that all my gold's been gobbled.

Then he and his wife went up to Gillings Bluff and passed on over Family Cliff.

One day Imsigull was inspecting his cornfields. He saw a bird called the sparrow – it's about the size of a tit. He thought the bird might have caused some serious damage, so he walked round the fields till he saw where the bird had picked a single grain from one of the ears. Then he said:

> See what that greedy bird has torn
> From my devastated corn,
> Ravaging a whole ear of grain!
> Can Totra's kin endure such pain?

Then he and his wife passed joyfully on over Family Cliff, unable to risk such another loss.

One day when Gautrek was seven years old, he noticed the fine ox outside, and stabbed it to death with a spear. Gilling was watching and said:

> He's killed my ox, has that young lad:
> The omens here are very bad.
> No such treasure will come my way,
> Never, though I grow old and grey.

'This has gone too far,' he added. And then he climbed up Gillings Bluff and passed on over Family Cliff.

Now there were only two of them left, Snotra and her son Gautrek. She made preparations for a journey, and off they went to see King Gauti. He gave his son a good welcome, and after that Gautrek was brought up at his father's court. He matured early in every way, and in only a few years he had reached full manhood. Then it happened that King Gauti fell ill and called his friends around him.

'You've always proved obedient and loyal to me,' he said, 'but now it looks as if this illness of mine is going to put an end to our friendship. I've decided to hand over my authority to my son Gautrek, and with it the title of king.'

His friends were all in favour of this, and after King Gauti's death Gautrek was made king over Gotaland. He's mentioned in many of the old sagas.

At this point we must shift our story north to Norway for a while and say something about the provincial kings who were ruling there at the time and also about their progeny. After this, our story will come back to King Gautrek of Gotaland and his sons, the same story that's told in Sweden and in many other lands.

3. Starkad the Old

There was a king called Hunthjof who ruled over Hordaland. He was the son of Frithjof the Brave and Ingibjorg the Fair. Hunthjof had three sons: Herthjof, who later was King of Hordaland; Geirthjof, King of the Uplands; and Frithjof, King of Telemark. All three brothers were powerful kings and great warriors, but King Herthjof was the more shrewd and a better leader than either of the others. He spent a lot of his time on viking expeditions, which earned him a great reputation.

At this time there was a king over Agder Province called Harald the Agder-King, a powerful ruler, with a young son of great promise called Vikar.

There was a man called Storvirk, the son of Starkad the Ala-Warrior. Starkad was a giant and had uncanny wisdom. After he had abducted a woman called Alfhild, from Alfheim, King Alf's daughter, King Alf called on Thor to bring his daughter back, so Thor killed Starkad and restored Alfhild to her father. She was carrying a child and her son was the boy Storvirk whom we've already mentioned.

Storvirk was black-haired and handsome, taller and stronger than other men. He was a great viking, and joined the court of King Harald of Agder Province, where he took charge of his defences. King Harald gave him Thruma Island in Agder and Storvirk owned a farm there. Sometimes he went on long viking expeditions, sometimes he stayed with King Harald.

Storvirk abducted Unn, daughter of Earl Freki of Halogaland, and after that he made his home on his island farm. They had a son called Starkad.

Earl Freki's sons, Fjori and Fyri, made an attack on Storvirk one night. They arrived unexpectedly with a force of men and burned down the farm, killing Storvirk and their sister Unn, and all the others inside the house at the time. The attackers had not wanted to risk opening the door in case Storvirk should escape. They sailed away the same night and travelled north along the coast, but late the following day they were overtaken by a sudden storm and ran on to a submerged rock off Stad, where they perished with all hands.

Storvirk's son, Starkad, was very young when his father was killed, and King Harald had him brought up at his court. Starkad himself refers to this:

> Only a little fellow
> was I when my father
> fell, by fire,
> with his men at the farm:
> there he lies, still,
> on Thruma Island,
> this mighty hero,
> King Harald's man.
> Fjori and Fyri,
> sons of Earl Freki,
> slew him, their own
> sister's husband –
> they were my uncles,
> the brothers of Unn.

4. *Vengeance*

King Herthjof of Hordaland and his army made a surprise attack on King Harald one night, killed him treacherously, and took his son Vikar as hostage. King Herthjof conquered all of Harald's kingdom, made hostages of a good many more sons of important men and collected tribute throughout the whole country.

There was an important man in King Herthjof's army called Grani Horsehair. He lived at Ask on Fenhring Island, off Hordaland. Grani took Starkad Storvirksson captive and brought him

home with him to Fenhring. Starkad was three years old at the
time, and spent the next nine years at Fenhring with Grani Horsehair. This is what Starkad says:

> Treacherous was Herjolf's
> treatment of his lord, Harald;
> he killed Agder's king,
> and captured his sons.

> To Hordaland Grani
> Horsehair carried me –
> I was only three:
> reared on Ask Island,
> nine long years I spent
> without sight of my family.

King Herthjof was a great warrior constantly at war, and there
was always trouble in his own kingdom. He had warning beacons
built on the mountains with watchmen in charge of them, so they
could light the fires as soon as war broke out. Vikar and two other
men looked after the beacons on Fenhring. At the first sign of
enemy forces the nearest beacon was to be lit, and then the rest, one
after another.

One morning shortly after he had taken charge of the
beacon, Vikar went over to Ask to see his foster-brother Starkad
Storvirksson. Starkad was an exceptionally big man, but he was a
layabout and slept among the ashes by the hearth. He was twelve
years old at the time. Vikar hauled him out of bed and gave him
some weapons and clothes. When he took Starkad's measurements
he was amazed to see how much he had grown since he had come to
live at Ask. Later they went aboard Vikar's ship and sailed away. As
Starkad himself says:

> I grew in power:
> like a pair of poles
> my legs grew longer:
> shaggy were my locks.
> Bored with it all
> I baked in the ashes:
> then came Herthjof's hostage
> from the hill-beacon,

> Vikar, he found me
> and forced me to my feet,
> grasped my arm, measured
> my wrist with his grip,
> just as hair had begun
> to grow on my cheek.

Starkad himself has said that although he was only twelve at the time he was already growing a beard. After Starkad had got off the floor, and Vikar had given him weapons and clothes, they went down to the ship and gathered a troop of men. He managed to get twelve, all warriors and duellists. In the words of Starkad:

> Then Vikar gathered
> a viking force,
> Sorkvir and Grettir,
> and Hildigrim,
> Erp and Ulf,
> An and Skuma,
> Hroi and Hrotti
> the sons of Herbrand,
> Styr and Steinthor
> from Stad in the North,
> and that old battler
> Gunnolf Blaze,
> twelve in our band,
> few better or bolder.

With these men, Vikar marched against King Herthjof. As soon as the king heard of this attack he got his forces ready. King Herthjof had a great house which was fortified as strongly as a castle or a town, and there he kept seventy warriors as well as all the farm-hands and other servants. The vikings wasted no time. As soon as they arrived they began ramming the gates and doors and breaking down the door-posts, forcing the locks and bars inside them. As the king's men fell back, the vikings were able to force their way into the house and a fierce skirmish began. As Starkad says:

> We reached the king's residence,
> rammed the gates,
> hacked and hewed
> the doors from their hinges:

> we unsheathed our swords,
> and smashed the locks,
> we set our faces
> not simply against slaves
> and workmen and water-carriers,
> but seventy royal warriors!

King Herthjof had many excellent fighting men, so he was able to hold out for a long time, but as Vikar had a choice company of the very best fighting men, Herthjof's troops had to give way. Vikar was always at the head of his men. Starkad has it:

> Vikar was ever
> in the vanguard of battle:
> hard to keep up
> with the hero ahead of us.
> We battered their helms
> and broke their heads
> and smashed and bashed
> their byrnies and shields.

Starkad and Vikar fought side by side against King Herthjof, and eventually they killed him. All Vikar's warriors fought like champions, killing many and wounding others. As Starkad says:

> Vikar was fated
> to foster his own fame,
> to pay back Herthjof
> and punish his wickedness.
> To some we dealt wounds,
> to others worse – death –
> and when we killed the king
> I was close to the action.

So Vikar won the victory, and King Herthjof fell, as we have said, along with thirty dead and many fatally wounded, but Vikar didn't lose a man.

After that Vikar took all the ships which had belonged to King Herthjof, and sailed east along the coast with all the men he could muster. When he came to Agder he was joined by those who had been his father's friends, so now he had a large body of men following him. Then he was made king over Agder and Jæderen

Provinces, and soon he laid Hordaland under him, as well as Hardanger and all the other districts King Herthjof had ruled.

King Vikar soon became a powerful war leader. Every summer, he used to go on viking expeditions. Once he brought his forces east to Oslofjord and landed the army on the east coast, plundering as far as Gotaland and creating havoc there. When he reached Lake Væner he came up against King Sisar of Kiev, who was a great warrior and had a formidable army with him. The two kings, Vikar and Sisar, fought a hard battle there. Sisar attacked and killed a number of Vikar's men. Starkad was there fighting on Vikar's side, and he moved up against Sisar. They fought for a long time, and neither had any reason to complain about the other's strokes. Sisar hewed at Starkad's shield, gave him two nasty head wounds and broke his collarbone. Starkad also got a wound on his side above the hip. In Starkad's words:

> You weren't with Vikar,
> east at Lake Væner
> when early one morning
> we met with Sisar:
> hard to imagine
> how mighty the task –
> he smashed my skull
> through shield and helm,
> cracked my collarbone,
> cut through to the jaw.

Then Starkad suffered another deep wound from Sisar's halberd on the opposite side. In his own words:

> The blade of the hero
> hewed at my hip:
> with his halberd
> he hacked at my body:
> the scars have healed
> but still you may see them.

Starkad struck back at Sisar with his sword, slicing off part of his side and wounding him badly in the leg below the knee. Finally he cut off Sisar's other leg at the ankle, and King Sisar fell. As Starkad says:

I cut a slice
out of his side,
with my sharp blade
slitting the body:
all the strength I could summon
was in that stroke.

There were many casualties in this battle, but Vikar won the victory, and the survivors of the Kiev forces were routed. After this victory King Vikar went back to his own kingdom.

5. Herthjof's Brothers

King Vikar heard that King Geirthjof of the Uplands had gathered a large force, intending to attack Vikar and avenge the killing of his brother Herthjof, so Vikar ordered a general levy throughout his kingdom, and marched against King Geirthjof of the Uplands. The battle between them was so fierce they fought for seventeen days without a break, but King Geirthjof was killed, and Vikar won the victory. He took over the Uplands and Telemark as King Frithjof of Telemark happened to be out of the country at the time.

Starkad also mentions that the Battle of Uplands was Vikar's third battle:

Courageous, the King
completed his third
war-game; next
he won in the Uplands,
when he killed Geirthjof
and cast him into Hell.

King Vikar left some of his men in charge of the kingdom he had won in the Uplands, and went back home to Agder; his power and his army had now become very great. He got himself a wife, and had two sons by her, the elder called Harald, and the younger Neri. Neri was the wisest of men, and all the advice he gave turned out for the best; but he was such a miser that he could never part with anything without immediately regretting it. In Starkad's words:

Two fine sons
had this famous King.

the elder, Harald,
took hold of Telemark;
the other, Neri
the Earl – known
for meanness with money,
but mighty in war
and shrewd in council –
controlled the Uplands.

Earl Neri was a great warrior, but his meanness is a household word, and all the most niggardly and the most reluctant with gifts to others have been compared with him ever since.

When Frithjof heard that his two brothers had been killed he went to the Uplands and took back the kingdom Vikar had previously won. Then he sent word to Vikar, ordering him to pay tribute from his own kingdom or suffer at the hands of Frithjof's warriors. As Starkad says:

Frithjof in a fury
sent to find
what the wise King
wished for most –
payment of his dues
or pitched battle?

As soon as Vikar got this message, he called a meeting and conferred with his counsellors about how he ought to reply. They discussed the problem at great length. As Starkad has it:

Though long the discussion,
there was no deception:
the King's own forces
declared he should fight.

Word was sent to King Frithjof that Vikar intended to defend his land, so Frithjof set off with his army to attack King Vikar.

There was a king called Olaf the Keen-eyed ruling over Næriki in Sweden, a powerful ruler and a great warrior. Olaf ordered a general levy in his kingdom and with this force he went to support King Vikar. It was a huge army that faced King Frithjof, formed up in a wedge-shaped column. As Starkad says:

Olaf the Keen-eyed
ruled his kingdom

east in Sweden,
organized a levy:
large was the force
his men formed.

After some hard fighting, Vikar's men pushed forward, since there were many famous warriors among them. First of all, there was Starkad Storvirksson, then Ulf and Erp and many more great fighters and brave champions. King Vikar made a fight of it. Starkad was without a coat of mail, and waded through the enemy army hewing about him with both hands. As the verse reports it:

> We strode eagerly
> into the war-din,
> Vikar's warriors
> in the vanguard of battle:
> Ulf and Erp
> were both in action:
> without aid of armour
> I used my hands.

Vikar and his men kept up the pressure until King Frithjof's resistance started to crumble and Frithjof was forced to ask King Vikar for mercy. In the words of Starkad:

> Frithjof planned
> to plead for mercy:
> Vikar, he knew,
> could never be vanquished,
> and Starkad Storvirksson
> was a tower of strength.

It had been a fierce battle and most of King Frithjof's men were dead, so when he asked for peace Vikar ordered his army to stop fighting. Frithjof made a peace settlement with King Vikar, the terms to be fixed by King Olaf. The final agreement was that King Frithjof should surrender his authority over the Uplands and Telemark. After that he went into exile.

King Vikar appointed his sons rulers of these territories. He made Harald king over Telemark and gave Neri the title of earl, and authority over the Uplands. Earl Neri became a friend of King Gautrek of Gotaland, and some books say that King Gautrek gave him that part of Gotaland to rule over which was closest to the Uplands, and that he was King Gautrek's earl and gave advice whenever the king was in need of it.

After this, King Vikar went back home to his own kingdom, and he and King Olaf parted great friends. So they remained for the rest of their lives. King Olaf went back home to Sweden.

6. The Farmer's Boy

There was a wealthy farmer called Rennir who lived on what came to be called Rennis Island, off Jæderen in Norway. He had been a great viking before he settled down on his farm. Rennir was married and had one son, called Ref.

When he was young Ref used to lie in the kitchen and eat twigs and tree bark. He was a marvellously big man, but never bothered to wash the filth off his body, and never gave anyone a helping hand. His father was very thrifty and took a poor view of his son's shiftless behaviour, so Ref earned his fame not by any wisdom or bravery but rather by making himself the laughing stock of all his sturdy kinsmen. His father thought it unlikely that Ref would ever do anything worthwhile, such as was expected of other young men in those days.

Rennir had one treasured possession which he valued more than anything else he owned, a big ox with magnificent horns. Both horns had been incised and inlaid with gold and silver, and the points decorated with gold. There was a silver chain stretched between the horns, bearing three gold rings. It was the finest ox of its kind in the land, both for size and splendour. Rennir made such a fuss of this ox that it was never allowed to go about unattended.

Rennir took part in many of King Vikar's battles, and they were good friends.

7. The Gods in Judgement

King Vikar became a great war leader and had with him a number of distinguished warriors, but Starkad was the most highly regarded of them all and the one best loved by the king; he sat next to him on the high-seat, acted as his counsellor and was in charge of the defences. King Vikar had given him many gifts, one of them a gold bracelet weighing three marks. In return, Starkad gave the king Thruma Island, which King Harald had once given to Storvirk, Starkad's father. He was with King Vikar for fifteen years. As Starkad himself says:

> Vikar gave me
> gold from abroad,
> the red bracelet
> that rings my arm,
> three marks weight.
> But I gave him Thruma,
> and fifteen years
> fought loyally for him.

King Vikar set out from Agder and sailed north to Hordaland with a large army. Then he ran into unfavourable winds and had to lie at anchor off a group of small islands. They tried divination to find out when the wind would be favourable and were told that Odin expected a human sacrifice from the army, the victim to be chosen by lot. So they drew lots throughout the army and every time, King Vikar's lot came up. They were all very shaken by this, and it was decided that all their leading men should have a meeting the following day to consider the problem.

Then just about midnight, Grani Horsehair woke up his foster-son Starkad and asked him to come along with him. They got a small boat, rowed over to another island, and walked through a wood until they came to a clearing where a large group of people was gathered for a meeting. There were eleven men sitting on chairs but a twelfth chair was empty. Starkad and his foster-father joined the assembly, and Grani Horsehair seated himself on the twelfth chair. Everyone present greeted him by the name Odin, and he declared that the judges would have to decide Starkad's fate.

Then Thor spoke up and said: 'Since Starkad's grandmother, Alfhild, preferred a clever giant to Thor himself as the father of her son, I ordain that Starkad himself shall have neither a son nor a daughter, and his family end with him.'

Odin: 'I ordain that he shall live three life spans.'

Thor: 'He shall commit a most foul deed in each one of them.'

Odin: 'I ordain that he shall have the best of weapons and clothing.'

Thor: 'I ordain that he shall have neither land nor estates.'

Odin: 'I give him this, that he shall have great riches.'

Thor: 'I lay this curse on him, that he shall never be satisfied with what he has.'

Odin: 'I give him victory and fame in every battle.'

Thor: 'I lay this curse on him, that in every battle he shall be sorely wounded.'

Odin: 'I give him the art of poetry, so that he shall compose verses as fast as he can speak.'

Thor: 'He shall never remember afterwards what he composes.'

Odin: 'I ordain that he shall be most highly thought of by all the noblest and the best.'

Thor: 'The common people shall hate him every one.'

Then the judges decreed that all that had been declared should come about. The assembly broke up, and Grani Horsehair and Starkad went back to their boat.

'You should repay me well, foster-son,' said Grani Horsehair to Starkad, 'for all the help I've given you.'

'That I will,' said Starkad.

'Then you must send King Vikar to me,' said Grani Horsehair. 'I'll tell you how to go about it.'

Starkad agreed, and Grani Horsehair gave him a spear which he said would appear to be only a reed-stalk. Then they joined the rest of the army, just a little before daybreak.

In the morning the king's counsellors held a meeting to discuss their plans. They agreed that they would have to hold a mock sacrifice, and Starkad told them how to set about it. There was a pine tree nearby and close to it a tall tree trunk. The pine tree had a slender branch just above the ground, but stretching up into the foliage. Just then the servants were making breakfast. A calf had been slaughtered and its entrails cleaned out. Starkad asked for the guts, then climbed up the trunk, bent down the slender branch and tied the calf guts around it.

'Your gallows is ready for you now, my lord,' he said to King Vikar, 'and it doesn't seem too dangerous. Come over here and I'll put a noose round your neck.'

'If this contraption isn't any more dangerous than it looks,' said the king, 'then it can't do me much harm. But if things turn out otherwise, it's in the hands of fate.'

After that he climbed up the stump. Starkad put the noose round his neck and climbed down. Then he stabbed the king with the reed-stalk. 'Now I give you to Odin,' he said.

At that Starkad let loose the branch. The reed-stalk turned into a spear which pierced the king, the tree stump slipped from under his feet, the calf guts turned into a strong withy, the branch shot up with the king into the foliage, and there he died. Ever since, that place has been known as Vikarsholmar.

This affair made Starkad a much-hated man among the common people, and because of it he was first banished from Hordaland, and later had to flee from Norway east to Sweden. He stayed for a long time at Uppsala with the kings there, Eirik and Alrek, the sons of Agni Skjalf's-husband and went on viking expeditions with them. When Alrek asked Starkad what he could tell him about his kinsmen or himself, Starkad composed the poem called *Vikar's Piece*, in which he described how Vikar died:

> The best years
> of my battle-time,
> I followed the first
> of famous kings;
> then we launched
> upon our last
> hateful venture
> to Hordaland.
>
> Thor shaped
> my shame, ordained
> me traitor, tied
> me to misery.
> I was not keen
> for killing: I
> was not apt
> for such evil.

Against my will
I gave to the gods
my true lord Vikar
high on the tree:
never such pangs
of pain for me
as when my spear
slipped into his side.

I rambled alone,
wretched, restless,
hated by all
in Hordaland,
a sorrowing man,
songless, without gold
or glorious lord,
lost without my king.

Next to Sweden
my path strayed,
east to Uppsala
home of the Ynglings:
long I'll remember
the lack of love,
the roughness
of those royal retainers.

It's only too clear from Starkad's poem that he thought the killing of Vikar the most evil and odious thing he had ever done in his life. None of the stories we have heard suggests that he ever came back to Norway.

While Starkad was at Uppsala, twelve berserks were there as mercenaries. They were very aggressive and used to make fun of him, in particular two brothers called Ulf and Otrygg. Starkad was a taciturn man, and the berserks used to say he was the reincarnation of a giant, as well as a traitor. This is what is said here:

They set me among
serving soldiers,
me an old man,
white-browed, a mockery.
Jesters and jokers

these jackanapes,
cruel and unkind
the cuts they gave me.

These monstrous scars
that are seen on me,
on the killer of Hergrim –
so they claim –
are what's left of the arms,
all eight of them, Thor
ripped from my trunk
on the northern rock-face.

Mankind mocks
my snout of a mouth,
the grim jaws, the grey
wolf's gross
bristle, the barked
arms, the bruised
skin knotted
and gnarled at the neck.

When Kings Eirik and Alrek settled down, Starkad went on plundering expeditions with the ship that King Eirik had given him, manned with Norwegians and Danes. He travelled widely, fought duels and battles in many lands, and always won: and now Starkad is out of our story.

King Alrek had a short life, and this is the way he died – his brother, King Eirik, struck him dead with a bridle when they had gone out to train their horses. After that King Eirek was the sole ruler of Sweden for a long time, as will be told elsewhere in Hrolf Gautreksson's Saga.

8. *King Gautrek's Rule*

Now there are two sets of events which have been taking place at the same time, so we must go back to the point at which we broke off, when King Gautrek had become ruler of Gotaland and established himself as an outstanding leader and fighting man. Yet the king felt it was a great defect of honour that he had no wife, so he decided to look out for one.

There was a king called Harald ruling over Wendland, a shrewd man but not much of a warrior. He was married and had a daughter called Alfhild, a fine-looking, well-mannered girl.

King Gautrek got ready for a journey and travelled to Wendland to ask for King Harald's daughter. His proposal was well received, and whatever was said, the outcome was this, that the princess was promised to King Gautrek, so he brought her with him back to Gotaland and celebrated their wedding. They had not been married long before Alfhild gave birth to a beautiful daughter. They chose a name for her and called her Helga. She was a girl who matured early. She grew up with her father, and was thought to be the finest match in all Gotaland.

King Gautrek had a number of prominent men with him. One of his friends was a great viking called Hrosskel. On one occasion King Gautrek invited him to a feast, and when it was over, he gave Hrosskel some excellent parting gifts: a grey stallion and four mares, all silk-pale and splendid. Hrosskel thanked the king for the presents, and they parted the best of friends.

King Gautrek ruled his kingdom in peace for a number of years. Then his wife fell ill, and had no relief till she died. King Gautrek was deeply grieved by this, and had a burial mound raised over the queen. Her death affected him so much, he paid no attention to matters of state. Every day he used to sit on her mound and from there he would fly his hawk. In this manner he would amuse himself and while away the time.

9. The Prince and the Peasant

Now we come back to Earl Neri, the ruler of the Uplands, whom we mentioned before. When he heard that his father, King Vikar, had been killed he arranged a meeting with his brother Harald, and there they discussed how they ought to divide their inheritance. They agreed that Harald, who was the elder, should take over all the kingdoms that King Vikar had ruled and have the king's title; but Earl Neri was to stay ruler of the Uplands and also get Telemark, which till then had been ruled by his brother Harald. The brothers parted on good terms. Earl Neri was so wise he was without equal, and all his schemes turned out well no matter what the problem. He would never accept a gift, being too mean to give anything in return.

One day the farmer Rennir we spoke of earlier was passing through his kitchen and tripped over the feet of his son Ref.

'It's a shocking disgrace to have a son like you,' Rennir told him, 'you bring nothing but trouble. Well, if you must behave like an idiot, you'd better get out of my sight, and don't ever show your face here again.'

'Since you're kicking me out,' said Ref, 'it's only fair I should take whatever it is you love and value most.'

'There's nothing I'm not happy to give for seeing the back of you,' said Rennir, 'you're the laughing-stock of the family.'

No more was said, but one fine day not long after, Ref rose to his feet and got ready to leave. He took the fine ox with him and led it down to the sea, then launched a large boat, intending to go over to the mainland. He didn't care whether or not the ox got wet, so he tied it to the boat, then settled down on the rowing bench and rowed over to the mainland. He was wearing a short cloak and breeches down to the ankles. When he had landed he set out with the ox behind him, travelling east through Jæderen and so by the usual route to the Uplands.

Ref journeyed on without a break until he arrived at Earl Neri's residence. The retainers told the earl that Ref, Rennir's idiot son, had arrived with the famous ox. The earl told them not to make fun of the boy. When Ref came up to the door of the hall where the earl usually sat, he told the doorkeeper to call the earl to come and talk with him.

'You're as big a fool as ever,' they said. 'The earl isn't in the habit of rushing out to talk with peasants.'

'You give him the message,' said Ref. 'He'll answer for himself.'

So they went inside to the earl and told him that Ref the Fool was asking for him to come out.

'Tell Ref I'll come and see him,' said the earl. 'You can never tell what may bring you luck.'

So the earl went outside, and Ref greeted him.

'What have you come here for?' asked the earl.

'My father's thrown me out,' said Ref. 'Here's an ox of mine I'd like you to have as a gift.'

'Haven't you heard,' said the earl. 'I never accept gifts, as I don't like having to give any.'

'I've heard you're so mean, no one can expect a gift in return for anything he's given you,' said Ref. 'Still, I'd like you to accept this ox. Maybe you could help me with your advice. Never mind the money.'

'Since you put it like that, I'll accept the ox,' said the earl. 'Come inside and stay the night.'

Ref let go of the ox and went into the house. The earl asked someone to bring Ref some clothes to make him look more decent, and when Ref had washed himself, he seemed a very handsome man. Ref settled there for a while.

The earl's hall was completely lined with overlapping shields, hanging with not an empty space between them. The earl took one of the shields, heavily inlaid with gold, and gave it to Ref.

Next day when the earl went to drink in the hall, he looked at the gap where the shield had hung, and said:

> On the wall-weave it would glitter,
> The bright shield in its place:
> But now it makes me bitter
> To see the empty space.
> This is the deadliest of rifts:
> All the riches that life yields
> Might vanish too, should another's gifts
> Threaten my precious shields.

The earl had his high-seat turned round, for it upset him deeply that the shield wasn't there any more.

When Ref realized this, he took the shield and went up to the earl.

'My lord,' he said, 'cheer up now, here's that shield you gave me. I'd like to give it back to you, for it's no use to me, I've no weapons to go with it.'

'Good luck to a generous man!' said the earl, 'now my hall will have its old splendour again, once the shield's back in its usual place. Here's a present I want to give you, and it may be you'll find it useful as long as you take my advice.'

The earl gave him a whetstone, 'but you'll think this a gift of little value,' he said.

'I can't see how it can be much use to me,' said Ref.

'The fact is, I won't feed any idler who hangs about with nothing to do,' said the earl. 'Now, I'm going to send you to King Gautrek, and you're to hand this whetstone to him.'

'This is the first time I've ever acted as an emissary between kings,' said Ref, 'and I don't see what possible use the king can have for this whetstone.'

'I'd hardly have a reputation for wisdom if I couldn't see further into the future than you,' said the earl. 'But this job won't in any way test your courage, since you're not even to talk to him. I've been told that the king often sits on the queen's burial mound, and flies his hawk from there. But as the day wears on, the hawk gets tired and then the king gropes round the chair for something to throw at the bird. Now if it happens that the king can't find anything to throw, you're to put the whetstone into his hand. And if he gives you something in return, take it and then come back to me.'

So Ref set out as the earl had instructed him and travelled on till he arrived at the mound where King Gautrek was sitting. Everything turned out precisely as Earl Neri had said it would. The king threw all the objects he could lay his hands on at the hawk. Ref sat down behind the king's chair. Then he realized his chance had come. When the king stretched his hand back, Ref put the whetstone into it, and the king hurled the stone at the hawk. The bird flew up as soon as the stone hit it. The king was so pleased with his success he didn't want his helper to go unrewarded, so without bothering to see who it was, he reached out behind him with a gold ring. Ref took it and went back to Earl Neri, who asked him how his trip had gone. Ref told him and showed him the ring.

'This is a valuable prize,' said the earl. 'It's a lot better to earn a thing like this than just sit around.'

Ref stayed there over the winter, and in the spring the earl asked him, 'What are you going to do now?'

'That shouldn't be difficult to decide,' said Ref. 'Now I can sell my ring for hard cash.'

'I'm going to take a hand in your affairs again,' said the earl.

'There's a king called Ælla who rules over England. You're to give him the ring, you won't lose by it. Come back to me in the autumn, I'll give you plenty of good food and advice even if I don't repay you for the ox any other way.'

'There's no need for you to bring that up,' said Ref.

Then he sailed over to England and went before King Ælla and greeted him courteously. On that occasion Ref was wearing fine clothes and weapons. The king wanted to know who this man was.

'I'm called Ref,' he said, 'and I'd like you to accept this gold ring as a present from me.'

Then he laid it on the table in front of the king.

The king looked at it. 'This is a great treasure,' he said. 'Who gave it you?'

'The ring was given me by King Gautrek,' said Ref.

'What had you given him?' said the king.

'A little whetstone,' said Ref.

'King Gautrek's a mighty generous man, to repay stone with gold,' said the king. 'I'm going to accept this ring, and invite you to stay with me.'

'Thank you, my lord, for your invitation. But I've decided to go back to my foster-father, Earl Neri.'

'You must stay here for a while,' said the king.

The king had a ship fitted out, and one day he asked Ref to come with him for a walk. 'Here's a ship I want to give you, with all the crew you need and a cargo of all the goods you'll find most useful,' said the king. 'Wherever you choose to go, I don't want you to be another man's passenger any longer. But this isn't to be compared with King Gautrek's gift when he repaid you for the whetstone.'

'This is a most generous gift,' said Ref. He thanked the king eloquently, then made ready for the voyage.

'Here are two little dogs I'd like to give you,' said the king.

They were remarkably small and pretty, and Ref had never seen anything like them. Each wore a halter of gold with a gold clasp round the neck, and there were seven small rings on the chain that linked them. No one had seen precious things quite like this before.

Then Ref sailed off till he came to the land ruled by Earl Neri, who went out to meet him and make him welcome.

'Come with all your men and stay with me,' he said.

'I've money enough now to pay our own way,' said Ref.

'Good,' said the earl. 'But you mustn't spend your money on that. You're to eat at our table, that's not too much to pay for the ox.'

'The one thing that annoys me is when you bring that subject up,' said Ref.

So Ref spent the winter with the earl, and got on well with people, and plenty of men used to follow him around.

In the spring the earl said to Ref, 'What are you going to do now?'

'Wouldn't it be possible for me to go on a viking expedition or else go trading,' said Ref, 'now I've plenty of money?'

'That's true,' said the earl. 'But I'm still going to take a hand in your affairs. Travel south to Denmark to see King Hrolf Kraki and give him the dogs. They're not the thing for common people. You won't lose money by it if Hrolf is willing to accept the gift.'

'I'll take your advice,' said Ref, 'though I've plenty of money already.'

10. King Hrolf

Ref made ready for a voyage and sailed over to Denmark. He went to see King Hrolf and greeted him, and the king asked him who he was. He said he was called Ref.

'Aren't you called Gift-Ref?' asked the king.

'It's true I've accepted gifts from people,' said Ref, 'and occasionally I've given presents to others.' Then he added: 'I'd like, Sir, to present you with these little dogs and their outfit.'

The king looked at them. 'These are very valuable,' he said. 'Who gave them to you?'

'King Ælla.'

'What had you given him?'

'A gold ring.'

'And who'd given you the gold ring?'

'King Gautrek.'

'And what had you given him?'

'A whetstone.'

'He's a remarkably generous man, King Gautrek, to repay stones with gold,' said the king. 'I'd like to accept the dogs. You must stay with us.'

'I'm going back to Neri in the autumn,' said Ref.

'There's nothing to be done about it then,' said the king. So Ref stayed there for a while.

In the autumn Ref made his ship ready. Then the king said to him, 'I've decided how to repay you. Like the King of England, I'm going to present you with a ship, fully manned, and laden with the best of cargoes.'

'I can't thank you enough for this magnificent gift,' said Ref, and got ready to leave.

'Here are two precious things I want to give you, Ref,' said the king, 'a helmet and a coat of mail.'

Ref took the gifts, both made of red gold, then he and King Hrolf parted good friends, and Ref went back to Earl Neri, this time in charge of two ships.

The earl welcomed him with open arms, and said his money had continued to increase.

'You'd better stay here with all your men over the winter,' he said, 'and even then I've only repaid you for the ox in a small way. But I'll never grudge you my good advice.'

'I'll accept your guidance in everything,' said Ref.

He stayed there over the winter enjoying lavish hospitality, and getting a reputation as a man of note.

11. Deception

In the spring Earl Neri asked Ref, 'What are you going to do this summer?'

'I'd like your advice, sir,' said Ref. 'Now that I've plenty of money.'

'I think you're right about that but there's still one more trip I'd like you to make,' said the earl. 'There's a king called Olaf who's always plundering. He has eighty ships and lies out at sea, winter or warm summer. You're to go and give him the helmet and the coat of mail, and if he accepts the gift, I expect he'll let you choose your own reward. Then you're to tell him that in return you want to command his forces for a fortnight and be free to take them wherever you like. The king has a counsellor called Ref-Nose, who's a thoroughly evil character. It's doubtful which will be the stronger, your good luck or his magic, but you have to take the risk whatever happens. Bring all Olaf's forces here, and then maybe I can repay you for the ox.'

'You're always on about that,' said Ref. And so they parted.

Ref put out to sea in search of King Olaf and found him with his fleet. He lay alongside the king's own ship, climbed aboard and presented himself. King Olaf asked him who he was, and Ref told him.

'Are you known as Gift-Ref?' asked the king.

'Some eminent people have given me gifts,' admitted Ref, 'and I've always given them something, too. Here are two precious things I'd like to present you with, a helmet and a coat of mail, both very fitting for a man like you.'

'Who gave you these precious things?' said King Olaf. 'I've never seen anything like them, nor even heard that such things existed, even though I've travelled all over the world.'

'King Hrolf Kraki gave them to me,' said Ref.

'What had you given him?' asked the king.

'Two little dogs with gold halters that King Ælla had given me.'

'What had you given King Ælla?'

'A gold ring Gautrek had given me in return for a whetstone.'

'Some kings are extraordinarily open-handed,' said King Olaf, 'but King Gautrek outdoes them all in generosity. Should I accept these gifts, Ref-Nose, or should I reject them?'

'I wouldn't advise you to accept them,' said Ref-Nose, 'if you don't know how to repay them,' and with that he grabbed those precious objects and jumped overboard with them.

Ref realized that it would soon be the end of him if he failed to recover the things, so he went after him. There was a sharp skirmish between them, and the outcome was that Ref managed to get the coat of mail, but Ref-Nose held on to the helmet and dived with it down to the bottom of the sea where he went raving mad. By the

time Ref managed to surface again, he was exhausted. Then someone said:

> The way it seems to me
> The counsels of Ref-Nose
> Were a lot worse than those
> Offered by Earl Neri.
> Gautrek the King, who gave
> To Ref the ring of gold,
> Didn't cast his wealth, I'm told,
> Into the ocean wave.

'You're a remarkable man,' said King Olaf.

'Well,' said Ref, 'I'd like you to accept this one remaining
treasure.'

'I'm glad to accept it,' said King Olaf. 'I'm just as grateful to you
as if I'd been given both treasures; and it was my mistake not to
accept them straight away. But there's nothing surprising about
that, it was an evil fellow's advice I was following. Now, I want you
to choose your own reward.'

'I'd like to command your ships and forces for a fortnight,' said
Ref, 'and take them wherever I please.'

'That's an odd choice,' said the king, 'but you're welcome to
them.'

Then they sailed to Gotaland to meet Earl Neri. They landed
there late in the day, and Ref sent messengers in secret to Earl Neri,
asking Neri to come and see him. The earl went to see Ref, who told
him all that had happened on his travels.

'Now the time has come, my friend, to put your good luck to the
test,' said the earl. 'I want you to marry King Gautrek's daughter
and form a family alliance with him.'

Ref said he'd trust the earl's judgement.

'The next time we meet,' said the earl, 'whatever I say to you,
don't show any surprise, and make sure you agree to anything I
suggest.'

Then the earl rode off, and didn't stop until he came to King
Gautrek's residence. It was just about midnight when the earl
arrived and he told the king that an invincible army had invaded his
country. 'These men intend to kill you and then lay the country
under their rule.'

'Who's the leader of this army?'

'A man we'd never have believed would ignore my advice: my foster-son Ref.'

'Your word still carries a lot of weight with him,' said the king. 'Would it be wise to gather an army against him?'

'If you don't make peace with them,' said the earl, 'it seems pretty likely to me that they'll have caused a great deal of damage before you can muster your forces. I think it would be more sensible to make them a generous offer and find out whether you can reach a peaceful settlement. It seems to me any kingdom is on the verge of ruin when men like these start getting too close.'

'We've always been guided by your advice,' said the king.

'I'd like you, sir, to pay heed to our conversation,' said the earl.

The king said he'd do as the earl advised. Then they set out with a small number of men, and when they saw the enemy fleet, the king realized how many there were and how hard it would be to stand up against them.

The earl called out from the shore, shouting: 'Is it true that my foster-son is the leader of this army?'

'That's so,' said Ref.

'I'd never have thought, foster-son, that you'd attack either my territory or King Gautrek's. Is there anything we can offer to keep the peace?' asked the earl. 'I'm willing to do everything in my power to enhance your reputation, and I'm sure King Gautrek will make the same promise on his own behalf. I'd like you to accept an honourable settlement from the king and leave his kingdom in peace. I realize that you'll be very exacting in your demands, and that's only natural, seeing that your grandfather was a powerful earl and your father a great fighting man.'

'I'll accept an honourable offer,' said Ref, 'if I get one.'

'I'm sure you can't be bought off cheaply,' said the earl. 'I think I know the sort of thing you have in mind: you want my earldom, the one I've held under King Gautrek, and you'll be expecting the king to give you his daughter as well.'

'You've grasped the situation perfectly,' said Ref, 'and this is what I'll agree to as long as the king is willing.'

The earl turned to the king. 'It seems the wisest thing to accept this offer rather than risk our very lives against these killers. Anyway, most likely they'd first help themselves to your kingdom and then take your daughter captive,' he said. 'It would be perfectly honourable for you to marry your daughter to an earl's grandson. I'll help Ref with my advice if he's trusted with the government of your kingdom, assuming you'll go along with these proposals.'

'Earl Neri,' said King Gautrek, 'your advice has always been a great help to us, and I'm still willing to trust your foresight. Besides, I realize this army's too big to handle.'

'My proposal is that Ref should be given proper status so that he'll be able to strengthen your kingdom,' said the earl.

This was agreed and sealed with oaths, exactly as the earl had laid down the terms. Then King Gautrek went back home.

'You've given me great support, King Olaf, and now you may go on your way, wherever you wish,' said Ref.

'They're shrewd men who've had a hand in this affair of yours,' said King Olaf, and after that he sailed away.

When the fleet had gone, King Gautrek said, 'I've been dealing with cunning men in this business, but I'll not break my oaths.'

The earl spoke to Ref: 'Now that you've only your own men left, you can see the value of my support. This advice was just the thing for you. It looks as though the ox has been paid off. All the same, I've been less generous than you deserve; you gave me all you had, while I'm still as rich as ever.'

King Gautrek had a feast prepared, and there Ref married Helga, King Gautrek's daughter. The king also gave him the title of earl. Everybody thought Ref a very enterprising fellow; he was descended from men of rank, and his own father had been a great viking and champion. So Ref ruled his earldom, though he didn't live very long.

Earl Neri died suddenly, and there's nothing more to tell about him in this story. King Gautrek gave a funeral feast for him. By now the king himself was getting old and infirm. He had won a great reputation for his generosity and bravery, but it's not said that he was a very profound thinker. However, he was well liked, exceptionally open-handed, and the most courteous of men.

And so we end Gift-Ref's Saga.

Halfdan Eysteinsson

1. King Eystein

Trondheim in Norway takes its name from a king called Thrand, son of Sæming, son of Odin who once ruled over Halogaland; and Namdal is so called after Sæming's wife Nauma. Thrand was a great chieftain. He and his wife Dagmær, sister of Svanhvit who was married to Hromund Gripsson, had a son called Eystein. Nobody knows who was the mother of Thrand's other son, Eirik the Traveller, who discovered Odainsakur.

Eystein married Asa, whose parents were Sigurd Hart and Aslaug, daughter of Sigurd Snake-in-the-Eye. Asa's dowry brought Eystein the provinces of Finnmark, Valdres, Totn and Hadaland, and he made a firm and capable ruler.

Eystein and his wife had a son called Halfdan, another great leader. He was a quiet, handsome-looking man and from the very first showed every quality that deserves praise, and is thought better lodged in a man than lacking in him. Halfdan was loyal and devoted to his friends, but chose them carefully. He was cheerful and enjoyed life, but for all his good nature, he could be a dangerous enemy to anyone who offended him, though he had a long memory rather than a quick temper. He was brought up by his parents, but when he was fifteen his mother fell sick and died – a sad loss to King Eystein as it was to everyone – and she was given a great funeral. After she died, the king hated to stay at home, so each summer he would set out on a viking expedition.

There was a farmer called Svip, a wealthy man but not very popular. He had three sons. One, Ulfkel the Wizard, was a great bully and not very bright. He used to go raiding with King Eystein, who had a high opinion of him and gave him command of five ships.

Svip's second son, Ulfar, acted as the king's counsellor. His attitude towards the king, as to everyone else, was friendly and accommodating. Svip's youngest son, Ulf the Evil, used to go plundering in the Baltic with a band of robbers, all the way up to Permia. Nobody was very fond of him.

One summer King Eystein went raiding in the Baltic along with his son Halfdan and Ulfkel the Wizard. They had thirty ships, all well manned, and Ulfkel's brother Ulfar had charge of the kingdom for as long as the expedition might last.

2. To Ladoga Town

The ruler of Ladoga Town at that time, King Hergeir, was getting on in years. He was married to Isgerd, daughter of King Hlodver of Gotaland, whose brothers were King Harald Fine-Hair's forecastleman Sigmund, and Odd the Showy, father of Gold-Thorir who figures in the Icelandic *Book of Settlements*.

King Hergeir and his wife had a daughter called Ingigerd, a fine-looking girl, as tall as a man and in everything she did the most gifted of women. She was fostered by Earl Skuli, who ruled over Alaborg and its earldom. People say that Skuli was the brother of Heimir, who fostered Brynhild Budli's-daughter and figures in Ragnar's Saga. In war and in wisdom, Skuli was a great man.

Skuli had a slave called Kol, a big, powerful man, equal to a dozen in any trial of strength. He was, you might say, the earl's most intimate adviser and very loyal. This Kol had a daughter called Ingigerd, the prettiest of girls and much like Princess Ingigerd to look at, though very different in spirit; for while the princess was a true lady, her namesake was a trollop – not that she was without ability, for the princess had let her spend a lot of time in her own boudoir and had taught her embroidery.

Earl Skuli was very fond of his foster-daughter. He himself was still unmarried, and had no equal in sport or skill.

3. *Eystein Kills Hergeir*

When King Eystein and his troops reached Ladoga Town, King Hergeir had only a small force with him, so Eystein led his army forward up to the town. Ill prepared as he was for battle, King Hergeir put up a brave defence, but the outcome was that he and most of his men were killed. After the fall of King Hergeir, King Eystein offered terms to all the enemy survivors, and once they surrendered the fighting came to an end. The king had the town cleaned up, then sent for the queen, but she was in a bitter mood. For a while the king looked at her closely, then he spoke.

'It's natural enough that you should take to heart all that's happened here,' he said, 'but for everything there's compensation: and now I'd like to become your husband. A man so old shouldn't be hard to replace.'

'Old age was no fault in him,' said the queen, 'and my heart tells me I'll not be true to his killer.'

'You've two choices,' said the king. 'Either I make you my concubine for as long as fortune will have it, or you marry me and hand over the whole kingdom, in which case I'll show you every respect, and never fear that you might betray me to my death, when my time comes.'

'The old saying is true,' she replied. ' "A hard choice makes for harsh terms", so I'll choose marriage.'

The king said that was the choice nearest his own liking, so the whole business was settled and that's how things were arranged – though they took longer than the telling.

4. *A Mission*

After that the king called all his men together and spoke to his son Halfdan and Ulfkel the Wizard.

'It's like this,' he said. 'Earl Skuli rules up north in Alaborg, where he's fostering King Hergeir's daughter Ingigerd. Skuli's a great warrior, so we can expect him to lead an army against us, which is why you must move east against him, conquer his earldom and bring the princess back to me. If you manage to get control, Ulfkel can take over the country as a reward for the way he's backed me up. I'll find him a good wife, and Halfdan can marry Ingigerd, if that's what he wants.'

Halfdan and Ulfkel got their troops ready and travelled without a break to Alaborg.

5. Victory

Earl Skuli had already heard what had happened at Ladoga Town and got together a great army, but just as it was assembled he fell seriously ill. By that time he had received reliable reports about the expedition of Ulfkel and Halfdan. He had a word with Kol.

'I want you to take command of our forces,' he said. 'You carry my banner and wear my clothes. I'll make you an earl and give you my foster-daughter Ingigerd if you win.'

Kol said he was ready and willing. Skuli gave his men full instructions about how matters were to be arranged, and when Kol led the troops against Halfdan and Ulfkel, everyone thought he was Skuli. Meanwhile Skuli himself was confined to bed in one of the villages, though slowly he was getting better.

Princess Ingigerd sent for her namesake, Ingigerd Kol's daughter, and had a word with her.

'I want to take you into my confidence,' she said, 'but you must never tell anyone about it as long as you live. Since we look very much alike, I want you to put on my clothes and say that you're King Hergeir's daughter, while I take your clothes and run off with the other maidservants. As long as the two of us are alive, never betray this secret. If the people attacking us win, either Prince Halfdan will ask to marry you – and you could hardly get a better husband – or Ulfkel will. So no matter what happens, you're in luck.'

Ingigerd agreed willingly, and they went ahead with the plan. When Halfdan and Ulfkel came up with their troops, Kol had the town gates opened and marched out with his own army. The battle began and many were killed. Kol was powerful and hard-hitting, and as he forced his way through the enemy ranks everyone assumed him to be Earl Skuli. One of the Earl's kinsmen, a man called Herbjorn, led the column against Halfdan, and though the battle was hard fought, in the end Herbjorn fell and his men were routed, running off into the woods with Halfdan after them.

Now to describe the clash between Kol and Ulfkel. Kol had already killed a good many men. Ulfkel had a standard-bearer called Snæulf who pushed forward bravely with the banner and fought like a true warrior. Ulfkel and Kol met face to face, and a ferocious combat began, each hacking away at the other's armour with none to come between them. Then Kol got in a powerful stroke on one side of Ulfkel's helmet, slicing off a quarter of it along with Ulfkel's left ear. The blow was so powerful that Ulfkel went down, but then Snæulf came up and struck Kol upon the face, slicing away his nose, lips and chin so that his teeth fell down in the grass. In spite of his wounds Kol didn't stay idle but hit back at Snæulf, slicing off his head. Now Ulfkel was back on his feet again, and lunged at Kol, piercing his chest right through to the shoulder-blade, whereupon Kol dropped down dead. At that, the troops began to run, with Ulfkel after them.

As Halfdan was returning to the town, he saw two old folk, a man and a woman, walking by. One of his men asked how the battle was progressing, and after they had described everything in detail they went on their way. The old man was so stiff that he had to lean on the woman's shoulders, and like that they dragged themselves into the wood. Halfdan asked his men who they had been talking to, and they said it was some poor old beggar.

'You can never be too careful,' said Halfdan. 'That old fellow means trouble to me: better to have killed him.'

They said that would have been a wicked thing to do, and since the old man had vanished into the wood by then, there was no point in looking for him.

Halfdan rode into the town. Ulfkel had arrived before him and had gone straight to Ingigerd's boudoir. Someone brought her to him.

'You've won a great victory,' she said, 'killing the ruler of the town. Now, if you're true warriors you'll shame neither me, nor any of the leaderless people here. May I go and see my mother?'

'You're right,' said Ulfkel, 'though we'll make amends for any injury we've done you or your mother. But you must promise to be faithful and true to us, to be meek and obedient and never turn against us.'

'The way things are,' said she, 'I don't think there's much scope for pride.'

They promised to treat her well, then opened up the treasure-chests, taking gold and silver and anything else they fancied, though they gave quarter to everyone. Then the dead were prepared for burial, and Earl Skuli – in reality, Kol – was laid to rest in a worthy grave. After subduing the entire earldom, they set out to rejoin King Eystein, taking Ingigerd along with them.

6. Ulfkel Marries Ingigerd

King Eystein learned that they had come back after winning a great victory, and gave them a generous welcome while they entertained him with an account of their expedition. The king thanked them handsomely, and asked Halfdan what he thought of the princess. Halfdan answered that, while he was no judge of women, he had to admit that she was a good-looking girl. Ingigerd had already gone to the palace to join the queen, who gave her a friendly welcome – rather less affectionate, however, than people might have expected. The king sent for mother and daughter, and when they came before him he spoke to Queen Isgerd.

'Now that your daughter's here,' he asked, 'I wish, with your consent, to grant you both the very highest honour. I'd like Halfdan to take my advice and marry Ingigerd, provided, madam, you're both in favour.'

'She's clever enough to speak for herself on matters like this,' said the queen.

'I've no plan to marry yet,' said Halfdan. 'Still, though I've not seen many princesses in my life, I think the man who wins Ingigerd will be making a fine match, and I hope you'll see her well married.'

Then Ulfkel spoke.

'I've given you long service, sir,' he said, 'and I'm sure you'll want me to have my reward. I would think it a great honour if you were to give this girl to me as my wife. I've put it to her already and she hasn't turned me down.'

The king asked Ingigerd how she felt about it, but she answered that she would leave the decision to him as long as her mother raised no objection.

'And after that, sir,' she added, 'perhaps you'll add to Ulfkel's titles.'

The king asked the queen what she thought of the idea, and she said that nothing would please her more than for him to make whatever arrangements he wished.

So the king gave Ingigerd in marriage to Ulfkel, then bestowed on him the title of earl, to rule over Alaborg and the earldom that went with it. They celebrated the wedding, and then Ulfkel travelled to Alaborg and took charge of the domain. As ruler of the earldom, he made tributary payments to the king: and that's how things stood for many years, while Ulfkel and Ingigerd grew to love each other dearly.

7. Two Strangers

King Eystein remained in his kingdom. He was very much in love with Queen Isgerd, and she conducted herself towards him like a true lady. So three years went by. Then one day a large trading vessel cruising off the coast of Finland vanished with all hands in a terrible gale. Everyone assumed that the ship must have foundered in the storm. Later that autumn, two strangers came to King Eystein's court, both very tall but shabbily dressed. People couldn't see their faces clearly as they were wearing long hoods. They came before the king and greeted him with respect – for, as always, the king was very approachable. When he asked who they were, they replied that they were both called Grim, were of Russian stock, and had lost all their money in a shipwreck: then they made a request to stay over the winter.

The king asked the queen what she thought. She answered that he must decide for himself, but added that strangers often spring surprises.

'No one can blame me,' she said, 'as long as I have nothing to do with it.'

The king said she had never been one to meddle.

'I won't begrudge food to visitors who've come so far,' he said.

The strangers were given seats between the retainers and the king's agents. They kept to themselves, but most people came to like them. Few of the men were taller than the older Grim, who was strong and agile at every sport and competed with the king's men at the butts, and at ball-games. He used his strength with discretion and never tried to outplay others, though he showed his power whenever anyone else turned on him. The younger Grim had a great talent for games, particularly archery, but never took part in trials of strength. He was a first-rate shot with handbow and crossbow, and so skilled at chess that no one could beat him. Prince Halfdan used to compete with him at both chess and archery, and kept such a sharp eye on the two Grims that even at night, when they were asleep, he would be awake, watching them out of the corner of his eye. So the winter passed, and Christmas came.

8. The Fair Hand

One day at Christmas, the retainers were playing a ball-game before the king, who was sitting on a stool, with the queen on another. The two Grims were taking part in the game, and the only player who could match the older Grim was Prince Halfdan. Throughout the winter, neither Grim had spoken a word to the queen. The older Grim was batting and it was the younger Grim's turn to chase the ball, but it rolled right under the queen's stool. Grim groped for the ball, and as he rose, whispered something in the queen's ear. Her face changed colour.

At lunch the game broke up and the retainers started drinking. The king had them served generously throughout the rest of the day, and those who couldn't drag themselves off to bed fell asleep on their seats. The king went on drinking late into the night with the queen beside him. He asked her what Grim had whispered to her, but she said she could make no sense of it. The king complained that she always wanted to keep things to herself and never bothered to tell him what was going on, so the queen warned him to be on his guard, and left. By now the two Grims had fallen asleep.

The king went to bed, and his son Halfdan came with him. When they reached the royal chamber, the queen was missing. The king lay on the bed fully dressed, with his sword beside him. The pages put out the lights, and Halfdan went back to the hall where the two Grims were fast asleep. He noticed that the younger Grim had taken off one of his gloves and the hand was bare. Never, he thought, had he seen such a fair hand on any man. Upon it was the most exquisite ring he had ever set eyes on, with a precious stone which he thought looked very mysterious. Halfdan coaxed the ring off the finger and dropped it into the glove. Then he asked for the lights to be brought up, and settled down beside the two Grims. By now, the lower part of the hall was shrouded in darkness. Holding the glove in his hand, Halfdan soon fell asleep. When he woke, all the lights were out, but then the younger Grim flashed a light into his eyes so dazzling that he was unable to see, and snatched the glove away from him.

'For this hand, this ring and this glove,' he said, 'you shall seek and pine without a moment's peace, until someone places them in your hand as freely as he has just now taken them from you.'

With that, he hurled the lamp towards the nearer door, and ran out through the other.

9. Murder

Halfdan sprang to his feet and rushed to the door where the lamp had been thrown, but found it locked. He tried the other door, shouting for the men inside to wake up, but that proved to be locked too and they had to break it down before they could get out. Halfdan made for the royal chamber and there he found the king dead, run through with a sword along with three of his young pages. A fourth had managed to scramble on to the crossbeam and he told Halfdan how the older Grim had come in and killed the king, along with the others.

'Tell Halfdan that Vigfus and Ofeig have avenged King Hergeir,' he had called out before he left.

Just at that moment the queen entered the chambers. She was so horrified by what had happened that she fainted, and everyone thought she was dying. The town was in an uproar, with men setting out by sea and land in search of the two Grims, but there was no sign of them. The search continued for a month, and there was a great deal of speculation about where they might be hiding, but gradually things calmed down. Most people wanted Halfdan to take over as king.

10. Halfdan Sets Out

Shortly after that, Halfdan called an assembly. When the chieftains had gathered they asked him to become their king, and this was his answer: 'In view of what has taken place here lately, it would be improper for me to assume the title of king as things stand, since I'm not the legal heir to the throne. Most of you will agree that my duty is to seek out the killer and avenge my father, so I think it best for the queen to send for her brother Sigmund, and rule the kingdom with him until I return, no matter what I may decide to do afterwards. I'm leaving now, and won't be back until I've found my father's killer and taken whatever vengeance fate permits.'

The queen gave her opinion that it would be best for the kingdom if he were to rule it, but in the end, no matter what people said, Halfdan got himself ready for the voyage with five ships, bravely manned. He sailed first to the Baltic where he won fame and plunder, but always, as he lay awake, he saw before his eyes the fair hand and the precious gold ring he had lost in Ladoga Town. So now, for the next five years, we'll leave him to sail wherever he chooses.

11. Fratricide

At this point we come back to Ulfkel and his wife Ingigerd, up north in Alaborg. When they heard the news of King Eystein's death, and how it had come about, Ingigerd asked Ulfkel if he meant to claim the kingdom left by her father Hergeir. He said he was ready and willing, so they made their preparations for the journey, then travelled without a break to Ladoga Town where Sigmund and Queen Isgerd were in control. Ulfkel laid formal claim to the kingdom, but the queen's answer was that he and his wife had enough land to rule, and instead of demanding more, they ought to be satisfied with what they had. After that they started threatening each other, and Ulfkel went home to gather forces.

At once, Sigmund set out north after them. They met off a headland called Krakuness and in no time at all the battle commenced, only to end with Ulfkel and his wife escaping in a single ship. They sailed northwards first, to Norway, where Ulfkel saw his brother Ulfar, and told him how he and Sigmund had parted, as well as all the other things that had taken place in the east Baltic. Ulfkel asked his brother to hand over the kingdom to him. Halfdan, he said, had even greater territories in the east. Ulfar ordered him not to speak of such treachery as the betrayal of his overlord. He told Ulfkel that it would be better to gather forces and fight for the kingdom beyond the Baltic which he claimed to be his, even offering Ulfkel his support. That wasn't enough for Ulfkel, and there were hard words between them.

The affair ended with Ulfkel killing his brother, taking over the whole kingdom and becoming its ruler: but in most people's eyes he had committed the worst of crimes, and he was universally hated for it.

12. Battle

Once Ulfkel had the kingdom, he started gathering ships and forces, then sailed his fleet east to the Baltic. He had thirty longships and a dragon head with seventy oars on each side. His army included vikings and outlaws and all the rogues he could muster. A man called Ivar Bundle was in charge of the dragon ship, a berserk and the worst of villains, with a brother called Hrafnkel, a strongly built man, Ulfkel's standard-bearer. Ulfkel had plenty more big, powerful men with him and they went about like brutes, attacking wherever they came and plundering the coastline without mercy.

On they sailed till they reached a place called Klyfandness, east of the Hlyn Forest and not far from Permia, where they ran into ten ships, all bravely manned, commanded by King Eystein's son Halfdan, who had heard all about what Ulfkel and his men had done on their expedition. As soon as they recognized one another, Halfdan asked Ulfkel why he had betrayed and murdered his own brother and usurped the throne. Ulfkel said that Halfdan and his men had taken even more than that – Ulfkel's kingdom in the east. Halfdan replied that he thought Ulfkel could lay claim to no proper realm at all.

Both sides reached for their weapons, and at once the battle began. The odds were so heavily against Halfdan that a lot of his men were killed, but a big powerful man called Svidi, Halfdan's principal counsellor, gave orders for the ships to be linked together. This was done with such skill that Ulfkel was unable to deploy all of his ships, not even those within shooting range. So the battle raged, with Halfdan putting up a great fight. But, seeing no point in wearing themselves out, he and Svidi decided to board Ulfkel's dragon ship. The first man they had to face was Ivar Bundle, and there were some hard exchanges. Ivar struck at Halfdan, landing a blow on his helmet which sliced right through the dome and shaved clean the top of Halfdan's head. He countered with a stroke which cut off one of Ivar's arms just below the shoulder, severing the standard-pole. Then Svidi killed Egil, Ulfkel's forecastleman, but now Ulfkel lunged at Halfdan unexpectedly, driving the spear into his armpit and giving him three broken ribs and a gash in the side. A stroke of Svidi's caught Ivar Bundle right in the eye and killed him. Ulfkel dodged a blow from Halfdan, but the sword landed on the deck and sliced off the big toe of Ulfkel's right foot. Ulfkel lunged back with a halberd but Halfdan leapt over the boom and the halberd stuck in the hatch. Halfdan gave it a kick, breaking the shaft in two.

Then a blow from Svidi across Ulfkel's shoulder-blades brought him to his knees, but Svidi himself was hit on the chest by a lump of rock and knocked overboard, where he landed in a boat floating along-side. At the same time, a mighty stroke with a club by Hrafnkel sent Halfdan overboard as well, but Svidi was close by, and picked up a boat-hook and heaved him out of the water. He was unconscious, wounded in six places, and in no condition for battle.

13. Strangers to the Rescue

Now several things were happening all at the same time. Suddenly, people saw twenty-five large ships rounding the headland, their crews in full battle-armour. Beside the mast of one stood a tall man in a sleeveless tunic and a fine coat of mail. He asked who the players were in such a one-sided game. Svidi told him everything and explained how matters stood.

'Would Halfdan accept our help?' asked the stranger.

Svidi inquired who he was, but he replied that it was none of Svidi's business. Svidi then said that he would be glad of their help, so the fighting began all over again, more fiercely than ever, and Ulfkel's men suffered heavy casualties. The tall stranger laid his own dragon ship alongside Ulfkel's, while Svidi attacked the smaller ships, the decks of which were soon cleared. Now it was Ulfkel's turn to face the heavier losses.

The tall stranger set to and boarded the dragon ship, and a long, hard fight with Ulfkel, the first man to confront him, was to follow. The tall man caught Ulfkel with a powerful stroke that split his shield right through, struck him on the foot and sliced off three toes. When Ulfkel hit back at the tall man's helmet, the sword snapped at the hilt and Ulfkel saw that he had no choice but to save his own life, so he leapt aboard the nearest ship and made off. Hrafnkel hurled two halberds together at the tall man, but he caught them both in flight and sent them back, killing a man with each of them. Then he turned against Hrafnkel with a halberd, drove it straight through the shield and both arms, and heaved him into the air and over-board. After that Ulfkel's men were so hard pressed that they had no choice but to ask for quarter, and all who asked were granted it, though the tall man refused to take them into his own service, and set them ashore in their underclothes.

Ulfkel fled to his wife in a single ship, and the victors seized the rest of his fleet and other booty. Those of Halfdan's men who had survived joined forces with the tall man.

14. Recovery

The tall man came up to Halfdan, who was lying badly wounded.

'It seems to me that Halfdan's wounds could be healed,' he said to Svidi, 'if he were to have a good physician, but I don't think he's strong enough to be moved around or make sea journeys. I'm going to have him carried ashore here to a friend of mine called Hrifling. He and his wife Arghyrna are great healers, but they've many mouths to feed on what little they can earn with their hands, which is why it's called a hand-to-mouth existence. If they can't help him, then he's not destined to live and they'd better come back to us.'

The tall stranger told his trusted men to ferry Halfdan ashore. He gave them a hundred marks in silver, and asked them to tell Hrifling and his wife to take as much care treating Halfdan as they would if he himself had sought their help. They were to let him know precisely where to find their patient once his wounds were fully healed. The messengers went and saw the old man and his wife, and told them what was expected of them, then handed over the money, but the old couple said they were doing no more than their duty. With that, the messengers returned, and Hrifling and his wife started treating Halfdan. His wounds were so badly swollen that it proved far from easy, but after eighteen weeks in bandages he made a complete recovery, though he still had to stay on for twelve months before he regained his strength. The time seemed to pass slowly, for he kept seeing in his mind's eye the beautiful hand, the gold ring, and the glove that he had lost.

15. *More about Ulfkel*

Now we take up the story at the point when Ulfkel the Wizard fled from the battle. He managed to get ashore with fourteen men, but the remainder of his army was lost. He made inquiries about where his brother Ulf might be and, learning that he was in Permia, set off to find him. The king there was Harek, who had a daughter called Edny. Ulf proposed marriage, but the king refused, so Ulf started raiding his kingdom. When the brothers met, they talked things over and agreed to go together for a word with King Harek. They sailed with sixty ships, put in at the harbour close to the royal palace, and then Ulfkel the Wizard set off to see the king and present his compliments. The king asked his name, and Ulfkel told him exactly who he was.

Then the king asked who commanded the great fighting force that had just arrived, and Ulfkel replied that Ulf the Evil was in charge.

'He and I are brothers,' said Ulfkel, 'and here's why I've come to see you: we'd like to offer to be your men. If you let Ulf marry your daughter, I'll give him Alaborg, Ladoga Town and all the territories under them, since they all belong to me. I daresay my brother and I would be a great source of strength to you and people would find us hard men to deal with when it comes to foul play.'

King Harek told Ulfkel that he needed time to consult his people, and Ulfkel made no objection. Then the king asked his daughter how she felt about it, and she said that in her opinion the brothers' war-record made the decision a difficult one – 'but if we can be sure about the territories, I think it's a very tempting offer.' She added that if the brothers were turned down, nothing would be too wicked for them, so the outcome was that Edny married Ulf, and he and his brother took over the Permian defences.

Ulfkel made inquiries about the man who had helped Halfdan against him in the battle, and Harek told him the man's name was Grim.

'He rules over Karelia, to the east of here,' said the king. 'He forced his way to power, but no one knows anything about his background. He has his foster-daughter with him, the best-looking girl anyone's ever heard tell of.'

'That's a man I'd like to have my revenge on, if I can,' said Ulfkel, 'and I'd be glad of your help and support.'

'It shouldn't be hard for us to come to terms,' said the king, 'since she's the girl I want to marry.'

Both brothers swore to stand by him and said they thought it was a good idea, so they sealed an agreement to go to Karelia once summer came, and not to leave till Grim was dead and the king had won the girl. And now for a while they took things easy.

In the spring they prepared their ships and gathered a great army. With them went two Lappish kings called Finn and Floki, both of them magicians. They travelled all the way to the Bay of Karelia, where they came face to face with Grim. To cut a long story short, they presented Grim with a choice, either to fight them on the spot, or to surrender and hand over the kingdom to Harek, along with Grim's foster-daughter.

Grim said that they wouldn't find things quite so easy. 'King Harek has no quarrel with us: and as for you, Ulfkel, it will be worse than the last time.'

They slept well overnight, and next morning Grim led all his troops out of the stronghold. A bitter struggle began and lasted till evening, when Grim retired into the stronghold, having lost many of his troops. In the morning they returned to the battlefield, leaving the fortress without a single able-bodied defender.

16. Hrifling Points the Way

Meanwhile, now that Halfdan's wounds had healed and he had recovered his strength, he had a word with old Hrifling and his wife, and told them that he was eager to leave. He asked who had actually sent him there to be healed, and to whom he owed his life.

'I know you're a gentleman,' said Hrifling, 'so I can give you an idea of where to find him. There's a man called Grim, a great warrior, ruling to the east in Karelia. He's the one who sent you to me, and now he's in bad need of strong men, so it's time to repay him for saving your life. King Harek of Permia, Ulf the Evil and Ulfkel the Wizard have arrived in Karelia to take revenge for the humiliation Ulfkel suffered at your hands. Now they're in the field with their whole army, and I'm told that King Harek wants to marry Grim's foster-daughter Ingigerd, the best-looking girl alive.'

'Well spoken, my friend,' said Halfdan. 'Now there's an even more important matter I'd like to settle. Who killed my father?'

'I can tell you that soon enough,' said the old man. 'His name's Skuli, and the honest truth of it is that he's the very same man who saved your life, so when you meet it's going to be a real test of your breeding. Anyone who takes him on in single combat is going to have his hands full, with a warrior like that.'

'What's the shortest route?' asked Halfdan. 'I'd like to get there as soon as I can.'

'Most of the routes from here are heavy going,' said Hrifling. 'What with vikings and pirates, it takes at least five weeks by sea. Then there's an easterly route through wild forest country and over mountains, but it's a long, hard road and I don't know if you'd make it. All being well, the third route would be the quickest and could get you there in about three weeks, but there are many obstacles. First there's a forest twenty leagues across called Kol's Wood, where a ruffian called Kol lives with his daughter, Gold-Ball. No one who meets them has much hope of survival. Just beyond is another forest called Klif's Wood, twenty-four leagues across, where another ruffian lives, Hallgeir, along with a wild boar that's a worse enemy than a dozen men. After that you come to a forest called Kalfar Wood, thirty-six leagues across, where there's nothing in the way of food apart from berries and sap, and there you'll meet yet another ruffian, who's called Sel and has a dog with him the size of a bull, that fights better than a dozen men and has a human brain. When you get out of that forest, you come to a river flowing east from the direction of Kjolen. Nobody knows its source, and only the best of swimmers can make it across, but once on the other side you're not far from Skuli's stronghold. With nothing to slow you down, you should get there near enough in time for the battle.'

Halfdan asked for his things to be made ready for the journey. By daylight he was all set to leave. He went to say goodbye to the old woman, who chanted various charms over him, then pulled a rag-bag from under her pillow and took out a short-sword as bright as a polished mirror. To Halfdan it seemed to drip venom from its edges. She told him that anyone carrying the sword would be sure of victory, for as long as it was properly handled its stroke would never fail. After that she hung a necklace strung with precious stones around his neck, and told him never to take it off. He gave her a kiss, and then her husband saw him on his way and told him which road to take. He gave Halfdan a lapdog and said he should follow whichever path the dog took, but never to go where the dog would not, since it knew how to keep clear of the ruffians.

Halfdan declared that no ruffians were ever going to kill him – 'and if you're hard up, take a look inside their shacks – I may have to take care of one or two of them, but I shan't be carrying anything away with me,' he said.

They wished each other the best of luck, and with that they parted.

17. The Three Ruffians

Halfdan made his way into the forest. After he had been walking for two days he noticed a hidden path. The dog wanted to take it, but Halfdan kept to the main road and in due course came to a homestead. The door was closed and Halfdan had to force it open. Inside was Gold-Ball, Kol's daughter. She struck at his neck with a sharp cleaver, but the blow landed on the old woman's necklace, and the cleaver broke in two with a loud bang. Halfdan picked her up, flung her down hard on the floor, took hold of her two legs, ripped her apart from top to toe and tossed her out of the house. At sunset when Kol came home, he stooped to get through the door. Halfdan swung a blow at his neck and that was the end of Kol.

That night while Halfdan was asleep, the two dead ones, Kol and his daughter, came inside and set on him. The dog sprang up, ripped Gold-Ball open at the groin and unravelled her guts. Halfdan went for the householder and they had a long wrestling match, but in the end Halfdan brought him down and broke his neck, then built a fire and burnt them both to ashes.

He stayed there for two nights, then went on his way without a pause until he entered Klif's Wood. There he came to a large dwelling with a door so heavy that he had to use all his strength to force it open. The bed was two yards longer than himself, and there was a sty as big as a cattle-stall. As it was getting dark, he heard a terrible noise outside and guessed that it must be the boar scream- ing. It sounded very ugly.

Halfdan went out of the house. The dog ran yapping at the boar, forcing it to back away, and with a stroke Halfdan sliced off the creature's tail. The boar turned and thrust its snout into Halfdan's crotch, tossing him in the air so that he lost hold of the sword, though he managed to land on his feet. Then the man of the house came up and took a swing at Halfdan with an iron-studded club. He dodged it, and since he couldn't reach the sword, grabbed the boar by the leg, and tugged it towards him so that the blow landed right between the boar's ears, smashing its skull. Halfdan ripped the leg off the boar and brought the ruffian to his knees with a blow to the ear, then charged him and laid him flat on his back. He grabbed hold of Halfdan and they began to wrestle furiously, now one on top and then the other. Halfdan's dog had a go at the ruffian's nose and snapped it off. Just then, Halfdan managed to lay hands on his sword and cut off the householder's head, then he made a fire and burnt him to ashes.

By this time he was feeling stiff and worn out. He passed the night there, and carried on next day into Kalfar Wood, where he came to the home of Sel. The door was jammed half-shut, and three times he tried to force it before it gave way. Then he sat on the householder's bed and took an oak stick, whittling it till both ends were sharp, before singeing them in the fire. Through the door of the hall he could see the householder coming, with the dog running ahead of him. Halfdan's own dog was scared and jumped up on to a crossbeam, but Halfdan himself went outside to face the man. As soon as Sel's dog saw him, he leapt at him with open jaws, howling horribly. Halfdan stuck his hand into the dog's mouth and twisted the stick inside with one end jammed up against the palate and the other downwards, so that the dog couldn't shut its mouth. Just at that moment Sel came up carrying a young whale on his chest and a bear on his back.

18. Death of Sel

Sel cast off his burden and lunged with a bear-hunter's knife at Halfdan, who parried with his sword and sliced the knife handle in two, cutting off all the fingers of one of Sel's hands as well. Sel picked up a rock and flung it at Halfdan, but he dodged out of its path and, getting close enough to Sel, managed to take a grip on the tooth jutting from his snout. Sel started away so violently that the tooth came out, and Halfdan gave him such a blow on the nose with it that it broke both the nose and the whole row of front teeth. The giant looked like nothing on earth – apart from himself, that is. He grabbed Halfdan and crushed his ribs so hard, blood gushed out of his ears and nostrils. But then Halfdan caught Sel with a heel-throw that put him flat on his back. Another of Sel's teeth struck the necklace, breaking one of the precious stones, and then Halfdan couldn't budge, but now Hrifling's dog joined in and clawed out both of Sel's eyes. At that, Halfdan broke free, cut off Sel's head, and dumped him in the nearby river. Then he went over to the ruffian's dog.

'Unless you show me the same loyalty that you showed Sel,' he said, 'that stick is never going to leave your mouth.'

The dog crept up to Halfdan and rolled over on its back. Halfdan took the stick from its mouth, and the dog was so happy that the tears ran down its snout. Halfdan had something to eat and then went to sleep. In the morning he got ready and set out for the lake. Sel's dog ran along the shore till it came to a heap of moss, where it began to burrow, and there Halfdan found a boat. Halfdan took it and rowed across the lake, then walked all day till it was dark.

19. Reunion

Next morning, Halfdan sighted the castle to which he had been directed. That very day, Earl Skuli had set out to face King Harek and the brothers, for the battle was to be fought some distance from the castle. Earl Skuli had much the smaller army, and not a single able-bodied man had been left behind, so when Halfdan arrived only women stood on the ramparts. He saw one young woman to whom he took a great fancy. She came down to the castle gate, greeting Halfdan by name, and he responded warmly.

'You must be thinking it's about time you saw the glove and the gold ring that you lost in Ladoga Town,' she said.

'Did you do that?' he asked.

'And there's plenty you can do about it,' she answered. 'My foster-father is engaged in battle, and in bad need of troops and the hand of friendship. I'd do anything to see him win.'

'I owe your foster-father nothing,' said Halfdan, 'but if you'll take me by the hand as a pledge of faith, I'll join the battle on his side.'

She threw him the glove and told him to keep it as her pledge – 'but the gold ring will stay with me until we meet again: no man will ever take this castle, even though there are only women to defend it.'

20. Victory

Then Halfdan marched into battle, where there was terrible carnage. Svidi, carrying Earl Skuli's banner, pushed forward bravely and killed King Harek's standard-bearer, Krabbi. Halfdan needed no urging on. First he assaulted the flank commanded by the Lappish king, Floki, where the king was shooting three arrows at a time and hitting a man with each one. Halfdan made for him and struck at the bow with his sword, breaking it and slicing off one of Floki's hands to that it flew up in the air. But the king held the stump upwards so that the hand fell right on to it and healed directly. Seeing this, the other Lappish king, Finn, turned himself into a whale. He hurled himself on top of the men who were fighting him and crushed fifteen of them to death beneath him. The dog Sel's-gift rushed at him, ripping him apart with its teeth, but as the whale opened its jaws, Hrifling's dog ran in right down to the belly, tearing at his innards, and bit away the heart. Then it ran out again and dropped down dead. Halfdan took his sword and turned once more against Floki, but Floki blew at him so hard that the sword went flying out of his hand and landed a long way off. Then he attacked Halfdan, but his sword struck the necklace and broke. Halfdan was wounded on the neck at the spot where the stone had been damaged, and had the necklace not been there to protect him, his head would have been off. He took a grip on Floki and flung him hard to the ground just as Ulfkel the Wizard came up, so Halfdan had plenty to think about. Then the dog joined in and tore off the whole of Floki's face while Floki, his arms clasped round its back, broke every bone in the dog's body, and there the pair of them lay, dead. Seizing what seemed to be his only chance, Halfdan went for Ulfkel, snatched the sword away from him, used the flat of it on Ulfkel's nose, and told him to defend himself. Halfdan managed to get back his own sword, and again the two of them set about one another. That was how Ulfkel the Wizard met his death.

By now, Earl Skuli had killed Ulf the Evil too, but King Harek of Permia came up to face Skuli and there was hard fighting between them. At a stroke Harek shattered Skuli's shield, wounding him in the fingers, though not too badly. Skuli hit back, slicing off one of the king's ears and all the flesh on one cheek, leaving his back teeth bare. Then Harek turned into a winged dragon and swung his tail at Skuli, laying him out completely. Up came a fighting man called Grubs and hacked off one of the dragon's legs, but the dragon hooked his remaining talons into Grubs's belly and ripped him open just above the loins. By then, Halfdan was back in action, and he struck at the dragon's neck, and so the creature died.

Now the vikings broke ranks and fled to their ships, three of which managed to get away. The ship carrying Ingigerd Kol's-daughter struck a submerged rock and all aboard were drowned. Halfdan returned to the battlefield, where there was great plunder to be shared out. Skuli was nowhere to be seen so Halfdan went back to the castle, where the wounded were dressed and the plunder carried inside.

Ingigerd greeted them warmly, and three days later called a meeting to which everyone in the castle came. Ingigerd herself came in and sat on Halfdan's knee, offering herself and all that she owned, and handing over the gold ring that was mentioned earlier.

'Now everything between us is settled, Ingigerd,' said Halfdan, 'on condition that you tell me what it was you whispered to your mother before my father was killed.'

'I asked her to leave the chamber door unlocked that night,' she said, 'and now I want to make amends, in any way you wish, for this and for anything else that might need setting to rights – though according to higher laws there's right on both sides.'

21. The Wedding

Just then they saw a man coming towards them and recognized Earl Skuli in full armour. He went up to Halfdan and took off his helmet.

'It's come to this, Halfdan,' he said. 'I'd like a reconciliation with you on your own terms. Name your compensation for any offence I've committed against you. I'd also like to offer you a pact of blood-brotherhood, sealed with a marriage to my foster-daughter Ingigerd. If you don't like my offer, I won't risk meeting you again, and each of us will have to make of it what he can.'

'It's no use running away and regretting it later,' said Halfdan. 'If you'd not stood by me so bravely when we fought Ulfkel, I wouldn't have lived to tell the tale.'

'Well, now you've squared the reckoning,' said Skuli.

At that, Ingigerd put it to them that they should settle their differences, which proved an easy matter to arrange. People were very happy about the settlement, and thought that both men had shown great spirit.

Next the loot was shared out. There was so much, it filled the pockets of many a pauper. Halfdan began preparations for the wedding, sending off meanwhile for all the wealth of the three ruffians, treasures of every kind, enough to load fifteen great ships. He also sent for Hrifling with all his household, and made him a wealthy man.

Now he celebrated the wedding, to which he had invited everyone of importance. Earl Skuli took charge of everything and the feast went off in grand style. All the guests were presented with gifts appropriate to their rank, and this made Halfdan so popular that everybody wanted to serve him.

22. *Expedition to Permia*

Next, Halfdan held a public meeting to announce a military expedition to Permia leaving within a month. People liked the idea, and after speedy preparations they all set out for Permia, where Earl Skuli joined them. There was little resistance and they took over the whole country.

Edny, King Harek's daughter, was taken captive by Halfdan, but Harek's son Grundi, who was only three years old at the time, was being fostered by Earl Bjartmar, the son of the same King Raknar who had built the ship *Raknarslodi*. Earl Bjartmar pledged his allegiance to Halfdan.

After all this was done, Halfdan got himself ready and sailed back to Ladoga Town. He had been away for five years and everyone was pleased to see him. The queen welcomed her daughter and thanked Halfdan and Earl Skuli for all their kindness towards her.

23. *Revelations*

Queen Isgerd's brother, Sigmund Hlodversson, who had been in charge of the Russian defences, came with a great retinue of men and was given a good welcome, after which Halfdan called a meeting. This is the speech he made.

'I've been here in the east now for sixteen years,' he said, 'and there are two points in particular that I want to make: that we came here to make war, and that our losses have been heavy. Each side has had to take a beating from the other, and we'll have to put a stop to it if we're going to live together as friends. As you know, the rumour has spread that Ulfkel the Wizard had married Ingigerd, King Hergeir's daughter, and now they're dead. What I'd like to find out from Queen Isgerd, and her brother Sigmund, and my blood-brother, Earl Skuli, is whether this Ingigerd I've brought along with me is Kol's daughter or King Hergeir's. If it had been up to me, I'd have picked a better bride for myself than the daughter of Kol.'

'In spite of the long, hard dealings between us, Halfdan,' said Queen Isgerd, 'I've no wish to cheat you in any way, since in all our affairs you've acted like a gentleman. I'm telling you, this Ingigerd you brought here is none other than my daughter and King Hergeir's, sole legal successor to the throne. Here I make proclamation: I give myself, my daughter, and this whole kingdom in full possession to Halfdan, and may each side make up for the wrongs done to the other. My great wish is that Earl Skuli be granted a position of such honour as will fully content him.'

24. The New Order

Now Earl Skuli told his story, saying how he had appointed Kol leader of the troops, how the two Ingigerds had changed places, and how he and the princess had been the old couple who fled from Alaborg when Halfdan had wanted to take them captive. Now, he said, both he and his realm were under the authority of Halfdan.

'Since all these lands have come into my power,' said Halfdan, 'I'll make clear how I'm going to arrange things. I'll give Queen Isgerd in marriage to Earl Skuli, along with her kingdom here in Russia. Both Permia and King Harek's daughter Edny are now under my authority, and provided both parties agree I want Sigmund to have the kingdom and the princess.'

Sigmund said that as long as the girl was in favour, it was all very much to his liking, and Edny said that she wasn't expecting a better offer – 'so it suits me very well'.

Halfdan announced that he was returning to his own kingdom in Norway – 'People', he said, 'are happiest with what they're born to.'

So that's how it went; the weddings were celebrated in style and afterwards the chieftains set out each to his own home. Halfdan spent the winter there with Ingigerd, both very much in love. They sent Svidi the Bold across to Karelia to run that country, under the overlordship of Earl Skuli.

In the spring, when the ice broke, Halfdan started gathering ships and men, then set out for Permia with Sigmund and Earl Skuli. Their expedition was a great success, for the people there offered no resistance: Sigmund became their ruler though he remained with Halfdan, while Earl Skuli went back to Alaborg. He and Isgerd loved each other deeply: they had a son called Hreggvid, father of Ingigerd who married Göngu-Hrolf.

25. Back to Norway

Now the time has come to tell how Halfdan sailed to Norway, along with Sigmund and his brother Odd the Showy, and a fine retinue of men. Halfdan received a friendly welcome from his kinsmen in Norway. He was made King of Trondheim and all the other provinces once ruled by his father Eystein, and was very popular with his subjects. He and Ingigerd had two sons, one called Thorir Hart and the other Eystein the Clatterer. Odd the Showy took charge of Halfdan's defences and proved himself a man of great spirit. In his old age he emigrated to Iceland, and many people there are descended from him.

Some of Sigmund's men arrived in Norway east from Permia with the report that vikings had been raiding in Permia and Novgorod, killing Svidi the Bold and laying Karelia and a large part of Russia under them. When Halfdan and Sigmund heard the news they started gathering forces and then set out east for Permia.

26. Fighting in Permia

At that time, the king ruling over Gestrekaland and all the provinces east of the Kjolen Mountains was a man called Agnar, married to Hildigunn, sister of the late King Harek of Permia. They had two sons, one Raknar, the other Val, both vikings, who spent their time in the Arctic Ocean attacking giants.

Raknar had a ship called the *Raknarslodi*. It had a hundred rowing spaces, and after the *Long Serpent* it was the biggest ever built in Norway, manned by every kind of blackguard, with fifteen sons of whores at either hand upon each bench. Raknar conquered the wild regions of Slabland and cleared them completely of giants.

His brother Val lived upon the Arctic Sea, and there is a great story about him. He and his brother believed they had inherited the

right to rule Permia from their uncle, Harek. Val had two sons, Kott
and Kisi, both big, powerful men. Val it was who had killed Svidi the
Bold and conquered Karelia. He had captured more gold than
anyone could count in marks from the giant Svadi, a son of the god
Thor, who lived on the mountain called Blesanerg, north of the
Arctic Sea. Val had a sword called the 'Horn-Hilt', heavily inlaid
with gold, and its stroke never failed.

Halfdan and Sigmund arrived east in Permia, and after inquiring
where Val might be found they located him north of the White Sea.
They went straight into battle. Two of Sigmund's men are specially
mentioned, one called Hauk and the other Gauk, both forecastle-
men. Raknar's son, Agnar, laid his ship alongside Halfdan's, and a
mighty battle began. Hauk and Gauk, sailing free in unlinked
vessels, attacked the outlying ships and cleared all their decks of
men. With Kott and Kisi in support, Val leapt aboard Sigmund's
ship and created havoc. Val gave Sigmund a blow that split his whole
shield, so that the sword went through and caught him on the
instep, slicing off a couple of toes. Sigmund struck back: his sword
cracked at the hilt on a gold helmet Val was wearing. Val stood
upright, ready to strike, but Sigmund rushed at him and he went
flying overboard, right down to the bed of the sea. When he surfaced
again his men hauled him aboard one of the ships.

Soon, Kott and Kisi fell back and withdrew to their own ship. Odd
the Showy, Gauk and Hauk came alongside and launched a fierce
attack on them. Now that Val was out of the fight, Kott and Kisi
made off in the one ship, but Odd went after them, forcing them
ashore at a place where a great river pours over a cliff into the sea.
Val was in their party and now he picked up a pair of chests so heavy
with gold that two men could scarcely have carried them. Odd raced
after him but when they reached the waterfall Val plunged right
over, and that is how they parted.

Next on the scene were Kott and Kisi, and Gauk and Hauk. When
they got to the waterfall, Kott took hold of Gauk and Kisi took hold
of Hauk and down they plunged into the waterfall; that was the
death of Hauk and Gauk. Behind the waterfall was a great cavern.
Val and his sons swam into it under water, lay down upon the
gold-hoard, and were changed into winged dragons. With helmets

upon their heads and swords carried beneath their fins, there they rested until the time Gold-Thorir conquered the waterfall.

Odd was the only one to come back alive, and by then Halfdan and Sigmund had killed all the vikings except for Agnar, who escaped in a single ship. He went to Halogaland and became a notorious troublemaker. He amassed a heap of riches and eventually built himself a huge grave mound, which he entered alive just as his father had done along with all his crew, and turned into a monster, money and all.

27. The End of the Story

Halfdan and Sigmund went back to Permia. Sigmund settled down there in his kingdom and Halfdan journeyed back to Norway. There's a long story yet to be told about him. Halfdan and Queen Ingigerd died in old age, and many great people are descended from them in Norway and Orkney.

And thus we end our tale; now go in peace.

Bosi and Herraud

1. Herraud's Family

There was a king called Hring who ruled over East Gotaland. His father was King Gauti, the son of King Odin of Sweden. Odin had travelled all the way from Asia, and all the noblest royal families in Scandinavia are descended from him. Hring's half-brother on his father's side was Gautrek the Generous, but his mother's family was just as distinguished.

Hring was married to a fine-looking, even-tempered woman called Sylgja, the daughter of Earl Seafarer of the Smalands. She had two brothers called Dayfarer and Nightfarer, both retainers of King Harald Wartooth, who at that time ruled over Denmark and the greater part of Scandinavia besides.

Hring and his queen had a son called Herraud. He was a tall handsome man, strong and talented, a man with very few equals. Everyone was very fond of Herraud, except his own father who had no great liking for him. As it happened, the king had another son, who was illegitimate, and he was fonder of him than he was of Herraud. This bastard son was called Purse and at this time he was a grown man, as the king had begotten him when he was still young. The king granted Purse large estates and made him his counsellor and tax collector. Purse was in charge of levies and fee-estates, and he controlled the king's revenues and expenses. Most people found him very grasping in collecting the money and equally tight-fisted when he had to pay it out. But he was loyal to the king and always had his interests at heart, and so his name became a household word and people are called Pursers who look after your interests and guard them with care.

To store the silver that was paid as dues to the king, Purse used certain money bags which have been known as purses ever since. But what he collected over and above the rightful amount he used to set aside in smaller money bags which he called profit-purses. He used this money for expenses, leaving the main tribute intact. Purse was not a particularly popular man, but the king was very fond of him and let him have his own way in everything.

2. Bosi's Family

There was a man called Thvari or Bryn-Thvari, who lived not far from the king's residence. He had been a great viking in his younger years and during his fighting career he had come up against an amazon, Brynhild, the daughter of King Agnar of Noatown. They had set about one another, and soon Brynhild was wounded and unable to carry on fighting. Then Thvari took her into his care, along with a great deal of money. He saw to it that her wounds were fully healed, but she remained bent and twisted for the rest of her life, and so she was known as Stunt-Brynhild. Thvari made her his wife, and although she wore a helmet and coat of mail at her wedding, their married life was a happy one.

After that Thvari retired from viking life and settled down on a farm. He and Brynhild had two sons. The elder, Smid, was not very big, but exceptionally good-looking, highly talented and extremely clever with his hands. The younger son, Bosi, was a tall strong fellow, swarthy and not so handsome. A cheerful, humorous man, he took after his mother in personality and looks. Whatever he started, he would see it through, and he never flinched, no matter whom he had to deal with. His mother was very fond of him, and so he was nicknamed after her and called Stunt-Bosi. He was a great joker both in what he said and did, so the name suited him well.

There was an old woman called Busla, who had been Thvari's concubine, and fostered his sons for him. Busla was highly skilled in magic. She found Smid more amenable than his brother and taught him a great deal. She offered to tutor Bosi in magic as well, but he said he didn't want it written in his saga that he'd carried anything through by trickery instead of relying on his own manhood.

The king's son Herraud and the brothers were much of an age, and they were also close friends. Bosi spent a lot of time at the royal court, where he and Herraud were always together. Purse often complained that Herraud used to give clothes to Bosi, since Bosi's clothes were always getting torn. Bosi was considered a bit rough when he was playing with the other boys, but no one dared complain about it because of Herraud who always took his side. In the end, Purse asked the king's men to give Bosi such a rough time that he'd stop playing.

3. Bosi Joins Herraud's Expedition

On one occasion when the ball-game was getting a bit out of hand, the king's men started pushing Bosi around but he hit back and one of them dislocated an arm. The next day he broke someone's leg. On the third day two men went for him and a number of others got in his way. He knocked out the eye of one of them with the ball, and threw the other to the ground, breaking his neck. The king's men rushed for their weapons with the idea of killing Bosi, but Herraud stood by him with all the men he could get. They came very close to fighting, until the king turned up. At Purse's insistence the king made Bosi an outlaw, but Herraud helped him to escape so he wasn't caught.

A little later Herraud asked his father to give him some warships and sturdy men as he wanted to sail away and, if possible, earn himself a reputation. The king put the matter to Purse, who answered that in his opinion the treasury would soon be empty if Herraud was to get all the outfit he wanted. The king said they would have to grant the request, and he got his own way. So preparations were made for Herraud's expedition and no cost was spared, for he was very particular about everything. He and Purse didn't see eye to eye over this.

Herraud set off with five ships, most of them old. He had brave men with him and a great deal of money, both gold and silver, and with this he sailed away from Gotaland south to Denmark.

One stormy day they saw a man standing on a cliff. He called out, asking them for a passage, but Herraud said he wasn't going out of his way for him, though he was welcome provided he could catch the ship. The man jumped off the cliff and landed on the tiller that jutted out from the helm, a leap of fifteen yards. Then everyone realized that it was Bosi. Herraud was delighted to see him and asked him to be the forecastleman on his own ship. From there they sailed to Saxony, plundering wherever they went, and getting plenty of money.

So it went on for five years.

4. Bosi Kills Purse

Meanwhile, back in Gotaland, after Herraud had gone away, Purse inspected his father's treasury. When he saw that the coffers and bags were empty, he said the same thing over and over again. 'I remember the days,' he said, 'when this treasury was a happier sight.'

Then Purse set off to collect the royal tributes and taxes and was very exacting in most of his demands. He came to Thvari and ordered him to pay his levies as others did, but Thvari answered that he was old enough to be exempt from the levy and refused to pay. Purse said that Thvari's responsibility was even greater than other men's, since it was his fault that Herraud had left the country. He also wanted compensation for the men Bosi had injured, but Thvari said that anyone who played in a game had to look out for himself, and that he wasn't going to throw away his money on that account. This led to a heated argument between them and eventually Purse forced his way into Thvari's store-room and took away two chests full of gold and plenty of other valuables, including weapons and clothes. After that they parted. Purse went back home with a great deal of money and told the king what had happened. The king told him it had been a mistake to rob Thvari as he would later find out to his cost, but Purse said that he wasn't in the least concerned.

Meanwhile, as Herraud and Bosi were getting ready to sail back home from their expedition, they heard about how Purse had robbed Thvari. Herraud decided then to try to set things right for Bosi and bring about a reconciliation between him and the king. They ran into a gale so fierce that their ships were driven apart, and all the ships that Herraud had brought from home were lost, but with two other ships he managed to reach Elfar Skerries.

Bosi's ship was driven to Wendland. Shortly before, Purse had also arrived there with two ships from the Baltic countries where he'd bought some fine treasures for the king. When Bosi realized this, he told his men to arm themselves, then went to see Purse and asked him when he was going to pay back what he'd stolen from Thvari. Purse replied that Bosi was making a pretty impudent suggestion, since he'd already been outlawed by the king, and ought to count himself lucky if he lost no more than this. Then both sides seized their weapons and started fighting. The outcome was that Bosi killed Purse, and then spared the lives of all the rest, but he seized the ships and all that was on board.

As soon as he got a favourable wind, Bosi sailed over to Gotaland, where he found his foster-brother Herraud and told him what had happened. Herraud said that this wouldn't exactly endear him to the king. 'Why come to me when you've dealt me such a near blow?' he said.

'I knew that I'd never be able to escape you if you wanted revenge,' said Bosi, 'and anyway, you seemed to be the only person I could turn to.'

'It's true enough,' said Herraud, 'that Purse was no great loss, even though he was my kinsman. I'm going to see my father and try to reconcile you.'

Bosi said he didn't expect any great consideration from the king, but Herraud said they ought to try everything they could. So he went to see his father, and greeted him respectfully. His father received him coldly, as he'd already been told what had happened between Bosi and Purse.

Herraud said to his father, 'You've every right to demand compensation from my friend Bosi, he's made a great deal of mischief. He's killed your son Purse, though it wasn't without provocation. We'd like to make a settlement and offer you as much money as you wish. In addition, we'll agree to pledge our loyal support and Bosi is willing to serve you in any way you like.'

The king replied angrily, 'Herraud, you're very determined to help this ruffian, but plenty of people would have thought it more your duty to avenge your brother and our disgrace.'

'Purse was no great loss,' said Herraud. 'I'm not even certain whether or not he was my brother, even though you were so fond of him. It seems to me you're showing me very little respect when you refuse to accept a reconciliation in spite of the plea I've made, and in my opinion, I'm offering a better man than Purse to take his place.'

The king had grown very angry and said, 'Your pleading on Bosi's behalf can only make matters worse. As soon as he's caught he'll be hanged on a gallows higher than any thief has ever been hanged before.'

Herraud was angry too. 'There are plenty of people,' he replied, 'who'll say you don't know where your honour lies. But since you're so reluctant to show me respect, you can take it that Bosi and I will share the same fate. I'll defend him as I would my own life, for as long as my courage lasts and till my dying day. Plenty of people will say that your bastard son was dearly bought if you decide to sacrifice us for his sake.'

Herraud was in a rage, and turned away. He didn't stop until he had found Bosi and told him what had happened between the king and himself.

5. *Busla's Prayer*

Hring had the alarm sounded to call his forces together, and then he went against the foster-brothers. The fighting began at once. The king had twice or three times as many men as they had, and though Herraud and Bosi fought bravely and killed a good many men, they were overpowered in the end, and shackled and thrown into the dungeon. The king was so furious he wanted to have them killed there and then but Herraud was very well liked and everyone pleaded for his life. Then the booty was divided and the dead were buried. A number of people put it to the king that he ought to make peace with Herraud, and eventually Herraud was led before him. The king offered to spare his life, and many people spoke in favour of this, but Herraud refused the offer unless Bosi were spared as well. The king said that was out of the question. Herraud threatened to kill anyone who put Bosi to death, even the king himself. The king said it would serve Herraud right if he got the punishment he asked for. He was so angry no one could talk to him, and ordered Herraud to be taken back to the dungeon and the two men to be killed the following morning. The king was adamant, and it seemed to most people that the situation was quite hopeless.

That evening, Busla had a talk with her husband and asked him whether he wasn't going to offer some money for his son. Thvari answered that he'd no intention of throwing his money away, he knew only too well that he couldn't save the life of a man doomed soon to die. Then he asked Busla what had become of her magic if she wasn't going to give Bosi any help; but she said that she'd no intention of competing with Thvari in meanness.

That evening, Busla appeared in the king's bedroom and recited a prayer which has been known as 'Busla's Prayer' ever since. It has become famous everywhere, and contains many wicked words unfit for Christian mouths. This is how the prayer begins:

> Here lies Hring,
> Gotaland's king,
> The stubbornest man
>   when in the wrong:
> He'll be the one
> To kill his own son,
> Beyond belief,
>   yet on every tongue!
>
> King, beware
> Old Busla's prayer,
> Soon it will echo
>   through the world:
> All who hear
> Shall live in fear,
> And into Hell
>   your soul be hurled.
>
> Demons will scatter,
> All values shatter,
> Cliffs will tremble
>   to their knees:
> Storms will batter,
> Crash and clatter
> Unless with Herraud

you make your peace,
And let my Bosi
  live at ease.

Soon I shall dart
Close to your heart
With poison snakes
  to gnaw your breast:
Deafen your ears,
Blind you with tears,
Unless you let
  my Bosi rest,
Embrace your son
  as an honoured guest.

When you set sail
May your rigging fail,
Your rudder-hooks snap
  in heavy seas:
The sheets will rip
On your sinking ship
Unless with Herraud
  you make your peace,
And let my Bosi
  live at ease.

When you ride, I'll make
Your bridle break,
Your horse go lame
  at my behest:
Straight from your door
To the demon's claw!
Unless you let
  my Bosi rest,
Embrace your son
  as an honoured guest.

You'll rest no more
Than on burning straw,
Your throne will be
Like a swollen sea;
And what a shame

When you play the game,
When she's on her back
But you've lost the knack:
Would you like some more . . .

'Shut your mouth, you filthy witch,' said the king, 'get out of here, or I'll have you tortured for your curses.'

'Now we're face to face,' said Busla, 'it's not likely that we'll part till I have what I came for.'

The king wanted to stand up, but he was stuck fast to the bed, and none of his servants could be roused from their sleep. Then Busla recited the second part of her prayer, but I'd better not write it here, as people repeat it only at their peril. If it's not written down, the prayer is less likely to be repeated. All the same, this is how it starts:

Sorceresses,
Elves and Trolls,
Goblins and giants
Will burn your halls:
Frost giants fright you
Stallions ride you,
Straws shall sting you,
Tempests bring you
To madness and Hell
If you break my spell.

When the second part was over, the king said to Busla, 'Rather than let you curse me any more, I'm going to let Herraud live. But Bosi must leave the country and if ever I lay hands on him I'll have him killed.'

'In that case, I'll have to deal with you further,' said Busla.

Then she started reciting the so-called 'Syrpa Verses' which hold the most powerful magic, and which nobody is allowed to sing after sunset. This stanza comes near the end:

Of strangers six
The names are here:
What they might mean
You must make clear:
Solve this riddle,
But if you fail
To satisfy me,

The dogs of Hell
Will tear your body
Bit by bit,
As your soul sinks down
To the burning pit.

ᚱ.ᚠ.ᚦ.ᚤ.ᚤ.ᚿ||||||| ᛆᛆᛆᛆᛆᛆ : 111111 : |||||| : ᚱᚱᚱᚱᚱᚱ :*

'Interpret these names correctly or all my worst curses will bite you, unless you do as I ask,' she said.

When Busla had completed her prayer, the king had no idea how he ought to react to her demands. 'What do you want, then?' he asked.

'You're to send Bosi and Herraud on a dangerous mission,' said Busla, '– who knows how it will end – and they're to be responsible for their own safety.'

The king told her to go but she refused to leave until he'd given his solemn word to carry out his promises to her; and then, Busla's prayer could do him no harm.

After that the old hag went away.

6. Bosi's Mission

Early next morning the king got up and had the alarm sounded to call people to a meeting, and then Herraud and Bosi were led before the gathering. The king asked his counsellors what should be done with the two men, and most of them pleaded with him to spare Herraud.

Then the king spoke to his son. 'You don't seem inclined to show me much respect,' he said, 'but in spite of that I'm going to do as my friends ask me: I'm going to spare Bosi's life. He's to leave this country and not come back until he brings me a vulture's egg, inscribed all over with gold letters, and then we'll be reconciled. If not, everyone can call him a coward. Herraud is free to go wherever he wants to, either with Bosi or on any other path he

* On these runes, see Claibourne W. Thompson's article, listed in the Bibliography.

chooses. After what's happened, I only want him to stay away from me.'

So the two men were set free. They went to Thvari and stopped with him over the winter. In the spring they got ready for a voyage with one ship and a crew of twenty-four. Mostly they let themselves be guided by Busla's advice. And so they set off and sailed east across the Baltic, and when they came to Permia they brought their ships in under cover of a thickly wooded wilderness.

7. A Night in the Wood

At that time the ruler of Permia was King Harek, a married man with two sons, Hrærek and Siggeir. They were great fighters, serving at the court of King Godmund of Glasir Plains, and they were also in charge of the country's defences. King Harek had a daughter called Edda, a beautiful girl, and very talented in most matters.

Now we must return to the foster-brothers, who were lying off Vina Forest in Permia where they'd set up a tent ashore in a remote and desolate spot.

One morning Bosi told his men he was going ashore with Herraud to explore the forest and see what they could find. 'Wait a month for us here, and if we're not back by then, you can sail wherever you like.' Their men weren't too happy about this, but there was nothing they could do about it.

The foster-brothers made their way into the wood. They had nothing to eat except what they could catch by shooting wild animals and birds; sometimes their only food was berries and the sap of the trees, and their clothes were badly torn by the branches.

One day they came upon a cottage. An old man was standing outside it splitting firewood, and he greeted them and asked who they were. They told him and asked him his name, and he said he was called Hoketil. Then he said they were welcome to stay the night if they wanted to, so they accepted his offer. The old man showed them to the living-room, where not many people were to be seen. The woman of the house was getting on in years, but there was an attractive young daughter. The girl pulled off their wet clothes and gave them dry things instead, then brought a basin so they could wash their hands. The table was laid, and the young woman served them with excellent ale. Bosi kept eyeing her suggestively and touching her foot with his toe, and she did the same to him.

In the evening they were shown to a comfortable bed. The farmer slept in a bed-closet, his daughter in the middle of the room and the foster-brothers in a bed under the gable beside the door. When the people were asleep, Bosi got up, went over to the young woman's bed and lifted the bedclothes off her. She asked who was there, and Bosi told her.

'What have you come for?' she asked.

'I wasn't comfortable enough in my bed as things were,' he said, and added that he'd like to get under the bedclothes with her.

'What do you want to do here?' she said.

'I want to temper my warrior,' said Bosi.

'What sort of warrior's that?' she asked.

'He's still very young and he's never been steeled,' he said, 'but a warrior ought to be hardened early on in life.'

He gave her a gold ring and got into bed beside her. She asked him where the warrior was, and he told her to feel between his legs, but she pulled her hand back and said he could keep his warrior and asked why he was carrying a monster like that on him, as hard as a tree. He told her the warrior would soften in the dark hole, and then she said he could do anything he wanted. So now he set the warrior between her legs. The path before him was rather narrow, and yet he managed to complete his mission.

After that they lay quiet for a while, as long as they pleased, and then the girl asked him if the tempering of the warrior had been a complete success. Bosi asked her in turn whether she felt like tempering him again, and she said she'd be only too pleased as long as he felt like it.

There's no record of how often they played the game that night, but it's believed that Bosi asked her, 'Have you any idea where I can find a vulture's egg inscribed with gold letters? My foster-brother and I have been sent to find out.'

She said the very least she could do in payment for the gold ring and a good night's entertainment was to tell him all he wanted to know.

'But who's so angry with you that he wants you to die, sending you on such a dangerous mission?'

'Evil motives aren't the only motives, and a man can't win a reputation without some effort,' said Bosi. 'Plenty of things seem full of danger to start with, but bring you luck in the end.'

8. The Vulture's Egg

'In this forest,' said the girl, 'there's a great temple belonging to King Harek, the ruler of Permia. The god worshipped there is called Jomali, and a great quantity of gold and jewels can be found there, too. The king's mother, Kolfrosta, is in charge of the temple. Her witchcraft is so powerful that nothing could ever take her by surprise. By her sorcery she's been able to predict that she won't live out the month, so she's travelled by magic east to Glasir Plains and carried off King Godmund's sister, Hleid, whom she means to take her place as the priestess of the temple. But that would be a loss indeed – Hleid's one of the most beautiful and well-bred of women – so it would be all for the best if it could be prevented.'

'What's the main problem about the temple?' Bosi asked.

'An enormous vulture,' she said, 'so savage it destroys everything that comes anywhere near it. The vulture watches the door and sees anything that comes inside. Not a living soul has a chance if the vulture's claws and venom come anywhere near him. Under this vulture lies the egg you've been sent to get. There's also a slave in the temple, who looks after the priestess's food – she eats a two-year-old heifer at every meal. And there's an enchanted demonic bull in the temple, shackled with iron chains. The bull's supposed to mount the heifer, poisoning her flesh, and then all those who taste it go crazy. The heifer is to be cooked for Hleid, and then she'll turn into a monster like the priestess. As things are, I don't think it's very likely you'll be able to beat these devils, considering all the sorcery you're up against.'

Bosi thanked her for telling him all this and repaid her

handsomely with yet another round of good entertainment. They were both very pleased with themselves, and slept till dawn. In the morning, he went over to Herraud and repeated what he'd been told. They stayed on for another three nights, and then the farmer's daughter directed them to the temple. She wished them luck, and they set out on their journey.

Early one morning they saw a tall man in a grey cloak leading a cow. They realized this must be the slave, so they attacked him. Bosi struck him a heavy blow with a club, and that was the end of him. Then they killed the heifer and skinned her, and stuffed the hide with moss and heather. Herraud put on the slave's cloak and dragged the heifer's skin behind him. Bosi threw his cloak over the slave's body and carried him on his back. When they came in sight of the temple, Bosi took his spear and drove it into the slave's backside up through the body so that it jutted out of the shoulder. They walked up to the temple and, wearing the slave's clothes, Herraud went inside.

The priestess was asleep. Herraud led the heifer into the stall, then untied the bull, and the bull mounted the heifer at once. But the moss-filled hide collapsed on impact, so that the bull fell forward against the stone wall, breaking both its horns. Herraud gripped the bull by the ears and the jaw , and gave the neck such a violent twist that it broke. At that moment the priestess woke up and jumped to her feet.

Bosi walked into the temple carrying the slave over his head by the spear. The vulture wasted no time and dived down from the nest, intending to make a meal of this intruder, but it only swallowed the upper part of the corpse, and Bosi gave the spear a firm thrust so that it went straight through the vulture's throat into the heart. The vulture set its claws hard against the slave's buttocks and struck the tips of its wings against Bosi's ears, knocking him out. Then the vulture crashed down on top of him, ferocious in its death throes.

Herraud made for the priestess, and there was quite a tussle between them, as she wore her nails cut jagged and tore his flesh down to the bone. The fight took them to the spot where Bosi was lying, the floor around him soaked with blood. The priestess slipped

in the vulture's blood and fell flat on her back, and so the struggle
continued as fierce as ever, with Herraud sometimes on top of her
and sometimes underneath.

Then Bosi came to, got hold of the bull's head and hit the old hag
hard on the nose with it. Herraud tore one of her arms off at the
shoulder, and after that her spirit began to weaken. Even so, her
final death throes caused an earthquake.

After that they went through the temple and searched it thoroughly. In the vulture's nest they found the egg, covered in letters
of gold. They found so much gold there they had more than enough
to carry. Then they came to the altar where Jomali was sitting, and
from him they took a gold crown set with twelve precious stones,
and a necklace worth three hundred gold marks; and from his knees
they took a silver cup filled with red gold and so big that four men
couldn't drink it dry. The fine canopy that was hung over the god
was more valuable than three cargoes of the richest merchantman
that sails the Ægean Sea, and all this they took for themselves.

In the temple they found a secret side-room with a stone door,
securely locked. It took them the whole day to break it open and get
inside. There they saw a woman sitting on a chair – never had they
seen such a beautiful woman! Her hair was tied to the chair-posts,
and was as fair as polished straw or threads of gold. An iron chain,
firmly locked, lay round her waist, and she was in tears.

When she saw the men, she asked them what had been causing all
the uproar that morning. 'Do you care so little for your lives that
you're willing to put yourselves into the power of demons? The
masters of this place will kill you the moment they see you here.'

They said there'd be plenty of time to talk about that later. Then
they asked her what her name was, and why she was being treated so
badly. She said her name was Hleid and that she was the sister of
King Godmund of Glasir Plains in the east.

'The ogress in charge here got hold of me by magic, and wants me
to become priestess here when she's dead and take over the sacrifice
in the temple. But I'd rather be burnt alive.'

'You'd be good to the man who helped you escape from here?'
asked Herraud. She said she didn't think anyone could possibly
manage that.

'Will you marry me if I take you away?' asked Herraud.

'I don't know a man on earth so loathsome I'd not prefer being married to him rather than worshipped in this temple,' she said. 'What's your name?'

'I'm called Herraud,' he said, 'and my father is King Hring of East Gotaland. You needn't worry any more about the priestess. Bosi and I have already given her a good send-off. But you understand, I feel entitled to some reward from you if I get you out of this place.'

'I've nothing to offer but myself,' she said, 'that is, if my family will let me.'

'I don't intend to ask them,' said Herraud, 'and I won't have any more evasion, since it seems to me that I'm every bit as good as you. So whatever you decide, I'll set you free.'

'Of all the men I ever set eyes on, there's no one I'd rather have than you,' she said.

Then they set her free. Herraud asked what she would prefer, to travel home with them and become his wife; or else to be sent east to her brother, never to see Herraud again. She chose to go with him, and so they pledged themselves to each other.

They carried the gold and treasures out of the temple and then set fire to the building and burned it to ashes so that there was nothing else to be seen there. After that they set off with all that they'd taken and didn't break their journey till they reached Hoketil's house. Nor did they stay there very long, but gave him a great deal of money, then carried the gold and treasure on a number of horses down to the ship.

Their men were delighted to see them.

9. The Battle of Brow Plains

They sailed away from Permia as soon as the wind was in their favour, and there's nothing to tell of their voyage until they arrived back home in Gotaland, having been away two years. They went before the king, and Bosi delivered the egg. The shell had cracked, but even the broken piece was worth ten gold marks. The king used the shell as a loving-cup. Bosi also gave him the silver cup that he'd taken from Jomali and now they were completely reconciled.

About this time the queen's brothers, Dayfarer and Nightfarer, came to the royal court. They had been sent by King Harald Wartooth to ask for support, as a time had been set for the Battle of Brow Plains. This battle was the greatest ever fought in Scandinavia, and is described in the Saga of Sigurd Hring, father of Ragnar Hairy-Breeks.

Meanwhile, Hring asked Herraud to go in his place, and offered to look after the bride. He also said that he and Herraud should be fully reconciled over all that had happened between them. Herraud did as his father asked. He and Bosi joined the brothers with five hundred men and went to King Harald. In this battle King Harald and one hundred and fifteen other kings were killed, as it says in his Saga, and many great champions as well, even greater men than the kings themselves. Both Dayfarer and Nightfarer were killed. Herraud and Bosi were wounded but managed to come out of the battle alive.

Meanwhile in Gotaland great changes had taken place while they were away, as will soon be told.

10. The Death of Hring

Since it's not feasible to tell more than one story at a time, we'd now better explain what had happened earlier on. We begin at the point where King Godmund's sister, Hleid, had vanished from Glasir Plains. As soon as the king realized she had disappeared, he had a search made for her by sea and land, but no one could find any trace of her. The two brothers, Hrærek and Siggeir, were staying with the king at the time. The king asked Siggeir to take charge of the search for Hleid, and as a reward he was to win her for his wife. Siggeir said that in his opinion Hleid would be very hard to trace, unless the priestess in Permia knew where she was. The brothers prepared to sail with five ships. When they reached Permia, they found King Harek and told him about their mission. He advised them to go to the temple, and said that if neither the god Jomali nor the priestess knew Hleid's whereabouts, there wasn't much hope of finding her. The brothers went to the temple and saw nothing but a vast heap of ashes, with not a sign of anything that should have been there.

The brothers scoured the forest until they came upon Hoketil's house. They asked if he or his household had any idea who could have destroyed the temple. The old man said he didn't know, but he mentioned that two men from Gotaland had been lying at anchor for a long time off Vina Forest, one called Herraud and the other Bosi. In his opinion they were the most likely men to have done such an extraordinary thing. The farmer's daughter said she had seen these men on their way to the ship, bringing King Godmund's sister with them, Hleid of Glasir Plains. They had told the girl that anyone who wanted to see Hleid should come to them.

When the brothers learned what had happened, they told the king, then gathered forces all over Permia, and with twenty-three ships they sailed to Gotaland. They arrived there about the time of the Battle of Brow Plains where the foster-brothers were fighting, so Hring had only a small force with him. Hrærek and Siggeir told him either to fight or else hand over Hleid to them. The king chose rather to fight, but the matter was soon settled as Hring and the greater part of his army were killed.

Then the brothers took the girl, stole all the money they could and sailed back without delay to Glasir Plains. King Godmund was delighted to get his sister back and thanked them generously for their mission, which was considered a great success. Siggeir made a proposal of marriage to Hleid, but she was unhappy and said it would be more fitting if she were to marry the man who had saved her from the monsters.

The king said that Siggeir fully deserved to have her and added that he himself was the one to settle her marriage. 'And no foreign princes are going to have you, even if you won't accept my decision.' So she had to do as the king wished.

And now we'd better let them get on with their wedding preparations, since they are looking forward to them so much, though it may happen yet that the feast won't go without a hitch.

11. Bosi's Adventures

Now we should explain that Herraud and Bosi arrived home in Gotaland a fortnight after Siggeir and his men had sailed away.

Their return was a great sadness to them, but they took stock of the situation and then Bosi went to his father to ask for advice. Thvari said there was no time to gather a whole army and the only way of rescuing Hleid was by means of carefully laid plans and swift action, so the outcome was that they prepared a single ship with thirty men aboard. It was decided that Smid should go with them and be in charge of the expedition. Thvari gave them plenty of sound advice, and so did Busla.

They set off as soon as they were ready. Smid always had a favourable wind whenever he was at the helm, so their voyage was much faster than anyone might have expected. Soon the brothers had reached Glasir Plains in the east. They cast anchor off a thickly wooded coast, and Smid threw a helmet of invisibility over the ship.

Herraud and Bosi went ashore and came to a small well-kept cottage. An old man was living there with his wife, and they had an attractive and well-informed daughter. The peasant gave them an invitation to stay the night, which they accepted. The cottage was quite comfortable, and the hospitality good. The table was laid, and the guests were served with excellent beer. The master of the house was silent and reserved, but his daughter, the most sociable member of the household, was the one who served the guests. Bosi was in a good humour and flirted with her a little, and she did the same with him.

In the evening they were shown to their beds, but as soon as the light had been put out, Bosi went over to the girl and lifted the bedclothes off her. She asked who was there, and Bosi told her.

'What do you want?' she asked.

'I'd like to water my colt at your wine-spring,' he said.

'Do you think you can manage it, my lad?' she asked. 'He's hardly used to a well like mine.'

'I'll lead him right to the edge, then push him in if there's no other way to make him drink,' said Bosi.

'Where is your colt, sweetheart?' she asked.

'Between my legs, love,' he said. 'You can touch him, but do it gently, he's terribly shy.'

She took hold of his prick, and stroked it and said, 'It's a lively colt, though his neck is far too straight.'

'His head isn't all that well set,' agreed Bosi, 'but his neck curves much better once he's had a drink.'

'Well, it's all up to you now,' she said.

'Lie as open as you can,' said Bosi, 'and keep calm.'

Then he watered his colt generously, completely immersing him. This pleased the girl so much she was hardly able to speak. 'Are you sure you're not drowning the colt?' she asked.

'He has to be given all he can possibly take,' said Bosi, 'he often gives me a lot of trouble when he isn't allowed to drink his fill.'

Bosi kept at it for as long as he wanted, then took a rest. The girl was wondering where all the fluid between her legs had come from, for the whole bed was lathering under her.

'Could it be your colt's drunk more than was good for him,' she asked, 'and then vomited up more than he's drunk?'

'Something's the matter with him,' said Bosi, 'he's as soft as a lung.'

'He's probably ale-sick,' she said, 'like any drunkard.'

'Could be,' he said.

So they entertained themselves to their satisfaction, the girl being now under him and now on top. She said she'd never ridden a more even-paced colt than this.

After many an entertaining turn, she asked him who he was. He told her and in turn asked her what was the latest news in the land. The very latest news, she replied, was that the brothers Siggeir and Hrærek had got back the King's sister, Hleid, from Gotaland and killed Hring.

'It's gained them such a reputation that no one here in the east can measure up to them,' she said. 'The king has promised his sister Hleid to Siggeir against her wishes, and the wedding is to be in three days' time. The brothers are very much on their guard, they've spies on every road and at every harbour. It's impossible to take them by surprise. They're expecting Herraud and Bosi to come at any time to fetch Hleid. The king has had a hall built, so huge there's a hundred doors in it, with the same distance between each of them, and a hundred men can sit in every space. There are two watchmen at every door, and no one is allowed to pass through unless he's been vouched for by one of the doorkeepers. Those who aren't recognized at any of the doors are to be kept in the dungeons until it's known who they are. There's a raised bed standing in the middle of the floor of the hall, with four steps leading up to it. The bride and bride-groom are to lie there, and all the retainers will be keeping watch round the bed, so it's impossible to catch them unawares.'

'Which of the retainers is the king's favourite?' asked Bosi.

'He's called Sigurd,' she said, 'the king's counsellor. He's a master-musician, there's nobody to compare with him anywhere, particularly at playing the harp. Just now Sigurd's visiting his concubine, a peasant's daughter living near the forest. She makes his clothes while he tunes his instruments.'

After that they dropped the subject and slept for the rest of the night.

12. A Wedding Feast

Early in the morning Bosi went back to Herraud and told him what he'd learnt during the night. They got ready to leave, and Bosi gave the young woman a gold ring. They followed her instructions about which way they should go, until they came in sight of the farm where Sigurd was staying. Then they saw him making for the royal palace with a servant. The foster-brothers stepped forward into their path. Bosi drove his spear through Sigurd, and Herraud strangled the servant. Afterwards, Bosi flayed the bodies. Then they went back to the ship, told Smid what they had done, and between them settled their plans. Smid put Sigurd's clothes and the skin of his face on Bosi, and wore the other mask and the servant's outfit himself.

Then they told Herraud what he had to do and walked up to the palace. They came up to the door where King Godmund was waiting, and he thought this was Sigurd, so he welcomed him and led him into the palace. 'Sigurd' took charge of the royal coffers, and of the ale supplies and wine cellars, too. It was he who decided what ale should be served first, and told the cup-bearers how generously they were to serve the drinks. He said it was most important that the guests should get as drunk as possible on the first night of the feast, since in that way they would stay drunk much longer.

All the important guests were shown to their seats, and the bride was escorted into the palace and led to her bench with a large company of elegant young women.

King Godmund sat on the high-seat. Beside him sat the bridegroom with Hrærek in attendance on him. It isn't said how the other noblemen were placed, but this much is known, that 'Sigurd' played the harp before the bride and her maidens. When the toasts were being served, 'Sigurd' played so well, everyone remarked that he had no equal, but he said this was only the beginning. The king told him not to spare his efforts. When the memorial cup consecrated to Thor was carried into the hall, 'Sigurd' changed the tune. Then everything loose began to move – knives, plates and anything else which no one was holding on to – and lots of people jumped up from their seats and danced on the floor. This went on for quite some time.

Next came the toast dedicated to all the gods. 'Sigurd' changed the tune again, and this time he played so loud, the music rang through the entire palace. All the people inside jumped to their feet, except the king and the bridal couple. All the guests were shuffling about and so was everything else inside the hall. This too went on for quite some time.

The king asked whether 'Sigurd' knew any more tunes. He answered that there were still a few less important ones and advised everybody to take a rest for a while. The guests sat down and carried on with their drinking. Then he played the tunes of the 'Ogress', the 'Dreamer' and the 'Warrior', and after that it was time for Odin's toast to be drunk. Then 'Sigurd' opened the harp. It was heavily inlaid with gold, and so big that a man could stand upright inside it. From inside he took a pair of white gloves, gold-embroidered, and played the 'Coif-Thrower'. Then all the coifs were blown off the ladies' heads, and danced above the crossbeams in the hall. All the men and women jumped to their feet, and not a thing remained still in its place.

When Odin's toast had been drunk, there was only one more left, the toast dedicated to Freyja. Then 'Sigurd' started plucking the one string that lies across the other strings, and told the king to get ready for the tune called 'Powerful'. The king was so startled at this tune that he jumped to his feet and the bride and the bridegroom too, and nobody danced more vigorously than they did. This went on for quite some time. Now Smid took the bride by the hand, led her a lively dance, and when he got the chance, picked up the table service and bundled it into the bridal sheets.

Now we come back to Herraud, who told his men to stove in all the ships along the coast, making them unseaworthy. He sent some others up to the town to collect the gold and jewels that Smid had put ready for them to carry down to the sea. By now it was growing very dark. Some of the men were on the roof of the palace, watching what was happening inside and hauling up through the skylight what had been thrown into the sheets. Others carried this down to the ship, which had been pointed out to sea.

13. *Abduction*

The next thing to happen was this. While the people in the palace were having their fling, a stranger walked inside, a tall, handsome man wearing a red scarlet tunic, with a silver belt round his waist and a gold band on his forehead. He was unarmed and started dancing like the others. When he came before the high-seat, he raised his fist and punched the king so hard on the nose that three teeth shot out of his mouth. Blood began to pour from the king's nose and mouth, and he fell unconscious on to the floor.

'Sigurd' saw what had happened, and threw the harp into the bed. Then he struck the stranger with both fists between the shoulder-blades. The man turned away, with 'Sigurd' after him. A good many followed, while others were attending to the king. Now 'Sigurd' took the bride by the hand, led her up to the bed and locked her inside the harp, and the men on the roof hauled her and Smid up through the skylight. After that they hurried down to the ship and went on board. The man who had hit the king was already there before them. 'Sigurd' stepped aboard as soon as he arrived, but Siggeir was right behind him with sword in hand. Then 'Sigurd' turned to face him and pushed him into the sea. Siggeir's men had to fish him out of the water, more dead than alive.

Smid cut the moorings, and the crew set sail. They tried to reach open water as fast as possible by rowing and sailing at the same time. Hrærek rushed down to the beach with a number of other men to launch their ships, but the coal-black sea poured in, and they had to make their way back to the shore. There was in fact nothing much they could do about it, as all of them were helplessly drunk.

The king was very shaky when he came to. He was offered some food, but he was still too weak to take any. The festivities had turned sour and sorry. Still, when the king had recovered, they made their plans. They decided not to disband but get themselves ready as quickly as they could to chase after the foster-brothers.

While they are busy getting ready, we must take up the story of the others. They sailed on their way till they came to the point where one route lies to Gotaland and the other to Permia. Then Bosi told Herraud to sail on to Gotaland and said he himself had some business in Permia.

Herraud said he was not going to leave him. 'What's your business there anyway?' he asked.

Bosi said this would become clear later. Smid offered to wait for them five days, and Bosi said that would be long enough. Then the two men rowed ashore in a small boat and hid it in a secret cove. They walked for a while until they came to a house belonging to an old man and his wife, who had a good-looking daughter. The foster-brothers were given a friendly welcome and served with excellent wine in the evening.

Bosi gave the girl a cheerful smile, and she eyed him in return. A little later they all went to sleep. Bosi went over to her bed, and she asked what he wanted. He said he wanted her to put a ring on his stump. She said she wondered what ring he could be talking about, and he asked her didn't she have one? She answered that she hadn't any ring that would fit him.

'I can widen it if it's too narrow,' he said.

'Where's that stump of yours? I've got a fair idea of what I can expect from my narrow little ring.'

He told her to feel between his legs, but she pulled her hand back and said he could keep his stump.

'What does it remind you of?' he asked.

'My father's steel-yard with the ring broken off.'

'You're very critical,' said Bosi. He took a ring off his finger and gave it her. She asked what he wanted in return.

'I want to put a stopper in your bung-hole,' he said.

'I can't think what you mean,' she said.

'Lie as open as you can,' he said.

She did as he asked, and he went between her legs and made a thrust deep into her body, almost up under her ribs.

She gave a jump, and said, 'You've pushed the stopper right through the hole, man.'

'I'll get it out again,' he said. 'How did you like that?'

'Nice as a drink of fresh mead,' she said. 'Keep the mop stirring in the flue.'

He kept nothing back, and she got so warmed up she began to feel a bit sick, so she asked him to leave off, and they took a rest. Then she asked him who he was, and he told her. He asked her whether she was by any chance on friendly terms with the king's daughter, Edda. She answered that she often visited Edda's boudoir and was always given a good welcome there.

'I'll take you into my confidence,' he said. 'I'm going to give you three marks of silver, and in return, you get the princess to join me in the wood.'

Then he took three walnuts from his purse, as bright as gold, and gave them to her. She was to tell the princess that she knew a grove in the forest where walnuts like these were plentiful.

The girl warned him that the princess wouldn't be afraid of just one man. 'There's a eunuch called Skalk who goes everywhere with her, and he's as strong as twelve men, and ready for anything.'

Bosi said he didn't mind as long as the odds were no worse.

Early next morning the girl went to see the princess, showed her the golden walnuts and told her she knew a place where they were plentiful.

'Let's go there right away and take Skalk with us,' said the princess, and that's what they did.

Bosi and Herraud were already in the grove and met them there. Bosi greeted the great lady and asked her why she was travelling with so small a retinue. She said there was no risk involved.

'That's what you think,' said Bosi. 'Now make your choice: either come with me willingly, or I'll make you my wife right now, here in the wood.'

The eunuch asked who the ruffian was that dared to mouth on like that. Herraud told him to shut up and not behave like an idiot. The eunuch hit out at Herraud with a heavy cudgel, and Herraud parried it with his shield, but it was such a powerful blow that the shield was shattered. Herraud rushed at Skalk but he gave a good account of himself. There was a hard tussle between them, but Skalk wouldn't budge an inch. Then Bosi came up to them and pulled Skalk's feet from under him. After that they put a noose round his neck and hanged him on an oak tree.

Then Bosi took the princess and carried her in his arms down to the shore where they rowed out to the ship and found Smid. The princess took it badly, but after Smid had had a few words with her she soon cheered up.

And so they sailed back home to Gotaland.

14. A Battle

While all this was going on, Siggeir and Hrærek had gathered and fitted out a huge army, but King Godmund was unfit to travel because of the punch Herraud had given him, so the brothers were in sole charge. They set off from Glasir Plains with forty ships, but added a good many more as they went along. They went to Permia to see their father, King Harek, just after Bosi and Herraud had left. By now King Harek knew for certain that the foster-brothers had gone off with his daughter. He had his own forces ready with fifteen large ships, so he joined his sons on their expedition, and between them they had sixty ships in all, and with this fleet they sailed to Gotaland.

Now we come back to Herraud and Bosi, who had begun to gather forces as soon as they arrived home, as they wanted to be ready in case they were being followed, though they meant to celebrate the double wedding as soon as they had the time and the opportunity. While they were away Thvari had had a lot of spears, axes and arrows made, and now the army began to grow.

When they heard that King Harek and his sons were approaching the coast, and things didn't look so good, Herraud ordered ships to be launched to meet them. He had a large force of hand-picked men, but it was much smaller than King Harek's. Smid attacked the king's ship, while Bosi went for Hrærek, and Herraud for Siggeir. There's no need to go into detail over what happened next. A fierce battle broke out, with both sides eager for action.

Shortly after the battle had begun, Siggeir boarded Herraud's ship and soon killed one of his men. Herraud had a forecastleman called Snidil, and he threw a spear at Siggeir, who caught it in flight and hurled it back at him. The spear went right through Snidil and into the prow, pinning him fast to the timbers. Herraud turned to meet Siggeir and lunged at him with a halberd. It broke through his shield but Siggeir gave it a powerful tug so that Herraud lost hold of the weapon. At the same time Siggeir hit back at Herraud, slicing off his ear and part of his helmet. Herraud picked up a great log that was lying on the deck and hit him on the nose, knocking the visor off the helmet and breaking his nose and all his teeth. Siggeir tumbled backwards into his own ship, and lay there unconscious for some time.

Smid fought bravely, but King Harek managed to board his ship with eleven men and they caused a lot of damage. Then Smid turned to meet him and lunged at him with a special short-sword that Busla had given him, since Harek couldn't be hurt by ordinary weapons. The blow caught him in the face, breaking all his teeth and cutting his palate and lips. Blood poured out of his mouth. This blow so upset King Harek that he turned into a flying dragon and spewed venom all over the ship, killing a number of men, then dived down at Smid and swallowed him in one gulp.

Next, they saw an enormous bird, called *skergipr*, flying down from the land. This bird had a nasty big head and it's often compared with the devil himself. The bird attacked the dragon, and a savage battle began. Eventually, they both came plunging down, the *skergipr* crashing into the sea and the dragon on to Siggeir's ship. Herraud was already there, letting fly with the log on either hand. He struck Siggeir on the ear, cracking his skull and knocking him overboard, and he never came up after that.

Then King Harek came to and transformed himself into a boar.

He snapped at Herraud with his teeth, tore the mail-coat off his body and bit into his breast, ripping off both nipples and all the flesh down to the bare bone. Herraud struck at the boar's snout, cutting clean through the head below the eyes. Herraud was now so exhausted that he collapsed on his back. The boar trampled on him but wasn't able to bite him as its snout had been cut off.

Next a monstrous bitch with enormous teeth appeared on the deck. She tore a hole into the boar's groin, unravelled his guts and jumped overboard. Harek reappeared in human form and dived into the sea after her. Both sank to the bottom of the sea and never came up again. It's commonly believed that this bitch would have been Busla, since after that she was never seen again.

15. Victory

By this time Bosi had boarded Hrærek's ship and was fighting like a true hero. Then he saw his father floating in the water just beside the ship, so he dived in and helped him aboard his own ship.

Hrærek was already aboard and had killed a good many men. Bosi was exhausted when he climbed aboard, but in spite of that he turned on Hrærek and hewed at his shield, splitting it in two and cutting off his leg at the ankle. The sword finished up in the yard-arm and broke in two. Hrærek hit back and struck at Bosi as he was turning. The sword caught him on the helmet and ran down on to the shoulder, ripping the mail-coat and wounding him in the shoulder-blade, and so right down his back. All his clothes were torn off so he stood there stark naked with the heel-bone sliced off his left foot. Bosi then seized a piece of the yard-arm, but Hrærek tried to jump overboard. He was leaning against the bulwark when Bosi struck at him, severing the body so that one part fell overboard and the other into the ship. By this time most of the enemy had been killed, but those still alive were spared.

The foster-brothers now took a roll-call of their troops. No more than a hundred were in any condition to fight, but they had won a great victory, and now they shared out what they had taken in the battle, and gave treatment to all the wounded who could benefit from it.

16. The End of the Story

After that Herraud and Bosi made arrangements for their weddings. There was no shortage of anything that was needed, and the feast lasted a month. When it was over, they gave all the guests splendid parting gifts. Herraud became king of all the territories his father had once ruled.

A little later they gathered their forces and went to Permia. Bosi demanded to be accepted as king there, since his wife Edda was legal heir to her father. Bosi told the people that this would be the best way of compensating the country for the men he had killed, that he could make them strong, with better laws and greater justice, and that since they now had no leader, the best solution would be to make him their king. Edda was well known to them and they knew all about her qualities, so Bosi became the king of Permia.

Bosi had a son by the girl who had tempered his warrior for him. He was called Svidi the Bold, and his son was Vilmund the Absentminded.

Bosi went east to Glasir Plains and made peace between King Godmund and Herraud.

Herraud and Hleid loved each other dearly, and their daughter was Thora Town-Hart, who married Ragnar Hairy-Breeks.

According to legend, a small snake was found in the vulture's egg which Herraud and Bosi had fetched from Permia. It was golden in colour, and King Herraud gave it to his daughter as a teething-gift. She put a piece of gold under the snake, and after that it grew and grew until it circled her bower. The snake was so savage no one dared come near it except the king and the man who fed it. The snake ate an old ox at every meal, and everyone thought it a thoroughly nasty creature. King Herraud made a solemn vow that he would only marry Thora to the man brave enough to go into the bower and destroy the snake, but no one had enough courage for this until Ragnar, son of Sigurd Hring, appeared on the scene. This Ragnar has since been known as Ragnar Hairy-Breeks, and his nickname is taken from the clothes he had made for himself when he went to kill the snake.

And so we end the Saga of Stunt-Bosi.

Egil and Asmund

1. Brynhild

There was a king called Hertrygg who ruled over Russia, a large, well-populated country lying between Hunland and Novgorod. He was married and had two daughters, both called Hild. They were fine-looking, even-tempered girls, very well brought-up, and the king was extremely fond of them.

Once when the king was away on a hunting trip, the elder Hild went with her maidens to a nut-grove. She was called Brynhild, because she had been trained in the skills of knighthood. As the women were getting ready to return home from the wood, a huge beast, called the *hjasi*, came up to them. This is an enormous, savage creature and of all the beasts the *hjasi* has the longest life, which explains the saying that a very old man is 'as old as the *hjasi*'; it's shaped like a monstrous dog, but with ears so large they touch the ground. The women scattered in all directions as soon as they saw the creature, but the *hjasi* got hold of the princess and ran into the wood with her.

The maidens went back home and told what had happened. The king was terribly distressed by the news and had a search made for his daughter, but they could find no trace of her anywhere. No one could tell him anything about her disappearance, and soon people began to lose interest in it.

So time passed till Christmas.

2. Bekkhild

At Christmas the king held a magnificent feast. The younger Hild, a clever girl – they called her Bekkhild because of her skill at embroidery – used to sit in her boudoir. On the first day of Christmas the king sent for his daughter, who made herself ready and went into the street with her maidens escorted by some gentlemen of the court. As they were passing a certain garden they heard a great uproar and saw a terrible vulture flying overhead. Its wings seemed to extend over the entire city. Then a great darkness fell and the vulture grabbed the princess and flew away with her. It struck two of her servants dead, and all the others were shaken with terror.

The news soon reached the royal palace. The king was extremely distressed and said, 'There seems no end to our misfortunes. I don't see what can be behind these monsters. I want you all to know that anyone who cares to search for my daughters shall not only marry one if he finds them, but get a third of my kingdom as well. Even if the searcher finds them dead, he can still have the best earldom in the country and choose any woman he wants as his wife.'

Some people called this a generous offer but added that there was a great deal at stake. After Christmas everyone went back home, deeply disturbed by what had happened.

Winter passed, and summer after. Late in the autumn it came about that a small ship, gold-painted above the water-line, put into the harbour with thirty men aboard, not including servants. The king happened to be at the harbour, and these men went before him to present themselves. He responded in a friendly way to their greetings and asked who they were. Their leader replied that his name was Asmund and that he was known as the Berserks-Killer.

'How old are you?' said the king.

'Sixteen,' said Asmund.

'I've never seen a more useful-looking fellow for your age,' said the king. 'Where have you come from?'

'A viking expedition,' said Asmund. 'But now winter's coming on and we'd like to have sanctuary here till spring. We're not short of money to pay our own way.'

The king said he was welcome to stay on, so Asmund had his cargo unloaded, and they were given a fine house to store their goods. Asmund, however, spent most of the time drinking in the king's palace. He and his men got on well with everybody.

3. Egil One-Hand

One day after Asmund had been staying there a month it happened that eighteen men came into the hall, every one of them wounded. Their leader, Rognvald, was in charge of the king's defences. The king responded warmly to his greetings and asked who had given him such a rough handling.

'There's a man called Egil come to your country,' said Rognvald, 'a hard man to deal with. He's been plundering your kingdom, so I went against him with five well-equipped ships, while he had just one ship and a crew of thirty. I didn't expect them to give me any trouble but the outcome of the battle was that I had to run for it, and all my men have been killed, apart from those here. He only has a single hand, and so he's known as Egil One-Hand, but he manages to do more with the one that's missing than with the other. Just above the wrist there's a sword fixed, made by dwarfs, and there isn't a man alive can stand up to his strokes.'

With that Rognvald went to his seat and dropped down dead. 'The thought that your death won't be avenged is not to be borne,' said the king.

'The best way to repay your hospitality,' said Asmund, 'would be if I went to see this Egil.'

'I'd like that,' said the king. 'You can take as many men as you want.'

'I'm not in the habit of taking on extra men when the odds are fair,' said Asmund. 'But if Egil has more men than I have, the farmers are sure to help us.'

4. The Encounter

Asmund set off to meet Egil, and told his men to row fully armed over to Egil's ship. Egil wasn't unprepared for this, and asked who was responsible for all that rowing.

Asmund gave his name. 'I've some business with you,' he added.

'Let's hear what you want,' said Egil.

'I want to exchange weapons with you,' said Asmund, 'and give you swords for axes.'

'We're not likely to refuse your offer,' said Egil. 'Do you have plenty of money aboard?'

Asmund said he hadn't. 'We're hoping to put that right with your help. How do you plan to compensate the king for your plunderings?'

'We're not in the habit of paying out money for the odd sheep my lads take for the table,' said Egil.

'In that case we'll have to use force,' said Asmund. 'The king's sent me for your head.'

'He must be pretty anxious to get rid of you,' said Egil. 'Why shouldn't we become sworn-brothers? Then we can kill the king and marry his daughters.'

'They're not available at the moment, they've both been abducted,' said Asmund.

'It would be a pity if our men were to kill each other,' said Egil. 'Let's fight a duel instead.'

Asmund said he was ready enough for that, so they went ashore to try out each other's skill, and were just about evenly matched. In the evening they all sat down to a joint drinking feast, and after that they slept through the night.

Next morning Asmund and Egil took up their weapons again and set to, each destroying three of the other's shields.

When the sun was due south, Egil said, 'Do you want to go on with the game?'

'Nothing's been proved either way yet,' said Asmund, 'and the king isn't going to think my mission's been properly carried out if we stop now.'

'Just as you wish,' said Egil.

'How old are you?' asked Asmund.

'Eighteen,' said Egil.

'Pick up your weapons if you want to live longer,' said Asmund.

So they fought another round, and it seemed to them as if every stroke was a death-blow. When the sun was in the south-west, Egil said, 'I think it would be better for us to stop this game now.'

'You must be getting scared,' said Asmund, who had already received one wound.

'Look out for yourself then,' said Egil.

So they fought the third round. Asmund could do no more than defend his life, and he'd already been wounded three times. He realized that this wouldn't do, so he threw down his sword and flung himself at Egil. It was difficult for Egil to use the mutilated hand, and the scuffle took them all over the field. At last Egil fell, and by then each had torn off the other's helmet.

'My sword's not to hand,' said Asmund, 'and it's too much trouble to bite your throat.'

'You've not much choice in the matter,' said Egil.

'I'm going to take a chance,' said Asmund, and ran for his sword and then back to Egil who lay as still as if he was having his hair cut.

Asmund said, 'You haven't any equal, Egil. Now stand up. I want to accept the offer you made, and become your sworn-brother.'

'It worries me a lot,' said Egil, 'that I owe you my life.'

'I'm not going to kill you,' said Asmund, 'But I want you to come with me to the king.'

Then their men arrived on the scene and pleaded with them to be reconciled. So they shook hands and each agreed to become the other's sworn-brother according to ancient custom.

5. Eagle-Beak

They got ready for the voyage and went back to King Hertrygg. Asmund greeted the king, who received him kindly and asked if he had met Egil One-Hand.

Asmund said he certainly had. 'I've never met a braver man. He's offered to take Rognvald's place, and we'll defend your country together.'

'If you're both willing to swear an oath of loyalty and take his place, I'll accept this offer as a settlement,' said the king.

Asmund said he was willing to do that, then Egil was called for, and they were put in charge of the country's defences, and stayed there over winter.

At Christmas the king gave a feast, and on the first day he asked whether anyone there could tell him what had happened to his daughters, but no one could. Then the king repeated the offer he had made before.

Egil said, 'This is a chance for a brave man to earn some money.'

After Christmas all the guests returned home.

Soon after midwinter Egil and Asmund launched their ship and selected a crew of twenty-four. They put a man called Viglogi in charge of those who were left behind. Egil and Asmund announced that they were not coming back till they had found the king's daughters, dead or alive. Then they put to sea, though they had no idea of where they should go. They spent the summer exploring outlying islands, skerries and mountains, and by the autumn they had reached as far north as Jotunheim. There they sailed close in by a forest, hauled their ship ashore and made themselves comfortable.

The foster-brothers told their men to stay there over the winter. 'Egil and I are going to explore this country,' said Asmund, 'and if we don't come back next summer, you're free to go wherever you like.'

They set off into the wood, shooting wild animals and birds for food. But months passed by, and sometimes they had no food at all. One day they came to a valley with a river flowing through it and low grassy banks on either side. The hillsides were wooded below and rocky higher up. There they saw a large number of she-goats and some well-fed males. They rounded up the herd and got hold of one of the fat goats with the idea of slaughtering it. Then they heard shouting up the slope, all the goats scattered, and they lost hold of the one they'd caught. They saw a monster up among the rocks, broader than it was high. It spoke in a shrill, bell-like voice and asked who was so bold that he dared steal one of the queen's goats.

'Who are you, oh beautiful, bed-worthy lady? Where's your queen's country?'

'My name's Skin-Beak,' she said, 'I'm the daughter of Queen Eagle-Beak who rules over Jotunheim. Her residence isn't very far from here, and you'd better go and see her before you start stealing things.'

'You're absolutely right,' said Asmund, and gave her a gold ring.

'I daren't accept this,' she said, 'I'm sure my mother will say that's my bed-money.'

'I'm not in the habit of taking back my gifts,' said Asmund, 'but we'd like you to find us a place to stay.'

She went ahead of them home to her mother, who asked her why she was so late. Skin-Beak said she had found two men who needed hospitality. 'One of them gave me a gold ring and asked me to find them lodgings,' she said.

'Why did you take money from them?'

'I was hoping you might repay them for it,' said Skin-Beak.

'Why didn't you invite them here?'

'I wasn't sure how you'd take it.'

'Ask them over,' said Eagle-Beak.

Skin-Beak ran back to them and said, 'My mother wants you to come and see her. You'd better be ready with the news, because she's very sharp about most things.'

So they went to see the old hag. She asked them their names, and they told her. She could hardly take her eyes off Egil. They said they'd not eaten for a whole week. The hag was skimming the milk. She had fifty goats yielding as much as cows, and an enormous cauldron, big enough to hold all this milk. She had a vast wheat-field too, and every day she took from it so much meal that the gruel she made with it filled the cauldron, and this was the food she and her daughter lived on.

'Skin-Beak,' she said, 'you'd better get some brushwood and make a good fire. Our hospitality wouldn't be up to much if we only offered them gruel to eat.'

Skin-Beak wasted no time, but even so her mother told her to hurry up and serve the food that was already cooked. So some game and venison appeared on the table.

The hag said, 'Let's not sit around with nothing to say, even though the hospitality does leave something to be desired. It'll be a long while before the gruel's ready. Now, Asmund, you can tell us the story of your life, and then Egil can tell us his. After that I'll entertain you at table with some stories about my own adventures. I'm curious to hear about your family background and the reason for your travels.'

6. Aran

Asmund began his story: There was a king called Ottar who ruled over Halogaland. He was married to Sigrid, daughter of Earl Ottar of Jutland in Denmark, and they had a son called Asmund. He was a fine big fellow, and while he was still young he was trained in all kinds of skills. When he was twelve he was considered a better man than any in the land.

Asmund had a good many playmates. One day when they'd gone riding into the forest, Asmund saw a hare and set his hounds on it. The hare ran away and the hounds couldn't catch it, but Asmund didn't give up, and when his horse collapsed from exhaustion Asmund ran with the hounds after the hare. In the end the hare jumped off a sea-cliff. Asmund turned back to look for his horse but he couldn't find it. Dusk had already fallen, so Asmund had to spend the night there, but in the morning a heavy mist had risen and he had no idea where he was.

For three days Asmund was completely lost in the wood, but then he saw someone coming towards him, a tall, handsome man, with a fine head of yellow silken hair, and wearing a scarlet cloak. It seemed to Asmund that he'd never seen a finer-looking man. They greeted each other, and Asmund asked the stranger's name. He said he was called Aran, the son of King Rodian of Tartary. 'I've been on a viking expedition,' he added.

'How old are you?' asked Asmund.

'Twelve,' said Aran.

'There can't be many like you,' said Asmund.

'Back home I had no equal,' said Aran, 'and that's why I made a solemn vow not to return until I'd found someone of my own age and as good as myself. Now, I've heard about a man called Asmund, the son of the king of Halogaland. Could you by any chance tell me anything about him? I've been told that there shouldn't be much between us.'

'I know him pretty well,' said Asmund. 'He's talking to you.'

'That's a bit of luck,' said Aran. 'And now we'd better try each other out.'

Asmund said he was ready.

They performed every athletic feat known to young men in those days, but were so equally matched there was no choosing between them. Next they wrestled. There was quite a tussle between them, but it was impossible to tell which was the stronger. When they broke off, they were both exhausted.

Then Aran said to Asmund, 'We must never test each other's skill with weapons, since we'd both end up dead. I'd like us to enter a sworn-brotherhood, each of us pledging himself to avenge the other, and sharing equally each other's money, now and in the future.'

It was also a part of their pact that the one who lived the longer should raise a burial mound over the one who was dead, and place in it as much money as he thought fit; and the survivor was to sit in the mound over the dead for three nights, but after that he would be free to go away.

Then they each opened a vein and mixed their blood, which was regarded as an oath. Aran invited Asmund to go with him down to the ships to see what a splendid outfit he had. Since Asmund was staying at that time in Jutland with his grandfather, Earl Ottar, he did as Aran wished.

7. Aran's Death

They went down to Aran's fleet, where he had ten longships, all manned with good fighting men. Aran gave Asmund a half-share of his ships and men; Asmund wanted them to sail first to Halogaland to get his own ships and their crews, but Aran insisted on sailing first to his own country and going from there to Halogaland so that people would see they were no common beggars. Asmund said he could have it his own way, and so they put to sea with a fair wind.

Asmund asked whether King Rodian had any other children. Aran said he had another son who was called Herraud. 'His mother's the daughter of the King of Hunland. Herraud's a brave man, very popular, and heir to the throne of Hunland. My father has two brothers, Hrærek and Siggeir, both berserks, very difficult to control, and pretty unpopular among the people. The king puts a lot of trust in them, since they do everything he tells them. They often go plundering and bring back treasures for the king.'

There's nothing more to tell of their voyage until they reached King Rodian's harbour, where they saw twelve warships and two dragon-headed longships, so splendid they'd never seen anything like them before. These ships belonged to two brothers from Ethiopia, called Bull-Bear and Visin, sons of Earl Gorm. They'd killed King Rodian, laid much of the country waste and created total havoc.

When the sworn-brothers heard of this, they had the alarm sounded, and as soon as the people realized that Aran had arrived they flocked to him in large numbers. The marauders rushed down to their ships and a fierce and deadly battle broke out. For a long time the issue hung in the balance. Aran jumped aboard Bull-Bear's ship and laid about him so that everyone on board began to fall back. Bull-Bear turned to meet him, so Aran struck a blow at his bald pate, but the sword failed to bite, particles flew from the skull and the sword broke at the hilt. Bull-Bear hit back at Aran's shield, splitting it right through and wounding him badly in the chest. A broken anchor was lying on the deck. Aran picked it up and drove it deep into Bull-Bear's head then pushed him overboard, and Bull-Bear sank down to the sea bottom.

Visin boarded Asmund's ship and hurled two spears simultaneously at him. Asmund tried to parry one with his shield, but it passed right through the shield and into Asmund's elbow, sticking fast in the bone. But Asmund caught the other spear in flight and hurled it back at Visin straight into his mouth, sinking it up to the middle of the shaft. The spear stuck in the mast as far as the barb, with Visin dangling from it, dead. After that the vikings surrendered, and Asmund had them all killed and thrown overboard. Aran and Asmund went into the town, and the people were very pleased to see Aran. Their wounds were seen to, and afterwards Aran was given the title of king. Then he announced his agreement with Asmund, and gave him a half-share in everything he owned.

Less than a month after their arrival Aran died suddenly one day as he was going into his palace. The corpse was dressed for burial according to custom. Asmund had a burial mound raised over Aran and beside the corpse he put in the mound Aran's horse with a saddle and bridle, his banners and armour, his hawk and hound. Aran was seated on a chair in full armour.

Asmund had another chair brought into the mound and sat himself down there, after which the mound was covered up. During the first night Aran got up from his chair, killed the hawk and hound, and ate them. On the second night he got up again from his chair, killed the horse and tore it to pieces; then he took great bites of horse flesh with his teeth, the blood streaming down from his mouth all the while he was eating. He offered to let Asmund share his meal, but Asmund said nothing. The third night Asmund became very drowsy, and the first thing he knew, Aran had got him by the ears and torn them off. Asmund drew his short-sword and sliced off Aran's head, then he got some fire and burnt Aran to ashes. Asmund went to the rope and was hauled out of the mound, which was then covered up again.

Asmund took all the treasures from the mound with him.

8. The Berserks

A little later Asmund called the people to a meeting and asked them whether they intended to honour the agreement he had made with Aran. Not many were in favour of the proposal and only the men Aran had given to Asmund were ready to support him.

At this point they happened to look out to sea and saw some ships sailing in. The leaders of this fleet were berserks, the brothers Hrærek and Siggeir. The people ashore weren't too happy about this. Asmund offered to be their leader, but no one was willing to put up a fight, so Asmund went back to his ships with his men.

When the berserks knew what had happened they claimed the whole country for themselves. Asmund told them about his agreement with Aran and said half the country belonged to him. The berserks told him to clear off if he wanted to live. Asmund challenged either of them to a duel, with the kingdom as the stake, but they shouted him down and told their men to get ready for a fight. A fierce battle began. Asmund had a smaller force, and the people didn't dare give him any help, so all his men were killed, and he himself was taken captive. This happened just towards evening.

The berserks decided that Asmund should be executed the following morning on top of Aran's mound and given to Odin as a victory offering, so Asmund was tied to the windlass, but all the others went ashore to see to their wounds and slept in the camp overnight. The brothers were sleeping in a small tent some distance away from the main camp and had only a few men with them.

Now we go back to Asmund, still tied to the windlass. He noticed an iron-lock jutting out from it. This had been given a great blow which had left a rough edge on the iron. Asmund rubbed the rope against this and managed to cut it through as the edge was so sharp. Now that his hands were free he broke the shackles off his feet.

The wind was blowing from the sea, so Asmund cut the anchor line and the ship drifted right up under the forest. In no time he was ashore, and it occurred to him that he might play a bit of a joke on the berserks before making off into the forest, so he made his way to their tent and pulled it down on top of them. Those inside jumped to their feet, but couldn't get out as the tent got in their way. Asmund struck Hrærek on the head, splitting it down to the jaw. Siggeir managed to get out and tried to run into the forest, but Asmund chased after him, and when Siggeir stumbled Asmund struck him from behind, just below the small of his back, slicing it clean through. After that Asmund went into the wood, having already killed ten men as well as the berserks. A search was made for him but he couldn't be found.

Before the day was done Herraud arrived with twenty ships, and everybody was very relieved to see him. He had already heard what had happened, and now he called the people to a meeting where he announced his ownership of the kingdom and asked to be accepted as king. No one spoke against him, so he was made king over the whole country. Those who had supported the berserks were driven away, and Herraud took their property.

Then Asmund went to see King Herraud and greeted him, and the king asked who he was. Asmund told him, and Herraud asked whether he was the man who had killed the berserks. Asmund said he was.

'Why have you come to me then?' asked the king.

'I couldn't think of anything better,' said Asmund, 'and it seemed to me that I'd dropped some pork into your cabbage. I came to see you since I knew very well I couldn't escape. Now I'd like to know what's going to happen to me. I'll defend myself while I can and try to save my life, but I'd accept a better choice if it were offered.'

'I've been told about your agreement with Aran,' said Herraud, 'and it seems a good idea to take you in my brother's place. In my opinion we're well rid of the berserks you killed.'

So Asmund stayed with Herraud, and they got on well together. Asmund asked Herraud to provide him with ships as he wanted to go plundering. Herraud told him to choose his ships and as many men as he liked. He also invited Asmund to come and stay with him whenever he wanted. Asmund picked thirty of Herraud's men and chose one ship. He and Herraud parted the best of friends, each vowing to treat the other as his own brother wherever they might meet again.

From then on Asmund was known as the Berserks-Killer. This is the end of my story, for I am that very man, Asmund.

'I liked that story,' said the old hag. 'How's the gruel getting on, my girl?'

'It's on the boil,' said Skin-Beak.

'It'll be a long while before it's ready,' said the queen. 'And what can you tell us, Egil?'

'Here's how my story begins,' said Egil.

9. The Giant

There was a king called Hring who ruled over the Smalands. He was married to Ingibjorg, daughter of Earl Bjarkmar of Gotaland. They had two children, a son called Egil, and a daughter called Æsa. Egil grew up at his father's court until he was twelve years old. He was quite a handful, troublesome, ambitious, and very hard to control. He used to go around with a crowd of boys and often went with them into the woods to shoot animals and birds.

There was a large lake in the wood, with a number of islands, and

Egil and his companions used to go swimming there as they'd grown
very skilled at all kinds of sports. One day Egil asked the other boys
which of them could swim the farthest into the lake. The outermost
island was so far from land that to see it they had to climb the
highest trees. So they set out swimming across the lake, thirty of
them in all. Everybody agreed that no one should risk going out
farther than was safe for him. They went on swimming out into the
lake, and some of the sounds between the islands were very wide.
Egil was the fastest swimmer and no one could keep up with him.
When they had swum a long way from the shore, a mist came down
on them so dark that none of them could see the others. Then a cold
wind sprang up, and they all lost their bearings. Egil had no idea
what had happened to his companions, and wandered about in the
water for two days. At last he came to land, now so weak that he had
to crawl ashore. He covered himself with moss and lay there
overnight, and in the morning he was feeling a bit warmer.

Then a great giant came out of the wood, picked Egil up and
tucked him under his arm. 'It's a good thing we've met, Egil,' he
said. 'Now I'm offering you a choice: either I kill you on the spot,
or else you'll swear an oath to look after my goats as long as I
live.'

Finding himself in this predicament, Egil didn't waste much time
coming to a decision.

They travelled for many days, and at last came to the cave where
the giant had his residence. The giant owned a hundred billy-goats,
as well as a good many she-goats. Keeping up their numbers was a
matter of life and death to him. Egil started herding the goats but
they gave him plenty of trouble. So it went on for some time, but
after Egil had been there for a year he ran away. As soon as the giant
discovered this, after Egil he went, being so smart that he could trace
footprints as readily in water as in snow. Egil had been gone four
days before the giant found him in a cave.

The giant said that Egil had treated him worse than he'd deserved.
'So now you're going to get something that'll be the worse for you,'
he added.

He took two stones, each of them weighing forty pounds,
fastened them with iron clamps to Egil's feet, then told him he could

drag this load behind him, and that's what Egil had to put up with for seven years.

The giant was always on his guard, so Egil could see no chance of killing him.

10. Escape

One day when Egil had gone to look for his goats he came across a cat in the wood. He managed to catch it and brought it home with him. It was late in the evening when he came back, and the fire was smouldering into ashes. The giant asked him why he was so late getting back. Egil answered that he wasn't all that comfortably dressed for walking, and anyway the goats were running all over the place.

'It's a marvel to me,' said the giant, 'how you can find what you're looking for in the dark!'

'That's because of my golden eyes,' said Egil.

'Have you got some other eyes, apart from the ones I've seen?' asked the giant.

'I certainly have,' said Egil.

'Let's have a look at these treasures, then,' said the giant.

'You won't steal them from me?' said Egil.

'They wouldn't be any use to me,' said the giant.

'They're no use to anyone,' said Egil, 'unless I fit them on.'

Then Egil lifted the hem of his cloak and across the fire the giant saw into the cat's eyes, which glittered like two stars.

'There's a treasure worth having,' said the giant. 'Would you sell me these eyes?'

'I'd be the poorer for it,' said Egil. 'But if you'll set me free and take off these shackles, I'll sell them to you.'

'Could you fit them well enough,' asked the giant, 'for me to get the full benefit of them?'

'I'll do my best,' said Egil, 'but you'll find the operation a bit painful, as I'll have to lift your eyelids quite a lot to fix the eyes where they ought to be. You'll always have to take them out as soon as it grows light, and only put them in after dark. Now I've got to tie you to this column.'

'You want to kill me,' said the giant, 'that's a dirty trick to play!'
'I'd never do such a thing!' said Egil.

So they made a bargain, and the giant took the shackles off him.

'You've done the right thing,' said Egil, 'and now I'll make you a promise to serve you for the rest of your life.'

Then Egil tied the giant to the column, took a forked rod and drove it into the eyes so that they lay bare on the giant's cheeks. The giant jerked so violently with pain that he snapped the ropes binding him. He fumbled about after Egil and tore the cloak right off him.

'Your luck's run out,' said Egil. 'The gold eyes have fallen into the fire and now they'll be no use to either of us.'

'You've played a dirty trick on me,' said the giant, 'but you'll starve to death in here, and never get out.'

The giant ran to the door and locked it securely, and Egil knew he was in a tricky situation. He had to stay in the cave four nights without food, with the giant on guard all the time.

Then Egil decided what to do. He slaughtered the biggest goat, flayed off the skin, then crept into the skin and sewed it up as tightly as he could.

On the morning of the fourth day Egil drove the goats to the entrance. The giant had placed his thumb against the lintel and his little finger on the doorstep, and the goats had to pass between. Their footsteps echoed on the cave floor.

The giant said, 'It's a sign of stormy weather when the hooves of my goats start to click.'

The goats ran out between his fingers, with Egil bringing up the rear. There wasn't a sound from his hooves.

'You're moving very slowly today, Horny-Beard,' said the giant, 'and you're pretty thick about the shoulders.'

Then he took hold of the goat's wool with both hands, and gave Egil such a shaking that he tore the skin and released him.

'It was lucky for you that I'm blind,' said the giant. 'All the same it's a pity we have to part without your getting some gift from me in recognition of your long service. So take this gold ring.'

It was extremely valuable, and Egil thought it a very fine ring, so he stretched out his hand for it. When the giant felt him take the ring, he pulled Egil towards him and struck at him, cutting off his right ear. Luckily for Egil the giant was blind. Egil cut off the giant's right hand and got the ring.

'I'm going to keep my word,' said Egil, 'and I won't kill you. You'll just have to put up with the pain, and may your last day be your worst.'

With that they parted, and Egil went on his way. For some time he slept out of doors in the wood. When he came out of the wood he saw some viking ships. Their leader was a man called Borgar. Egil joined them and proved himself the bravest of men. They spent the summer plundering, and at Svia Skerries they fought a berserk called Glammad. He had one excellent weapon, a halberd, which could pick out any opponent as soon as the bearer knew his name. Soon after the battle started Glammad jumped aboard Borgar's ship and ran him through with the halberd. Egil was standing near by, his spearhead broken off the shaft. He raised the shaft and drove it hard against Glammad's ear, knocking him overboard. Glammad sank to the bottom with his halberd, and neither ever came up again. Then the vikings stopped fighting and made Egil their leader. He picked out thirty-two men, and went plundering in the Baltic. Plenty happened on his campaign.

11. *The Dwarf*

On one occasion Egil lay at anchor in a certain harbour because of bad sailing weather. He went ashore alone and came to a clearing in a wood, where he saw a mound and on it a giant fighting a giantess over a gold ring. She was much weaker than her opponent, who was giving her a hard time. She was wearing a short dress, and her genitalia were very plain to see. She tried to hang on to the ring as best she could. Egil struck at the giant, aiming for the shoulder, but the giant turned quickly so the sword slid down the arm, slicing off a piece of the biceps so big that one man couldn't have lifted it. The giant struck back at Egil and caught him on the arm, cutting it off at the wrist, so that the sword and the hand fell to the ground together. The giant prepared to strike at Egil a second time so Egil had no choice but to run. The giant went after him into the wood, but Egil managed to escape and so they parted. Egil went back to his men with one hand missing and they sailed away.

Egil suffered a lot of pain from the arm. Two days later they came to another harbour and spent a night there. Egil couldn't stand the pain any longer so he got out of bed and took a walk into the forest. He came to a stream and seemed to get some relief by holding the arm in the water and letting it wash over the wound. Then Egil saw a dwarf child coming out of a rock with a pail to fetch water. Egil picked a gold ring off his finger with his teeth and let it slip into the bucket, and the child ran with it back into the rock.

A little later a dwarf came out of the rock and asked who had been so kind to his child. Egil told him his name and added that the way things stood, gold wasn't much use to him.

'I'm sorry to hear that,' said the dwarf. 'Come with me into the rock.' So that's what Egil did.

The dwarf began dressing the stump, and soon the pain had completely gone. In the morning the wound was healed. Then the dwarf set about making him a sword, and from the hilt he made a socket so deep, it reached up to the elbow, where it could be fitted to the arm. So now Egil found it as easy to strike with the sword as if he still had the whole arm. The dwarf gave him a good many more things of value, and they parted the best of friends. Then Egil went back to his men.

'So this,' said Egil, 'is my story up to date, because I'm the very same man as this Egil whose story I've been telling.'

'You seem to have got yourself into plenty of trouble,' said the queen. 'How is the gruel getting on, my girl?'

'I think it's properly cooked now,' she replied, 'but it's far too hot for anyone to eat while it's like this.'

'I think it'll have cooled by the time I've told my tale, though nothing much has ever happened to me,' said the queen.

12. Queen Eagle-Beak's Tale

There was a giant called Oskrud, who came from Jotunheim. His wife was called Kula, and he had two brothers called Gaut and

Hildir. My father Oskrud had eighteen daughters by his wife, and I was the youngest. Everyone agreed I was the best-looking of them all. My father and mother fell ill and died, and then they were put underground and given back to the trolls. We sisters inherited all the money they left, but Gaut and Hildir took the kingdom. They didn't get on with each other.

My father had owned three remarkable treasures: a horn, a chess set, and a gold ring. The brothers took the horn and the chess set, but we sisters managed to hold on to the ring, which was a very valuable thing to have. My sisters used to bully me and I had to wait on them all. Whenever I tried to argue they used to hit me. In the end I felt I couldn't bear it any longer so I made a vow to Thor to give him any goat he wanted if he'd even things up between my sisters and me.

Thor paid us a visit, and went to bed with my eldest sister. He lay with her all night, but my other sisters were so jealous of her that they killed her next morning. Thor did the same to all my sisters, he slept with them all in turn, and they were all killed. But each of them managed to utter a curse on the next, that if she had a child by Thor it would neither grow nor thrive.

Eventually Thor slept with me and gave me this daughter you can see, and the curse has worked well enough on her because she's a yard shorter now than when she was born. Thor gave me everything the sisters left, and he's always been very helpful to me. So I got all the money, but ever since I've been driven by an urge so strong that I don't seem able to live without a man.

One of the men I had to have was Hring, son of the king of the Smalands. I set out to see him, but he'd gone off to Gotaland to ask for the hand of Ingibjorg, the daughter of Earl Bjarkmar. I hurried on my way but when I arrived in Gotaland, Hring was already celebrating his wedding feast and his bride was about to be led into the hall. I lay down in the street intending to play her some dirty trick, but she saw me first and gave me a kick that broke both my thigh-bones. Then she was led into the hall to her seat. I followed her inside, turned myself into a fly, and crept under her clothes with the idea of ripping her belly open at the groin. But she recognized me right away, banged me in the side with a knife handle and broke three of my ribs, so I thought I'd better get out of there.

The day passed, and when the bride was being led to her bed and the bridegroom ushered out of the hall, I picked him up in my arms, and it seemed to me as if I was running down to the sea-cliffs to drown him so no one else would be able to enjoy him. But while I thought I was throwing him off the cliffs, all I did was fling him behind the bed-curtain. He landed on the bed alongside his bride, and I was captured, with no chance of escape. To save my life I was to go to the Underworld and fetch three treasures: a cloak that fire couldn't burn, a drinking horn that could never be emptied, and a chess set that would play by itself whenever anyone challenged it.

13. *The Underworld*

So I went down to the Underworld and saw King Snow, and for sixty goats and a pound of gold I bought the horn from him. A poison-cup the size of twelve casks had been prepared for his queen, and I had to drink this on her behalf as well. Ever since then I've always been a bit troubled with heartburn.

From there I went to Mount Lucanus where I found three women (if you could call them women, for I looked like a baby compared with them), in charge of the chess set. I managed to get half of the chess set off them, but when they found it missing and realized it was me, they asked me to give it back. I refused and challenged any one of them to take it away from me, staking the chess set against all the gold I could carry. They thought this wouldn't be too hard for them, and so one of them made for me, grabbed hold of my hair and tore half of it off along with my left ear and the whole of my cheek. She was hard on me, but I didn't give in, I put my fingers into her eyes and gouged them out. Then I tried to throw her, but she caught her foot in a rock crevice so I dislocated her hip joint. With that we parted.

Then the second sister rushed at me and gave me a punch on the nose, so that she broke it. It's been regarded as rather a blemish on my looks ever since, and I lost three teeth as well. I got hold of her breasts and tore them both off down to the ribs and then the flesh of her belly and the entrails too.

Next the third sister attacked me, the smallest of them. I meant to gouge her eyes out just as I'd done to the other, but she bit off two of my fingers. I put her down with a heel-throw, and she fell flat on her back. She begged for mercy, and I told her that I'd only spare her life if she gave me the whole chess set. She didn't waste any time over that. Then I told her to get up, and as a parting gift she gave me a magic glass. If a man looks into it, I can give him the shape of anyone I choose. If I want I can blind whoever looks into it.

Next I went to the Underworld to fetch the cloak, and there I met the Prince of Darkness. As soon as he saw me he said he wanted to sleep with me. I guessed he must be Odin because he only had one eye. He told me I could have the cloak if I was willing to fetch it from where it was kept. I had to jump across a huge fire to get it. First I slept with Odin, then I jumped over the fire and got the cloak, but ever since I've had no skin to my body.

After doing all this I went back home to Hring and Ingibjorg and gave them the treasures, but before we parted I had to swear an oath never to avenge myself on them. So, not feeling too happy about the affair, I came back to my own home. I'll remember that girl in Gotaland as long as I live. Later I'll tell you about the little games I've had to play with my brothers. How's the gruel getting on, girl?

'I think it's just about cool enough,' she said.

'Serve it up then,' said the hag.

After they had finished their meal the foster-brothers were shown to their bed, and slept through the night.

14. Recovery

In the morning the brothers woke up early. The old hag joined them, and when they asked her what time it was, she told them that they could stay there all day. So they got up and dressed. The old hag was very hospitable. They sat down to a meal, and now she offered them good ale and fine cooking, and inquired where they were going and what business they had. They told her all about their business and asked her whether she could give them any idea of what had happened to King Hertrygg's daughters.

'I don't know how successful you'll be in your search for them,' she said. 'But first of all, I'd better tell you what happened after the death of the giant Oskrud. The brothers didn't agree about which of them should be king, they both felt they had the right. Anyway, they did agree that the one who could get the more nobly born and talented princess should be king. Gaut was the first to go and he carried off King Hertrygg's elder daughter Hild; then Hildir went and carried off Bekkhild. Both girls are here now in Jotunheim, but I don't think they'll be easy to get free. They're to be married at Christmas, and all the giants will be gathered to decide which of the sisters has the greater skill.

'Things are looking up,' said Asmund, 'now we know where the sisters are. It would make all the difference if you'd help us.'

'The only reason why I keep up my family ties with Gaut and Hildir,' she said, 'is so that I shouldn't be under any obligation to them. It's due more to my own good faith than to anything on their part. You'd better take a rest here for today, and I'll show you my treasures.'

This suited them very well. When the table had been cleared, the old hag led them into a large side-chamber off the main cave. Inside stood a number of boxes which she unlocked, full of a great many rare and precious things, which they very much enjoyed looking at. Finally, the old hag picked up a small casket and opened it. A sweet fragrance came from it and, inside, Egil recognized his hand with his gold ring on the finger. It seemed to him as if the hand was still warm and steaming, and the veins throbbing.

'Do you know anything about this hand, Egil?' asked the old hag.

'I certainly do,' said Egil, 'and I recognize this gold ring my mother once gave me. But how did you come by my hand?'

'I can tell you about that,' said the old hag. 'My brother Gaut came and asked me to sell him my precious gold ring, but I wouldn't part with it. Some time later when my daughter was out tending the goats, he went to her and gave her a certain drink, which started her screaming and she couldn't be stopped until I brought the ring to her where she was lying on top of a mound. When I arrived with the ring Gaut appeared and wanted to take it away from me. I stood up to him, and there was quite a tussle between us. I was just about to loosen my hold on the ring when a stranger came out of the wood – very much like you, Egil. He took a great swing at the giant but the giant cut off his hand, and after that both of them ran off into the wood. I picked up the hand and ever since then I've looked after it and kept it wrapped in life-herbs so that it wouldn't die. I think we agree, Egil, that this man must have been you. If you'll risk letting me reopen the wound, I'll try to graft the hand on to the arm.'

'I don't see any risk in that,' said Egil. She took the socket off his arm and deadened the arm so that Egil didn't feel any pain when she trimmed the stump. Then she put life-herbs on it, wrapped it in silk and held it firmly for the rest of the day. Egil could feel the life flow in. The old hag put him to bed and told him to stay there until his hand was healed. It was fully healed in three days, and now he found the hand no stiffer than it had been when the arm was still whole, though it appeared to have a red thread around it.

They asked the old hag what she would advise them to do, and she told them to stay there till the wedding.

'My partner, Skrogg, lives not far from here and if we manage to outwit my brothers, I'd like Skrogg and myself to profit from it.' So time passed till Christmas.

15. The Wedding

Now we take up the story at the point where the brothers Gaut and Hildir called the giants together to a meeting, to which they came from all over Jotunheim. Skrogg, as the giants' lawman, was there as well. The two princesses were led before the gathering with the masterpieces they had created. Brynhild had made a carpet with this remarkable property, that you could fly on it through the air and land wherever you wanted. You could even carry a heavy load on it. Bekkhild had made a shirt that no weapon could bite, nor would anyone wearing it ever grow tired when swimming.

Now an argument started about which of the sisters had shown the greater skill. The final decision was a matter for all the giants, but they couldn't reach an agreement, so Skrogg was asked to make the award. His verdict was that Brynhild was the more beautiful of the two, and that her carpet was made with the greater skill, 'and so Gaut shall be the king and marry Brynhild, but each brother rule over half the kingdom.'

After that the assembly broke up.

The brothers invited the leaders and all the most important people to the double wedding.

Skrogg came back home and told the old hag what had happened at the assembly and when the wedding was to be. They talked things over for some time and she told him that she wanted to help the brothers. She asked him to come with a large following and whatever else they needed. Skrogg said he would do as she wanted.

When the time had come for the wedding the old hag, and the foster-brothers with her, got ready to go. One of them was to be called Fjalar and the other Frosti. She made them look into the mirror, and then they seemed the size of giants, though much better-looking. She provided them with the right sort of clothes, and so they travelled on till they came to the brothers' residence called Gjallandi Bridge. The giants were drinking; and when the old hag walked into the cave, each glanced at the other. She went up to Gaut and gave him a polite greeting.

He made a proper acknowledgement. 'This is something that's never happened before, your paying us a visit,' he said.

'Things aren't quite as they should be,' she answered. 'Relations have been pretty cool between us till now, and I won't deny that I'm to blame for that. I realize now, my dear Gaut, that you've good luck on your side: you've found an excellent wife, and as my contribution I'd like to offer something we've quarrelled over in the past. I'm going to give you that fine ring, a perfect bed-gift for your wife, and my friendship with it. We owe it to our family ties to be generous to each other.'

Gaut said he was truly grateful '– and, by the way, where did you find these good-looking men?'

She told him they were the sons of King Dumb of the Dumb Sea, 'and you won't easily find anyone in Jotunheim to equal them, particularly in matters of etiquette. I'd meant them to be in attendance at your wedding.'

Then she handed the ring over to Gaut who thanked her for it. She was to serve at the wedding, everything was to be done exactly as Fjalar and Frosti wanted, and they were given keys to all the money boxes.

The guests were now beginning to arrive and soon there was a large gathering. The old hag was in charge, and everything had to be done according to her instructions. Skrogg the Lawman was the most respected of all the honoured guests.

The old hag explained in a whisper to the sisters who her companions were. 'So you can cheer up, now,' she added.

This made them very happy, for they hadn't felt particularly enthusiastic about their wedding, but the giants were delighted to see them in a cheerful mood and thanked their kinswoman for her good services. When all the guests had been settled and the brothers had sat down, the brides were led inside. The giants were making boorish jokes in loud voices. Skrogg the Lawman was sitting on one side with the farmers, and Gaut and Hildir on the opposite bench with their own followers. Eagle-Beak was sitting next to the brides, and helped by some other huge ladies she gave them advice about how they should conduct themselves. Fjalar and Frosti served the ladies and there was no shortage of strong drink.

So as the evening wore on, the guests were becoming quite drunk. Then Eagle-Beak got to her feet and called the lawman and the foster-brothers over to her, telling them to bring in the wedding presents. The magic carpet, the shirt, the fine chess set that belonged to the brothers, the fine ring that had belonged to Eagle-Beak, and many other things of value were carried into the cave. Skrogg the Lawman handed over the wedding presents, and the old hag took them into her charge. She spread the carpet on the ground, put the other treasures on top, and told her daughter Skin-Beak to fetch the gold and silver.

Eagle-Beak went back into the cave and asked Frosti to come with her. They went to the place where Gaut and Brynhild were meant to sleep. She told Frosti that behind the bedpost he'd find Gaut's famous sword, the only weapon that could wound him. She also said that Fjalar and Hildir would be meeting again in another place, and warned the foster-brothers to be ready for a test of their manhood.

After that Eagle-Beak went back to the main cave and called out that it was bedtime for the brides. Fjalar and Frosti took the brides by the hand and settled them down on the carpet. Then the old hag made the carpet take off. She gave her daughter the mirror and told her to go to the entrance of the cave and hold the mirror to the face of all those who came out. The sisters soared in the air on the carpet, along with everything that was on it.

Now a lively dance started up in the cave as the bridegrooms were about to be led outside.

16. Casualties

The cave had three doors. Skrogg the Lawman with his party was in charge of one of them and Skin-Beak was in charge of the door through which the common people went. The bridegrooms were led through the third door and just outside it were two smaller caves on either side, hung with fine tapestries, where they were to sleep.

When the two giants had passed through the door, each of them went into his own room. Egil accompanied Hildir into one, walking ahead. As Hildir entered the cave Egil turned on him, got hold of his hair and swung his short-sword, aiming at the throat, but Hildir struck back at him quickly, so Egil was knocked against the rock face, and the skin of his forehead broken. It was quite a wound and bled freely, but the short-sword caught the giant's nose and sliced it off. The severed piece was big enough to make a full load for a horse. Hildir managed to get outside and shouted that he had been tricked. The giants inside heard this and made a rush for the exit, but didn't find it easy to get by. At one door Skrogg the Lawman killed all who tried to get out and at the other Skin-Beak blinded everyone with the mirror. So the giants ran to and fro inside the cave, not knowing which way to turn and roaring and banging about.

Gaut heard this and realized what must have happened. When he came to his private cave he saw that the bride was missing, so he rushed over to the bed intending to grab his sword, but found it missing too. Asmund raised the sword and aimed at Gaut, though he didn't take account of the low ceiling, so the sword caught the rock and bit through it. But the point of the sword caught Gaut's eyebrow, cut down through the eye, the cheekbone and collarbone, and sliced clean through the breast to sever the ribs. Gaut managed to get outside where he picked up a huge boulder and hurled it at Asmund, hitting him in the chest and knocking him flat. Gaut made an effort to rush towards him but his entrails got tangled up with his feet and he dropped down dead.

Asmund stood up and began looking around for Egil. At last he came to where Egil and Hildir were fighting it out. Blood was pouring out of Egil's eye from the wound he'd received, and his strength was obviously failing. Asmund caught hold of both Hildir's feet, Egil held on to his head and between them they broke his neck. That was the end of him.

Asmund and Egil went back to Skrogg the Lawman. He'd killed ninety giants, and the rest of them were begging for mercy. The giants who went out through the door guarded by Skin-Beak walked straight over the cliff and killed themselves.

The foster-brothers spent the night in the cave and Eagle-Beak joined them there. In the morning they got hold of all the valuables in the cave and went back home with the old hag. The sisters had already arrived and were delighted to see them. They all stayed there over winter and enjoyed the finest hospitality.

In the spring they got ready to set out and rejoin their own men, but before parting they gave Jotunheim to Eagle-Beak and Skrogg the Lawman. Everyone parted the best of friends. The foster-brothers took away with them all the treasures mentioned above. They came to their own men in the last week of winter and there was a happy reunion between them.

As soon as the wind was favourable they put to sea and kept going until they got back to King Hertrygg.

17. *Another Wedding*

King Hertrygg gave them and his daughters a great welcome. They brought him a good many treasures and told him exactly what had happened to them on the trip. The king thanked them handsomely for the journey they had made.

A little later the king called the people to a meeting, and reminded them of the promise he had made to the man who found his daughters. The king asked the foster-brothers whether they'd prefer to get their reward in gold and silver, but both gave the same reply, that they'd rather have his daughters as long as the girls were willing to marry them. The girls knew that the foster-brothers had saved their lives and said they wouldn't want any other men for husbands if they could marry these. So the outcome was that Egil married Bekkhild and Asmund married Brynhild.

The king had preparations made for a wedding feast. Egil said he wanted first to go back home to see if his father was still alive and what his hopes might be concerning the throne, which he thought he had a right to. Asmund said he wanted to go east to Tartary to invite his foster-brother Herraud to the wedding. The time for the wedding was fixed and also the time for their return. There's nothing to say about their travels except that they went well.

When Egil arrived in Gotaland, he went to see his father who completely failed to recognize him, as he thought he must have died long before. He told his father in detail what had happened to him (as we've already described it here) and showed the scar on his wrist where his hand had been cut off. He showed him too the socketed sword the dwarf had made him. They asked the dwarf Regin to fix a handle on it, and after that it was a fine weapon. Egil invited his father, mother and sister to the wedding and when they came to King Hertrygg, Herraud and Asmund had already arrived.

The king gave them all a splendid welcome and it wasn't very long before a great feast was in full swing. There were many different kinds of musical instrument to be heard there and many distinguished people to be seen. No expense had been spared to get the best of everything available in that part of the world.

During the feast Egil and Asmund entertained the guests with stories about their travels, and it's said that to prove the truth of their tale, both Skin-Beak and Eagle-Beak were there and vouched for their story. Queen Ingibjorg recognized Eagle-Beak, and they were fully reconciled.

The feast lasted a whole month, and when it was over all the guests went back home with splendid gifts. Egil gave Herraud the shirt that Bekkhild had made and Asmund gave him the ring that had belonged to the old hag and the sword as well, that had belonged to Gaut.

King Hertrygg was getting on in years, so he asked Egil to stay with him. He said he didn't expect to live much longer. Egil said he wanted first to go home to Gotaland but that he would be back within twelve months, and the king gave his permission. Asmund invited Herraud to come with him to Halogaland and Herraud agreed to go.

Eagle-Beak went back home to Jotunheim: Queen Ingibjorg gave her a butter-keg so big she could only just lift it and said they would think it a rare thing in Jotunheim. Asmund gave her two flanks of bacon so heavy they weighed a ton. The old hag appreciated these gifts more than if she'd been given a load of gold, and they all parted the best of friends.

18. The End of the Story

Asmund and Herraud embarked, and sailed off in the fine dragon-headed longship that had belonged to Visin and Bull-Bear. There's nothing to tell of their voyage until they arrived north in Halogaland. When the people there saw their dragon ship King Ottar remarked on how far these men must have come.

As soon as they landed, they pitched their tents ashore. Asmund went with eleven men to see his father and greeted him respectfully. The king failed to recognize him, but his mother knew him at once and put her arms round him. The king asked who was this stranger his wife was being so friendly to and Asmund gave him the answer. Soon an excellent feast was under way, and they spent a month there enjoying the best of hospitality. They told the king all about their travels and he thought they'd had plenty of success and good luck.

Herraud told Asmund that he wanted them to go east together to Gotaland to ask for the hand of Æsa, Hring's daughter. Asmund thought this a good idea, and as soon as the wind was favourable they sailed east to Gotaland. Egil and Hring gave them a great welcome. Herraud spoke up and asked for Æsa's hand. This was well received and she was given to him with a large dowry. The wedding was celebrated at once and the feast went very well.

After the feast Egil and Herraud sailed to the Baltic, but Asmund stayed behind as he was to be king of Gotaland should Hring die. By the time they got back to Tartary King Hertrygg was dead, so Egil was made king, and he and Bekkhild lived there from then on. Herraud took over his own kingdom a little later. Neither of them came north to Scandinavia after that.

Asmund went back home to Halogaland and ruled there for many years. His son Armod married Edny, daughter of King Hakon Hamundarson of Denmark, and a great progeny has come down from them. This Armod was killed in his bath by Starkad the Old, and that was Starkad's last crime.

Brynhild didn't live long, so Asmund married again. His second wife was the daughter of Sultan, the king of the Saracens. Asmund was supposed to come to the wedding in a single ship, as they intended to trick him, but Asmund had a ship built that he called the *Gnod*, the biggest ship known to have been built north of the Ægean Sea. Because of this ship he was nicknamed Gnod-Asmund, and he is considered the greatest of all the ancient kings who did not rule over the major kingdoms.

Asmund was killed near Læso Island and over three thousand men with him. It's said that Odin ran him through with a spear and that Asmund jumped overboard, but the *Gnod* sank to the bottom with its cargo and nothing of the ship or the cargo has ever been found.

And so we end this story.

Thorstein Mansion-Might

1. Mansion-Might

About the time Earl Hakon Sigurdarson was ruler of Norway, there was a farmer called Brynjolf Camel living in Gaulardale, a landed man and a great fighter.

Brynjolf was married to Dagny, the daughter of Jarnskeggi of Yrjar, and they had a son called Thorstein, a tall strong man, harsh-minded and unflinching, no matter who he was dealing with. Thorstein was the biggest man in Norway, so big that in the whole country there was hardly a door he could walk through without some difficulty, and since he seemed to be a bit too well-developed for most houses he got the name of Thorstein Mansion-Might. Thorstein was so unfriendly, his father gave him a ship with some men, and he spent the time alternately plundering and trading, and was equally successful at both.

It was about this time that King Olaf Tryggvason came to the throne of Norway, after Earl Hakon's throat was slit by his own slave Thormod Kark. Thorstein became Olaf's retainer, and the king thought highly of him for his courage, but the other retainers had no great liking for him. He seemed to them too rough and unyielding. The king used to send Thorstein on dangerous missions that other retainers refused to undertake, but sometimes Thorstein would go on trading trips to buy things of value for the king.

2. To the Underworld

One morning, when Thorstein was lying off the Finnish coast waiting for a favourable wind, he went ashore, and when the sun was in the south-east he came to a clearing. There was a beautiful mound in the clearing and on top of it stood a bald-headed boy.

'Mother,' he was calling, 'hand me my crooked stick and gloves, I want to go for a witch-ride. They're having a celebration down below in the Underworld.'

Then a crooked stick, shaped like a poker, was thrown out of the mound. The boy put on the gloves and sat astride the stick and started riding it, as children often do.

Thorstein went up on to the mound and repeated the boy's words. Right away a stick and a pair of gloves were thrown out, and a voice asked, 'Who is it wants these?'

'Your son, Bjalfi,' said Thorstein.

Thorstein got astride the stick and rode after the boy. They came to a wide river and plunged into it and it was as if they were wading through smoke. After some time the mist cleared before their eyes and they came to where the river was cascading over a cliff. Thorstein saw a thickly populated district and a large town.

They made their way towards the town, and found the people there sitting at table. They walked into the palace where crowds of people were drinking from silver cups. There was a table standing on the floor. Everything seemed to be golden in colour, and nothing was drunk but wine. Then Thorstein realized that they were both invisible to the people there.

The bald-headed boy moved along the tables picking up from the floor all the titbits that fell down.

A king and queen were sitting on the throne, and all the people inside were enjoying themselves. Then Thorstein saw a man come into the hall and greet the king. The newcomer said he had been sent by the earl who ruled over Mount Lucanus in India, and explained to the king that he was an elf-man. He presented the king with a gold ring. The king thought he had never seen a more exquisite ring and it was passed around the hall for everyone to admire. This ring could be taken apart in four sections. Thorstein noticed another fine thing that appealed to him very strongly, and that was the cloth on the royal table. It had stripes of gold and was set with twelve precious stones, the best there are. Thorstein had to have the tablecloth, and it struck him that he might try out King Olaf's luck, and see whether he could get the ring. Now Thorstein saw that the king was about to put the ring on his finger, so he grabbed it and with the other hand took hold of the cloth, spilling all the food into the mud. Then Thorstein ran for the door, leaving the crooked stick behind.

At once a great uproar broke out. Some men ran outside, saw which way he had gone and started after him. He could see now that they might soon catch up with him, so he called out, 'If you are as good, King Olaf, as my faith in you is strong, help me now.'

Thorstein ran so fast that the pursuers couldn't intercept him before he came to the river, but there he had to stop. They set on him from all sides, but Thorstein gave a good account of himself, and had killed a number of them when his companion appeared with the crooked stick, and at once they both plunged into the river.

Eventually they got back to the mound they had started from, and now the sun was in the west. The boy threw the stick into the mound and the sack as well, which he had filled with choice food, and Thorstein did the same. The bald-headed boy ran into the mound but Thorstein waited outside at the skylight. He saw two women in the mound, one of them weaving a precious cloth and the other rocking a baby.

The younger one said, 'What can be holding up Bjalfi, your brother?'

'He didn't come with me today,' said the bald-headed boy.

'Who took the crooked stick?' she asked.

'That was Thorstein Mansion-Might,' said Bald-Head, 'King Olaf's retainer. He got us into a lot of trouble by stealing those treasures from the Underworld, the like of which aren't to be found in Norway, and we came very close to being killed when he threw his stick right into their hands. While they were chasing him to his death I brought the stick back to him. He's certainly a very brave man and I've no idea how many he may have killed.' With that the mound closed.

Thorstein went back to his men, and sailed off to Norway. He found King Olaf in Oslofjord, gave him the treasures and told the story of his travels, which made a great impression on everyone. The king offered to give Thorstein big estates, but he said he wanted to take one more trip to the east. Then he stayed with the king over winter.

3. *The Dwarf*

In the spring Thorstein made his ship ready and gathered a crew of twenty-four men. He sailed first to Jamtland, and one day when he was lying in harbour there he went ashore for a stroll. He came to a clearing and saw a hideous-looking dwarf standing there beside a huge boulder, screaming at the top of his voice. It seemed to Thorstein as if the dwarf's mouth was twisted up to the ear on one side, and on the other side the nose overlapped the mouth. Thorstein asked the dwarf why he was acting like a madman.

'No wonder, man!' said the dwarf. 'Can't you see that great eagle flying over there? It's got hold of my son. It must be a devil sent by Odin himself. It would kill me to lose that child.'

Thorstein aimed a shot at the eagle, hitting it under the wings, and the bird dropped down dead. Thorstein caught the dwarf's boy as he fell and gave him back to his father. The dwarf was very happy and said, 'My son and I owe you a great debt for saving his life, and now I'd like you to choose your own reward in gold and silver.'

'You'd better see to your son first,' said Thorstein, 'and anyway, I'm not in the habit of taking money just for showing my talents.'

'That doesn't make my duty to repay you any the less,' said the dwarf. 'I don't suppose you'd consider accepting my sheep's wool shirt? You'll never get tired at swimming and never be wounded as long as you wear it next to your skin.'

Thorstein tried on the shirt and it was a perfect fit although it had seemed too small for the dwarf. He also took a silver ring from his purse and gave it to Thorstein, warning him to take good care of it, for he would never be short of money as long as he kept the ring.

Then the dwarf gave Thorstein a black flint. 'If you hide this in the palm of your hand no one can see you. There aren't any other useful things I can give you, except for a bit of marble I want you to have just for your amusement.'

He took this bit of marble from his purse and with it a steel point. The marble was triangular in shape, white in the centre and one of the sides was red, with a yellow ring around it.

The dwarf said, 'If you prick the white part with the point, a hail-storm will come, so fierce no one will be able to face it. When you want to thaw out the snow, you have only to prick the yellow part and the sun will shine and melt it all away. But when you prick the red part, fire and flames and a shower of sparks will come flying out that no one will be able to bear. Besides that, you can hit anything you aim at with the point and the marble, and they'll both come back into your hands when you call for them. This is all the reward I can give you for now.'

Thorstein thanked him for the gifts and went back to his men, feeling that this trip had not been altogether wasted. Then they got a favourable wind and sailed on to the east, but soon they ran into fogs and lost their bearings. For a whole fortnight they had no idea where they were going.

4. Giantland

One evening they realized that they were close to land, so they cast anchor and lay there overnight. In the morning the weather was fine, with bright sunshine. They saw that they were in a long narrow fjord, with lovely wooded slopes on either side. No one on board could identify this land. They could see no living thing anywhere, neither beast nor bird. So they set up their tents ashore and made themselves comfortable.

The following morning Thorstein said to his men, 'I'll tell you what I have in mind. Wait for me here for six days while I go and explore this country.'

They weren't at all happy about this and insisted they wanted to go with him, but Thorstein wouldn't have it. 'If I don't come back before the seventh sunset,' he said, 'you're to sail back home and tell King Olaf that it's not my fate to return.'

They walked with him as far as the wood and then he vanished out of sight. They made their way back to the ship and waited there as they had been told.

Thorstein walked on through the forest all day without noticing anything particular, but towards evening he came to a wide road and followed it till dusk. Then he turned off the road and made for a huge oak tree. He climbed it and found there was plenty of room to lie down, so he slept there through the night.

At sunrise he heard a great deal of noise and some voices and saw twenty-two men riding hard past the tree. Thorstein was amazed to see how big they were – he had never seen men of this size before. He put on his clothes, and the morning passed till the sun was in the south-east.

5. Godmund of Glasir Plains

Then Thorstein saw three horsemen riding up, fully armed and so enormous, he had never seen such men. The one in the middle was the tallest, and was wearing gold-trimmed clothes and riding a pale dun horse. His two companions wore scarlet clothing and rode on grey horses.

When they were opposite the tree where Thorstein was hiding the leader said, 'What's that moving in the oak?'

Thorstein climbed down to meet them but when he greeted them they all burst out laughing. The tall man said, 'It's not every day that we see someone like you. What's your name, and where are you from?'

Thorstein gave his name, and added that he was also known as Mansion-Might. 'My family belongs to Norway, and I'm King Olaf's man.'

The tall man smiled and said, 'This regal splendour of his must be a great lie, if he has nobody braver-looking than you. In my opinion you ought to be called Mansion-Midget, not Mansion-Might.'

'Give me a naming-gift, then,' said Thorstein.

The tall man took a gold ring off his finger and gave it to Thorstein.

'What name are you called by?' asked Thorstein, 'What's your background, and what's the name of this country?'

'I'm called Godmund, and I'm the ruler of Glasir Plains; this country's a dependency of Giantland. I'm a king's son, and these are my companions, Full-Strong and All-Strong. Did you by any chance see some riders pass by this morning?'

'Twenty-two men rode past here,' said Thorstein, 'and they weren't exactly unobtrusive.'

'Those would be my lads,' said Godmund. 'The neighbouring country's called Jotunheim and there's a king called Geirrod ruling it just now. We're tributaries under him. My father, Ulfhedin Trusty, was known as Godmund, as all the other rulers of Glasir Plains have been. He travelled over to Geirrod's town to hand over his tribute to the king, but during this trip my father died, so King Geirrod has asked me to a funeral feast in my father's honour, and to take my father's titles as well. But we're not happy about being ruled by giants.'

'Why did your men ride ahead of you?' asked Thorstein.

'There's a great river that divides our countries. It's known as the Hemra and it's so deep and swift the only horses that can ford it are the three we're riding on. The rest of my men have to ride as far as the source of the river, but we'll all meet tonight.'

'It could be amusing to go with you and see what happens there,' said Thorstein.

'I'm not so sure about that,' said Godmund, 'I suppose you're a Christian.'

'I can take care of myself,' said Thorstein.

'I shouldn't want you to come to any harm on my account,' said Godmund. 'But if King Olaf will give us his good luck, I'm willing to risk taking you with us.'

Thorstein gave his word, so Godmund told Thorstein to get up behind him, which is what he did.

They rode as far as the river. On the bank there was a hut and from it they took a set of clothes for themselves and their horses. These clothes were made so that the water couldn't touch them, for the river was so cold that it would cause instant gangrene to any part of the body that came into contact with the water. They forded the river, with the horses struggling hard, but Godmund's horse stumbled, so Thorstein got his toe wet, and gangrene set in at once. When they got out of the river they spread their clothes on the ground to dry. Thorstein cut off his toe, and they were immensely impressed by his toughness. Then they rode on their way.

Thorstein told them there was no need for them to hide him. 'I can make myself a helmet of invisibility, so nobody can see me,' he added. Godmund said this was a useful skill to have. When they arrived at Geirrodstown, Godmund's men came to meet them, and they rode all together into the town. They could hear the sound of all kinds of instruments, but Thorstein didn't think much of the tune. King Geirrod came out to meet them and gave them a good welcome. They were shown to a stone-house or hall where they were meant to sleep and their horses were taken to the stable.

Godmund was escorted into the royal palace where the king was sitting on the throne and beside him Earl Agdi, ruler of Grundir which lies between Giantland and Jotunheim. Agdi had his residence at a place called Gnipalund; he was a sorcerer and his men were more like giant trolls than human beings.

Godmund sat down on a footstool beside the high-seat opposite the king. It was their custom that no prince could take his seat on the throne until he had assumed his father's titles and the first toast had been drunk.

Soon an excellent feast was well under way, with everyone drinking and having a good time. When it was over the guests went to sleep, and as soon as Godmund came back to his quarters Thorstein made himself visible again. They all laughed at him until Godmund told them who he was and asked them not to make fun of him.

So they slept soundly through the night.

6. Drinking

Early in the morning they all got up, and Godmund was led to the royal palace. The king gave him a good welcome. 'What I'd like to know now,' he said, 'is whether you're willing to show me the same obedience as your father. If so, I'm willing to add to your titles and let you keep Giantland as long as you swear me an oath of loyalty.'

Godmund answered, 'It isn't lawful to demand oaths of a man as young as me.'

'Have it your way,' said the king.

Then he took a cloak of precious material and laid it over Godmund and gave him the title of king. Geirrod picked up a large drinking-horn and gave a toast to Godmund, who took the horn and thanked the king. Then Godmund stood up, stepped on to the foot-board in front of the high-seat before the king and made a solemn vow that he would neither serve nor obey any other king as long as Geirrod lived. The king thanked him for that and said it pleased him more than if he had sworn him formal oaths. Then Godmund emptied the horn and returned to his seat. Everyone was cheerful and happy.

Earl Agdi had two men with him, called Jokul and Frosti, both very jealous men. Now Jokul took hold of an ox-bone and hurled it at Godmund's men. Thorstein saw this, caught it in flight, and sent it back where it came from, hitting a man called Gust right in the face, breaking his nose and every tooth in his mouth, and knocking him senseless.

This annoyed King Geirrod and he asked who was hurling bones over his table, adding that before it was all over they would find out which of them had the strongest throwing-arm.

Then King Geirrod called over two men, Drott and Hosvir.

'Go and fetch my gold ball, and bring it here,' he told them.

Off they went, and came back with a seal's head weighing two hundred pounds. It was red-hot, with sparks flashing from it like a forge fire and fat dripping from it like burning tar.

The king said, 'Take the ball now and throw it to each other. Anyone who drops it will be made an outlaw and forfeit all his property: and anyone afraid to throw the ball will be thought a coward.'

7. The Ball-game

Now Drott hurled the ball at Full-Strong who caught it with one hand, but Thorstein realized that Full-Strong's strength was not quite sufficient so he threw his weight against the ball. Together they flung the ball at Frosti, because all the champions were standing in front of the benches on either side. Frosti caught the ball with firm hands but it went so close to his face that the cheek-bone was broken. He threw the ball back at All-Strong who caught it with both hands, but his knee would have given way had Thorstein not supported him.

All-Strong hurled the ball at Earl Agdi who caught it with both hands, but the burning fat from the ball splashed on to his beard, setting it on fire, so he was in a hurry to get rid of the ball and hurled it at King Godmund, who threw it at King Geirrod, but he dodged out of the way so the ball hit Drott and Hosvir, killing them both. The ball travelled on through a glass window and splashed into the moat that surrounded the town. Flames erupted from it, and that was the end of the game. Earl Agdi said he felt shivers down the spine every time he came anywhere near Godmund's men.

In the evening Godmund and his men went to sleep. They thanked Thorstein for all his help and protection from danger. He told them it was nothing – 'but what sort of entertainment can we expect tomorrow?'

'The king will make us wrestle,' said Godmund. 'They'll try to get their own back on us, since they're much stronger than we are.'

'King Olaf's luck will strengthen us,' said Thorstein. 'Don't forget, let the scuffle take you over towards me.'

So they slept through the night.

In the morning everyone went to his own favourite kind of entertainment while the servants were laying the tables. King Geirrod asked the guests whether they would like to wrestle, and they said they would if that was what he wanted, so they stripped and the wrestling match began. It seemed to Thorstein that he'd never seen such a clash, for whenever someone was thrown the whole place shook. It was obvious that Earl Agdi's men were losing the contest.

Frosti stepped on to the floor and said, 'Who's going to take me on?'

'I daresay someone will,' said Full-Strong.

They set about each other and there was a fierce struggle between them. Frosti was much the stronger, and the scuffle took them close to Godmund. Frosti heaved Full-Strong up to his chest, but had to bend his knees. Then Thorstein kicked him behind the knees so Frosti fell flat on his back with Full-Strong on top. The back of Frosti's head was broken, and so were his elbows.

He got slowly to his feet and said, 'You're not playing singles in this game. And what makes you smell so foul?'

'Your nose is too close to your own mouth,' said Full-Strong.

Now Jokul got up and All-Strong turned on him. Their clash was the hardest yet, but Jokul seemed the more powerful and dragged All-Strong to the bench where Thorstein was. Then Jokul tried hard to force All-Strong away from there, but Thorstein held on to him. Jokul pulled so hard that his feet sank into the floor, ankle-deep, then Thorstein suddenly pushed All-Strong away from him, so that Jokul fell flat on his back and dislocated his leg.

All-Strong went back to his seat, but Jokul got slowly to his feet and said, 'We can't see everyone on that bench.'

Geirrod asked Godmund whether he wouldn't join in the wrestling, and Godmund said that although he'd never wrestled before he wouldn't turn down the offer. The king ordered Earl Agdi to avenge his men, and he replied that although he'd given up wrestling long ago, he would do what the king wanted.

So they stripped off their clothes. Thorstein thought he had never seen a body more inhuman than Agdi's, for it was black as death. Godmund rose to his feet to meet him, and his skin was very white. Earl Agdi went for him in a rage, and gripped Godmund's ribs so hard he went right through to the bone. They staggered about all over the hall and when they came to Thorstein, Godmund tried to put down the earl with a hip-throw and swung him hard around. Thorstein threw himself under the earl's feet, toppling him over so he crashed on his nose. Not only his thieving nose was broken, but four teeth as well. The earl stood up and said, 'An old man always takes a nasty fall, but never nastier than when it's three to one.'

At that they put their clothes back on.

8. More Drinking

After this the king and his guests sat down at table. Earl Agdi and the others said they must have been tricked in some way. 'I always feel hot under the collar whenever I'm in their company.'

'Leave it be,' said the king; 'someone will turn up to make us wiser.'

Then the drinking began, and two horns were carried into the hall. They belonged to Earl Agdi and were very precious. The horns, called the Whitings, were two yards long and all inlaid with gold.

The king sent one horn to either side. 'Each man is to empty the horn in one go and anybody who can't manage it shall pay the steward an ounce of silver.'

Only the champions could drink it up in a single draught, but Thorstein saw to it that none of Godmund's men was penalized. When this was over, the drinking continued in a lighter mood for the rest of the day, and in the evening the men went to sleep.

Godmund thanked Thorstein for all his help, and Thorstein asked him when the feast would be over.

'My men have to leave in the morning,' said Godmund. 'I know the king will try to get his own back when he shows off his treasures. He'll have his great drinking horn brought into the hall, called Grim the Good, a magnificent treasure, ornamented with gold, and with magical powers. There's a man's head on the narrow point, with flesh and a mouth, and it can talk to people and tell them what the future holds for them and warn them when there's trouble ahead. It will be the death of us all if the king finds out that we've had a Christian with us. We'll have to be very generous to Grim.'

Thorstein said that Grim wouldn't be able to say any more than King Olaf would let him. 'I think Geirrod's a doomed man. If you'll take my advice, you'll do as I tell you from now on. Tomorrow I'm going to show myself.'

They said it would be a terrible risk, but Thorstein replied that Geirrod wanted them all out of the way. 'What else can you tell me about Grim the Good?' he asked.

'First, that the horn is so long, an average man can stand upright in the curve. The ornamental rim round the opening is a yard wide and while their greatest drinker can drink so deep into the horn, only the king can finish it all in one go. Everybody is supposed to give Grim something valuable, but the greatest honour you can show him is to empty the horn in one go. I know I'm supposed to be the first to drink from the horn, but there isn't a mortal man good enough to finish it off in one.'

Thorstein said, 'You'd better put on my shirt, because if you do, nothing can harm you, not even poison in the drink. Take the crown off your head, give it to Grim the Good and whisper into his ear that you'll show him much greater honour than Geirrod does, and then pretend to be drinking. But since there's going to be poison in the horn, pour the drink under your clothes, and then it won't hurt you, but when all the drinking is over you'd better arrange for your men to ride away.'

Godmund told him to have it his way. 'If Geirrod dies, the whole of Jotunheim belongs to me, but if he lives much longer, we're sure to be killed.'

So they slept through the night.

9. Grim the Good

In the morning they were up early and dressed. Then King Geirrod came and asked them to drink his health, which they did. First they drank from the Whitings and then from the loving-cups. After that the toasts dedicated to Thor and Odin were drunk. Then various musical instruments all came playing into the hall, and two men, both rather smaller than Thorstein, carried in Grim the Good between them. All the people got to their feet, then knelt down before him, but there was an ugly look about Grim.

Geirrod spoke to Godmund, 'Take Grim the Good and let this toast bind you to your pledge.'

Godmund went over to Grim, took off his gold crown, put it on Grim's head, and whispered into his ear as Thorstein had instructed him. Next, he poured the poisonous drink into his shirt. After he had drunk in this way to King Geirrod's health, he kissed the point of the horn and Grim was taken away from him with a smile on his face.

Geirrod took the full horn and asked Grim to bring him good luck and warn him if there was any danger about. 'I've often seen you in a happier mood,' he said.

He took a gold necklace he was wearing and gave it to Grim, and then he drank a toast to Earl Agdi. It was like a sea-wave crashing over a skerry as the drink cascaded down his throat. He drank it all up, but Grim only shook his head. Then the horn was carried over to

Earl Agdi who gave Grim two gold bracelets and asked him for mercy. He drank it up in three draughts and handed the horn back to the cup-bearer.

Grim said, 'The older the man, the feebler.'

Then the horn was filled yet again, this time for Jokul and Full-Strong to drink from. Full-Strong was the first to drink. Jokul took it from him, looked into it and said he had drunk like a weakling, then hit at Full-Strong with the horn, but he hit back and drove his fist against Jokul's nose, breaking his thievish chin, and scattering his teeth. This caused quite an uproar. Geirrod told them not to let it be put about that they'd parted on such bad terms, so they were reconciled and Grim the Good was borne out.

10. *Geirrod's Death*

A little later a man came walking into the hall. Everyone was amazed to see how tiny he was, but it was Thorstein Mansion-Midget. He turned to Godmund and told him his horses were ready now. Geirrod asked who that little child was.

Godmund said, 'This is my servant-boy that Odin sent me. He's a real king's treasure and knows a trick or two. If you think you could use him I'm willing to give him to you.'

'He seems a striking little lad,' said the king. 'I'd like to see him in action.' He asked Thorstein to perform some trick or other.

Thorstein took his marble and point and when he started pricking the white part, there was such a terrible hail-storm that no one dared open his eyes, and snow piled up in the hall ankle-deep. This made the king laugh. Then Thorstein pricked the yellow part of the marble, and blazing-hot sunshine burst out over the hall, thawing all the snow in a moment. With this came a sweet fragrance and the king said that Thorstein was indeed a clever fellow.

Thorstein said he had still one more trick up his sleeve, one called the Scourge. The king wanted to see it, so Thorstein stepped into the middle of the floor and pricked the red part of the marble. Sparks began flashing from it, and Thorstein ran all over the hall to every seat, with more and more sparks flying from the marble, so that everyone had to cover his eyes; but King Geirrod only laughed. The fires grew until everyone felt it was getting beyond a joke. Thorstein had warned Godmund beforehand that this was the time for him to go outside and get away on horseback.

Thorstein ran up to Geirrod and asked, 'Do you still want more of this game?'

'Yes, let me see more, boy,' he said.

So Thorstein pricked harder than ever and the sparks flew into Geirrod's eyes. Thorstein rushed to the door, and threw the marble and point straight into Geirrod's eyes, knocking him dead on to the floor. When Thorstein got outside Godmund had already mounted.

Thorstein said they must ride off at once. 'This is no place for weaklings,' he said.

They rode over to the river and by that time the marble and point had come back. Thorstein told them that Geirrod was dead. So they forded the river and rode on to the spot where Thorstein had first met them.

'Now we must part,' said Thorstein. 'My men will be thinking it's time for me to join them.'

'Come home with me,' said Godmund, 'I'll repay all the help you've given us.'

'I'll come for that some other time,' said Thorstein. 'But you'd better go back to Geirrodstown with plenty of men. You can take control of the whole country now.'

'Whatever you say,' said Godmund. 'Give King Olaf my regards.'

Then he handed Thorstein a golden bowl, a silver dish and a gold-embroidered towel to take to King Olaf. Godmund asked Thorstein to come and visit him, and they parted the best of friends.

11. Back to Norway

Next Thorstein caught sight of Earl Agdi who was storming along in a titanic fury. Thorstein followed him until they came to the large farmstead where Agdi lived. There was a young woman standing at the gate to the orchard, Agdi's daughter. Her name was Gudrun, and she was a tall, good-looking girl. She greeted her father and asked him the news.

'There's news enough,' he said. 'King Geirrod's dead. Godmund of Glasir Plains has tricked us all and hidden a Christian there called Thorstein Mansion-Midget. He's thrown fire into our eyes, but now I'm on my way to kill his men.'

Earl Agdi threw down the Whitings and ran into the wood as if he were out of his mind.

Thorstein went up to Gudrun. She greeted him and asked him his name and he told her he was called Thorstein Mansion-Midget, one of King Olaf's men.

'His biggest must be very big indeed, if you're the midget,' she said.

'Will you come with me and embrace our faith?' said Thorstein.

'There's not much here to keep me happy,' she said. 'My mother's dead. She was the daughter of Earl Ottar of Novgorod, and she wasn't a bit like my father in temperament. There's a lot of the giant about him. I can see now that he's doomed, so if you promise to bring me back here, I'll go with you.'

She collected her things, and Thorstein took the Whitings. They went into the wood and saw Agdi going about screaming, with his hands over his eyes. Two things had happened simultaneously; as he caught sight of Thorstein's ship he felt a terrible pain in his thief's eyes and went blind.

It was sunset by the time Thorstein and Gudrun reached the ship and his men were ready to sail. When they saw Thorstein, they were overjoyed. He stepped on board and they put to sea at once.

Nothing remains to be told of his voyage till he arrived home in Norway.

12. *The Wedding*

That winter King Olaf was in residence at Trondheim, and Thorstein went to see him at Christmas to bring him the gifts which Godmund had sent him and also the Whitings and many other valuable things besides.

Thorstein told the king about his travels and introduced Gudrun to him. The king thanked him warmly and everyone was very impressed and praised his courage. The king had Gudrun baptized and instructed in the Christian faith. At Christmas Thorstein played the Scourge and everyone thought it great entertainment. The Whitings were used when toasts were being drunk, with two men sharing each horn. The loving-cup Godmund had sent the king was so big that no one could drink from it except Thorstein Mansion-Midget. The towel wouldn't burn even when it was thrown on the fire: the flames only made it cleaner than before.

Thorstein mentioned to the king that he intended to marry Gudrun. The king gave his consent and there was a splendid feast. On their wedding night when they had just gone to bed, the curtain came crashing down, the panelling over Thorstein's head burst open, and through it appeared Earl Agdi whose intention was to kill Thorstein, but he was hit by such a wave of hot air he didn't dare go inside. Then King Olaf came and thumped Agdi's head with a gold-trimmed staff, hammering him right into the ground. After that, the king kept watch throughout the night.

In the morning the Whitings had vanished, but the wedding feast went ahead without a hitch. Thorstein stayed the winter with the king and he and Gudrun loved each other dearly.

In the spring Thorstein asked permission to sail to the east to see King Godmund, but King Olaf said he couldn't go unless he promised to return, so Thorstein gave his word. The king asked him to keep his faith well. 'And put more trust in yourself than in those people to the east,' he added.

They parted the best of friends, and everyone wished Thorstein good luck, as he had now become a very popular man. So he sailed to the Baltic, and as far as is known the voyage went smoothly for him. He arrived finally at Glasir Plains and Godmund gave him a good welcome.

'Have you heard anything from Geirrodstown?' asked Thorstein.

'I went there myself,' said Godmund, 'and they surrendered the country into my hands. My son Heidrek Wolf-Skin is ruling over it.'

'What happened to Earl Agdi?' said Thorstein.

'After you left, Agdi had a burial mound built for himself,' said Godmund, 'then retired into it with a great deal of money. Jokul and Frosti were drowned in the river Hemra on their way back home from the feast, so now I'm in full control of the district of Grundir as well.'

'What matters to me,' said Thorstein, 'is how much of it you're prepared to let me have, since it seems to me my wife's entitled to all the inheritance after her father, Earl Agdi.'

'You can have it all if you become my man,' said Godmund.

'Then you won't interfere with my faith?' said Thorstein.

'That's a promise,' said Godmund.

So they went to the district of Grundir and Thorstein took charge of it.

13. The End

Thorstein rebuilt the house at Gnipalund as Earl Agdi had come back from the dead and destroyed the old home. Thorstein became a great chieftain, and a little later Gudrun gave birth to a fine big boy who was called Brynjolf.

Earl Agdi couldn't restrain himself from playing tricks on Thorstein. One night Thorstein got out of bed and saw Agdi wandering about, but Agdi didn't dare go through any of the gates as there was a cross on every one of them. Thorstein went over to his mound. It was open, so he went inside and picked up the Whitings. Then Agdi came into the mound, and Thorstein ran out past him and put a cross in the doorway. The mound closed up, and since then nothing has ever been seen of Agdi.

The following summer Thorstein went back to Norway and gave King Olaf the Whitings, then got permission to go back to his own possessions. The king told him he should keep his faith well. Since then we have not heard anything about Thorstein, but when King Olaf disappeared from the Long Serpent the Whitings vanished.

And so we end the story of Thorstein Mansion-Midget.

Helgi Thorisson

1. The Woman

There was a man called Thorir farming at Raudaberg near Oslofjord in Norway. He had two sons, Helgi and Thorstein, both fine men, though Helgi was the more talented of the two. Their father was a man of some rank and enjoyed the friendship of King Olaf Tryggvason.

One summer the brothers went on a trading voyage north to Finnmark, with butter and bacon to sell to the Lapps. Their trade went very successfully, and late in the summer they sailed back south again. One day they came to the headland called Vimund where there are fine woods. They went ashore and cut themselves a certain maple tree. Helgi happened to stroll deeper into the wood than the rest of his men. Suddenly a heavy mist came down over the forest, so that he couldn't find his way back to the ship that same evening, and soon night fell and it grew very dark.

Then Helgi saw twelve women come riding through the wood, all of them on red-coloured horses and wearing red costumes. They dismounted, and all their riding-gear shone with gold. One woman was far lovelier than all the others, and they were in attendance upon this great lady.

They put out their horses to graze, then the women set up a splendid tent, with stripes of alternating colours and embroidered everywhere with gold. The points of the tent were ornamented with gold, and on top of the pole which stood up through the tent there was a great golden ball. When the women had made these preparations, they set up a table and laid it with all kinds of choice food. Then they took water to wash their hands, using a jug and basins of silver, inlaid everywhere with gold.

Helgi was standing near the tent watching them, and the great lady said to him, 'Come over here, Helgi, have something to eat and drink with us.'

So that's what he did, and he could see that the food and wine were delicious, and the cups quite splendid. When the table had been cleared, and the beds were made – these beds were much more ornate than those of other people – the great lady asked Helgi whether he would prefer to sleep alone or share a bed with her. He asked her name.

'I'm called Ingibjorg. I'm the daughter of Godmund of Glasir Plains,' she said.

'I'd like to sleep with you,' he said.

So they slept together for three successive nights.

On the third morning the weather was fine, so they got up and dressed.

'This is where we part company,' she said. 'There are two boxes here, one full of silver, the other of gold. I'm going to give you these, but you must on no account tell anyone where you got them.'

Then the women rode off the same way as they had come, and Helgi went back to the ship. They gave him a great welcome and asked him where he'd been, but he wouldn't tell.

They sailed on south along the coast until they came home to their father with plenty of money. Helgi's father and brother wanted to know where he'd got all this money in the boxes, but he said nothing.

2. The Strangers

So time passed till Christmas, and then one night a terrible gale began to blow. Thorstein said to his brother: 'We'd better get up and see what's happening to our ship.'

So that's what they did, and saw the ship was secure.

Helgi had had a dragon-head fitted on to their ship's prow, and the whole stem was decorated above the sea-line. This is how Helgi had invested part of the money Ingibjorg had given him, but some of it he'd locked in the neck of the dragon.

The brothers heard a loud crash, then two riders suddenly appeared and carried Helgi off with them. Thorstein had no idea what could have happened to him. When the weather cleared up, Thorstein went home to tell his father what had happened, and everybody thought it terrible news.

Helgi's father went at once to see King Olaf, told him all about it and asked him to find out what had happened to his son. The king said he'd do as Thorir wished but added that he very much doubted if Helgi would ever be much use to his family again. After that, Thorir returned home.

The year went by, till it was Christmas again. That winter, King Olaf was in residence at Alreksstead. On the eighth day of Christmas, in the evening, three strangers came into the hall before King Olaf as he was sitting at table. They greeted him respectfully, and the king returned their greetings. One of these men was Helgi, but no one recognized the other two.

The king asked them their names, and each said he was called Grim. 'We've been sent to you by Godmund of Glasir Plains,' they said. 'He sends you his compliments and also these two drinking-horns.'

The king accepted the horns. Precious things they were, all inlaid with gold. King Olaf owned two other drinking-horns, called the Hyrnings and thought to be great treasures, but the horns from Godmund were far better than those.

'What King Godmund wants, my lord, is for you to be his friend. He sets a higher value on your friendship than that of any other king,' they said.

The king didn't answer that, but had them shown to their seats. The king had the two horns (both also called Grim) filled with good ale and after that had them blessed by a bishop. Then the king had the horns called Grim brought to the two men called Grim, so they could take the first draught.

King Olaf said:

> These drinking horns,
> One for each guest,
> For Godmund's men
> While here they rest:

Each Grim shall drink
From his namesake,
To test the worth
Of the ale we make.

The two Grims took the horns and now they realized what the bishop must have sung over the drink.

'It's just as our King Godmund told us,' they said. 'This king is full of tricks, he exchanges evil for good, while our king treats him with the greatest honour. Let's get up and go.'

And that's what they did, causing a great stir in the hall, as they spilled the drink and put out all the lights. Then everybody heard a great crashing sound. The king prayed for God's protection, and told his men to get up and put an end to the noise, but by this time the two Grims and Helgi had got outside. When the lights were relit in the king's hall, they saw three men had been killed, with the Grim-horns lying beside their bodies.

'This is a strange business,' said the king. 'Let's hope it doesn't happen too often. People tell me Godmund of Glasir Plains is a great sorcerer and a bad man to have as an enemy. It's no joke for anyone to get into his power, even if we could do something about it.' Then the king told his men to take care of the horns and carry on drinking from them, and they gave no trouble to anyone.

The mountain pass the two Grims had travelled through on their way west down to Alreksstead is now known as Grim Pass and no one has ever used that route since.

3. The Victim

Winter passed, and the rest of the year, till it was the eighth day of Christmas once more, and the king was in church with his retainers attending Mass. Then three men came up to the church door, and one of them stayed on, but the other two went away again. This is what they said before they left: 'We've brought a skeleton for your feast, my lord, and you'll not so easily get rid of it again.'

The retainers saw that this man was Helgi. When the king went in to eat and his men tried to talk to Helgi, they realized he was blind. The king asked how things were with him and where he had been all this time. Helgi told him the whole story, how he'd met the women in the wood, how the Grims had brought the gale on him and his brother when they were trying to save their ship, and how the Grims had finally brought him to Godmund of Glasir Plains and handed him over to Ingibjorg, Godmund's daughter.

'How did you like it there?' asked the king.

'Very well,' he said. 'There's nowhere I've liked better.'

Then the king asked him about the way King Godmund lived, how many men he had, and what kind of things he did. Helgi spoke very highly of everything and answered that there was much more to be said about King Godmund than he could ever tell them.

'Why did you leave in such a hurry last winter?' said the king.

'King Godmund sent the two Grims to fool you,' said Helgi, 'and he only let me go because of your prayers, so that you could learn what had happened to me. The reason we left in such a hurry last year was that the Grims weren't able to drink the ale once you'd had it blessed. It put them into a rage to be beaten like that. They killed your men because Godmund had told them to, if they couldn't harm you personally. But he sent you the horns just to make an impression, and to take your mind off me.'

'Why did you go away this time?' asked the king.

'Because of Ingibjorg,' said Helgi. 'She said she couldn't sleep with me without feeling uneasy whenever she touched my naked body, that's mainly why I had to leave. In the long run, King Godmund didn't want to argue when he realized you were so keen to get me away from there. As for King Godmund's style and splendour, I haven't the words to describe it, nor the great numbers he had with him.'

'Why are you blind?' asked the king.

'Ingibjorg gouged out both my eyes when we parted,' said Helgi. 'She said the women in Norway wouldn't enjoy my company very long.'

'Godmund needs to be taught a proper lesson for all those killings of his, God willing,' said the king.

Then Helgi's father, Thorir, was sent for, and he couldn't thank Olaf enough for getting his son out of those monsters' hands.

Thorir went back home, but Helgi stayed on with the king and lived for exactly one more year.

King Olaf took the Grim-horns with him when he set out on his last journey. It's said that when King Olaf disappeared from the Long Serpent, the horns vanished too, and no one has ever seen them since. And this is all we can tell you about the Grims.

Appendix:
Sources and Parallels
of Arrow-Odd

Arrow-Odd has a number of features in common with other Icelandic sagas; those for example of Grim Hairy-Cheek and Ketil Trout, Odd's legendary father and grandfather. The account of how Grim Hairy-Cheek was conceived in Lappland and the story of the magic arrows are both told in these sagas. *Heidrek's Saga*, too, shares an important episode with *Arrow-Odd*, the love story of Hjalmar and Ingibjorg.

Another parallel is in the well-known *Story of a Guest* (Norna-Gestsþáttr) which describes a stranger who suddenly turns up at the court of King Olaf Tryggvason. This guest proves to be a three-hundred-year-old pagan. He can remember far back and has known many of the heroes of Germanic legend, but he also remembers his own childhood, and it is in these memories that most of the parallels with *Arrow-Odd* are to be found:

'I was brought up by my father at a place called Græning. My father had plenty of money and a splendid house. At that time there were witches who used to travel through the land, called prophetesses, and they would tell people's fortunes. That's why people used to invite them to feasts and give them gifts when they left. This is what my father did, and the witches came to him with their retinue. They were supposed to tell my fortune. I was lying in my cradle when they were discussing my fate, and there were two candles burning just above me. Two of the sorceresses spoke to me and said that I would be a very lucky man, greater than my parents or the sons of the other chieftains in the country; they ordained that all my life should turn out just like that. The youngest witch thought she was treated as someone inferior to the other two, since they failed to consult her on such momentous prophecies. And as it happens there was a group of very rough men there who pushed her out of her seat so that she fell on the floor. This made her furious, and she shouted at the others to stop giving me such favourable prospects. "I decree that he shall live no longer than it takes this candle beside him to burn up." Then the senior witch grabbed the candle and told my mother to take good care of it and not to light it until the last day of my life. After that the prophetesses went away with the young one in shackles; my father gave them handsome presents before they left. When I was a grown up man, my mother gave me this candle for safe keeping. And here it is,' said the guest.

Later in the tale King Olaf asks his guest when he would like to die, and the guest says soon. He lights the candle, and when it burns out, he dies.

Another story with affinities to *Arrow-Odd* is *Orm's Story* – incidentally, Orm is supposed to be a descendant of Ketil Trout, Odd's grandfather. Orm is brought up in Iceland, but his great friend is a Dane named Asmund, the same name as Odd's first and closest friend. There is also an episode involving a prophetess, closely resembling the episode in *Arrow-Odd*:

It was the custom in those days that women called prophetesses would travel round the country to foretell people's futures, and to forecast the weather for the next season and other things people wanted to find out about. A prophetess with her retinue came to Virfil [i.e. Asbjorn's father]; she was given a good welcome, for there was a splendid feast on. In the evening when the people had gone to their seats, they started asking the prophetess about their future. She said that Virfil would farm there till old age and always be regarded as a worthy farmer. 'The young man sitting beside you, farmer, should be glad to hear about his fate, for he'll travel widely and be considered the greatest man wherever he comes. He will accomplish many great things and die of ripe old age – provided that he doesn't go to Nordmore in Norway or to the country north of that.'

Further parallels to *Arrow-Odd* can be found outside the sagas. For instance, there is a Russian account of the death of King Oleg which tells the same story as that of Odd:

Now Autumn came on, and Oleg bethought him of his horse which he had ordered to be fed yet not mounted. For he had made enquiry of the wonder-working magicians: 'From what shall death come to me?' One magician replied: 'O, Prince, the steed which you love and on which you ride, from him you shall meet your death.' Oleg then took this to heart and said: 'Never shall I mount him or look upon him again.' So he gave command that the horse should be properly fed, but never led into his presence. He thus let several years pass not seeing him until he attacked the

Greeks. And having returned to Kiev, and having passed four years, on the fifth he thought of the horse through whom the magicians had foretold that he should meet his death. He thus summoned his head groom, and enquired as to the whereabouts of the horse which he had ordered to be fed and well cared for. The groom answered that he was dead. Oleg laughed and mocked the magicians, exclaiming: 'Sooth-sayers tell untruths, and their words are naught but falsehood. The horse is dead, but I am still alive.'

Then he commanded that a horse should be saddled. 'Let me see his bones,' said he. He rode to the place where the bare bones and skull lay. Dismounting from his horse, he laughed and remarked: 'Am I to receive my death from this skull?' and he stamped upon the skull with his foot. But a serpent crawled forth from it and bit him in the foot, so that in consequence he sickened and died. All the people mourned for him in great grief. They bore him away and buried him on the hill which is called Shchekovitsa. His tomb is there to this day. It is called the Tomb of Oleg.*

And, as with the other legendary tales, certain episodes in *Arrow-Odd* can be paralleled in Saxo Grammaticus' *Danish History*. One is the description of Permia and its inhabitants:

It is a region of eternal cold, covered with very deep snows, and not sensible to the force even of the summer heats; full of pathless forests, not fertile in grain and haunted by beasts uncommon elsewhere. Its many rivers pour onwards in a hissing, foaming flood, because of the reefs embedded in their channels. (Book VIII, Elton's translation.)

And, as in *Arrow-Odd*, the inhabitants of Permia have remarkable powers:

[The Permians] cast spells upon the sky, stirred up the clouds, and drove them into most furious storms. (Book IX.)
[The Permians] by their spells loosed the sky in clouds of rain, and melted the joyous visage of the air in dismal drenching showers. (Book I.)

But the closest link between *Arrow-Odd* and Saxo is this specific reference to the death of Hjalmar and the heroism of 'Arvarodd':

[The sons of Arngrim, i.e. Anganty and his brothers] followed the business of sea-roving from their youth up; and they chanced to sail all in one ship to the island Samso, where they found lying off the coast two ships

---

* Quoted in N. K. Chadwick, *Beginnings of Russian History* (Cambridge, 1946), pp. 23–4; from Samuel H. Cross, *The Russian Primary Chronicle* (Cambridge, Mass., 1930), p. 58. Mrs Chadwick discusses the relationship and possible modes of transmission.

belonging to Hjalmar and Arvarodd the rovers. These ships they attacked and cleared of rowers; but, not knowing whether they had cut down the captains, they fitted the bodies of the slain to their several thwarts, and found that those whom they sought were missing. At this they were sad, knowing that the victory they had won was not worth a straw, and that their safety would run much greater risk in the battle that was to come. In fact, Hjalmar and Arvarodd, whose ships had been damaged by a storm, which had torn off their rudders, went into a wood to hew another; and, going round the trunk with their axes, pared down the shapeless timber until the huge stock assumed the form of a marine implement. This they shouldered, and were bearing it down to the beach, ignorant of the disaster of their friends, when the sons of Eyfura, reeking with the fresh blood of the slain, attacked them, so that they two had to fight many; the contest was not even equal, for it was a band of twelve against two. But the victory did not go according to numbers. For all the sons of Eyfura were killed; Hjalmar was slain by them, but Arvarodd gained the honours of victory, being the only survivor left by fate out of all that band of comrades. He, with an incredible effort, poised the still shapeless hulk of the rudder, and drove it so strongly against the bodies of his foes that, with a single thrust of it, he battered and crushed all twelve. And so, though they were rid of the general storm of war, the band of rovers did not quit the ocean. (Book V.)

In *Arrow-Odd* the prophecy that Odd will 'wander from land to land' is used to the full, as the hero travels through Europe and Asia, and west to Slabland Waste (probably Baffin Island). But of all the lands travelled by Odd, Permia makes the most lasting impression. As we have seen in the passage from Saxo, Permia, or Perm, to the east of the White Sea, was known to be a cold and inhospitable land, but with plenty of fur-giving beasts. From reliable historical sources we know that the Norwegians, from the ninth century onwards, had been trading with the Permians. The earliest references to such contacts is to be found in King Alfred's Old English version of *Orosius*; Alfred adds to the Latin original a chapter on Lappland and Permia based on the account of a Norwegian who lived in Halogaland, in the north of Norway. King Alfred's informant, Ohthere, lived furthest north of all Norwegians. 'He said however that that country extended very far to the north from where he lived; but it is all uninhabited except that, in a few places, here and there, Lapps are encamped, hunting in winter and, in summer, fishing in the sea.'[*]

* A. J. Wyatt, *An Anglo-Saxon Reader* (Cambridge, 1948), p. 12.

In Chapter 66 of his *Hakon's Saga* Sturla Thordarson describes a punitive expedition led in 1222 by some Norwegians against Permia. 'The men of Halogaland fell out with the King of Permia, and in the winter the Permians attacked them and killed the entire crew.' But one of the Norwegians stayed behind and in the autumn went east to Suzdal with his companions and goods, then west to Novgorod, and from there all the way to Jerusalem. 'From there he travelled back to Norway, and this journey made him famous.'

Two other Norwegians went to Permia to take vengeance for what had been done to their fellow-countrymen. 'They caused a great deal of damage, killing people and plundering. They won a lot of loot, grey furs and purified silver, but later they lost a good deal of it.' Sturla concludes the chapter by saying, 'since then no trip has been made to Permia.' If we accept his word, no one must have travelled from Norway to Permia during the period 1222 to 1265.

Apart from this account, there are plenty of other stories in early Icelandic literature about Scandinavian voyages to Permia in early times. In Chapter 133 of *St Olaf's Saga*, for example, we have a vivid description of such a voyage. St Olaf (King of Norway 1015–30) sent a certain Karli one spring north to Halogaland and Lappland. Karli went all the way north to Permia where he attended a market; he started trading with the natives, buying grey furs, beaver skins and sable furs. After the trading Karli and his men sailed down the river Dvina. The truce being over, Karli decided to make some easy money. He found out that when a rich man died, his chattels were divided between the dead man and his heirs, according to Permian custom. The dead man was supposed to keep one-third or even as much as a half, but sometimes less. 'That money was brought into the forest, put into a mound and mixed with earth.' The Norwegians went inland to a clearing where there was a palisade and a locked door, with two native watchmen on guard in shifts; what follows is again reminiscent of *Arrow-Odd*. 'The Norwegians got inside the fort just as the guards were changing. Inside the mound there was gold and silver and earth all mixed together. The Permian god Jomali stood there; they stripped the god and took a lot of silver besides. They were attacked by the

Permians but escaped and sailed across the White Sea and back home.'

There are many parallels to the prophecy of Odd's long life and death in the sagas, and it seems that the best way of looking at it is to see it as a vatic pronouncement, a mixture of prophecy and curse. Without the witch's utterance Odd's life would have taken a different course. Thus it is in her power not only to foresee events (in this respect her pronouncements on the weather and the future prospects of the men of Berurjod seem no more impressive than the trivialities of a modern fortune-teller), but, a more sinister power, to modify their course.

Stories of prophetesses are known from other sagas, for example the one in *Eirik's Saga*:

There was a woman in the settlement called Thorbjorg; she was a prophetess, and was known as the Little Sybil. She had had nine sisters (and they had all been prophetesses) but she was the only one left alive. It was her custom in winter to attend feasts; she was always invited, in particular by those who were most curious about their own fortunes or the season's prospects . . . Thorkel invited the prophetess to his house and prepared a good reception for her, as was the custom when such women were being received. A high-seat was made ready for her with a cushion on it, which had to be stuffed with hens' feathers.

She arrived in the evening with the man who had been sent to escort her. She was dressed like this: she wore a blue mantle fastened with straps and adorned with stones all the way down to the hem. She had a necklace of glass beads. On her head she wore a black lambskin hood lined with white cat's fur. *

The prophetess in *Arrow-Odd* has certain striking features in common with the Lappish sorceress in *Vatnsdaela Saga*. Ingjald, who is the foster-father of the principal hero, Ingimund, gives a feast to which he invites a certain Lappish sorceress with the specific intention of finding out his own and others' futures. Nearly all the guests approach her, one after another, and she tells them what lies in store for them, but Ingimund and his blood-brother ignore her. When the sorceress asks why they are not coming forward like the

* *The Vinland Sagas*, translated by M. Magnusson and H. Pálsson (Penguin, 1965).

rest, Ingimund tells her bluntly that he is not interested in finding out beforehand what will happen to him, and anyhow he can't see how her tongue has anything to do with his fate. In spite of the rebuff, she tells his future, that he will emigrate to Iceland. Ingimund resents the prophecy, and remarks that if his foster-father had not been involved, he would have avenged himself on her. When she has gone away, Ingjald explains that he had only good motives for inviting her, but Ingimund says that he is certainly not going to thank him for it. After that Ingimund goes away, and travels to his father, just as Odd does.

List of Proper Names

The following abbreviations are used: *AO* (*Arrow-Odd*), *EA* (*Egil and Asmund*), *BH* (*Bosi and Herraud*), *Gautr* (*King Gautrek*), *HE* (*Halfdan Eysteinsson*), *HTh* (*Helgi Thorisson*), *Thorst* (*Thorstein Mansion-Might*). The numbers refer to chapters, not pages. Hjalmar's companions mentioned in Chapter 14 of *Arrow-Odd* are omitted. These two lists are not exhaustive.

Personal Names

ÆLLA, king of England, *Gautr* 9–11.

ÆSA, sister of Egil One-Hand, *EA* 9, 18.

AGDI, earl of Grundir, *Thorst* 5, 7–9, 11–13.

AGNAR, a berserk, *AO* 10, 27.

AGNAR, king of Noatown, *BH* 2.

AGNAR, king of Gestrekaland, *HE* 26.

AGNAR RAKNARSSON, *HE* 26.

AGNI, father of Eirik and Alrek, *Gautr* 7.

ALF, a berserk, *AO* 10, 27.

ALF, king of Alfheim, *Gautr* 3.

ALF BJALKI, king of Bjalka, *AO* 28–9.

ALFHILD, grandmother of Starkad, *Gautr* 3, 7.

ALFHILD, wife of Gautrek, *Gautr* 8.

ALL-STRONG (*Allsterkr*), one of King Godmund's men, *Thorst* 5, 7.

ALREK, king of Sweden, *Gautr* 7.

AN, one of Vikar's men, *Gautr* 4.

ANGANTYR, leader of twelve viking brothers, *AO* 14.

ARAN, son of King Rodian, *EA* 6–8.

ARGHYRNA, *HE* 14.

ARMOD, son of Asmund Berserks-Killer, *EA* 18.

ARROW-ODD (ODD, BARKMAN), *AO passim*.

ASA, mother of Halfdan Eysteinsson, *HE* 1.

ASLAUG, grandmother of Halfdan Eysteinsson, *HE* 1.

ASMUND BERSERKS-KILLER, son of King Ottar, *EA passim*.

ASMUND, a berserk, *AO* 10, 27.

ASMUND, Odd's blood-brother, *AO* 1–13, 27, 31.

ASMUND, son of Arrow-Odd, *AO* 31.

BARKMAN (an alias for Arrow-Odd), *AO* 24–7.

BARRI, brother of Angantyr, *AO* 14.

BEARD, see RED-BEARD

BEKKHILD, daughter of King Hertrygg, *EA* 2, 14–15, 17.

BILD, brother of Angantry, *AO* 14.

BJALFI, an alias for Thorstein, *Thorst* 2.

BJARKMAR, earl of Gotaland, *EA* 9, 12.

BJARTMAR, *HE* 22.

BORGAR, a viking leader, *EA* 10.

BOSI (STUNT-BOSI), son of a retired viking, *BH passim*.

BRAND, a berserk, *AO* 10, 27.

BRUNI, king of Lappland, *AO* 1.

BRYNHILD, daughter of Budli, *HE* 2.

BRYNHILD, daughter of King Hertrygg, *EA* 1 (14), 15, 17.

BRYNHILD (STUNT-BRYNHILD), mother of Bosi, *BH* 2.

BRYNJOLF, son of Thorstein Mansion-Might, *Thorst* 13.

BRYNJOLF CAMEL, father of Thorstein Mansion-Might, *Thorst* 1.

BRYN-THVARI, see THVARI.

BUDLI, father of Brynhild, *HE* 2.

BUI, brother of Angantyr, *AO* 14.

BULL-BEAR, son of Earl Gorm, *EA* 7, 17.

BUSLA, foster-mother of Bosi, *BH* 2, 4–5, 14.

DAGMÆR, wife of King Thrand, *HE* 1.

DAGNY, mother of Thorstein Mansion-Might, *Thorst* 1.

DAYFARER (*Dagfari*), one of King Harald Wartooth's men, *BH* 1,
    9.

DROTT, one of King Geirrod's men, *Thorst* 6–7.

DUMB, king of the Dumb Sea, *EA* 15.

EAGLE-BEAK (*Arinnefja*), queen of Jotunheim, *EA* 5, 15–17.

EDDA, daughter of King Harek, *BH* 7, 13, 16.

EDDVAL, king of Suzdal, *AO*, 30.

EDMUND, king of England, *AO* 12.

EDNY, daughter of King Hakon, *EA* 18.

EDNY, daughter of King Harek, *HE* 15, 22, 24.

EGIL, Ulfkel's forecastleman, *HE* 12.

EGIL ONE-HAND, son of King Hring of the Smalands, *EA passim*.

EIRIK, son of King Thrand, *HE* 1.

EIRIK, king of Sweden, *Gautr* 7.

ERP, one of Vikar's men, *Gautr* 4, 5.

EYFURA, mother of Angantyr, *AO* 14.

EYSTEIN, king of Trondheim, *HE* 1, 3, 5, 6, 7, 11, 12, 25.

EYSTEIN, son of Halfdan, *HE* 25.

EYTHJOF, a viking, *AO* 19.

FINN, king of the Lapps, *HE* 15, 20.

FINN, one of Ogmund's men, *AO* 19.

FJALAR, Egil One-Hand in disguise, *EH* 15.

FJOLMOD, one of the backwoodsmen, *Gautr* 1–2.

FJORI, son of Earl Freki, *Gautr* 3.

FJOSNI, one of Ogmund's men, *AO* 19.

FJOTRA, sister and wife of Imsigull, *Gautr* 1–2.

FLOKI, king of the Lapps, *HE* 15, 20.

FREKI, earl of Halogaland, *Gautr* 3.

FREY, the pagan god, *AO* 29.

FREYJA, the goddess, *BH* 12.

FRITHJOF THE BRAVE, *Gautr* 12.

FRITHJOF, king of Telemark, *Gautr* 3, 5.

FROSTI, one of Earl Agdi's men, *Thorst* 6–7.

FROSTI, Asmund Berserks-Killer in disguise, *EA* 15.

FULL-STRONG (*Fullsterkr*), one of King Godmund's men, *Thorst* 6, 9.

FYRI, son of Earl Freki, *Gautr* 3.

GARDAR, Odd's blood-brother, *AO* 19–23.

GAUK, Sigmund's forecastleman, *HE* 26.

GAUT, uncle of Queen Eagle-Beak, *EA* 12, 14–15.

GAUTI, son of King Odin; grandfather of Herraud, king of West Gotaland, *Gautr* 1–2; *BH* 1.

GAUTREK, king of West Gotaland, *Gautr* 1–2, 5, 8–11; *BH* 1.

GEIRRID, wife of Ogmund, *AO* 23.

GEIRROD, Geirrid's father, *AO* 23.

GEIRROD, King of Jotunheim, *Thorst* 5–11.

GEIRTHJOF, king of the Uplands in Norway, *Gautr* 3–5.

GILLING, one of the backwoodsmen, *Gautr* 1–2.

GLAMMAD, a berserk, *EA* 10.

GODMUND, king of Glasir Plains, *BH* 7–8, 10, 12, 14, 16; *Thorst* 5–12; *HTh* 1–3.

GODMUND, father of King Godmund, see ULFHEDIN TRUSTY.

GODMUND, son of Hildir, *AO* 18.

GOLD-BALL, daughter of Kol, *HE* 16–17.

GOLD-THORIR, *HE* 2, 26.

GÖNGU-HROLF, the eponymous hero of a viking romance, *HE* 24.

GORM, earl of Ethiopia, *EA* 7.

GRANI HORSEHAIR, Odin in disguise, *Gautr* 4, 7.

GRETTIR, one of Vikar's men, *Gautr* 4.

GRIM, an alias for Earl Skuli, q.v.

GRIM, an alias for Princess Ingigerd, q.v.

GRIM, one of King Godmund's messengers, *HTh* 2.

GRIM HAIRY-CHEEK, father of Arrow-Odd, *AO* 1, 3–4, 6–9, 14, 24, 27.

GRIMHILD, mother of Ogmund, *AO* 19.

GRUBS, a warrior, *HE* 20.

GRUNDI, son of King Harek, *HE* 22.

GUDMUND, brother of Arrow-Odd, *AO* 3–10, 12, 17.

GUDRUN, daughter of Earl Agdi and wife of Thorstein Mansion-Might, *Thorst* 11–13.

GUSIR, king of the Lapps, *AO* 4.

GUST, one of King Godmund's men, *Thorst* 6.

HADDING, two namesakes, brothers of Angantyr, *AO* 14, 27.

HAK, one of Ogmund's men, *AO* 19.

HAKI, a viking, *AO* 14.

HAKI, one of Ogmund's men, *AO* 19.

HAKON HAMUNDARSON, king of Denmark, *EA* 18.

HAKON SIGURDARSON, earl of Norway, *Thorst* 1.

HALFDAN, a viking, *AO* 7, 27.

HALFDAN EYSTEINSSON, *HE passim*.

HALLGEIR, *HE* 16.

HARALD, king of Agder in Norway, *Gautr* 3–4, 7.

HARALD, king of Wendland, *Gautr* 8.

HARALD, a chieftain in Norway, *AO* 1.

HARALD FINEHAIR, king of Norway, *HE* 2.

HARALD VIKARSSON, ruler of Telemark in Norway, *Gautr* 5, 9.

HARALD WARTOOTH, king of Denmark, *BH* 1, 9.

HAREK, king of Permia, *AO* 19; *HE* 15–16, 19–20, 22, 24, 26; *BH*
    7–8, 10, 14.

HAREK, one of King Herraud's retainers, *AO* 27–9, 39.

HAUK, Sigmund's forecastleman, *HE* 26.

HEID, a witch, *AO* 2.

HEIDREK WOLF-SKIN, son of King Godmund, *Thorst* 12.

HEIMIR, brother of Earl Skuli, *HE* 2.

HELGA, daughter of King Gautrek and wife of Ref, *Gautr* 8, 11.

HELGI THORISSON, one of King Olaf Tryggvason's men, *HTh*
    1–3.

HERBJORN, Earl Skuli's kinsman, *HE* 5.

HERGEIR, king of Russia, *HE* 2–5, 11, 23.

HERGRIM, a victim of Starkad, *Gautr* 7.

HERRAUD, son of Hring, *BH passim*.

HERRAUD, son of King Rodian, *EA* 7–8, 17.

HERRAUD, king of Greece, *AO* 24, 29.

HERRAUD, son of Arrow-Odd, *AO* 31.

HERTHJOF, king of Hordaland in Norway, *Gautr* 3–5.

HERTRYGG, king of Russia, *EA* 1, 5, 14, 16–18.

HERVARD, brother of Angantyr, *AO* 14.

HILDIGRIM, one of Vikar's men, *Gautr* 4.

HILDIGUNN, sister of King Harek, *HE* 26.

HILDIGUNN, daughter of Hildir, *AO* 18, 21.

HILDIR, a giant, *AO* 18, 32.

HILDIR, uncle of Queen Eagle-Beak, *EA* 12, 14–16.

HILDIRID, wife of Hildir, *AO* 18.

HJALMAR, a viking hero, *AO* 8–15, 27.

HJOROLF, king of Gaul, *AO* 30.

HJORVARD, brother of Angantyr, *AO* 14, 27.

HJOTRA, sister and wife of Fjolmod, *Gautr* 1–2.

HLEID, sister of King Godmund, *B H* 8, 10–11, 16.

HLODVER, king of Gotaland, *HE* 2, 29.

HLODVER, king of Sweden, *AO* 8, 10, 15.

HLODVER, a viking, *AO* 14.

HOKETIL, a backwoodsman, *BH* 7–8, 10.

HOLMGEIR, king of Novgorod, *AO* 30.

HOSVIR, one of King Geirrod's men, *Thorst* 6–7.

HRÆREK, brother of King Rodian, *EA* 7–8.

HRÆREK, son of King Harek, *BH* 7, 10–15.

HRAFNHILD, grandmother of Arrow-Odd, *AO* 1.

HRAFNKEL, standard-bearer of Ulfkel, *HE* 12–13.

HRANI, brother of Angantyr, *AO* 14.

HREGGVID, son of Earl Skuli, *HE* 24.

HRIFLING, *HE* 14, 16, 21.

HRING, king of East Gotaland, *BH* 1, 5, 8–11.

HRING, king of Denmark, *AO* 32.

HRING, king of the Smalands, *EA* 9, 12–13, 18.

HROAR, king of Gaul, *AO* 30.

HROI, one of Vikar's men, *Gautr* 4.

HROLF, King Hreggvid's son-in-law, see *Göngu-Hrolf's Saga*,
    HE 24.

HROLF GAUTREKSSON, eponymous hero of a legendary saga,
    Gautr 7.

HROLF KRAKI, eponymous hero of a legendary saga, *Gautr* 9–10.

HROMUND GRIPSSON, eponymous hero of a legendary saga, *HE* 1.

HROSSKEL, one of King Gautrek's men, *Gautr* 8.

HROTTI, one of Vikar's men, *Gautr* 4.

HUNTHJOF, king of Hordaland in Norway, *Gautr* 3.

IMSIGULL, one of the backwoodsmen, *Gautr* 1–2.

INGIBJORG, Hjalmar's beloved, *AO* 10, 14–15.

INGIBJORG, mother of Egil One-Hand, *EA* 9, 12–13, 17.

INGIBJORG, daughter of King Godmund, *HTh* 1–3.

INGIBJORG THE FAIR, wife of Frithjof the Brave, *Gautr* 3.

INGIGERD, daughter of King Hergeir, *HE passim.*

INGIGERD, daughter of Hreggvid, *HE* 24.

INGIGERD, daughter of Kol, *HE* 2, 5–6, 11, 20, 23.

INGJALD, a berserk, *AO* 10, 27.

INGJALD, a foster-father of Arrow-Odd, *AO* 1–3, 29, 31.

INGJALD, one of King Herraud's retainers, *AO* 24–7.

ISGERD, daughter of King Hlodver and wife of King Hergeir, *HE* 2,
   6–7, 23–4.

IVAR BUNDLE, a berserk, *HE* 12.

JAPHET, son of Noah, *AO* 30.

JARNSKEGGI, grandfather of Thorstein Mansion-Might, *Thorst* 1.

JOKUL, one of Earl Agdi's men, *Thorst* 6, 9.

JOLF, Odin in disguise, *AO* 24, 29.

JOMALI, pagan deity worshipped in Permia, *BH* 8–10.

KÆNMAR, king of Kiev, *AO* 30.

KETIL TROUT, grandfather of Arrow-Odd, *AO* 1, 3–4.

KISI VALSSON, *HE* 26.

KOL, *HE* 16.

KOL, slave of Earl Skuli, *HE* 2, 5, 20, 23, 24.

KOLFROSTA, mother of King Harek, *BH* 8.

KOTT VALSSON, *HE* 26.

KRABBI, king Harek's standard-bearer, *HE* 20.

KULA, mother of Queen Eagle-Beak, *EA* 12.

LOFTHÆNA, mother of Arrow-Odd, *AO* 1, 3.

MAGOG, son of Japhet, *AO* 30.

MARRO, king of Muram, *AO* 30.

NAUMA, wife of King Sæming, *HE* 1.

NERI, earl of the Uplands in Norway, *Gautr* 5, 9–11.

NIGHTFARER (*Náttfari*), one of King Harald Wartooth's men, *BH* 1, 9.

ODD THE SHOWY, son of King Hlodver, *HE* 2, 25, 26.

ODIN, *HE* 1; *AO* 14, 17, 23, 29; *Gautr* 1, 2, 7; *BH* 1, 12; *EA* 8, 13; *Thorst* 3, 9–10.

OFEIG, alias for Skuli or Ingigerd, *HE* 9.

OGMUND EYTHJOF'S-KILLER, *AO* 13, 15, 19–24, 27.

OLAF THE KEEN-EYED, king of Nærike in Sweden, *Gautr* 5.

OLAF, a warrior king, *Gautr* 11.

OLAF TRYGGVASON, king of Norway (995–1000), *Thorst* 1–2, 4–5, 7–8, 10–12; *HTh* 1–3.

OLVIR, one of Arrow-Odd's victims, *AO* 27.

OLVOR, wife of Arrow-Odd, *AO* 11–12.

OSKRUD, father of Queen Eagle-Beak, *EA* 12, 14.

OTHJODAN, *AO* 12.

OTRYGG, a berserk in Sweden, *Gautr* 7.

OTTAR, retainer of King Herraud, *AO* 24–7.

OTTAR, earl of Halogaland and father of Asmund Berserks-Killer, *EA* 6, 18.

OTTAR, earl of Jutland, *EA* 6.

OTTAR, earl of Novgorod, *Thorst* 11.

PALTES, king of Polotsk, *AO* 30.

PRIESTESS, THE, wife of King Alf Bjalki, *AO* 28.

PURSE, illegitimate son of King Hring, *BH* 1–4.

QUILLANUS, alias for Ogmund, *AO* 30.

RAGNAR HAIRY-BREEKS, eponymous hero of a legendary saga, *BH* ·9, 16; *HE* 2.

RAGNHILD, daughter of Arrow-Odd, *AO* 12, 32.

RAKNAR AGNARSSON, *HE* 22, 26.

RED-BEARD, Odin in disguise, *AO* 19–23.

REF (*Rennisson*), a farmer's son from Norway, *Gautr* 6, 9–11.

REF-NOSE, an adviser to King Olaf, *Gautr* 11.

REGIN, a dwarf, *EA* 17.

RENNIR, father of Ref, *Gautr* 6, 9.

RODIAN, king of Tartary, *EA* 6–7.

RODSTAFF, king of Rostof, *AO* 30.

ROGNVALD, in charge of King Hertrygg's defences, *EA* 3, 5.

SÆMING, son of Odin, *HE* 1.

SÆMUND, a viking, *AO* 16, 27.

SEAFARER, earl of the Smalands, *BH* 1.

SEL, *HE* 16–18.

SIGGEIR, son of King Harek, *BH* 7, 10–11, 13–14.

SIGGEIR, brother of King Rodian, *EA* 7, 8.

SIGMUND, son of King Hlodver, *HE* 2, 10, 11, 23–7.

SIGRID, mother of Asmund Berserks-Killer, *EA* 6.

SIGURD, a retainer of King Herraud, *AO* 24–7.

SIGURD, a musician at King Godmund's court, *BH* 11–12.

SIGURD, Bosi in disguise, *BH* 12–13.

SIGURD HART, Halfdan's grandfather, *HE* 1.

SIGURD HRING, eponymous hero of a legendary saga, now lost, *BH* 9, 16.

SIGURD SNAKE-IN-THE-EYE, *HE* 1.

SIGURD, cousin of Arrow-Odd, *AO* 3–8, 10, 12, 17.

SILKISIF, wife of Arrow-Odd, *AO* 24, 26, 29, 31, 32.

SIRNIR, blood-brother of Arrow-Odd, *AO* 19–24.

SISAR, king of Kiev, *Gautr* 4.

SJOLF, retainer of King Herraud, *AO* 24–7.

SKALK, a eunuch, *BH* 13.

SKIN-BEAK, daughter of Queen Eagle-Beak, *EA* 5, 8, 16–17.

SKINFLINT, king Gautrek's grandfather, *Gautr* 1–2.

SKJALF, wife of King Agni, *Gautr* 7.

SKOLLI, a viking in England, *AO* 12.

SKROGG, lawman of the giants, *EA* 14–16.

SKULI, earl of Alaborg, *HE passim*.

SKUMA, one of Vikar's men, *Gautr* 4.

SMID, brother of Bosi, *BH* 2, 11–14.

SNÆULF, standard-bearer of Ulfkel, *HE* 5.

SNIDIL, forecastleman on Herraud's ship, *BH* 14.

SNOTRA, mother of Gautrek, *Gautr* 1–2.

SNOW, king of the Underworld, *EA* 13.

SORKVIR, one of Vikar's men, *Gautr* 4.

SOTI, a viking, *AO* 8.

SOTI, partner of Hjalmar, *AO* 14.

STARKAD THE ALA-WARRIOR, grandfather of Starkad the Old,
    Gautr 3.

STARKAD (*Storvirksson*) THE OLD, the tragic hero, *Gautr* 3–7; *EA*
    18.

STEINTHOR, one of Vikar's men, *Gautr* 4.

STORVIRK, father of Starkad the Old, *Gautr* 3, 7.

STUNT-BRYNHILD, see BRYNHILD.

STYR, one of Vikar's men, *Gautr* 4.

SULTAN, king of the Saracens, *EA* 18.

SVADI, son of Thor, *HE* 26.

SVANHVIT, wife of Hromund Gripsson, *HE* 1.

SVART, son of Arrow-Odd, *AO*, 23, 30.

SVIDI THE BOLD, son of Bosi, *BH* 16; *HE* 12, 13, 14, 20, 24–6.

SVIP, a farmer in Norway, *HE* 1.

SYLGJA, mother of Herraud, *BH* 1.

THOR, the god, *Gautr* 3, 7; *BH* 12; *EA* 12; *Thorst* 9; *HE* 26.

THORA TOWN-HART, wife of Ragnar Hairy-Breeks, *BH* 16.

THORD PROW-GLEAM, blood-brother of Arrow-Odd, *AO* 8–10,
    12–13, 27.

THORIR, father of Helgi, *HTh* 1–3.

THORIR HART, son of Halfdan, *HE* 25.

THORMOD KARK, Earl Hakon's slave and murderer, *Thorst* 1.

THORSTEIN MANSION-MIGHT (*Mansion-Midget*), *Thorst passim*.

THORSTEIN THORISSON, brother of Helgi, *HTh* 1–2.

THRAND, king of Trondheim, *HE* 1.

THVARI (*Bryn-Thvari*), father of Bosi, *BH* 2, 4–6, 11, 14.

TIND, one of Ogmund's men, *AO* 19.

TIND, brother of Angantyr, *AO* 14.

TJOSNI, follower of Ogmund, *AO* 19.

TOKI, brother of Angantyr, *AO* 14.

TOKI, follower of Ogmund, *AO* 19.

TORFI, follower of Ogmund, *AO* 19.

TOTRA, King Gautrek's grandmother, *Gautr* 1–2.
TYRFING, brother of Angantyr, *AO* 14.

ULF, a giant, *AO* 18.
ULF, one of Vikar's men, *Gautr* 4, 5.
ULF, a berserk in Sweden, *Gautr* 7.
ULFAR SVIPSSON, *HE* 1, 11.
ULFHEDIN TRUSTY, father of King Godmund, *Thorst* 5.
ULFKEL SVIPSSON, *HE* 1, 4–6, 11–13, 15–16, 20–21, 23.
ULF SVIPSSON, *HE* 1, 15–16, 20.
UNN, mother of Starkad, *Gautr* 3.

VAL AGNARSSON, *HE* 26.
VIDGRIP, son of King Alf Bjalki, *AO* 28–9.
VIGFUS, alias for Skuli or Ingigerd, *HE* 9.
VIGNIR, son of Arrow-Odd, *AO* 18, 21–2.
VIKAR, king of Agder in Norway, *Gautr* 3–7.
VILMUND THE ABSENTMINDED, eponymous hero of a romance,
   BH 16.
VISIN, son of Earl Gorm, *EA* 7, 18.

YLFING, a giant, *AO* 18.

Place Names

ÆGEAN SEA, *BH* 8; *EA* 18.
AGDER, province in Norway, *Gautr* 3, 4, 7.
AGNAFIT, near Stockholm in Sweden, *AO* 14.
ALABORG, *HE* 2, 4, 6, 11, 15, 24.
ALFHEIM, in south-east Norway? *Gautr* 3.
ALREKSSTEAD, royal residence in Norway, *HTh* 2.
ALSACE, *AO* 17.
ANTIOCH, *AO* 29.
AQUITAINE, *AO* 17, 27.
ASIA, *BH* 1.
ASK, a farm on Fenhring Island, *Gautr* 4.
ATALSFELL, *AO* 27.

BALTIC, *EA* 10, 18; *Thorst* 12; *HE* 1, 10–12, 23.

BERURJOD, farm in south Norway, *AO* 1–3, 31.

BJALKA, *AO* 28.

BLESANERG, in the Arctic, *HE* 26.

BOLM, island in Sweden, *AO* 14.

BROW PLAINS (*Brávellir*), in the south of Sweden, *BH* 9–10.

DENMARK, *AO* 11–12, 19–20, 22–3; *Gautr* 10; *BH* 1; *EA* 6, 18.

DUMB SEA (*Dumbshaf*), the Arctic regions, *EA* 15; *HE* 26.

DVINA, river in north Russia, *AO* 4.

EAST GOTALAND, now part of Sweden, *BH* 1, 8.

EIKUND, in south Norway, *AO* 29.

ELFAR SKERRIES, off the west coast of Sweden, *AO* 7, 13; *BH* 4.

ELFAR SOUND, *AO* 27.

ENGLAND, *AO* 12, 19, 27; *Gautr* 9.

ERMLAND, later part of East Prussia, *AO* 30.

ESTONIA, *AO* 30.

ETHIOPIA (*Blökkumannaland*), *EA* 7.

FAMILY CLIFF (*Ætternisstapi*), *Gautr* 1–2.

FINNMARK, in north Norway, *HTh* 1; *HE* 1.

FINNISH COAST, *Thorst* 2.

FENHRING ISLAND, in Norway, *Gautr* 4.

FLANDERS, *AO* 14, 20.

FRANCE, *AO* 17, 20.

GAUL (*Gallia*), *AO* 30.

GAULARDALE, in Norway, *Thorst* 1.

GEIRRODSTOWN (*Geirröðargarðar*), mythical, *AO* 23; *Thorst* 5, 10, 11.

GESTREKALAND, in Sweden, *HE* 26.

GIANTLAND (*Risaland*), mythical, *AO* 18, 21; *Thorst* 5–6.

GILLINGS BLUFF (*Gillingshamarr*), *Gautr* 1–2.

GJALLANDI BRIDGE (*Gjallandabrú*), mythical, *EA* 15.

GLASIR PLAINS (*Glasisvellir*), mythical, *BH* 7, 8, 10, 14, 16; *Thorst* 5, 11–12; *HTh* 1–3.

GNIPALUND, mythical residence of Earl Agdi, *Thorst* 5, 13.

GOTALAND, now part of Sweden, *AO* 16, 19, 23–4, 27; *Gautr* 1–2, 4–5, 8, 11; *BH* 4–5, 9–11, 13–14; *EA* 9, 12–13, 17–18.

GOTA RIVER, in Gotaland, *AO* 10–11.

GREECE, *AO* 29–30.

GREENLAND SEA, *AO* 21.

GRIM PASS (*Grímaskarð*), near Alreksstead in Norway, *HTh* 2.

GRUNDIR, mythical, *Thorst* 5, 12.

HADALAND, province in Norway, *HE* 1.

HALOGALAND, province in Norway, *AO* 1, 10; *Gautr* 3; *HE* 1, 26; *EA* 6–7, 18.

HARDANGER, in Norway, *Gautr* 4.

HAUKSNESS, *AO* 27.

HEMRA, mythical river, *Thorst* 5.

HLYN FOREST, *HE* 12.

HORDALAND, a province in Norway, *Gautr* 3, 4, 7.

HRAFNISTA, in Norway, *AO* 1, 3, 6–10, 12, 17, 24, 27, 31–2.

HUNLAND, *EA* 1, 7.

ICELAND, *HE* 2, 25.

INDIA, *Thorst* 2.

IRELAND, *AO* 11–12, 32.

JÆDEREN, a province in Norway, *AO* 2, 29, 31–2; *Gautr* 4, 6.

JAMTLAND, now part of Sweden, *Thorst* 3.

JORDAN, river *AO* 17.

JOTUNHEIM, mythical, *EA* 5, 12, 14–16; *Thorst* 5, 8.

JUTLAND, *EA* 6.

KALFAR WOOD, *HE* 16–17.

KARELIA, in Finland, *AO* 30; *HE* 15–16, 24–6.

KIEV (*Kænugarðr*), *Gautr* 4; *AO* 30.

KJOLEN MOUNTAINS (*Kjölr*), in Scandinavia, *Gautr* 1; *HE* 16, 26.

KLIF'S WOOD, *HE* 16–17.

KLYFANDNESS, *HE* 12.

KOL'S WOOD, *HE* 16.

KRAKUNESS, *HE* 11.

KURLAND, part of Latvia, *AO* 30.

LADOGA TOWN, *HE* 2, 3.

LÆSO ISLAND, in Denmark, *AO* 11, 27; *EA* 18.

LANLAND, *AO* 30.

LAPPLAND, *AO* 4–5, 19.

LIVONIA, *AO* 30.

MOUNT LUCANUS, said to be in India, *EA* 13; *Thorst* 2.

MUNAR CREEKS, *AO* 14.

MURAM, in Russia, *AO* 30.

NÆRIKI, a province in Sweden, *Gautr* 5.

NAMDAL, in Norway, *HE* 1.

NOATOWN (*Nóatún*), mythical, *BH* 2.

NORMANDY (*Valland*), *AO* 17.

NORTH SEA, *AO* 11.

NORWAY, *AO* 1, 27, 31; *Gautr* 1–2, 6–7; *HE* 1, 11, 24–7; *Thorst*
    1–2, 5, 11, 13; *HTh* 1, 3.

NOVGOROD (*Hólmgarðr*), *AO* 30; *Thorst* 11; (*Garðaríki*), *EA* 1;
    (*Nógarðar*), *HE* 25.

ORKNEY, *AO* 11; *HE* 27.

OSLOFJORD, *AO* 1, 7; *Gautr* 4; *Thorst* 2; *HTh* 1.

PERMIA (*Bjarmaland*), Arctic Russia, *AO* 3–4, 7, 9, 12–13, 19, 21,
    27; *HE* 1, 12, 15–16, 22, 24–7; *BH* 6–10, 13–14, 16.

POLAND, *AO* 30.

POLOTSK (*Palteskjuborg*), *AO* 30.

RAUDABERG, farm near Oslofjord, *HTh* 1.

REFALAND, *AO* 30.

RENNIS ISLAND, in Norway, *Gautr* 6.

ROSTOF (*Ráðstofa*), *AO* 30.

RUSSIA (*Garðar, Garðarríki, Rússía, Rússland*), *AO* 24, 30, 32;
    HE 7, 25; *EA* 1.

SAMSO ISLAND, in Denmark, *AO* 14, 20, 27.

SAXONY, *AO* 20, 29; *BH* 3.

SCANDINAVIA, *AO* 22; *BH* 1, 9; *EA* 18.

SCOTLAND, *AO* 11.

SKAANE, now part of Sweden, *AO* 11.

SKIEN (*Skiða*), in South Norway, *A O* 8, 12, 27, 32.

SKUGGI, in Slabland, *AO* 21–2.

SLABLAND (*Helluland*), Baffin Island? *AO* 21–2, 27; *HE* 26.

SMALANDS, a province in Sweden, *BH*1; *EA* 9, 12.

STAD, in Norway, *Gautr* 4.

SUZDAL, in Russia, *AO* 30.

SVIA SKERRIES, near Stockholm, *AO* 27; *EA* 10.

SWEDEN, *AO* 8–10, 12–16, 20; *Gautr* 1–2, 5, 7.

TARTARY, *EA* 6, 17–18.

TAFESTLAND, in Finland, *AO* 30.

TELEMARK, province in Norway, *Gautr* 3, 5, 9.

THRUMA ISLAND, in Norway, *Gautr* 3, 7.

TOTN, province in Norway, *HE* 1.

TRONDHEIM, province in Norway, *HE* 1, 25; *Thorst* 12.

TRONU CREEKS, *AO* 13, 17, 27.

ULFSFELL, *AO* 27.

UNDERWORLD, mythical, *EA* 12–13; *Thorst* 2.

UPLANDS, a province in Norway, *Gautr* 1, 3, 5, 9.

UPPSALA, in Sweden, *AO* 13–15; *Gautr* 7.

VÆNER, lake in Sweden, *Gautr* 4.

VALHALLA, home of the heathen gods, *Gautr* 1–2.

VALDRES, province in Norway, *HE* 1.

VIKARS ISLAND, in Norway, *Gautr* 7.

VIMUND, headland in Norway, *HTh* 1.

VINA FOREST, in Permia, *BH* 7, 10.

VIRLAND, part of Estonia, *AO* 30.

VITLAND, *AO* 30.

WENDLAND, *AO* 30; *Gautr* 8.

WEST GOTALAND, now part of Sweden, *Gautr* 1.
WHITE SEA, *HE* 26.
WOLF ISLES (*Vargeyjar*), *AO* 18.

YRJAR, in Norway, *Thorst* 1.

ZEALAND, in Denmark, *AO* 10, 27.